37INK

SIMON &
SCHUSTER

ALL THE WORLD CAN HOLD

JUNG YUN

37INK

SIMON & SCHUSTER

NEW YORK AMSTERDAM/ANTWERP LONDON TORONTO

SYDNEY/MELBOURNE NEW DELHI

An Imprint of Simon & Schuster, LLC
1230 Avenue of the Americas
New York, NY 10020

First 37 INK/Simon & Schuster hardcover edition March 2026

Interior design by Carly Loman

Manufactured in the United States of America

3 5 7 9 10 8 6 4 2

Library of Congress Control Number has been applied for.

ISBN 978-1-6682-0059-9
ISBN 978-1-6682-0061-2 (ebook)

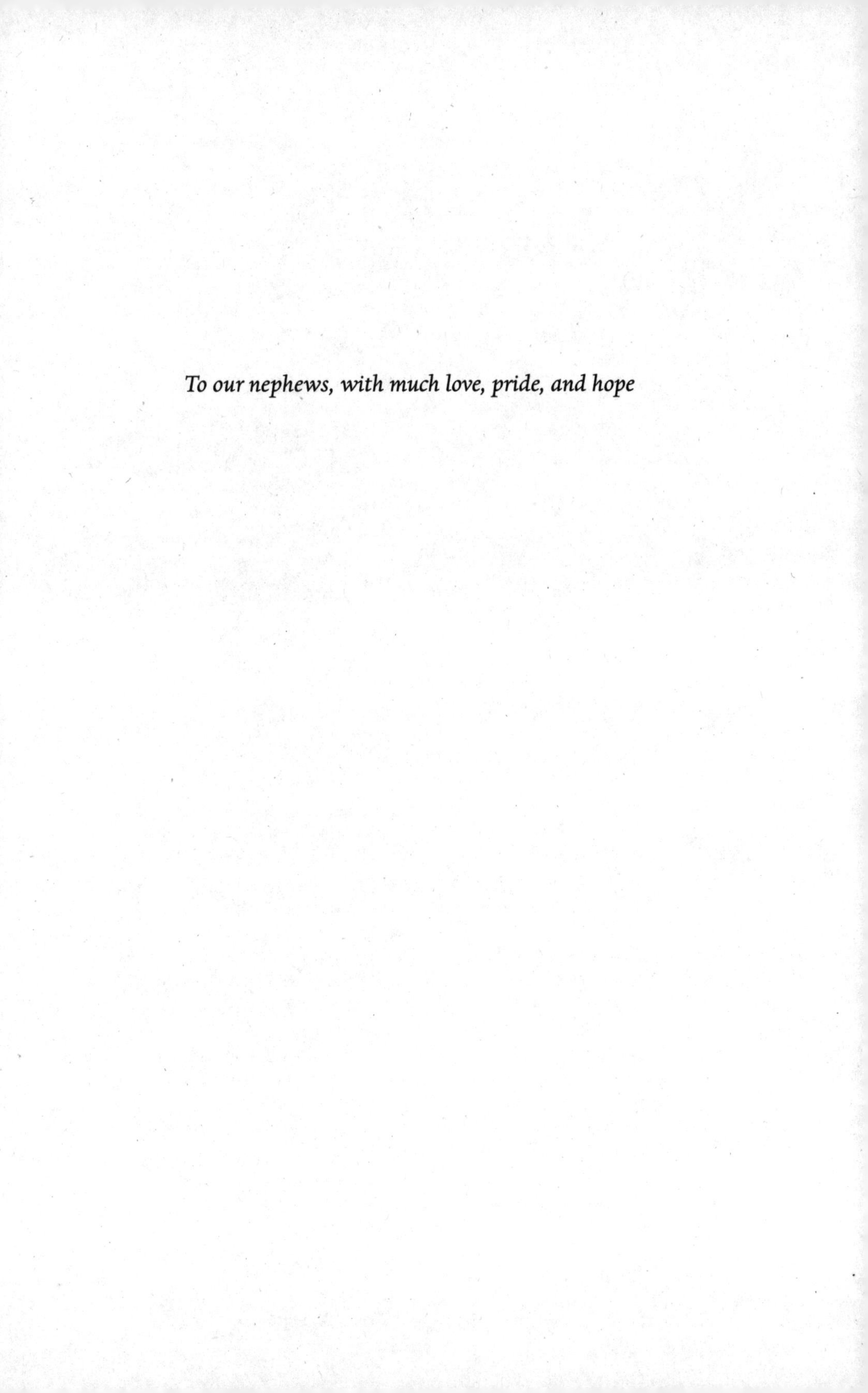

To our nephews, with much love, pride, and hope

The future is unwritten.

—JOE STRUMMER

Sunday, September 16

DEPART FROM ~~NEW YORK PASSENGER SHIP TERMINAL, NEW YORK~~
BLACK FALCON CRUISE TERMINAL, BOSTON

1.

The man from Guest Services is named Jimmy. Jimmy from Indonesia, two seemingly incompatible facts engraved on his brushed satin name tag. Franny is convinced that "Jimmy" isn't his real name. She assumes he shortened it—or the cruise line told him to shorten it—from something long and unpronounceable to something effortless and "American."

Jimmy is all smiles and small talk as he shows them around the suite, opening doors to reveal the bathroom, the closet, the mini fridge, the personal safe, and voilà—he actually says "voilà" as he pulls back a curtain and gestures grandly with his arm—the private balcony.

Their view of the port is unremarkable. The port, in general, is unremarkable. Under the late afternoon clouds, the water appears murky, too dark to hold a reflection of the soot- and algae-stained warehouses on the pier. Franny leans toward the sliding glass door for a better look at a nearby ship, a mega-liner twice the size of their own. She's about to call her husband over when she notices him kneeling in front of the television set on the bureau. He's aiming the remote at it, pressing random combinations of buttons too hard.

"This thing's not broken, is it?" Every channel Tom turns to is black, loud with static and filled with diagonal snow. "There's no way I can go a whole week without the news."

Jimmy, who had just started telling them about their daily fruit basket delivery, seems slightly wounded by the interruption. "I'm sorry, sir. We're having a problem with the satellite right now." He walks over to their luggage, which the porters brought in before they boarded and arranged on folding metal racks. He gives one of the suitcases a gentle nudge, squaring the edges off against the wall. "It should be fixed very shortly. And every morning, you'll receive a complimentary copy of the *Herald Tribune*."

"No *New York Times* or *Wall Street Journal*?" Tom asks.

"I'm sorry, sir. No."

"Not even the *Post*?"

"It's the *International Herald Tribune*," Jimmy says, emphasizing the word "international."

Tom glares at Franny as if she's responsible for the ship's selection of newspapers. Then he sinks into the sofa, crossing his arms over his chest. His stiff khaki shorts ride up indecently, well past midthigh, but he either doesn't notice or care. Three years they've been married, and Franny can count on one hand the number of times she's seen him in shorts. He said his legs were too white to wear them—a strange, circular argument that never made sense until now. It's the last week of summer, and compared to Jimmy, whose evenly tanned skin is the color of gingerbread, Tom looks unseasonably pale.

"Here in this armoire, sir and madam, you'll find your complimentary bathrobes and slippers." Jimmy opens the door to a large closet. A light turns on inside, revealing two plush robes and several plastic bags hanging from a hook. The bags are labeled and require no explanation, but he explains them anyway, noting that laundry, dry cleaning, and shoeshine services all have a guaranteed turnaround time of eight hours or less.

"Muy rápido," he adds.

The sudden switch to Spanish appears to be too much for Tom, who jumps up from his seat. He flips open his wallet, thumbing through his dwindling supply of small bills. Ever since they left the hotel this morning, he's been tipping people left and right—the housekeeper, the bellman, the concierge who called for their taxi, the man at the port who tossed their luggage into some kind of wheelbarrow and then took off running toward the ship. Tom's expression is the same now as it was then—slightly pinched and put out, in a way that suggests he's more inconvenienced by the need to tip than grateful for the service.

"All right, thank you. I think we can figure out the rest from here."

"Yes, thank you so much," Franny adds, brightening the sound of her voice to make up for the coldness in his. "That was very helpful."

The faint indentations on each side of Jimmy's mouth sharpen into creases when he smiles. He bows deeply from the waist as he accepts the twenty-dollar bill from Tom's outstretched hand, palming it with the skill and speed of a magician. They follow him to the door, where Jimmy stops at the threshold and flashes them another smile before offering two final reminders. The first is about the celebratory champagne toast, which will be served poolside right before departure. And the second is to ring him if they need anything—"absolutely anything"—a line he's probably required to repeat to all the passengers in his section of the deck.

Tom turns the lock and dead bolt as soon as Jimmy leaves. "You actually thought that was helpful?" he asks. "Like we've never seen a coffeemaker or a minibar before?"

"I was trying to be polite." She's tempted to say that it can't be easy repeating the same script with such enthusiasm, especially when people aren't listening. "Plus, he was thorough" is all she can manage.

Franny unwinds the silk scarf from her neck and pulls back her long hair, which is still damp with sweat from the rush to board. According to Jimmy, they were among the last passengers to arrive, which wasn't the accident he assumed it to be. There was no snarl of traffic that kept them, no confusion about the recent change of port. Just another argument that stretched on for longer than it should.

"So this is the Royal Ocean Suite," Tom says, in a tone that suggests there's nothing royal about it.

"Suite" probably isn't the right term to describe the cabin, which has a combined sitting room and bedroom, but Franny is relieved by how bright and airy it is, not cramped at all. Whoever designed the space tried to make the most of the light by adding built-ins and furniture in white lacquered wood, upholstered in muted shades of salmon and seafoam. She's glad that Tom insisted on getting a suite and wonders if she should tell him so. If they're going to survive this trip, she needs to find a way to smooth things over, even though the trip—the timing of it, at least—is what he's so upset about. Despite his many protests in recent days, Franny refused to postpone their plans, which left him no choice but to come.

"Celebratory champagne toast," he says. "Did you catch that?"

"It's his job, Tom. He's supposed to tell us about the events."

"Celebratory."

He shakes his head at her. Once again, it feels like an accusation. She worries that he's about to resume the fight that began at the hotel, which was really just a continuation of the same fight they'd been having all week.

"I'm going to the bar," he announces instead.

"What? Now? You're not going to unpack?"

"I can do that whenever."

At least three or four times a month, sometimes more, Tom has to travel for work. He says that having a routine helps him keep his bearings. Whenever he arrives in a new city, he hangs his clothes in the closet to air out the wrinkles. As soon as he returns home, he empties his suitcase and sorts everything into piles, one for the laundry and one for the cleaners. He's not the type of person to live out of a suitcase, or watch TV when he travels, or sit around in some bar.

"But don't you want to . . . Your tux—"

He gives Franny a withering look that warns her not to say another word about his tux, which she brought even though he told her not to. When he found the garment bag discreetly tucked in between their suitcases and carry-ons that morning, he asked if she'd lost her mind. Did she really think he was in any sort of mood to wear black tie and take her dancing?

Franny scans the cabin, searching for something else to talk about, something that will keep them in each other's presence, if only for a little while longer. They'll never resolve this unless they try. She picks up the brochure on the coffee table and flips through its glossy pages, landing on the maps of all the decks.

"So which bar are you going to?" she asks.

"Whichever one has a working TV."

Every set on the ship probably relies on the same satellite signal, which isn't worth pointing out to him. She understands that he just needs something to do.

"Well, let me come with you," she says. She's surprised when he doesn't turn her down.

THE *SONATA* IS the oldest ship in Aria Cruise Lines' fleet, something Franny didn't know—something she couldn't possibly have known—when her brother and his girlfriend convinced her to book passage on the five-day cruise to Bermuda. According to the historical section of her brochure, the ship entered into service in July 1980, making it just over twenty-one years old. Franny now realizes what it was about the mega-liner that made her so curious. Not only was it substantially bigger, but it also looked newer, more modern, *nicer*. In comparison, the *Sonata* seems like a budget ship, the kind that appeals to a certain type of traveler, like her perpetually underemployed brother. That's probably why their suite was so affordable, why suites were even available at all.

On their way to the elevators, Franny can't help but see signs of the *Sonata*'s age everywhere she looks. Tuscan color schemes of gold and terra-cotta; velvet wallpaper and paisley-patterned carpet; cherub-faced wall sconces dripping crystals shaped like teardrops; and along every corridor, elaborate chandeliers filled with soft white bulbs, giving the appearance that all the gilt and gold leaf surrounding them is lit by candlelight. When Jimmy first showed them to their cabin, she was too anxious to focus on the décor, which struck her in passing as excessive and old-fashioned. But now she sees it more clearly for what it is: tacky and old.

Tom walks at a brisk clip, following the signs to the elevators. He seems determined to get to a bar as quickly as possible, passing hotel-quality paintings of fruit bowls and fat, lyre-playing angels. Franny's chest tightens. She remembers what he said when she first mentioned the trip, before she hinted and asked and eventually pleaded with him to do this for her. *But we're not cruise people.* She wonders what exactly she's gotten them into. The busyness of their surroundings is such a contrast to their home, a Fifth Avenue co-op that's as spare and serene as the *Sonata* is baroque. Although Tom's not religious, she's certain that if he believed in hell, this ship is probably what it would look like.

At the elevator bank, three older couples are huddled in conversation, waiting to go up. Tom presses the down button like he's ringing a doorbell, impatient for someone to answer.

A woman with a great white pouf of hair turns to him. "I think that's the wrong way."

"Pardon?" he asks.

"The bubbly—it's on the Lido Deck. Deck ten."

"Oh . . . we're not going to that."

The woman tips her head to the side and frowns at him as if he just said something silly. "But they only do free champagne when we're about to leave. Plus, you're going to miss a pretty good view of Boston."

"We're not really int—"

Franny places a hand on his shoulder, aware that making small talk with strangers might lead to a subject she wants to avoid. "We're not going to that *right now,*" she interrupts. "We just wanted to take a quick look at the lower decks." She hopes this will be the end of it even though she suspects it's probably not.

"You young people." The woman seems delighted. "Already checking out the bars and nightclubs, aren't you?"

Franny and Tom are both thirty-eight. Not quite "young people," but younger than most of the people she's seen on board. Franny smiles politely, not certain what to say. The woman smiles back, motioning toward Franny's wedding rings with her chin.

"Well, aren't you a lucky girl?"

Under the twin chandeliers—one in front of each elevator—the emerald-cut diamonds appear even larger and brighter than usual, illuminated from the outside in. Franny quickly lowers her hand from Tom's shoulder.

"Are you two newlyweds?"

The word "newlyweds" attracts the attention of the woman's friends, who turn in unison to examine them.

"Just married?" a man with a hearing aid says to no one in particular.

"They're very good-looking," another woman whispers to her friend, but not quietly enough. "They'll have beautiful babies. Our neighbor's baby is half Oriental."

Tom's older relatives make comments like this at every holiday gathering, immune to his reprimands about not calling Franny "Oriental" or assuming that all married couples want children. He often seems more bothered by this kind of talk than she is, though Franny appreciates his willingness to correct people so that she never has to. She's not certain if he heard what the woman said because his expression registers no reaction now. He just stands there, staring at the bronze-paneled elevators. There's an arrow above each set of doors, slowly ticking toward them. Both cars seem to be stopping on every deck.

"No, we're not newlyweds," Franny says, scanning the area for stairs.

"First-timers though?" the woman asks. "To cruising, I mean."

To confirm this will only invite more conversation. But better this subject than the alternatives, she decides. "Yes. We're here with my family . . . for my mother's seventieth birthday." She omits the words "to celebrate," aware that Tom is sensitive to the idea of celebrating anything right now.

Like "newlyweds," this information earns a murmur of approval from the couples, who chime in with "wish my kids would do that" and "my son would never" in that way of people who are actually quite proud of their adult children but don't want to seem too proud.

"How wonderful. So where are they?" The woman looks around like they should all be together.

Franny has no idea. Her brother, Jae, and his girlfriend, Esther, were in an earlier boarding group with Ma. They never got a chance to make arrangements about where to meet or when. She doesn't even know what their cabin numbers are, which was terrible planning on her part. But despite a sudden pang of guilt for losing track of her family, she's grateful to have some alone time with Tom before the cruise starts, to make sure he remembers why they agreed to do this in the first place, even if the timing is no longer right.

"My mother's resting," she guesses. "My brother too."

"*Resting*? But they're going to miss departure. You all must be first-timers, aren't you?"

The up elevator arrives with a soft chime. When the doors open, Franny is disappointed to see that the car is nearly full.

"What did I tell you?" the woman says to Tom. "Everyone's heading to the pool."

She and her friends size up the situation and wonder aloud if half of them should get on or all six of them could squeeze in together. They bicker back and forth, eventually deciding that they don't want to get separated in the crowds, not like they did on that cruise to Alaska when they couldn't find Fred for an hour. The people in the elevator are surprisingly patient, as if they all have a Fred of their own to deal with. They hold the doors open until the woman finally waves them on.

"So where are you folks from?" she asks.

And there it is. The subject that Franny was hoping to avoid. The question was clearly directed at Tom, perhaps as a way of drawing him into the conversation. Franny stares at him in profile, hoping he can sense her thoughts like he sometimes does at parties when he decides it's time to leave before she even has to ask. *Don't answer her*, she tries to tell him now. *Just lie*. But of course, this is what Tom has wanted to talk about all along.

"We're from New York," he says.

The woman's eyes widen. "New York City?"

He nods.

The couples stop chattering. The wife of the man with the hearing aid almost shouts at him: "They're from *New York City*." At this, the man's whiskered gray face collapses.

Whatever excitement the couples were just feeling, heading up to the Lido Deck for champagne and a view of the port, is instantly extinguished. Instead, they study their sandals, fumble with the cameras slung around their necks, glance impatiently at the elevators they were content to wait for just moments ago.

"It's so awful," the woman says quietly. "What happened there, it was just so awful."

"That's why I'm trying to find a TV," he says. "We both work downtown. Our offices are right in that area . . . I want to know what's going on."

On Franny and Tom's first date—a setup by former classmates from law school—she appreciated how quick he was to pick up on subtle cues about things she'd rather not discuss. Her siblings, for example. What her father did for a living. It's rare for Tom to misread a social situation, but it's obvious that that's what he's done. The woman seems nervous all of a sudden, wringing the bamboo handles of her purse like a wet rag. She doesn't want to continue talking about what happened in New York any more than her friends do. She just wants to acknowledge their shared grief and move on.

"Try to have a nice time with your family," she says, patting him gently on the cheek. "There's no use sitting in front of a TV, just watching those planes hit the towers over and over again."

THE BAR, WHICH is called the Grotto, is nearly empty when they arrive. The bartender is the third person to remind them about the champagne toast by the pool, prompting Franny to wonder if free champagne is a big deal on every cruise, or just this one.

"Do those work?" Tom asks, pointing at the TVs mounted from the ceiling. All three sets are turned off.

"Sorry, mate. Problem with the satellite." The bartender's accent sounds fake, but his name tag confirms that he really is from Australia. "Should be fixed very shortly. What would you like to—"

The end of his question is cut off by the sound of a horn—two long, slow blasts from somewhere nearby. Tom sits down and orders a round of club sodas, which Franny interprets as an invitation, even though she dislikes club soda and always has. She slides in next to him, not certain where to begin. What can she say that she hasn't already said? Despite Tom's recent accusations to the contrary, she does understand that the timing of their trip is terrible. Insensitive and inappropriate, to use his terms. But they agreed to do this three months ago when Jae and Esther first suggested they come, back when the world seemed safe and all they risked losing was five days at sea.

The bartender returns with their drinks and a fish-shaped bowl of nuts. "Anything else I can get for you?"

"Do you know if the Internet on the ship is working?" Tom asks.

"In the business center? No, that runs off the satellite too."

"Then what about phone calls?"

"From one cabin to another? You just dial—"

"No. What if I want to call someone who's not on the ship?"

The bartender glances at Franny, and then back at Tom. "Sorry, mate. That's also—"

"Don't tell me. The satellite." He mutters "unbelievable," but not quietly enough to escape notice.

Franny's jaw tenses. The bartender's does too. He waits for something more to follow, then reverts to the same script he used before.

"It should be fixed very shortly, sir. Anything else I can get for you?"

Tom is no longer paying attention. He's resting his chin on his fist, staring at a long bank of windows facing the pier. The question hangs there, suspended for a few seconds too long before Franny responds with an apologetic smile.

"No, thank you," she says.

It bothers her to see Tom behaving so rudely, especially to someone who makes his living serving others. As a teenager, she waited tables at her mother's Korean restaurant after school. The people who treated her like she was invisible were the worst. Franny downs most of her club soda, fighting the urge to tell him to be more polite. She resents the need to, but she reminds herself that nothing about his behavior—or hers, for that matter—is normal right now. Normal spun off its axis on Tuesday. The two of them rarely disagree, much less argue, but that's all they've been doing for the past five days—arguing about why she wants to be here and he wants to be home.

"You smell like cocoa butter," she says, just to hear herself say something.

"What?"

"I think that woman we were talking to, when she touched your face—I think some of her suntan lotion got on you."

He rubs his cheek and brings his fingers to his nose with a frown. "Did you notice her reaction, by the way?" He dips a napkin into his glass and wipes off his skin. "She would have stood there all day, just talking nonstop. But the minute I mentioned where we were from, it was like she couldn't get away from us fast enough."

The loudspeaker squelches. Franny clears her throat, raising her voice to be heard over an announcement. "People have different ways of coping, Tom."

This is something she's always known, but never understood as clearly as she does now. Tom's way seems to involve watching CNN play the same footage on loop, or reading every word of every article he can get his hands on about the attacks. Franny doesn't have the stomach for it, any of it. She looks up at the black television screens, grateful that the satellite isn't working. She hopes it stays that way. She doesn't need to see or read the news to know what happened. Every time she closes her eyes, it happens. The planes strike the towers, the smoke billows out, and then the people—the people start to jump.

"Look," he says quietly, his voice gentler than she's heard it in a while. "I know I've been giving you a hard time about this trip, but, Franny, even you have to admit, this is . . ."

He pauses, then waves his hand at the cavernous Grotto. She's not sure what he's gesturing at. It could be anything, or everything. The glittery faux rock walls, the waterfall spilling out into the indoor lagoon, the boulder-shaped speakers piping in soft island Muzak. Franny glances at the entrance, where more people are starting to filter in, dressed in bright floral shirts and billowy caftans that graze the floor.

"This is what?" she asks.

He shakes his head. "I don't know. After everything we've been through, this all just feels so . . . wrong."

As if on cue, a group of middle-aged women at the far end of the bar start to cheer. The bartender is putting on a show for them, rattling a metal cocktail shaker in each hand with exaggerated vigor. The women are laughing and smiling, having themselves a time. Franny knows what Tom means, but his word choice is telling. She wouldn't have said "wrong," which implies that there's a right and wrong. "Surreal" is actually what comes to mind. Being on this ship while Lower Manhattan continues to burn, while the death toll continues to mount, is absolutely surreal. But what can she do about what they left behind? Nothing.

"Maybe if you and your mom were close, I'd get why this was so important to you, but half the time, you barely get along."

There's no point trying to deny this, so Franny slowly rests her hand on his, not certain if he'll pull away. "Please. We're here now. Please just make the best of this with me."

Tom stares at his empty glass, nodding like he agrees, or at the very least, understands. But he still seems conflicted. Franny wonders what more she has to say to convince him. She already explained how meaningful birthdays are to elderly Koreans, who celebrate each decade of old age as if they didn't expect to survive. The *chilsun*—the seventieth—is widely considered to be the most important birthday of all. But given Ma's resistance to gifts, spending money, and being the center of attention, postponing the trip was effectively the same as canceling it. They would never get a second chance.

"Remind me again. What happened to the trip insurance you bought? Why wouldn't the cruise line let us use it?"

Franny holds the sigh in her chest as she recites the exact same answer that she gave him twice before. Their trip insurance policy specifically disallowed acts of war from coverage, and it defined "acts of terrorism" as incidents that occurred exclusively overseas, not on U.S. soil—language she hadn't given much thought to a few months earlier. That same language now makes everyone who purchased a policy ineligible for a refund, not that she and Tom really need one. It's not about the money for Tom; it never has been. It's about wishing he had an out.

"This is my way of coping," she says hesitantly. "Helping my mom have a nice birthday for a change—this is something I can actually do, something we can both do together."

Tom continues to nod as if it's finally sinking in. Franny forces herself to wait, aware that she's been doing most of the talking and now she has to listen. She watches the bartender work valiantly to entertain the small crowd gathered around him. He spins a lazy Susan and fills four rotating coupe glasses with peach-colored liquid, prompting everyone to break out into applause.

"Excuse me, sir?" A young man with messy brown hair leans over the bar. He waves his empty glass in the air, signaling that he wants another. "Sir?"

The bartender seems slightly annoyed by the man's tone of voice and insistent posture, encroaching on his space behind the bar. He focuses on the drinks in front of him, plucking flower petals out of a plastic container with tweezers and floating them on the surface of the cocktails.

"*Sir,*" the man repeats, louder this time.

"There's a line over here, sweetheart," a woman says good-naturedly.

"I'll be right with you." The bartender doesn't lift his head from his work.

Franny is beginning to suspect that the man isn't a man at all. He looks more like a college student, or possibly even a teenager, someone too young to be served alcohol.

"Excuse me, sir." The kid is almost shouting now. "I just need some water."

She turns to Tom, wondering if he's watching this interaction too. But he's staring at the bank of windows again, his expression as sad as she's ever seen it. It takes a few moments to realize what he's looking at, but eventually, like clouds slowly drifting in the wind, the tiny changes in the scenery become more obvious to her. The pier is moving. Or more accurately, the ship is moving away from the pier.

The *Sonata* has departed.

2.

His agent probably shouldn't be his agent anymore. But at sixty-two, with only a handful of recent screen credits to his name, Doug knows he'll never do better than Annette, whose reputation still manages to open some doors for him, albeit fewer and fewer each year. Now in her late seventies, maybe even her early eighties, Annette routinely forgets things and sends him inscrutable messages from her BlackBerry that she says she didn't mean to send. She also falls out of contact, sometimes for weeks at a time, which would be fine if she still employed her legion of terrified-looking assistants to take his calls. But those days are long gone.

Doug blames Annette for his current predicament, sitting in a dark corner of the Grotto, a place he thought he'd never return to again. But here he is, trying not to hyperventilate and failing miserably. He sinks into his seat, head buried in his hands, telling himself to inhale, one-two-three. Exhale, one-two-three.

This is the third panic attack he's had in as many days, an unusually high number for him. The worst of them was on the flight from LAX to JFK, right after U.S. airspace reopened for commercial air travel. The stewardesses actually had to give him oxygen from a tank as he lay on the floor. Doug was mortified for causing such a commotion, in full view of everyone in coach, no less. He apologized profusely when the stewardesses removed the mask and sat him up, his gray hair so charged with static, he could see the electrified strands in his peripheral vision. The redheaded one squeezed his arm and told him not to be embarrassed. Then she gestured toward the half-empty cabin and said he wasn't alone. Everyone was so nervous about flying now. Although Doug agreed with this—he'd caught himself guiltily eyeing a Middle Eastern man during boarding—he couldn't bring himself to tell her that his fear came from an entirely different source.

The last time Doug set foot on the *Sonata*, it was 1982. Ronald Reagan was president. The Berlin Wall was still standing. He had a bit part in *Raiders of the Lost Ark* that ended up on the cutting room floor. He didn't miss being on the ship, not at all. In fact, he suspects that some of the worst moments of his life took place in this very room. He's both grateful and horrified that he was too drunk or high to remember most of them now. It's a testament to Annette's prickly, persuasive nature that she finally convinced him to book a *Starlight Voyages* reunion cruise, returning to the same ship where his best-known television series was filmed. She argued that it was great money for just an appearance—the most anyone was ever going to offer him, he was stupid to keep turning it down—plus it came with an ocean-view suite and legions of fans who were willing to pay top dollar to meet one of their favorite stars from the show.

"Wouldn't that be nice?" Annette had asked, nearly a year earlier when she first told him about the job. "Being adored again? In sunny Bermuda?"

Doug remembers thinking the whole thing seemed a little sad. Some of his former castmates had carved out a decent living doing

Starlight Voyages–related appearances. But at least they'd had real roles on the show, actual storylines that went somewhere and required them to act. Doug's character, a bartender aptly named Mack, was known for delivering line after line of strangely wholesome innuendo to female passengers while wearing uncomfortably tight shorts. Still, he received more fan mail than many of his castmates combined. When filming wrapped on *Starlight Voyages*'s ninth and final season, Doug liked to imagine that Mack had fallen off the ship in a drunken stupor and drowned, never to be seen again, while he—Doug Clayton—moved on to the film career that everyone expected him to have.

He wonders how many of Annette's older clients actually fell for that line about being adored again. Having experienced adoration during the early part of his career, Doug considers it overrated, the kind of thing that people want when they don't know what they need. These days, he just hopes to make a decent living, save for retirement, and earn enough credits to hang on to his health insurance from the actors' union.

"Here, Uncle Doug." Gideon returns from the bar with a glass of water. "Sorry that took so long."

Although his photo hasn't appeared in the tabloids in ages, he scans the room to make sure no one is watching. Then he quickly slaps two Xanax into his mouth with an open palm and chases them with water. Technically, Doug is in recovery. Technically, recovery can mean a lot of different things.

He closes his eyes and slows his breathing again. *Inhale, one-two-three. Exhale, one-two-three.* Whenever he takes his medications, he uses an old visualization technique that he learned at a wellness retreat in Big Sur. He tries to imagine the pills traveling through his esophagus, entering his stomach, and dissolving into millions of tiny particles as they enter his bloodstream. Whether the relief this exercise provides is real or psychosomatic, it doesn't matter. In the throes of a panic attack, all that matters is that it ends.

Doug opens his eyes to find his nephew staring at him. He looks so much like his dad—Doug's younger brother—at the same age, right down to the lanky build and unruly tangle of hair. Gideon is a good, smart kid. Always has been. Quite possibly the best of the whole Clayton clan. Doug doesn't regret trading in his ocean-view suite for two windowless interior cabins so he could bring him along as a guest.

"It's okay, Gid. I'm fine now. I really am."

"Oh, I'm not worried," he says, clearly worried. The crease between his eyebrows, the one that forms whenever he frowns, is deep enough to wedge a dime into. "Should I get you another glass of water?"

"No, I'm all set. Thanks."

Doug feels the need to say or do something more to reassure his nephew, so he breathes in deeply and sticks out his chest, playfully beating it like a drum. Halfway across the room, he notices two young women staring at their table. One of them takes a sip of her drink and smiles at Doug over the rim of her glass. He sinks down in his seat again, not ready to be recognized yet, not certain if he'll ever be ready again.

"So, do you mind if I ask . . ." Gideon twists the bracelet on his wrist. It's a white and yellow one, the woven kind that used to be called friendship bracelets back in the eighties. "What happened to . . . I mean, what triggered that?" He says "that" delicately and twists the bracelet harder, like he's referring to some unfortunate, unmentionable disease.

"I'm not really sure, Gid."

He was fine during check-in, the tour of their cabins, and the lap around the Lido Deck before it started to fill. At first, he was even fine sitting in the Grotto. But things quickly went downhill after the twin horns sounded, signaling their departure. He has no idea why that particular noise set him off when crossing the ship's threshold didn't.

"I wish I could explain it, but I can't."

Gideon nods. He stops fussing with his bracelet and glances around the room. "We were talking . . . before, you know . . . about whether this place has changed a lot."

The Grotto is basically the same cave-like monstrosity it used to be, not that Doug can remember all the details. "It doesn't seem any different. That thing is still there." He points at the lagoon, a huge, asymmetrically shaped fountain with a thick layer of coins on the bottom. "I'm pretty sure I fell into that once."

"You did?"

Gideon seems like he's trying to look interested, but Doug can tell how exhausted he is, too exhausted for someone his age. "Our trip's off to a pretty rough start, isn't it?" he asks, finally acknowledging the obvious.

He's referring not to the panic attack so much as the last-minute scramble to get to Boston by train. When they'd arrived at the ship terminal in New York that morning for early boarding, a uniformed man with a machine gun slung over his chest told them the port had been closed since the eleventh and all cruise ships scheduled to depart from New York had been rerouted to Boston. In addition to being physically intimidating, the man seemed irritated and somewhat skeptical that Doug hadn't received word directly from the cruise line. "Like every other passenger," he said emphatically. He was unmoved by Doug's explanation that his agent had been communicating with Aria on his behalf and vice versa, and she hadn't told him about the change.

As far as lapses in the agent-client relationship went, this one was bad. Someone with more options probably would have considered it unforgivable, but Doug hadn't been that kind of person in a while. Maybe Annette was avoiding him after he left all those voicemails on Tuesday, asking if he could cancel his appearance on the ship. Maybe she didn't want anything to interfere with her ten percent cut. Or maybe—and this is the possibility that worries him most—maybe she just forgot.

THE WOMAN SIDLES up to their booth so quickly, Doug nearly jumps out of his seat when she says hello—a reaction that she seems to think is hilarious.

"Oh! I'm so sorry! I didn't mean to scare you," she says, laughing. "I just wanted to introduce myself. I'm Tabby Sullivan, the assistant entertainment director."

"Abby?"

"No. Tabitha. Tabby." She raises her hands in front of her chest, curling them into claws. "Like the cat."

Her energy is off-putting, but Doug recognizes the type. Small-town theater kid, just happy to be anywhere other than home. He used to be the same way once. More looks than talent, more desire than sense. He resolves not to hold it against her.

"Nice to meet you, Tabby. This is my nephew, Gideon."

"Yes, hello! Someone mentioned you were bringing a guest." After exchanging handshakes, Tabby hugs her clipboard tightly, as if she's ready to burst. "I was so excited when I found out you were joining us. My entire family used to get together on Friday nights to watch *Starlight Voyages*. It was like the highlight of our week."

Although he's heard some variation of this a thousand times before, Doug smiles and nods appreciatively. "And where's your family from, Tabby?"

"Carterville, Missouri."

He nods again, vaguely familiar with Carterville, one of those Route 66 side-of-the-road towns similar to Galena, where he grew up in Kansas.

Tabby, still bubbling over, rocks back and forth on the balls of her feet. "My Grandma Sullivan—she wouldn't believe I'm standing here having a conversation with Mack Mitchell. Boy, did she used to *love* you."

Fans of the show often talk to him this way, like the best part of him exists only in the past. He tries not to take it personally, though it gets harder and harder every year. Normally, he'd ask if she wanted an autograph or a photo, something to send to the folks back home. But Tabby's curious phrasing makes him think that Grandma Sullivan might be dead now. Either that, or she's transferred her affections to someone else.

"If you were watching when we were on prime time in the seventies, then you must have been a baby."

Tabby laughs and swats him on the shoulder with her clipboard. The gesture is playful and coquettish—too familiar given how recently they've met. Doug prays that she doesn't think he was flirting with her.

"My nephew here, he just graduated from college. He was also a baby when the show was on the air."

He turns to Gideon, hoping he'll jump in and help carry some of the conversation. Instead, he catches his nephew staring at Tabby's breasts, which are quite large and noticeable despite how plainly she's dressed—black turtleneck, black pants—like a stagehand who moves furniture in between acts. Doug uncrosses his legs, accidentally kicking the underside of the table and rattling their water glasses.

"Pomona," he almost shouts. "Gid just got his degree in English and American Studies at Pomona."

"Congratulations!" Tabby nods agreeably, seemingly unaware of being ogled. "Is the cruise a graduation gift from your uncle?"

"Kind of," Gideon says, also seemingly unaware of being caught. "I always wanted to see where the show was filmed."

Doug arranges his face into a tight smile, which probably looks as awkward as he feels. He reminds himself that his nephew is a young man, and Tabby—though a few years older—is a young woman. It's not wrong for Gid to think she's attractive. Doug just doesn't like the way he did it.

"So . . ." She glances at her watch. "I imagine you'll be heading over to the atrium for the signing session now?"

"Signing session?"

"Yes. With the Captain's Club." She pauses, then adds, "You know, the rewards club for frequent cruisers?"

Doug shakes his head. "I'm sorry. I wasn't told—I don't know anything about a signing."

"But it was in your itinerary."

The speed with which this rolls off her tongue is alarming. It's obvious that he should have seen and read the itinerary already. He hesitates to tell her that he never received one; he didn't even know there was one. Annette didn't forward him anything, although it's possible she tried. There was a week in late August when he remembers hearing the shrill screech of a fax machine every time he picked up his phone. In retrospect, he can easily imagine Annette, with her cataracts and ever-thickening glasses, trying to fax something to his phone line instead of his fax line. He should probably just explain all of this to Tabby, but he's loath to make Annette look bad. To be represented by someone who's unreliable and irresponsible might suggest that he's also unreliable and irresponsible, a reputation he's worked too hard to reform.

"I've been traveling quite a bit for work," he says, glancing at Gideon, who doesn't seem to register the lie. "No fixed address to receive mail or faxes."

Tabby flips through the documents on her clipboard and pulls one out from the bottom of the stack. "Well, here then. You can have mine."

The itinerary is printed on bright yellow paper, and there are multiple pages—at least a dozen of them, all stapled together. Doug pats the breast pocket of his shirt. Finding it empty, he squints at the text, most of which is in a microscopic font. The only thing he can make out is that there are a lot of words. A lot of pages.

"I don't have my reading glasses with me." He swats at his pants pockets to be sure. "This is . . . this is just the general schedule, right? This isn't all for me?"

Tabby looks slightly concerned. "No. That's all you, see? Doug Clayton." She points at something on the top of the page, which must be his name.

Doug squints. His arms aren't long enough to hold the paper any farther. "Wait. Does this say *dance lesson*? I can't teach a dance lesson."

"Oh, you're not teaching it. We have professionals for that. You'll just be taking it."

He slides the itinerary across the table to his nephew. "Here. Can you make any of this out for me?"

Gideon scans the document, flipping through the pages with a confused frown. "It looks like they have you doing a lot of events, Uncle Doug. Cooking classes, photo session, Talent Night emcee . . ."

For years, Doug's AA sponsor had tried to convince him to wean off Xanax, arguing that benzos might lead to impaired judgment, which might lead to another relapse. He's glad he refused on the grounds that it was medically prescribed, no different from his statins or beta-blockers. If not for the Xanax in his system, his heart probably would have arrested by now.

"Tabby . . ." He glances at Gideon and back again. He's not sure how to express what he wants to say without seeming totally uninformed or just plain terrified. "Since this is my first time on one of these cruises, could you tell me . . . I guess I'm just curious . . . why am I doing all these activities *with* the passengers rather than, say, a discussion hour or a Q and A about the show?"

The radio on Tabby's belt chirps. A woman's voice warns that someone named Kevin is on the warpath again. She reaches down to lower the volume. "Well, it gives our guests a chance to really interact with you, to get to know you as a person rather than a performer they're just watching on a stage. That's why we pay our talent so well for these reunion tours. We really want you to be present and show our guests a good time."

"Karaoke." Gideon points at a line in the itinerary. "It says here that you're supposed to do karaoke."

"Yes, but, Tabby . . ." Doug feels himself grasping at anything he can, trying to convince her that he shouldn't have to do the things they hired him to do, none of which Annette ever discussed with him. He would have refused the job if he'd known. "Are people really interested in these types of activities right now? I mean, given what happened? Isn't the mood a bit more . . . somber these days?"

Tabby pauses, considering the question. "I suppose, but they all made the choice to come, right? Maybe the somberness is what they're trying to get away from."

To prepare for the trip, Doug spent months trying to visualize the things he'd actually enjoy doing while on board. Jogging around the Lido Deck instead of plodding along on his usual treadmill at the gym. Meditating outdoors, breathing in the clean ocean air. Free yoga classes and spa cuisine. A big stack of books. Meals with Gideon in the café instead of the main dining room with its stuffy formal seating arrangements. Somewhere in between, he knew he'd have to show up for his scheduled appearances—on time, looking dapper, with a smile on his face like the professional that he is—but suddenly he realizes that this cruise, this entire cruise, is just one long appearance.

THE FORMAT OF each fifty-minute episode of *Starlight Voyages* was always the same. There were three storylines, ranging from comedic to dramatic, featuring a combination of regular cast members, who played the crew, and several guest stars—usually actors plucked from other shows on the network—who played the passengers. All three storylines reached some form of resolution by the end of the cruise, which coincided with the end of the episode. Then the credits ran over a long shot of the crew waving from the upper deck as the passengers disembarked and returned to their regular, presumably improved, lives.

Near the entrance to the atrium, there's a life-size cardboard cutout of the cast on the same upper deck, right hands raised in midair as if posed for the long shot. Passengers are gathered around the display, posing for photos of their own, so Doug stops several feet away, prompting Gideon to stop with him.

"Wow. You were so young there, Uncle Doug."

Whenever he sees pictures of himself from the *Starlight Voyages* era, he cringes at his fake tan and volumized hair and one-size-too-tight uniform. He looks like a punch line now. But he wonders if he wasn't also a punch line then. A man well into his thirties, pretending to be a man barely in his twenties, with a small army of makeup artists, hairstylists, and costumers plying their trade to make the ladies swoon.

"Young and stupid," he says.

Of the six regular cast members, five are still living. Doug hasn't been in touch with any of them since the eighties, not because he dislikes them or has any hard feelings about the past. He actually suspects it's the other way around. He knows he probably said and did some things under the influence, many things, that caused his former costars to banish him from their lives. He just doesn't remember most of them. This is the fist wrapped around Doug's heart as he enters the atrium, where a long line for the signing has already formed.

"Are you sure you want to do this?" Gideon asks.

"I don't really have a choice."

"But can't you call your agent and complain about all the stuff they're making you do?"

There's too much history between him and Annette to go over in the time that he has, so Doug doesn't even try. "I signed the contract though. Let that be a lesson to you, Gid—always read the contract."

Gideon's forehead crease deepens, and Doug thinks it's hardly fair, making him worry like this. The trip was supposed to be a nice bonding experience for the two of them, not something they both had to endure.

"You should go explore the ship now. Have some fun," Doug suggests.

"You don't want me to stick around?"

"It's a signing line. I'll just meet up with you later." He pats Gideon on the shoulder and walks away, hoping this will encourage him to leave.

A murmur begins to build as Doug wades through the crowded atrium, a greenhouse-like space filled with sunlight and overgrown plants. Middle-aged women whisper to each other, "It's Mack!" and snap photos of him as he passes. Instinctively, he smiles and waves, smiles and waves, reminding himself that he now has enough Xanax in his body to calm a horse.

"Is that Doug Clayton?" a woman asks.

This voice is different from the others. Louder, brassier, almost theatrical in the way it projects across the room. It belongs to someone who wants to be noticed. He turns to see Renee Bostwick walking toward him, looking much like she did two decades ago. Blond, tan, trim. A knockout. Before he has a chance to prepare for what might happen, Renee gives him a long, perfumed hug that he didn't expect, and the fist wrapped around his heart begins to loosen, allowing him to breathe again.

"I saw your name on the schedule, but I just didn't believe it." She stands back and takes him in. "God, it's hardly fair. Your hair goes gray and it makes you even more handsome and distinguished, and here I am, still dyeing mine."

"Renee," he croaks, taken aback by the warmth of her greeting.

"It's nice . . . nice to see you again." He's aware of many sets of eyes on them and adds, "You look as beautiful as ever."

"Well, I should. I married a plastic surgeon." She laughs, and the people around them laugh with her.

Doug doesn't know if she just told a joke, but he laughs as if he's in on it too. "Are you still dancing these days?"

On the show, Renee played Donna, the ship's lead dancer and the closest thing to Mack's female counterpart. She often appeared onscreen dressed in brightly colored leotards, as if her life on the ship was just one big rehearsal. Unlike Doug, however, she actually had a chance to demonstrate her talents on every episode, which usually featured a few seconds of a dance routine on the main stage before cutting away to a scene in the lounge.

Renee pats her left side, flashing gold and gemstones on every finger. "I'm as good as new ever since I got this hip replaced."

A crew member tells them that the event is about to begin and ushers them to the table at the front of the room. Doug helps Renee into her seat before taking his own.

"Was someone else supposed to be here?" he asks, pointing at the empty chair on the end.

"Alan." Renee leans toward him and whispers behind her hand, "He hasn't boarded yet and no one's heard from him. Apparently, his brother's a firefighter in New York . . ." She leaves the sentence unfinished, but he understands what she meant to imply.

Doug, Alan, and the other two male cast members—Ron and Peter—used to spend most of their off-hours drinking together. After filming the show's exterior scenes on the *Sonata*, they gathered at the Grotto, usually staying until last call. After filming the interior scenes at the studio, they hit their regular circuit of West Hollywood nightclubs and bars. Nine years they did this, traveling back and forth from the ship to Los Angeles, yet Doug didn't even know that Alan had a brother. Or maybe he did know and had allowed himself to forget.

"You still keep in touch with everyone?" he asks.

"I do." Renee uncaps her pen. "Hello," she says brightly to a woman holding an old cast photo. "Would you like me to personalize that or just sign it?"

Doug wants to know how the others are doing, but the line has begun to move toward them. It loops around velvet-roped stanchions and stretches all the way out the door. He's not sure what he expected from this event, only that he didn't expect this. Back home in L.A., people rarely ask for his autograph anymore. He hasn't dealt with actual lines of fans since the show went off the air nineteen years ago, and the minor guest star spots and voice-over work that he does to pay the bills haven't exactly kept him in the public eye.

"Hello," he says, following Renee's lead. "Should I make this out to you, or just sign it?"

Thanks to the trio of watchful crew members running the event, the line moves at a brisk pace. Efforts to engage in too much small talk and requests to take new photos are politely but promptly shut down, which Doug is grateful for. "Let's make sure everyone has a chance to get their items signed," the crew says. Or: "You'll have plenty of time for photos with our stars this week." And most ominously to Doug: "Don't worry, this is just your first shot at them."

The people in line are mostly women of a certain age, with a handful of men scattered in between. Their enthusiasm for the show—and him—is unsettling. Embarrassing, even. It was just a show, he wants to tell them. Make-believe. But here they are, paying good money to sail on the tired old *Sonata*, confirming what he's always known about die-hard *Starlight Voyages* fans. They're strange. Even the things they ask him to sign are strange. He doesn't understand why anyone would still have his headshot from 1975 or a cast photo from the episode they filmed in France or a miniature metal replica of the ship. His only saving grace is the steady, numbing rhythm of the line, which makes him feel like a factory worker. Smile, sign, thank, repeat; smile, sign, thank, repeat—over and over again until there's no more line left.

When the session ends, exactly one hour later, Renee stands up and stretches. "Great job, ladies," she calls out to the crew as they scatter to collect the stanchions. "You ran that like drill sergeants."

"Yes, thank you." Doug checks his watch twice, stunned by how quickly the time passed. He actually didn't mind it as much as he thought he would, in large part because of Renee, with whom he chatted and joked in between autographs.

"Do you have any plans now?" he asks.

"Plans?"

"I was thinking it might be nice to get a cup of coffee somewhere and catch up without the crowds."

Renee is massaging her signing hand, which probably aches like his does. She stops and looks at him. "Are you kidding?" There's something not quite right about her expression. She almost seems put out by the suggestion.

"If you're free," he says. "But I understand . . . the schedule doesn't really leave much room . . ." He wonders if they have another event to go to and she's annoyed with him for being unaware, or perhaps inconsiderate. He had a bad habit of sleeping through his call times back in the day, inconveniencing everyone on the set.

"What did I tell you, Doug?"

"When?"

"All those years ago, when you called in the middle of the night. What did I tell you?"

He shakes his head, his mind the usual blank. He doesn't remember what call she's referring to. "I'm sorry. I'm not really sure . . ."

"I said don't"—Renee scans the room, lowering her voice as she walks away—"don't you ever come near me again."

3.

The safety presentation is about to begin when Lucy realizes her cell phone is still on. She squints at the screen, not recognizing any of the strange letters or symbols that appear in the upper-right-hand corner. "LE," it says, followed by a lightning bolt with a line drawn through it and a circle—or possibly a zero—she's not entirely sure.

"You know that thing doesn't work when we're at sea, right?" A man standing at a nearby cocktail table grins at her with straight white teeth.

She knows. She definitely knows. Lucy slips the phone back into her purse. "I just forgot to turn it off."

"If you need to reach somebody, they got a satellite phone on board, but I heard it's broken now. Plus, it's like thirteen or fourteen bucks a minute, I think."

The people on board the ship are chatty. Lucy has never experienced anything quite like it. Being alone is apparently a siren call for strangers to make random conversation. And being a first-time cruiser, which everyone seems to assume about her, is an invitation for all sorts of unsolicited advice. Back home in Boston, Lucy would probably find this kind of behavior patronizing, or at the very least, off-putting, but the old man seems harmless enough in his bucket hat and Bermuda shorts. He even has a ladies' tote bag hooked over his arm—raffia, oversize, with a cluster of red flowers embroidered on it.

"It's my wife's," he says, noticing her noticing the bag. "She forgot her life preserver, so she had to run back and get it." The man rakes his eyes up and down over Lucy's outfit—a white button-down shirt, sleeves rolled up to the elbows; black dress pants; and black slingback heels. "Did you board the boat straight from work or something?"

At her roommate Mariah's suggestion, Lucy had ditched the matching Brooks Brothers blazer in their cabin. But even without the top half of her pantsuit, she knows she stands out among the elderly white passengers gathered by the pool, dressed in their huge floral prints and mad plaids and gauzy linen guayaberas too thin to conceal the wiry chest hair underneath.

"I came from a job interview," she says.

"On a weekend? What kind of company interviews people on a Sunday?"

The kind of company that people are desperate to work for, she thinks. "We were originally supposed to meet on Tuesday, so everything had to be rescheduled. I was going to change once I got on the ship, but the porters lost my suitcase." She scans the crowd for Mariah, who insisted on leaving the first bar they went to so they could get to the safety presentation early. Then she promptly disappeared in search of more drinks.

"That happened to me once. Regency Cruise Lines, I think. If your bag doesn't show up after a certain number of days, they'll give you money—"

"Attention, all passengers." The announcement that's been playing on and off for the past twenty minutes starts again, but this time, the prerecorded voice is blasting out of the loudspeaker directly above Lucy's head. "Please report to your assigned muster station by seventeen hundred hours with the personal flotation device located in your cabin. Thank you for your cooperation with this mandatory safety drill."

Lucy looks at her watch. It's 5:02 now, but she doesn't see any crew members yet. She's used to things starting on time.

"You mind me asking what kind of job you interviewed for?"

"Oh, it was just a software engineering position." This is her default answer, the simplified version that she gives to people who aren't engineers.

The man looks Lucy over again, reassessing her. He seems both surprised and impressed. As the only Black female graduate student in her department, she's used to this reaction, but also tired of everything it implies.

"What do you have to study in school to get a job like that?"

"Computer science. I also majored in art."

"Art?"

"Attention, all passengers . . ."

The announcement loops back to the beginning. The volume is earsplitting, so she mouths a hasty *nice to meet you* to the man, puts on her life preserver, and throws Mariah's over her shoulder to search for a quieter place to stand. As she makes her way through the crowd, Lucy gets heady whiffs of suntan lotion, aftershave, perfume, and occasionally, menthol rub—the combination of which makes her slightly sick to her stomach. She veers toward the railing, where the crowd is thinnest and the air just smells faintly of brine. The sun is finally out from behind the clouds, dappling the opaque black water with light. She stares at the inkiness of the Atlantic, wondering why oceans are always blue on maps and globes. Never in her life has she seen a blue ocean.

Mariah returns a few minutes later, carrying two frozen drinks in fishbowl-size goblets. "Why are you wearing that?" she asks, laughing as she hands Lucy her glass. The pineapple wedge on the rim falls on the deck with a splat, so Mariah kicks it over the edge with her flip-flop.

"What do you mean?"

She reaches over and tugs on the nylon strap of Lucy's life preserver.

"The announcement said we're supposed to bring it."

"Look around though," she says, still laughing. "'Bring it' definitely doesn't mean wear it."

The pool area is awash with bright orange, but Mariah is right. Most of the people assembled in muster station 4 have a cocktail in one hand and a life preserver casually hanging from the other. Lucy reddens as she pulls the vest off over her head, nearly hitting herself in the eye with a dangling buckle. She thinks the awkward size and shape actually make it easier to wear than hold, but she doesn't want to stand out any more than she already does.

At 1707 hours, several crew members appear, dressed in crisp white uniforms. A woman with a bullhorn asks everyone to gather around. Some of the passengers take a step or two toward her, but most—including Mariah—stay where they are.

"I know you all want to get back to enjoying yourselves," the woman says, "so my crewmates are going to come around and check your names off the list while I quickly run through the safety features of our ship. In the event of an emergency, you'll hear an announcement instructing you to assemble at your assigned muster stations with your flotation devices, exactly as you've done here . . ."

Mariah turns her back to the woman and raises her glass. "Here's to our impromptu adventure," she says.

"Shouldn't we listen to the presentation?"

Mariah seems amused by the question, possibly even on the verge of laughing again. "Do you listen to the stewardesses when they do their safety demos on planes?"

The correct answer is clearly no. "Not really, but . . ."

"Then don't worry about it. This is like my twentieth cruise and I've never seen anything close to an emergency."

Lucy doesn't find this particularly reassuring, but she clinks her glass against Mariah's anyway. Her drink is so watered down, all she can taste is artificial coconut, syrupy and cold in a bath of melting ice.

"So, what do you think?" Mariah asks. "Is it what you expected?"

Two days ago, Lucy didn't know she was coming on this trip. There wasn't enough time to build up her expectations. She's still struggling to believe that she's here, while trying not to think about what she's done.

"It feels like we're the youngest people on board."

"Yeah, it's always like that. Plus, this is some kind of theme cruise that my grandma was into, and they tend to run even older."

"What's the theme?"

Mariah shrugs. "No clue. Gran just asked if I wanted to sail to Bermuda with her this week and I said yes."

The idea of this is so strange to Lucy. Every summer, her parents rent a small beach house on the eastern shore of Maryland where her father catches up on his reading and her mother cooks three meals a day, the same as she does at home. Most of the families that

Lucy grew up with vacationed the same way, fleeing D.C.'s heat and tourists for a glimpse of water, which usually meant the shore or a nearby lake or river. She didn't know anyone who'd ever been on a cruise before, so she was surprised to learn that Mariah's grandmother took her on one every year. Also surprising was Mariah's last-minute invitation to join her—for free—on the cruise to Bermuda. Her grandmother, a retiree who lived in Wisconsin, was afraid to fly now. She was especially afraid to fly into Boston, where two of the hijacked planes had originated.

At first, Lucy said no. She couldn't possibly go on a cruise. The fall semester—her last at MIT—had just started. She'd recently endured a gauntlet of first-round job interviews during a weeklong recruitment event, and if all went well, she'd soon advance to several more. She also had a dissertation that needed a final chapter and an adviser who expected her to be in the lab whenever she wasn't writing. But here she is instead, no longer able to see land, drinking a piña colada and wishing there was more rum in it.

"I can't believe I'm here," she says, not so much to Mariah as to the ocean.

"I know. Until I saw you board, I wasn't sure you'd actually come." Mariah lowers her sunglasses to examine a man walking past. "But I'm so glad you did, Luce."

Lucy dislikes this new nickname that Mariah's been throwing around ever since they boarded. *Luce.* She already goes by too many names to have another. Her grandparents call her Lulu, like they did when she was a child, while her parents refer to her as Lou. Meanwhile, everyone from college and grad school knows her as Lucy, which is how she knows herself. At least she thought she knew herself. But if that were true, then how does she even begin to explain what she's doing here?

* * *

AFTER RETURNING THEIR life preservers to the cabin, they stop at the Guest Services desk. An apologetic woman with a thick Irish accent tells Lucy that the porters still haven't found her suitcase, but her bag is their "number one priority." Lucy doubts this, but it's hard to complain after the woman gives her a toiletry kit sealed in plastic and a hundred-dollar voucher good at any of the shops in the *Sonata*'s galleria.

On their way to the elevators, they walk through a corridor filled with posters of the onboard entertainers. There's a hypnotist, a magician, a jazz singer, a dance troupe, a trio of rhythmic gymnasts, and several more. The heavily made-up faces, framed by words in giant, attention-getting fonts, stare down passersby from one end of the corridor to the other, beckoning everyone to experience a SPECTACULAR display of magic or a DAZZLING revue of Broadway's biggest hits. Lucy didn't realize that productions like this were available on the ship. It occurs to her that she has no idea what people actually do on cruises, other than cruise, so she asks Mariah.

"You won't have much chance of getting bored, if that's what you're worried about. They have activities going on pretty much twenty-four seven."

"What do you usually do?"

Mariah shrugs. "I'm a fan of laying out by the pool with a book and a cocktail. Oh, by the way, we can charge all our drinks to the suite. They still have my grandma's card on file."

Lucy tries to count up how many she's consumed since boarding. "But aren't the drinks free on cruises?"

"Only the nonalcoholic stuff. The rest, they'll bill at the end of the trip, but it's fine. Gran won't care."

Lucy isn't much of a drinker. And she's never really cared for swimming pools, the way the chlorine wreaks havoc on her hair. "Is there anything else you like to do?" she asks.

"Sometimes I'll go to an exercise class or a dance lesson. Gran also likes to see the shows after dinner, so I usually keep her company."

Lucy mentally catalogs all the things she'll need to take part in these types of activities: a bathing suit, comfortable shoes, a fresh change of clothes that doesn't look so out of place on the ship. Suddenly, her hundred-dollar voucher doesn't seem so generous anymore.

"What do you recommend doing on the first day?"

A pair of uniformed men walk by. The taller of the two nods at Mariah, gently touching the brim of his cap. Mariah smiles and cranes her head at him as if she has an extra joint in her neck, then turns back around.

"Mostly I just scope out where everything is and try to find my shipboard crush."

Lucy must look confused by this because Mariah adds: "You know, find some random guy to spend the week making eyes at. Forget the other passengers, by the way. Your best bet's always the crew."

Lucy has no intention of making eyes at anyone. She doesn't even enjoy flirting on land, not that she has many opportunities. Most of the men in her department are already married or have girlfriends, and the rest fall into the general category of "antisocial," which includes men who don't like to talk and men whom Lucy doesn't like to talk to. She wonders if any of them will notice that she's gone this week, not that she really cares. It's her adviser she's most worried about. She stiffens at the thought of Dr. Jimoh's reaction when he opens her email, which she sent just minutes before leaving for the cruise terminal. It was the same terse message she'd sent to her parents, simply cut and copied and readdressed. *I'm sorry for the short notice,* it said. *I'm going on a cruise to Bermuda with my roommate. I'll be gone for five days.*

They squeeze into a crowded elevator where a man with cigar breath is bragging to his friends about all the fish he recently caught in Baja. He holds his hands about two feet apart and explains how the Mexican girls at his hotel cleaned and cooked nearly a dozen of them for just a couple of pesos.

"Best fish tacos I've ever had," he says, pausing to study Lucy's outfit, which she desperately wants to change out of.

"The flirting can be pretty epic on cruises." Mariah picks up where she left off once they exit on deck five. She glances at the directional signage in the elevator bank, then takes a left toward the galleria. "The crew's really friendly because they're supposed to show you a good time, but all these ships have strict 'no fraternizing' policies, so they can only take it so far or else they'll get fired."

Lucy looks over at her. "You actually like that? Flirting even though it can't go anywhere?"

"It's just harmless fun, right?" Mariah winks. "Something to pass the time. So far, I think the Aussie's definitely in the running for hottest guy."

"Who?"

"The Australian bartender, the one from the first bar we went to."

Lucy only saw him from a distance, registering the bare minimum of details—tall, with white-blond hair like a Norwegian or a Swede. She wouldn't have guessed he was Australian. Then again, the lighting was dim and she was trying not to stare. The one time she glanced over at Mariah's suggestion, an old man sitting in her line of sight clearly thought she was looking at him. Rather than appearing flattered by the attention, he just seemed horrified, which made Lucy wonder what about her made him react that way, whether it was her looks or her age or the color of her skin. It hasn't escaped her attention that most of the passengers on the *Sonata* look like Mariah, while certain members of the crew—not the uniformed ones so much as the waitstaff and cleaners—look like her.

"I couldn't really see the Aussie," she says. "Bad light."

"We'll have to go back and sit at the bar next time."

All this neck craning and talk about shipboard crushes seems a little juvenile to Lucy, who was never particularly boy crazy, not even as a teenager. It reminds her that she and Mariah have known each other for years, but don't really know each other. They reconnected two months ago when Lucy posted an ad for an apartment share in the Wellesley alumnae magazine and quickly heard back from Mariah, whom she remembered. As undergrads, they ran in very different circles—Mariah, with a crew of New York City rich kids who liked poetry and weed, and Lucy, with a high-achieving, future summa cum laude set that led the Black Student Union, went out for multiple clubs, and pledged Alpha Kappa Alpha or the Deltas like their mothers.

Since Lucy spent more time in the lab than at home, she had few criteria for replacing her last roommate, who had recently graduated. Whoever took the empty second bedroom just had to be female, be tidy, and pay her share of the rent on time. She never intended to socialize with the person who moved in, which makes her presence on this cruise even odder.

"If they don't find your bag soon, do you at least have a change of clothes in your carry-on to get you through tomorrow?"

Lucy shakes her head, too embarrassed to admit that the only things in her carry-on are a notebook, a copy of her résumé, and a thick folder of background information on the company she interviewed with before boarding.

"Well, feel free to use my face wash and shower gel and that kind of stuff." Mariah looks at Lucy's feet. "What size shoes do you wear?"

"Seven and a half."

"I'm an eight, so you can borrow some of my sandals if you want. That's one less thing you'll have to buy." She turns and scans Lucy's chest and hips. "You're also welcome to borrow my clothes, if you think anything will fit." Her expression stiffens slightly. "Sorry, Luce. That came out wrong."

If not for the apology, Lucy probably wouldn't have registered anything worth being sorry for. It seems fairly obvious that borrowing clothes isn't an option. Mariah is tall and model slim, whereas Lucy is short with curves. Even if they were similar in size or shape, she doesn't think she could pull off some of the crazy white girl outfits that Mariah usually wears. The crop tops under vintage dresses, the unitards and flowy, flowery skirts, like some 1970s bohemian who just fell out of bed and threw on whatever random clothes she could find.

"I know what you meant," she says. "It's fine."

And it is fine. The seed of irritation growing within Lucy has nothing to do with Mariah. It has more to do with her feet, which are sore and blistered after hours of walking around on hardwood decks in slingback heels. The mere mention of borrowing Mariah's sandals, which Lucy has no intention of doing, is making it hard to continue ignoring the pain or the wet, sticky substance—blood, she imagines—pooling near one of the sharply pointed toes. She knows she should jump at Mariah's offer to loan her a pair of sandals, but Lucy's parents always took pride in outfitting her with new clothes and shoes at the start of every school year, not hand-me-downs from friends or relatives like some of the families who went to their church. She grew up believing there was something quietly shameful about wearing someone else's things.

The longer her own things are missing, the more their absence begins to weigh on her. Lucy is especially bothered by the fact that when she checked in at the terminal, she did exactly as the crew instructed and threw her bag into a large rolling cart, the same as all the other passengers.

"Don't worry," the Guest Services reps called out as people boarded the ship. "The porters will deliver your luggage to your cabins very shortly." Those were their exact words. *Don't worry.*

AS A CHILD, Lucy sometimes dislocated her right shoulder in her sleep. Tired of so many late-night trips to the emergency room, her father, a pharmacist who'd once dreamed of becoming a doctor, decided to pop it back into place himself. The first time he did it, the sensation was so bright and breathlessly sharp, Lucy passed out for several minutes. Repetition, however, made the pain routine, so by the time she went to college, she was able to pop the wayward shoulder back in on her own, usually with a single hard shove against the wall. Once, her roommate's boyfriend saw her do this and called her a "badass," a description so unlike her that she's been clinging to it ever since.

Despite her higher-than-average tolerance for pain, Lucy's blistered feet are making it hard to keep up with Mariah. For once, she doesn't mind being stuck in a slow-moving crowd, even though most of the people in the galleria seem to lack a basic understanding of pedestrian etiquette. Every few seconds, someone stops short to admire the trompe l'oeil walls, which have been painted to resemble an old Italian streetscape. Then someone else stops to study the elaborately decorated store windows that could rival Filene's at Christmastime.

The shops in the galleria sell everything from lingerie to bathing suits to evening wear, which should come as a relief to Lucy, but the clothes on display are all of a particular style. Most are pastel, animal print, tie-dyed, bejeweled, or otherwise embellished in some unappealing way. Mariah calls it the "*Golden Girls* aesthetic," reminding Lucy of the show that her mother used to watch in the eighties—old white ladies in Florida, always eating cake in their muumuus.

"Let's go to this one," Lucy says, stopping in front of a boutique called the Villa.

"Don't you want to do a full lap first?"

She doesn't. She's fairly certain that both of her big toes are bleeding now, so she points at the sign in the window. "They're having a sale."

A pair of saleswomen descend upon them with greetings as soon as they enter. They're both young, immaculately groomed, and speak perfect English through a layer of vaguely Eastern European accents. Lucy assumes they work on commission because they seem unusually eager to help, not like the sour-faced teenagers lurking behind the registers at the outlet mall where she shopped for her interview clothes. Mariah says they're just browsing, but the women continue to hover nearby, straightening displays that don't need to be straightened, probably in the hope of answering a question or unlocking a dressing room door.

Lucy makes her way toward the back of the store where she spots two tower racks filled with flip-flops. Even the adult sizes have bows or flowers or ladybugs attached to the wishbone-shaped straps, but she's in too much pain to be picky. She spins both towers and quickly chooses the plainest pair she can find—black and white stripes, but no ornament—for twenty dollars.

"Those are two for thirty-five." One of the saleswomen has crept up on her to share this information, even though it's clearly marked on the sign.

Lucy nods, trying to focus on how good it will feel to change into flats, not the fact that she could buy flip-flops in Chinatown for two bucks a pair.

"Thank you," she says, glancing at the woman's name tag, which reads KATYE on one line and ESTONIA on the next.

"Would you like me to help you find another pair?" she asks. "One for the pool maybe?"

Up close, it's impossible not to notice how pretty Katye is with her giant green eyes and heart-shaped face. She looks out of place in the Villa, hawking clothes that she's too young to wear. Lucy wonders if working on a cruise ship is considered a good job in her country, or if it's simply better than any of the jobs she could actually get.

"I only need one pair," she says, grateful for the arrival of new customers, who draw Katye back to the entrance.

Mariah calls her over to a large clearance rack of swimsuits, waving a hanger with a strawberry print bikini dangling from it. "These are actually a really good deal," she says. "I think I might get one."

Now that Lucy has something to put on her feet, she wants to focus on finding a change of clothes. But the swimsuits are surprisingly cheap, marked down multiple times with layers of orange stickers, one on top of the other. She rifles through the rack and pulls out a one-piece that's similar in style to the navy blue tank she packed in her suitcase. This one is black with a small gold anchor in the middle of the chest, which she doesn't love, but it's cut right for her figure and on sale for thirty dollars.

"Do you have this in a ten over on your side?" She holds up the suit for Mariah to see.

"I think you could probably fit into an eight, don't you?"

It's unclear whether Mariah actually believes this or if she's just trying to make amends for her earlier comment, but it doesn't matter. Lucy finds a ten. She also finds a plain black sarong that could double as a skirt or a swimsuit cover-up. Now all she needs is something to wear on top. The two of them move from rack to rack, one on each side as they sift through the expensive, unattractive blouses, most of which are made of shiny polyester. Occasionally, Mariah holds up an item that she thinks might work, but Lucy rejects her suggestions for being too red, too purple, too bare, too fitted, too floral, or too geometric.

"Oh, hey." Mariah motions toward the clock on the wall. "First seating is about to start. We better get going soon."

"What's first seating?"

"They serve dinner in the main dining room twice. Once at six and then again at eight-thirty. Gran always signs us up for the earlier group."

"But can't we go a little late?"

Mariah shakes her head. "No way. The people at our table won't order until everyone gets there, especially on the first night. They'll be annoyed about it too."

Lucy isn't sure what bothers her more—eating dinner with strangers, or not having time to change beforehand, assuming she even finds what she needs in the Villa. She scans the store to see how many more racks they have to go through. She's about to suggest they split up, convinced she'll go faster on her own without so many interruptions, when Mariah suddenly yelps.

"Here! I found it. No loud print, no weird cutouts. Just a plain white T-shirt with a tiny rhinestone heart on the hem. You could probably even pick the rhinestones off."

She hands the shirt to Lucy, who looks at the price tag first. Unlike the end-of-season swimsuits, the clothes are still full price, and the markups are ridiculous. Cruise ship prices for people with money to burn.

"But it's fifty dollars. And the voucher's only for a hundred."

Mariah shrugs. "Well, you'll probably have to spend some of your own money. It's not like you won't be able to afford it soon."

All afternoon, Lucy has been trying not to think about the jobs she recently interviewed for. Nine in all, each one more different than the next. Because of her research on the use of programmable spiders to index the web, her adviser accurately predicted that she'd be in high demand from government agencies, think tanks, and the private sector. But it's obvious that he's been trying to steer her toward the company she met with earlier today, a search engine that recently surpassed Netscape and Yahoo! in user hits.

"The upside there is huge," Dr. Jimoh keeps telling her. "They'll have to offer stock options to afford you, and if they ever go public, those could really be worth something one day."

Despite the luxe suite of conference rooms rented by the HR reps visiting from California, and the twenty-eight-dollar eggs Benedict that the head recruiter treated her to this morning, she's still having a hard time taking the company seriously. It's that idiotic name. *Google.* A play on a mathematical term that nonetheless reminds her of a babbling baby. She also hates their logo, with each letter spelled out in primary colors like it was written in crayon by a child.

"I just did first-round interviews. I don't have a job yet."

"Come on. A Black female computer scientist with a doctorate from MIT? You'll have your pick of jobs." Mariah smiles brightly, unaware of the insult she just levied.

The men in Lucy's grad cohort talk like this too. But unlike Mariah, they're not trying to be encouraging or optimistic. They want her to know that she'll get a good job after commencement, maybe before some of them do, maybe even at their expense, but not because of merit. Lucy slips her hand into her purse, reaching for her phone again before she remembers that it's useless now.

"What's wrong?" Mariah asks.

"What do you mean?"

Mariah draws a circle around her face with her finger. "You look totally freaked out all of a sudden."

"Oh. It's just . . . I just wish the phones on the ship were working so I could check my voicemail."

"I wouldn't worry about it. They'll probably get them fixed soon. And if not, we'll be in Bermuda in a few—"

"No. You don't understand. If someone leaves a message about a second interview and I don't call back right away, they'll probably assume I wasn't interested and move on." It's not the first time Lucy has had this thought, but it's the first time she's said it out loud. Hearing it almost makes it feel like a certainty. "They get a lot of applications for these positions. They move really fast. The tech companies especially."

Mariah continues browsing. "Okay, so just tell them you were delayed because you had a death in the family. Only a terrible person wouldn't understand something like that."

"But wouldn't I be a terrible person for lying about it?"

Mariah blinks at her innocently, as if she's never considered this.

She pulls out a shiny green blouse, takes one look at it, and quickly returns it to the rack. "Then tell them you needed a minute because of everything that happened this week. Like a mourning period, or whatever, but obviously, you wouldn't use that phrase."

"That's even worse, don't you think?"

"Why?"

"Because no one I know died or went missing." The fact that she has to explain this to Mariah irritates her. "What am I supposed to do, tell some recruiter I was sad after watching the news?"

"But it's true, right? Aren't we all sad?"

Are you? Lucy wants to ask.

4.

The headwaiter is deeply concerned about Franny's salmon. Is it not cooked properly? Is the sauce not to her liking? How can he help make it right? Franny wishes he'd stop asking so many questions, but it's obvious that Johannes is too serious about his job to take "It's fine" or "I'm not hungry" for an answer.

"My stomach's a little off," she says, placing a hand over her midsection as if to prove it. "It's my first time on a ship."

"I see." Johannes nods solemnly. "Then let me get you some ginger lozenges."

Before she can tell him not to bother, he's speed walking through the dining room, a blur in tuxedoed black and white.

Her brother's girlfriend leans over to show Franny something on her wrist. It looks like a rubber band, red with a small white button on it. "You should get one of these acupressure things in the gift shop," Esther says. "They really help with seasickness."

Physically, Franny feels fine. She's just too distracted to eat, surrounded as she is by her mother, brother, Esther, Tom, and some random couple and their granddaughter who were assigned to fill out their eight-person table. She didn't realize this was a common practice on cruise ships and wishes that Esther, who's quick to share lessons learned from her past travels, had warned her in advance. The presence of strangers upsets a dynamic that's already awkward enough.

Bob and Kathie Bowman are from Edina, Minnesota. When they first introduced themselves, they explained that the cruise was a gift for their granddaughter, Allison, who had recently graduated from high school. Perhaps to avoid any embarrassing questions about college, Bob, a retired CPA, quickly added that Allison was taking a gap year, hooking his fingers in the air when he said "gap year" as if he didn't believe what the kids were into these days.

Despite their being warm and personable, Franny suspects the elder Bowmans are glad to have Tom, another white person, at the table. And Tom seems equally glad for their company. After a brief attempt at small talk with Ma and Jae—he asked how they were settling in, if they liked their cabins, if they had any problems on the drive from New Jersey to Boston—the conversation quickly dried up, as it usually did when they were together. In Tom's defense, no one else tried very hard either. Now the circular table has cleaved in two and Franny feels like the odd man out, stuck between Tom, who's chatting with the Bowmans on her left, and Esther, who's talking to Jae and Ma on her right.

Franny picks at her entrée, flaking the salmon with a fork so it appears that she's eaten more than she actually has. Except for her and Allison—a vegetarian—everyone ordered the surf and turf special at Johannes's recommendation. Most of the fist-size filet mignons are gone now and the lobster tail shells are empty of their meat. She hopes this means dinner will be over soon, but then she remembers Johannes telling them to leave room for a special table-side dessert to celebrate their embarkation. Franny sinks into her chair.

"I have some Dramamine in my cabin," Esther says. "You want me to run back and get it for you?"

She has mixed feelings about Jae's girlfriend of the past year, the only semiserious one he's had in a while. Esther is a would-be musician like he is—a bad influence as far as Franny is concerned—but she appreciates the fact that Esther's making an attempt to be civil, unlike Jae, who's barely said ten words to her all night. Franny assumes he's still upset about the plans she made for Ma's *chilsun* on Wednesday, her actual birthday. When she first told him she'd rented a private party room and set up a meeting with the on-board catering manager, he said they didn't need to do anything that formal—the cruise was supposed to be their gift. But Franny argued that Ma had catered hundreds of events for people celebrating the sixtieth or seventieth birthday of a loved one. How could they not give her a proper celebration of her own?

She looks across the table to where Jae is whispering in Ma's ear—about what, she wishes she knew. As the baby of the family and also the only son, he's always had an easier relationship with their mother. Jae even moved back in with Ma a few years ago, something he tried to pass off as filial but was surely motivated by his finances. Neither he nor Ma seems to understand or care that it's bad manners to whisper at the dinner table. Twice, Franny notices Kathie Bowman glancing at them with just the slightest hint of judgment cracking through her Midwestern nice veneer. She's not sure what she finds more upsetting about this—the fact that they're being rude to strangers or the fact that they're being rude to her. If not for Franny, neither of them would even be here.

A month earlier, when the balance for Jae's fare and his half of Ma's was due, he called to tell Franny he was short. The admission was followed by a long, embarrassed silence that made it clear he wasn't a few hundred dollars short. He was *short*. Franny realized this was probably why he'd invited her to come in the first place, as insurance. She can't remember whether Jae asked for help or she offered to help, because what choice did she have? It was too late to plan something else and she knew Ma wouldn't go on the cruise without him. Bermuda had been his idea, after all. Or Esther's, at least. Franny agreed to pay off her brother's balance if he went along with her plans for the *chilsun,* a condition she knew he'd accept, however resentfully, because it would allow Ma to believe that the cruise was a gift split equally by her children. She wonders if Esther knows who actually paid her fare and if that's why she's being so nice to her now.

"I don't need any Dramamine. But thank you for offering."

"Well, make sure you hydrate," Esther says. "It takes most people a day to get their sea legs. Longer, if the water's really rough. One time, I was on this cruise to the Bahamas and the tail end of a hurricane—Floyd, I think, or maybe it was Mitch—anyway, the tail end of it started moving toward us . . ."

As she describes how high the squalls were, how violently they rocked the ship, Franny catches herself staring at the ring in Esther's nose, a small gold hoop circling her left nostril. She tries to look elsewhere, but every time her eyes land on a new location, something else claims her attention. A tiny black star tattooed on the outer edge of her heavily penciled eyebrow. A larger constellation of them peeking out from the collar of her shirt. Platinum blond streaks in her hair, one framing each side of her classically round Korean face. Nothing about Esther makes any sense. She doesn't look like the type of person who would ever go on a cruise, much less be a card-carrying member of the Captain's Club for Frequent Cruisers. She's too young, for starters. Too inked and pierced and bleached.

She also doesn't look like the nice Korean girl that Ma always wanted Jae to bring home. And yet Ma genuinely seems to like Esther, to feel as comfortable around her as she does with Jae.

". . . that was it. But it's so cheap to travel during hurricane season. I can't pass up a deal."

Franny snaps to attention, wondering if it's hurricane season now, if this is one more thing Esther didn't bother to mention before they booked this trip. She's about to ask when Johannes slides a small saucer in front of her.

"For you, miss. Ginger to help settle your stomach."

There's a pyramid of individually wrapped lozenges in the center of the gold-rimmed plate, each block perfectly stacked on top of the last. Franny feels guilty about the effort it must have taken to carry it undisturbed across the length of the dining room. She didn't mean for Johannes to go to so much trouble, but she barely gets a chance to thank him before he's off to tend to another diner.

Tom, who's been talking to Bob about the midterm elections, looks over at her plate. "Are you seasick?"

Even if she was, she'd never admit it, not to him. She squeezes his leg under the table. It's not an answer so much as a confirmation that he's still there.

"Aren't we lucky to have Johannes as our headwaiter?" Kathie asks Franny. "He's so attentive." She starts to laugh. "I wish I could say the same thing about us. We've been doing such a terrible job of getting to know you over here."

After the initial introductions, the Bowmans immediately turned to Tom, making the usual small talk—was he new to cruising? Had he ever been to Bermuda before? What did he do for a living? Franny had worried that he'd be sullen and unsociable during dinner, but as soon as he and the Bowmans discovered a shared interest in wine, they began paging through the leather-bound cellar list together, trying to decide what to order for the table. Five bottles later, and they all seem like old friends.

"I blame this setup," Kathie continues. "They put eight people at these giant rounds for ten."

Franny hadn't noticed how spread out they were, but now it seems obvious. The dining room is cavernous, a confection of pink and pearl and crystal that resembles the inside of a seashell. The room was clearly designed to hold at least twice its current capacity, which might explain why there's so much space between their seats and the individual tables. The cruise supposedly sold out in early August, but it doesn't look or feel sold out to Franny. She suspects that a large number of people who were scheduled to come backed out after the attacks, forgoing whatever they paid for their fare, insurance be damned.

"Have you taken many cruises?" Franny asks.

"Since we retired, yes. This is our twelfth."

"My mother retired last month."

"Oh! Congratulations!" Kathie raises her empty wineglass at Ma. "Bob!" She reaches over and shakes her husband's forearm, interrupting his conversation with Tom. "Bob, she just retired."

Franny wishes she hadn't said anything because suddenly everyone at the table is looking at Ma, raising their glasses at her.

"Congratulations, Nancy!" Bob almost shouts, using Ma's American name, which is how she introduces herself to strangers. "What line of work were you in?"

Ma reddens. Back home in Fort Lee, New Jersey, with its large Korean American population, she often goes for days without speaking English. Sometimes, Franny thinks she can actually see how stressful it is for her to try. Ma's accent isn't as bad as she says it is, but there's no convincing her of that. Around native-born English speakers, including Tom, she's reserved and self-conscious, almost painful to watch.

"A restaurant," Ma says. "I owned it and made the food."

Jae leans forward to add that it was voted "Best Korean Restaurant in Bergen County" for five years in a row. His pride in the recently shuttered family business is both surprising and irritating. Unlike Franny, who worked there every day after school starting in junior high, his involvement had always been minimal. When Ma needed another server, Jae begged her to let him go out for track and band instead. He also said his friends would make fun of him for waiting tables—a woman's job—an excuse that Ma actually let him get away with.

"Ah. I wasn't sure if you folks were Chinese or Korean. *Awn-yong-ha-say-yo!*" Bob says, hammering each syllable like a toddler playing the piano.

Ma responds to his hello with a flicker of a smile. Franny glances at the Bowmans' granddaughter, who hasn't said much during dinner. Allison's expression betrays nothing. No annoyance, no embarrassment even. She just continues twirling the last few strands of spaghetti around and around on her plate, making a scratching sound with her fork that all of them can hear.

"Wine!" Tom suddenly knocks on the table. "Come on now. We can't have a toast like this." He points at all the empty glasses. "Let's order some more wine."

FRANNY REGRETS MENTIONING Ma's retirement. In addition to embarrassing her mother, who occasionally glances at her in a way that doesn't feel very kind, the Bowmans turn the toast into an opportunity to go around the table, lobbing questions at everyone they haven't interrogated yet. First, they start with Esther, who tells them that she plays lead guitar in a band. When Kathie asks if they have any albums that Allison and her friends could buy at Tower Records, she says not yet. Franny notes that Esther doesn't mention the day job that actually pays her bills—working at the front desk of a recording studio in Jersey City.

The Bowmans soon turn their attentions to Jae, who says he's in "management," a claim that probably seems dubious given his shaggy, unkempt appearance. Franny thinks the term sounds as vague as his career. When asked how he and Esther met, he says his band—a grunge band called Teargas—used to play at the same clubs that hers did, but he's taking a break from performing to start a new business.

"Telecom industry," he adds.

This is news to Franny. She's grateful to Bob for asking what his business will do so that she doesn't have to.

"License ringtones," Jae says. "For cell phones."

Everyone around the table nods as if they understand what he's talking about, but it seems obvious that they don't.

"You mean license . . . the what? The sounds?" Bob asks.

Jae gives Esther a split-second look, the same look that used to infuriate Franny when they were younger. He always thought he was so much smarter than everyone else.

"I'm going to license the music to make the sounds. See?" He pulls his cell phone out of his pocket. "This thing—your basic, entry-level Motorola—it comes with like twenty ringtones, but they're all kind of boring, so my company's going to let people buy ringtones that sound like instrumental versions of their favorite songs."

"So . . . instead of ringing, Bob's phone could play 'A Hard Day's Night' whenever someone called?" Kathie asks.

"If I bought the license for that, sure."

Everyone nods again, but the idea isn't much clearer than it was before. Franny wonders if Jae's been carrying his signal-less phone around, just waiting for someone to ask what he does for a living. The way he talks about his new venture—casually, with a prop in his hand—seems very practiced. Her shoulders tense at the thought of him asking for another loan. "Investments," he calls them. After six unpaid ones—seven, if she counts the money for the cruise—she hopes he wouldn't risk that kind of embarrassment again. But then she glances at Ma, who's listening intently to the conversation, and a whole different kind of worry sets in. She wants to believe that Jae isn't the type of person who would ask their mother—newly retired and living on a fixed income—for a loan, but what she wants to believe and what she has reason to believe are two very different things.

"Hang on." Tom frowns. "How would you make any money doing something like that? Doesn't it cost a fortune to license a Beatles song?"

"I'll structure the agreements so I don't have to pay up front. Once someone buys a ringtone, then I'll split the proceeds with the musician or whoever holds the rights, sort of like a royalty payment."

This time, when Tom nods, it seems like he might actually get it. Worse, his expression suggests that he might even think it's a good idea. Franny nudges him under the table. When he turns to her, she stares at him meaningfully. *Do not encourage this. Do not encourage him. You know how this will end.* Tom blinks back at her. His eyes are glazed and slightly bloodshot. She scans the table to make sure no one is looking, then moves his half-full wineglass away from him. He smiles at her, impish, and quickly moves it back.

"It sounds kind of cool," Allison suddenly pipes up. "I'd buy a ringtone."

Bob laughs. "This, coming from somebody who doesn't even have a cell phone. Or a job, for that matter."

Franny watches for a reaction, but again, the girl's face is completely expressionless. She wonders how many times Allison has been annoyed by her grandfather to reach this state of not caring. She wonders if people ever look at her and Tom the same way.

"One day, we'll all have cell phones," Jae continues. "Ten, fifteen years from now, they won't make the kind that plug into the wall anymore. Every phone will be a cell phone."

Bob laughs even harder. "It sounds like a great idea, then."

Ma perks up at this, but Jae clearly knows the difference between an encouraging comment and a patronizing one. He sinks into his chair, losing the inches of height he seemed to gain while talking about his plans. Franny isn't sure whether to feel sorry for him or relieved to see him shut down, but then the usual resentment starts to seep in, crowding out the possibility of anything else. Her brother is thirty-five years old and still behaving like dead weight.

Just as Franny senses the spotlight of the Bowmans' attention shifting in her direction, Johannes returns to the table. Behind him is another tuxedoed waiter pushing a wheeled cart with a large metal dome on it.

"And for your dessert this evening, we have bananas flambé," he says proudly, doing the same grand sweep of his arm that Jimmy, their room steward, did earlier.

The other waiter lifts the dome to reveal a pan filled with sliced bananas steeping in butter and sugar. Kathie, who's been more excitable ever since Tom poured her another glass of wine, cups her cheek and says, "Oh, myyyyy" in a way that makes bananas seem thrilling. The waiter splashes some rum into the pan and ignites it, swirling and shaking the blue flames over a portable gas burner.

Just as the flames are about to go out, he sprinkles them with something from a small spice shaker—cinnamon, Franny assumes from the smell—and the pan emits a bright, crackling fireball before the flames quickly settle down again. Out of the corner of her eye, she sees the same two-man show taking place all over the dining room.

The dessert service is courteous but brutally efficient, no different from the salad or entrée courses. Johannes and the other waiter work swiftly as a team, spooning the caramelized bananas into small bowls and topping them with ice cream and cherries. The presentation and distribution take only a few minutes before they offer a synchronized bow and move on to the next table.

"So, Franny . . ." Bob clears his throat.

She takes a bite of treacly banana, bracing herself.

"Your husband tells us you're both lawyers. Do you work for a developer too?"

It's strange how people present themselves, she thinks. Tom doesn't work for just any developer. He works for his father, who owns and develops commercial properties all over the country. His two older brothers work for their father as well, ensuring that Tom will always have a job if he wants one, but never the top job, which he says he doesn't mind. His brothers are professionally and socially ambitious in a way that he finds distasteful, married off to women from families as wealthy as their own. Tom has always liked the fact that Franny is from a working-class background. He used to tell people stories about all the jobs she had in college until she finally asked him to stop.

"My firm specializes in trusts and estates," Franny says.

"That's an area you don't hear about much." Bob waves away a server as he attempts to fill his water glass. "What got you into that?"

Ordering more wine was a mistake, she thinks. Bob is as bright as a beet, with wine-stained teeth that remind her of a rotting jack-o'-lantern. Even if he were sober, Franny wouldn't tell him about her father and eldest brother, how they died in a car accident when she was eight.

"I did an internship in law school."

"Now, see?" Bob says to his granddaughter. "That's smart."

Before her interview, Franny had barely been interested in estate law. She assumed that estate planning attorneys usually tended to the whims of the rich and elderly—people who wanted to control this son or that niece by writing them in and out of their wills. She was also aware that in exchange for slightly more humane hours, they earned less than other types of lawyers. The only reason Franny went on the interview was to practice. But then the founding partner explained that the firm's mission was to guard families from disaster, an idea that appealed to her for obvious reasons.

"I guess one thing just led to another," she says.

"You're probably going to see a real uptick in new clients now, aren't you?"

At first, Franny is too distracted by Tom helping himself to another glass of wine—his sixth? Maybe even his seventh?—to understand what this means. Across the table, she notices that Ma is watching him too.

"Uptick?" she asks.

"Well, if I didn't already have a will, this whole sad business on Tuesday would have sent me running to an estate lawyer. I bet lots of folks feel the same."

Kathie pats his hand gently. "Honey, that's morbid. We're on vacation."

"But I'm just saying—all those people who died, who were probably unprepared . . ." Bob wags his spoon at them. "You know, we had a friend whose wife died without a will, and he just had a hell of a time getting things sorted out afterward. Franny here knows what I mean. The probate courts aren't going to make it easy—"

"*Grandpa* . . ." Allison says firmly, in a tone she hasn't used before. "Jesus Christ. Nobody wants to talk about that now."

TOM IS INCREDULOUS. "You're mad at *me*?" he whispers.

"Lower your voice."

"No, seriously. You're mad," he repeats, more declaration than question this time. "At me."

Everyone from the first seating is spilling out of the dining room into a long corridor. Uniformed crew members await them with ready smiles, shouting like carnival barkers: "This way to the main theater, folks. This way to tonight's entertainment!" Franny slows down, trying to put more distance between them and Ma, who's walking with Jae and Esther several feet ahead.

"I asked you to help me make the best of this," she says.

"I *am*. Didn't you see me talking to everyone at dinner?"

"To the Bowmans, you mean."

"Franny, it's not my fault that your mom is impossible to talk to."

She doesn't have a good response to this. It's true, after all. Ma has never been easy to communicate with. Despite living in the States for over forty years, Korean is still her preferred language, while Franny is more comfortable with English. She imagines this is why Ma never wants to leave Fort Lee and acts like an invitation to visit her and Tom in Manhattan is an expedition to a foreign country. It doesn't help that Ma has been borderline exhausted for most of her life. Before the accident, when there were two incomes to rely on, she worked long hours at the restaurant to help make ends meet.

After the accident, she fired her employees and worked even more, which allowed her to keep the house and hold off the debt collectors. When she wasn't working, she was sleeping, and vice versa—a cycle that she kept up until her recent retirement, even though the threat of losing everything had long since passed.

"Well, you didn't have to ply people with alcohol," Franny says under her breath.

"Are you serious?" Tom almost laughs out the words as he says them. "All I did was help choose the wine and try to have a toast for Nancy, to make her feel special. Isn't that what you wanted this trip to be about?"

He did more than that, she thinks. Whether he intended to or not, he did more than that, and now he's trying to make it sound like something else. Unlike her austere, conservative firm, Tom's company has a culture of boozy holiday parties and client dinners, thanks to his father and older brothers. She knows he doesn't particularly enjoy these events, but he pretends to because that's what's required of him. Usually, this means drinking excessively and encouraging everyone else to do the same, a strategy she's certain he was employing tonight.

"Didn't you even notice how drunk you got those people?"

"Bob and Kathie are consenting adults. I didn't *get* them drunk. And seriously, if you're going to be mad at anyone for making things awkward, then how about the bratty teenager cursing out Grandpa at the dinner table?"

"Please, Tom. Lower your voice."

No one knew what to say after Allison's outburst. Bob did his best to laugh it off, but it was obvious that dinner had taken a turn for him, and Kathie too. Their mouths set firmly; their thin lips disappeared into hard, straight lines. Franny realized it was the first time they'd stopped talking all night. A few minutes later, Bob balled up his napkin—a little too roughly, she thought—and tossed it onto his plate.

"A great first meal," he said. "Just great." But he could barely look anyone in the eye as he stood up from the table.

Allison, meanwhile, returned to her default state. Not embarrassed, not angry. Just wholly unperturbed.

Franny scans the crowd, wondering if the Bowmans are also headed to the theater. It seems like everyone from the first seating is. Crew members continue to direct them from the sidelines, promising "a fantastic lineup tonight, folks" and "some extra-special guests." Esther was the one who kept insisting they go to a show after dinner because they couldn't miss the onboard entertainment. Franny wishes she'd asked what exactly they're about to see.

"So, is this how the entire trip is going to be?" Tom whispers. "The two of us constantly arguing? Because this just isn't us, Franny."

Although they don't often argue, it's not because they always agree. Franny simply refused to give in this time. She continues staring straight ahead, unwilling to look at him. If she does, it's possible she'll lose it. How good that might feel, to just open her mouth and shout, not caring who sees or hears her do it. *Jesus Christ.* Maybe a release like that would be helpful, clearing out the buildup so it can accumulate again.

Near the entrance to the *Avventura!* Main Stage, the caravan thickens into a crowd and comes to a standstill. Crew members with bullhorns apologize as they direct traffic. There's apparently a bottleneck due to a broken set of doors leading into the theater, forcing everyone to squeeze in through one entry point. As people close in around her, Franny loses sight of Tom. Even in high heels, she's so much shorter than everyone. She holds her hands out in front of her, trying to create some space for her body, but it's no use. She stumbles against someone's shoulder, then stumbles again off someone else's back. The only thing that prevents her from pinballing through the crowd is its density. It feels like she's no longer moving of her own free will but being carried along in spite of it. She can hear crew members saying, "Plenty of seats, folks. Plenty of seats. No need to push." But everyone is pushing.

By the time Franny clears the threshold and enters the theater, her heart is pounding—the same frantic, blood-in-her-ears kind of pounding that she experienced on Tuesday. And suddenly she's transported to the corner of Church and Fulton, where there's a partial view to the west. Franny is standing in a crowd of people, clutching her briefcase to her chest as she watches smoke billowing out of the South Tower. Sirens and security alarms are going off everywhere. The woman behind Franny is crying, then praying, then crying again. The men beside her can't help but speculate. *If there were two planes, then it wasn't an accident.* Time stops and speeds up, stops and speeds up, over and over until a sharp *crack* rips through the air, followed by *crackcrackcrackcrackcrack,* like the loudest and heaviest doors on earth, all slamming shut in rapid succession. When the chorus of "Oh God" starts, Franny hears it before she understands the source of it, before she feels the force of the tower's impossible collapse, and then everyone takes off running from the wall of dust and debris hurtling toward them, through the makeshift wind tunnel formed by the buildings on Church.

Franny understands how it happened now, how the momentum of the crowd ferried her into the lobby of that bank when all she wanted to do was stand outside and watch. She squeezes her eyes shut and tells herself to wait. All of this has to wait until she returns to New York. This week, she's here to celebrate Ma's birthday and retirement. This week, everything has to be about Ma. Franny repeats these words to herself, fists clenched as she walks through the front of the theater where the crowd disperses almost as quickly as it formed.

The crew wasn't lying—there are plenty of seats, arranged to create a lounge-like atmosphere with sofas and cocktail tables instead of traditional rows. Just off the stage, she spots Ma sitting on a love seat surrounded by empty chairs.

"Where are Jae and Esther?" she asks. "Where's Tom?"

"Your brother went to the bar." Ma glances up from her program and lowers her reading glasses. "Ay, what's the matter with you?"

Franny shakes her head. She wonders what she must look like to warrant such a question. "Nothing."

"Were you crying?"

"I wasn't crying." She sits down and touches her face to make sure it's dry, which it is.

The love seat is upholstered in plush blue velvet. Franny brushes her hand back and forth against the grain. The sensation is calming, like stroking a cat. The curtains drawn across the stage are made of the same material, the edges fringed with aqua blue to resemble the ocean, which is calming too. She suspects that Ma is still staring at her, so she picks up a program and casually tries to read it, but she can't focus long enough to understand what any of it says. It feels like she's looking through the words instead of at them.

She's about to go to the restroom and check her face in a mirror when she notices Jae and Esther returning from the bar. Curiously, they don't have any drinks with them. Even more curiously, Tom is trailing close behind. When they sit down, reeking of cigarettes, it's obvious what the three of them have been up to. She breathes in deeply, aware that Tom hates smoking and does it only when he's stressed at work. She should probably feel more sympathy toward him than she does, but she's reminded of their conversation in the Grotto when he said it was wrong to be on a cruise "after everything we've been through." What *we*? Franny wants to know. Who's *we*? He was in Philadelphia for a client meeting when the planes hit. By the time he was able to rent a car and return home, she'd thrown out her dust-covered clothes and showered and bathed and showered again.

"We've got to cancel that cruise for your mom," he said, just minutes after walking through the door. And the way he said it—like it had already been decided—gave her sudden pause.

Franny had been waiting to tell him about her day in person. She didn't trust herself to do it on the phone, not without worrying him more. But in that moment, she knew there would be no cruise if she were truthful about where she'd been and what she'd seen that morning.

"Are you all right?" he asks.

She turns to him as the houselights flicker three times, signaling the start of the show.

He leans over and whispers in her ear, "I'm sorry. I didn't mean what I said before."

When he kisses her on the cheek and asks if she forgives him, Franny breathes in the awful smell of smoke.

5.

"Reading glasses?" Doug whispers. "Does anyone have an extra pair of reading glasses I can borrow?"

A dancer in an oversize headdress hustles past him, brushing the side of his face with peacock feathers. Another dancer's feathers go straight into his mouth. Doug steps back and tucks himself into a nook formed by a wall and two rolling wardrobes. He senses that he's in the way, that he shouldn't be wandering around asking anyone for anything right now. Ever since the show started, the energy backstage feels very different. Gone are the buzzy, lighthearted conversations that he observed just a few minutes ago. In their place are laser-focused stares and elaborately costumed bodies moving into their assigned positions. Most of these bodies belong to very fit, very attractive young women. He'd guess at least three dozen in all, made up with the same shimmery eyes and bright red mouths.

The size of the *Sonata*'s company of performers has grown quite a bit since the seventies, but the costumes have become noticeably smaller and more revealing—so much so that Doug makes a concerted effort not to stare. The first group of dancers went onstage dressed in black satin corsets and fishnet stockings. The peacocks preparing to enter on stage right are wearing low-cut green leotards with provocative tail feathers. And the mermaids' long blond wigs are strategically glued over certain parts of their flesh-colored bodysuits. Predictably, the half dozen or so male performers are fully clothed as pirates.

Being backstage during a live performance is still a relatively new experience for Doug. He's done only two plays, both of which were regional theater productions with small casts and modest black box sets. He's never performed on Broadway, off Broadway, or even off-*off*-Broadway before, though he used to dream about the stage when he was young. In the mid-eighties, he had a brief window of opportunity when Annette decided her aging client roster was landing better roles in theater than in television. After moving her entire operation to New York, she invited Doug to visit and sent him on several auditions with well-known producers and casting directors. That was his last relapse—a brief one thanks to Annette, who actually paid for his stint in rehab because she could back then, and also because she felt so responsible. Whenever he's frustrated with her, he tries to remember that she's capable of great acts of kindness like this, although doing so is having very little effect on him now.

The audience applauds as the women in corsets return backstage, clip-clopping in their shiny black tap shoes. Then out go the peacocks—heads up, smiles wide, feathers bouncing in unison to the sound of "Something Wonderful." Doug looks at the index cards that Tabby handed him when he arrived at call time. Once again, the text is impossibly small, sized for much younger eyes. He has a general understanding of what the cards say but wishes he could make out the actual words. Ad-libbing while sober was never his strong suit. He considers asking around for glasses again but decides against it. No one paid much attention to him the first time, and now the women who were wearing corsets are frantically tearing them off.

Doug realizes that he probably looks like a lech, hidden—but not hidden—between the wardrobes during a costume change. He scans the area for a better place to stand and spots Renee stretching in front of a mirrored wall while listening to music. With the exception of her bright yellow Walkman, which has been replaced by a portable CD player, it's the same ritual she used to follow before every performance on the show. It occurs to him that she's probably the only person backstage who's actually old enough to own a pair of reading glasses, but he doesn't dare go anywhere near her.

Since their last conversation, he's been trying to figure out what he could have done to Renee to make her dislike him so much. Unfortunately, it's not that hard to guess. He slept around a lot during the *Starlight Voyages* era. His definition of the word "girlfriend" was extremely loose, allowing him to juggle two or three at a time without any cost to his conscience. Growing up, this was what he thought famous men did, and there was no shortage of women willing to confirm. Doug is fairly certain that he never had sex with Renee—for years, she had an on-again, off-again relationship with their castmate Ron, who played the ship's captain—but who knows? He wasn't a particularly trustworthy person when he was drinking, so it wouldn't surprise him to learn that he'd tried.

Out of the corner of his eye, Doug sees a flash of pale white breast as the once-corseted women quickly change into disco-themed costumes—shiny short-shorts, sequined T-shirts, and roller skates. He pulls the cards out of his pocket and pretends to read them, lowering his head to avoid seeing anything else he shouldn't. Things aren't the way they used to be during the height of *Starlight Voyages'* popularity. Back then, he went through dancers and extras like uppers—behavior that seems so horrifying in 2001 but was commonplace in the seventies. At least once a month, there was some sort of "incident" that required the director or producer to lecture Doug and his male costars about keeping their language clean, keeping their hands to themselves, or keeping it in their pants. But aside from these lectures, none of the men ever experienced any consequences for their behavior. Only the women did. At least a handful of dancers were fired at Doug's request for being too clingy or emotional after a brief romance fizzled. Maybe some of them were Renee's friends. Maybe that's why she's so angry with him now. He wonders if it would help to confess that he's angry with himself too, angry and regretful about things that can't be forgiven.

The peacocks return to the sound of whistles and applause, signaling the end of the second number. Then the mermaids and pirates take to the stage, accompanied by a song he recognizes from *Penzance*. Tabby said all he had to do was greet the audience and introduce the finale, which would feature a dance solo by Renee. He must have looked nervous about this because she patted him on the shoulder and said very encouragingly, as if speaking to a child, that he'd never come across a friendlier audience.

"Everybody loves you out there," she said. "Plus, I jotted down some suggestions if you need them."

He glances at the blurry cards again and wonders if Tabby had any luck finding reading glasses in the costume shop. She thought there might be a pair left over from an old production and ran off to check. That was several minutes ago, and he hasn't seen her since. What he does see is a very irate-looking man walking straight toward him, not breaking eye contact. Doug suspects this must be Kevin, the infamous entertainment director who everyone's been whispering about backstage, as in "Kevin, that dick" or "Kevin's such an asshole."

The name tag on the man's Aria Cruise Lines polo shirt confirms Doug's guess. KEVIN HANNA, UNITED KINGDOM. He stops in front of the wardrobes, effectively trapping Doug in the nook, and holds out his hand to shake. Kevin has the most ferociously upturned nose that Doug has ever seen on an adult human being. The word "pugnacious" instantly comes to mind. Both the feature and the description suit him. It's obvious that he's upset about something, about a million different things, which probably comes with the territory of overseeing all the entertainment on the ship, from the elaborate ensemble productions to the sleepy afternoon bingo games.

The *Sonata* went through several entertainment directors when the show was on the air. None of them stayed with Aria for very long. Doug remembers little about them except that having a Jekyll and Hyde personality seemed like a requirement of the job. With the passengers, the EDs were always the life of the party, walking around on the public decks with smiles from ear to ear, encouraging the paying customers to let loose and enjoy themselves. But with the in-house entertainers, they had to be the authority figure, the one who ran the rehearsals, gave the performers notes, and told everyone to stop fucking around or fucking each other. Doug isn't exactly a passenger, but he isn't a member of the repertory either. He's not sure where this leaves him.

"I'm sorry I haven't had a chance to introduce myself yet." The British accent makes Kevin seem uptight, even more uptight than his severe side part and polo shirt buttoned up to his throat. "You boarded much later than I expected and I've had at least a dozen fires to put out today."

"Nice to meet you," Doug says. He's familiar with this personality type, the kind that can't apologize without pointing out how the other person was at fault too. They shake hands for what feels like a few seconds too long.

"May I ask . . ." Kevin clears his throat. "May I ask what you're doing here right now?"

Doug doesn't know what he means by "here." Here in the nook? Here on the ship? Where else is he supposed to be? "Tabby gave me these, but I can barely make out what they say." He holds out the cards to show him, even though Kevin can probably read them just fine. He's young. Not as young as the dancers, but in his thirties still. "I was hoping someone might have a pair of reading glasses I could borrow since I misplaced mine."

Kevin takes the cards and flips through them, frowning. "Why would she even bother writing these?" He crumples the paper in his fist and throws it on the floor. "No one wants to see Doug Clayton read from *cards*. They want to see those famous blue eyes of yours when you thank them for coming on a reunion sail with Aria. After that, just turn it over to Renee for the final number. That's it, thirty seconds tops. You can do that, can't you?"

Doug nods. Even if he couldn't do it, there's something about Kevin's personality that makes him feel like he has to agree.

"Good then. Now let's get you back in the greenroom where you belong."

"There's a greenroom?" Doug asks.

Kevin's eyes widen. "Did Tabby . . . did she not show you where the greenroom was when you arrived?"

She didn't. But Doug senses that Kevin has it in for poor Tabby, who's actually been quite nice to him. He worries that he keeps getting her in trouble every time he opens his mouth. "She offered to . . . yes. But I insisted . . . I insisted on getting this situation with the glasses taken care of first. She's trying to find some for me now. She's very helpful, you know."

Kevin nods at him, dubious. "Well, stars usually wait in the greenroom." He backs up a step and gestures toward a door near the performers' lockers. "Shall we?"

Doug follows him, uncertain if he should. Only on the *Sonata* would anyone ever refer to him as a star. Only on the *Sonata* did he ever feel like one, which had been nothing short of dangerous.

AT FIRST, HE doesn't understand what he's looking at. But the longer he stands there, blinking the warmly lit room into focus, the more obvious it is. The busy, colorful wallpaper—it's not really wallpaper. It's a collection of old photographs from the show. Doug's eyes move from left to right, floor to ceiling, wall to wall. He's stunned by the volume of headshots, candids, Polaroids, production stills, and publicity images gathered in one place. He suspects there must be hundreds, possibly thousands of them, all faded and yellow with age.

"This is the largest collection of *Starlight Voyages* memorabilia in the world," Kevin says. "Unofficially, that is. Maybe there's a fan out there who has more, but I doubt it." He's smiling, which suggests that he's proud of this space, but Doug feels like a character in a movie who just wandered into his stalker's lair, only to discover the full extent of his obsession.

"Did you . . . did you do all of this?" he asks, grateful that he took an extra Xanax before arriving backstage.

"No, I can't take credit for any of it. One of my predecessors got the idea after the show went off the air. I believe he worked with someone from the network." He rests his hands on the back of a makeup chair, one of three in the room, and gives it a gentle spin. A patch of silver duct tape on the vinyl shines as it rotates under the lights. "Corporate was planning to renovate and take all this down a few years ago, but I'm glad they didn't. *Starlight*'s such a big part of the *Sonata*'s history. It's probably the reason why most of us wanted to work for Aria in the first place. It was my reason, at least."

Now that they're alone, Kevin has noticeably softened. It seems clear that he's a fan. But Doug is too overwhelmed by his surroundings to mumble more than a terse, ungracious "thank you." Someone documented an entire decade of his life, a decade he thought he'd lost, and now here he is, witnessing all those years at once. It's a strange, almost out-of-body experience. Doug knows that he's the person in these images, but it feels like he's looking at someone else. In shot after shot, he sees himself doing things and visiting places that he doesn't really remember. The episode they filmed in Egypt. The fifth anniversary special. Renee's thirtieth birthday with the giant heart-shaped cake. The champagne toast to celebrate the end of season seven.

He scans the assemblage of young, happy, deeply tanned faces on the nearest wall. Everyone looks like they're having such a good time, especially him. There he is with the dancers, wearing one of their top hats and kicking his leg in the air as they laugh. And there he is with the crew, grinning mischievously at a table filled with poker chips, crushed beer cans, and overflowing ashtrays. There's even one of him, Renee, and their costar Catherine dressed for a night out at the clubs in their tightest leather and spandex. How different his life used to be. Just one big party, usually with him at the center of it all. Now he goes to silent yoga and meditation retreats, and takes long, solitary hikes in the Santa Monica Mountains. He reminds himself that it's better this way. He's not convinced that people are good for him and he's certain that he's no good for people.

Doug leans in and narrows his eyes at a photo of his costar Alan's bachelor party in Mexico. Alan is wearing a sombrero and there's a busty brunette perched on his lap. Doug is standing behind them, laughing with his arms around the shoulders of two men who are obviously Alan's brothers. They all share the same rugged good looks, the same slightly crooked smile. The party comes back to him in big, jagged pieces—the secret plan to fly the brothers to Mexico on the producer's private plane, the way Alan actually wept with happiness when he saw them. Doug wonders which one is the missing firefighter and feels a surge of shame course through his body. Not only did he know that Alan had a brother, he'd actually met them both.

"This one was probably my favorite episode of all time."

Kevin has sidled up next to him at the wall. Doug doesn't know which episode he's talking about until he notices Kevin's index finger tapping on a cast photo in front of the Sydney Opera House.

"I always wondered if you got a chance to enjoy the locations you filmed in. Or was it just nonstop work?"

To the right of Kevin's finger is a Polaroid of Peter MacNamee, who played the show's first officer. He's leaning against the railing, smiling as he points at the skyline of Sydney in the distance. Doug's chest tightens. He has no specific memory of taking this photo, but he's convinced that he did. He's distraught to see Peter captured in a moment when he was still young, still healthy, still alive. These days, Doug can barely remember what it felt like to have someone in his life who knew him as well as Peter did. During the first season of the show, they quickly bonded over their similar upbringings—two southern farm boys, raised by hard, unhappy parents whose lives they had no desire to replicate. Neither of them could believe his good luck to join the cast. Not only did *Starlight* pay more than they ever expected to earn, but it also made them famous, gave them a chance to see the world, and got them into any restaurant, nightclub, or party they wanted to go to. They were determined to make the most of their time in the spotlight, as if they both knew it wouldn't last.

"So . . . did you actually get a chance to enjoy being in Sydney?" Kevin asks again.

Doug realizes that he ignored the question the first time. "I don't . . . It really depended on the location, I guess. Is that—is that what you wanted to know?" He pauses, flustered. "I'm sorry. It's just so much to look at. Most of these pictures—I had no idea they even existed."

Kevin nods. "No need to apologize. I should just let you enjoy them. Maybe we can talk about the show another time." He's about to leave when he seems to remember something that he's supposed to say but hasn't yet. "You have water over there if you need it." He points at a carafe on one of the makeup tables. "And an intercom system if you want to reach a member of the production team. You can also watch the show on closed circuit if you'd like." He turns on the monitor hanging from the ceiling and a grainy black-and-white image of the stage appears. The dancers are roller-skating around a giant disco ball, encouraging the audience to clap along with them. "Don't worry though. I'll send someone to get you when it's time."

Doug is still studying the photos when he hears the door click shut. He's not sure if he said "thank you" or even "goodbye," which would normally bother him—such a big part of being professional is simply being polite—but he doesn't dwell on the lapse for long. Instead, he tries to find all the images in which he and Peter appear.

The people who tacked and taped the photos to the walls must have started in the corner closest to the door because Doug feels like he's witnessing them age a full decade as he circles the room. By season two, neither he nor Peter ever appear in a candid without a drink in hand. By season four—the year they discovered that coke was more enjoyable than speed—their weight loss, particularly Doug's, starts to become noticeable. In the pictures where they're not in full makeup, the circles under their eyes grow larger and darker over time. By the end of the series, they've both aged considerably, but not so considerably that women wouldn't still find them attractive.

Several minutes pass before Doug returns to the wall where he started, thinking about all the moments that haven't been accounted for in this makeshift shrine. The lectures that he and Peter received from Annette, who represented them both, warning them to cut the shit and clean up their act. The weeks and months they spent in rehab, sometimes in the same program at the same time, which never led to any good. The tabloid coverage of Peter's death and the photos of his prized red Mustang, crushed like an accordion at the bottom of a cliff in Palos Verdes.

If Doug tries hard enough, he can almost forget that Peter is gone. But this kind of forgetting—the kind he actually wants—never lasts for long, mostly because the shock eventually catches up with him, followed by the guilt. On the *Starlight* set, Doug was known as the instigator. He was the first to experiment with pot, then pills, then coke, and he was generous with his stashes, making them freely available to all. He was always the one who drank more and partied harder and encouraged the people around him, including Peter, to keep up. He dragged so many of his friends down into the abyss with him, but not all of them were able to get back out.

"Hello?" a woman shouts. "I hope you're decent."

The door squeaks open and he turns to find Tabby poking her head in.

"Sorry to bother you. I've been out here knocking for a while."

"Is it time?" he asks.

"Almost." She opens the door wider and enters without being invited. "No luck with the glasses, but Kevin said I should come find you and apologize."

He can almost see the lump slide down her throat as she says this. He studies her face, confirming that her eyes are pink and her cheeks are blotchy, as if she's been crying recently. He assumes that Kevin was terrible to her but decides it's best to just play dumb. "What could you possibly have to apologize for?"

"I was supposed to get you settled in the greenroom when you arrived. I'm sorry . . . I know celebrities like their privacy, but Ms. Bostwick . . ." She hesitates. "I'm sorry, but Ms. Bostwick told me not to bring you back here with her. She made me promise, and it really didn't seem like my place to ask questions."

Doug nods. He thinks he understands, although he's not sure why Renee was doing her warm-up routine out in the open area if she was trying to avoid him. "Please tell Kevin that Ms. Bostwick can have this room to herself for the rest of the week. I'm happy to wait backstage with everyone else."

At first, Tabby seems confused by this, but then she looks up at the monitor with a start. "We should get going now. This song's almost over. Are you ready?"

He reminds himself to inhale, one-two-three. Exhale, one-two-three. But his breath catches as a fluttering sensation begins to spread from his chest to his stomach, then from his hands to his feet—little signal fires telling him he's not ready. He's never been less ready. But what choice does he have except to perform?

* * *

"THANK YOU . . . THANK you, everybody . . . You're very kind . . . Thank you so much."

Doug keeps repeating these words into the mic, but he doesn't know if anyone can actually hear him over the applause. He glances at the wing, where Renee and Kevin are standing. Behind them are dozens of dancers dressed in shiny gold tuxedos, waiting for him to wrap up so they can go on.

He continues waving and smiling until the noise finally begins to subside. Then a woman in the back of the theater shouts, "We love you, Mack!" and something wired deep in the base of his brain kicks in, prompting him to shout, "Well, I love you too," and the audience starts clapping all over again. He touches his heart as if he's moved by the response instead of alarmed by it, and tries to settle the crowd down, but it's no use. When Kevin introduced him, he said it had been nearly two decades since Doug was last on the *Sonata*—information that elicited audible gasps throughout the theater—and now the audience seems intent on clapping for every one of those lost years.

"Thank you so much . . . Thank you, everybody . . . You're very kind . . ."

Doug lifts his hand over his head, trying to get a moment's relief from the relentless beam of light directed at him. Twice, he's done this, but the people in the booth still haven't taken the hint. It feels like he's being broiled to death, standing there in his sports coat and collared shirt. Sweat trickles down the side of his face while fat beads collect above his upper lip. Doug desperately wants to wipe himself off, but he knows better. No one in the audience can see how badly he's sweating, just as he can't see the audience beyond their faceless figures, outlined by the light.

Time feels slow all of a sudden. He's not sure how long he's been onstage, only that his cheeks are starting to ache from smiling too long and too hard. He wishes he had the kind of public persona that would allow him to say "shut up," which he once saw a female comedian do while he was filming a guest spot in Las Vegas. "Shut up so I can get this over with and cash my check," she barked, and everyone laughed and then complied. He just isn't that person. Among this crowd, he's Mack, the friendly, funny bartender, the one to whom all the passengers on the show confided their problems while he mixed their daiquiris and mai tais. Aside from this, the writers never really gave Mack that much to do. There was rarely an episode in which he even had an arc. His role was simply to provide comic relief and listen, creating an opportunity for the passengers to listen to themselves, which led to countless moments of epiphany.

During the last season of *Starlight*, when Doug made the disastrous decision to pose for *Playgirl*, a staffer at the magazine convinced him to answer the questionnaire as Mack might. With Annette's encouragement, he included "listening" in his list of turn-ons, further cementing his image as a sensitive hunk both on and off the show. He wonders how many of the middle-aged women in the audience saw his centerfold—a soft-core photo that involved very strategically placed satin sheets—and his face feels as red and shiny as the sheets were. He looks down for a moment to collect himself and notices that several large drops of sweat have landed on his sports coat, darkening the pale beige fabric. He worries that someone sitting up close might actually be able to see the inkblot-like discolorations on his sleeve.

"Let's lower that spotlight a little," he says, gesturing toward the booth. "I want to take a look at this fantastic crowd."

For some reason, several people in the audience hoot and whistle at the prospect of this as the light dims. Doug raises the blade of his hand over his eyes. Near the front of the theater, in house left, he thinks he can make out Gideon's curly hair. Doug told him he didn't need to come, but Gid said he wanted to, which he's grateful for. His other nieces and nephews are all much older with families of their own now, and he's convinced they have memories of him as a ghost who was never present or a drunk when he was. Not surprisingly, Gideon is the only one he still has a relationship with, the only one with whom he has nothing to repair. His presence makes Doug want to do well tonight.

"What a beautiful, amazing crowd," he says, even though he can make out only dark shapes and shadows, the occasional reflection of glasses being lifted and lowered in the light. "Thank you so much for coming."

He glances at the wing, halfway expecting to see Kevin gesturing frantically at his watch. But Kevin seems thrilled with the extended applause, a sharp contrast to Renee and the dancers, who wait in various states of crossed arms and hooded stares. They were probably warmed up before he went onstage, and now they've been standing around too long. As the applause finally starts to die down, Doug reminds himself not to say or do anything that might get it going again.

"We love you, Mack!"

He thinks this might be the same woman from earlier and refuses to take the bait. Not only will it rile up the audience but he worries that she's some sort of obsessed loon who'll show up at every dance lesson and cooking class this week, ogling him until she gets her money's worth. The thought of this is so nerve-racking it makes Doug want to drink, not that it takes very much to inspire this impulse.

Years ago, Gideon asked what it was like to be an alcoholic—a question that caught Doug off guard. Gid couldn't have been more than eleven or twelve at the time, an age that seemed too young to know about the existence of such a word, much less that it applied to his uncle. Doug was glad that Gid felt comfortable enough to bring it up—he wanted the two of them to have the kind of relationship that allowed them to talk about anything—but he'd never been asked to explain himself so directly before, not even in therapy. He eventually sputtered out a response about his desire to drink being more powerful than his desire for money, success, family, health, friendships, a life. Gid nodded as if he understood, but how could he? He was a child, and Doug hardly understood it himself. Even now, fifteen years after his last drink, he occasionally finds himself surrounded by people and feeling the urge as if it's been only fifteen minutes.

"Thank you, everybody. So here we are . . ."

As the last of the applause subsides, he mentally runs through the list of things that Kevin told him to mention. Reunion. Aria. Renee. Final number. Thirty seconds tops, he said.

"So here we are on this reunion sail with Aria . . ." Doug reaches into his coat pocket, expecting to touch the worn cover of his AA handbook, a miniature abridged version of the Big Book that he always carries with him. Instead, he finds the slick, glossy surface of a Polaroid. He pauses, resting his hand on the image of Peter in Sydney, which he peeled from the greenroom wall and secreted away.

"Reunions," he says hoarsely. "I guess reunions are about the people who show up, aren't they?" He can see several heads in the audience nodding in agreement. "But they're also about the people who didn't. Or couldn't, maybe . . ." He drifts off, aware that he's not striking the right tone. Far from it. When he realizes that he hasn't said anything in a while, he clears his throat and hears a few people in the audience do the same. "What I meant to say is that reunions give us a chance to think about the people who didn't make it and why."

He glances at the wing, where Renee is staring at him, more concerned than annoyed now, while Kevin's expression has turned rigid.

"So . . . it's a strange time to be getting together like this, don't you think?" He asks the question lightly, punctuating it with a nervous laugh, but no one laughs with him, not even the loon in the back. He digs his hands deeper into his pockets, feeling Peter's photo in one and his miniature book in the other. He has no idea where he was going with that question, only that it was the wrong one. Who wants to be reminded about what they're sailing away from?

"Alan Dennehy was supposed to be here this week. He played the ship's chief medical officer. You remember Alan, don't you?"

The absence of a response confirms that it's an idiotic question. Of course, they remember Alan. Doug hears people shifting in their seats and clinking the ice around in their glasses, which makes him wish that he was holding one too. It wouldn't even need to be a full glass, or a glass that used to contain alcohol. Just feeling the weight of an empty one would be such a comfort. Before he allows himself to get too caught up in this thought, he looks at house left again, searching for the outline of Gideon's head to help him focus.

"Did you know that Alan's brother was a firefighter in New York?" A few people mutter "oh, no" or "oh my God." He decides it's better than nothing, better than silence. "I met him once—the brother. In Mexico. He was . . . is a great guy, just like Alan. A hero, really." At this, several members of the audience clap, which Doug instinctively seizes upon. "He's missing now—that's why Alan couldn't join us. There are lots of brave men and women like him still missing, so . . . so how about on the count of three, we give them a round of applause, all right? Let's give a big round of applause for Alan's brother, for his courage, for all the families like Alan's who are still waiting to hear from their loved ones."

When Doug counts to three, the theater erupts with a roar unlike anything he's ever heard before. The wall of sound is so high and wide, it forces him back several steps. He doesn't know if the volume of the audience members' reaction is the product of their grief or of the guilt they feel about sailing off to Bermuda while the rest of the world grieves. But Doug leaps at the opportunity to exit while he has it, mumbling "thank you" into the mic and quickly walking offstage. The audience continues to clap and whistle and shout as he disappears into the wing, unable to look Kevin or Renee in the eye as he passes. He just elbows his way through the company of tuxedoed dancers, reaching the far end of the gauntlet before it occurs to him that he forgot to introduce Renee.

Monday, September 17

AT SEA

6.

When Lucy blinks awake, the first thing she sees is a toilet. A metal toilet, the kind that a hospital or prison might have. Beside it, her shoes are lying in a twisted heap, all straps and heels and dried brown streaks of blood. She feels terrible, a strange kind of terrible that she's never felt before—dizzy and dehydrated, with a head full of cotton and a mouth filled with sand. She tries to sit up but can't summon enough energy, so she sinks back onto the floor. The gray marble tiles are freezing, which is probably why someone—Mariah, she assumes—covered her with bath towels while she slept. Lucy rolls over, pulling the makeshift blankets all the way up to her chin.

"Hello?" she calls out.

Her voice barely registers under the whir of the exhaust fan. She clears her throat, wondering what time it is, whether Mariah is awake yet or in the suite at all. The bathroom door is open, letting in a pale beam of light that suggests morning. Lucy has never craved orange juice before, but suddenly she wants some, despite knowing that acid is probably the worst thing to put in her stomach right now. What she really needs is plain water and lots of it. The sink is only two feet away, close enough to get up and quickly fill a glass. But two feet might as well be two hundred in her state, and just the thought of a liquid, any kind of liquid, sloshing around in her gut is enough to make her ill all over again.

The queasy feeling began the day before, not long after the *Sonata* left Boston. At first, it was mild and easy to confuse with something else. When she and Mariah sat down to dinner, Lucy assumed she was just having a reaction to day-drinking in the sun, so she ordered soda instead of wine. She also ordered a heavy entrée in preparation for all the cocktails they'd probably consume in the bar afterward. But by the end of the second course, Lucy felt so much worse. She kept staring at the empty lobster shell on her plate, regretting her decision to eat a whole surf and turf special. Twice, she considered returning to the suite, but she resisted the impulse. After all, she had risked so much—possibly screwed up so much—to come on the cruise. The least she could do was be present for it, so she ordered more ginger ale and continued chatting with the people seated at their table, right up until the point when she threw up on it.

Lucy pulls the towels over her face, still mortified by the thought of her dining companions' goggle-eyed expressions and the way heads at other tables began to snap and spin in her direction. She'd been raised to avoid drawing attention to herself unless it was to collect compliments or praise, and this was definitely the wrong kind of attention. But worse than her dining companions' reactions was how kind the waiters and busboys were to her. Within seconds, a group of them surrounded the table and removed all the plates and glasses and linens to eliminate any evidence of her mess. When she apologized for causing them so much trouble, they responded in hushed tones and accented voices that it was no trouble, no trouble at all, miss. Even her tablemates were sympathetic once they recovered from the shock. One of the women said seasickness was extremely common for people new to cruising, while another laughed and said at least one passenger always threw up at dinner on the first night of a cruise. Noticeably, Mariah was the only person who didn't try to console Lucy before she excused herself and returned to their suite, where she's been ever since.

It's getting hot under the towels, so she pushes them away and lets her eyes readjust to the light. On the wall, directly above the toilet, there's a framed print of a Botticelli painting, his most famous. From Lucy's angle, it almost seems like Venus, perched high on her seashell, is staring down at her, perhaps even judging her, which would serve her right. The last time she saw *The Birth of Venus*, she was a college junior, spending the year abroad in Italy, which had arguably been the best year of her life. At first, her father didn't understand why she wanted to study in Florence when he was paying tuition for her to go to Wellesley. She tried to argue that Italy was home to some of the world's most important museums, but he worried aloud that maybe he'd indulged Lucy too much or given her the wrong idea when he allowed her to double-major in comp sci and art. "The art was just supposed to be the fun thing on the side," he said. "Nobody gets jobs doing art." This was always her father's greatest concern. He insisted that Lucy's education, the one he was paying so dearly for, had to lead to something that put a roof over her head and good money in the bank. They weren't rich enough or white enough to be frivolous, he was fond of saying.

He came around only after she told him about the spider, which at that point was little more than a long series of what-ifs rattling around in her head. Major museums like the Uffizi and the Accademia were just starting to put digitized images of their holdings online. What if she could program a spider to search the Internet and automatically index those images, pairing them with links to articles and critical essays about the work? What if she built an artificial intelligence element into the spider that could weed out good sources of information from bad? And what if her spider was sophisticated enough to continuously find, evaluate, and update the world's knowledge of art as more museums began to put their collections online? Lucy's undergraduate adviser thought her idea had great potential for commercial application and said so in a letter, written at her request to share with her parents. The stamp of approval from a faculty member was enough to convince her father, while her mother eventually decided that study abroad sounded sophisticated—an advantage she never had but wanted for her child.

Lucy is certain that the presence of Venus in the bathroom is some kind of sign, but she's too ill and addled to figure out what it means. She props herself up on her elbows to examine her clothes, confirming that she's still dressed in the same outfit as the day before. Her once white, once crisply ironed shirt is badly wrinkled and stained with something that unfortunately resembles vomit. She wonders if the Guest Services desk is open yet. Tracking down her missing bag might be the only thing that motivates her to get up off the floor. This time, she'll have to be more assertive, not so easily swayed by soothing Irish accents or gift certificates or complimentary toiletry bags.

In the next room, something quietly rattles. Then a cabinet or closet door slowly squeaks. Lucy suspects this is what she sounds like at home, trying to get ready to leave for campus every morning without disturbing Mariah, who usually sleeps in. Lucy isn't certain what to say to her now that they're both up. She understands that she was invited on the cruise as a fun travel companion, a role she's been failing miserably at, so she feels the need to make it up to Mariah somehow. Lucy is about to call out to her when she distinctly hears Mariah say the words "bring" and "store" and then a long pause, like she's talking to someone on the phone. She tries to listen in, bracing herself to discover that she's being complained about.

". . . this cruise . . ."

Should she get up? she wonders. Just walk out and say "good morning" like she didn't get sick at the dinner table or spend the whole night on the bathroom floor?

"Maybe we can . . ."

Or start the day with an earnest apology for what a disappointment she's been?

"I really . . ."

The longer Lucy listens, the clearer it is that there are two voices in the suite, and they're both coming closer. One is Mariah's. The other belongs to a man.

"When can I see you again?" he whispers.

"Whenever you're free."

"Same as last night, then?"

Lucy lies very still, pretending to sleep while they make plans. The man has an accent. She's almost certain that it's an Australian accent. But that can't be, she thinks.

DURING HER FRESHMAN year of college, Lucy roomed with a girl named Shawna who'd been homeschooled for most of her life. At first, they seemed so well suited to each other. They were both quiet, studious, and tidier than the average teenager. They were even interested in the same clubs and activities. But then Shawna found a boyfriend, whom she often snuck into their room at night, and Lucy was forced to feign sleep while they had sex under the covers.

She worries that she's about to relive that embarrassment all over again as Mariah and her visitor kiss outside the bathroom door, occasionally bumping against the wall. They've been at it for several minutes now—too long for Lucy to do anything other than continue to play dead.

"You think she'll be all right?" the visitor whispers.

"I don't know. I hope so."

Both of them laugh quietly.

Lucy peeks through a barely open eye. She didn't realize they'd stopped kissing or moved into the doorway, where she can make out Mariah's slippered feet and the lacy hem of her robe. Beside her is a man wearing large black sneakers. Lucy can hardly blame them for laughing at her, if that's what they were doing. She's not the kind of person one would expect to find sleeping on a bathroom floor. Whenever things like this happened in the movies, it was usually after many long hours of partying, a thought that leaves Lucy feeling somewhat cheated. She didn't even enjoy herself last night.

The cabin door clicks shut after Mariah and her visitor walk away. Lucy is relieved to be able to open her eyes again, but when she tells herself to get up, the signal between her brain and her body still isn't working. The longer she lies there, the more judgmental Venus's expression seems. Lucy studies her upturned lips, her slightly narrowed eyes, the way she leans forward on one foot, as if to get a better look. Her seashell platform is scalloped, which reminds Lucy of scallops, which remind her of clams, then shrimp, then crab, and finally, the lobster she ate last night—big, fleshy chunks of it, dipped in warm melted butter. She bolts upright, scrambling onto her knees to brace herself as she heaves into the toilet. Once, twice, three times, her voice echoing loudly off the metal. Although nothing comes up, not even water, the threat lingers for a while, so she continues hovering over the bowl. Toward the tail end of the wave, she realizes that someone is rubbing slow circles onto her back.

"Jesus, Luce. What a night you've had."

Lucy resists a sudden urge to cry. She wipes her face on her sleeve, leaving a long streak of makeup that will probably never come out. She sits back against the wall, hugging her knees to her chest while Mariah leans against the sink. The bathroom is too small for them both, but Mariah shows no sign of leaving.

"I guess I don't have to ask how you're feeling." She digs in her toiletry bag and pulls out a toothbrush. "We need to get some fluids in you, quick. And maybe some toast or a banana."

Lucy waves her hand in the air, as if to swat away the mention of food.

"But you have to eat something bland, otherwise it's just bile floating around in there." Mariah starts brushing her teeth. "I thought you said you'd been on the water before. Do you always get so seasick?"

There's a hint of annoyance, possibly even accusation, in her voice, like dealing with a sick roommate wasn't the kind of vacation she had in mind.

"I've been on the water a lot. On the Chesapeake. But nothing like this has ever happened."

"The Chesapeake Bay?" Mariah spits into the sink. "That's a totally different kind of water."

Lucy rubs the sleep out of her eyes while her stomach continues to churn. Their conversation is making her even more irritable than she already feels. "Who were you talking to just now? I thought I heard a man."

Mariah smiles and the toothbrush angles sharply out of her mouth. "The Aussie from the bar. His name's Iain."

"Ian?"

"No. *Iain,*" she says, pronouncing the word "Eeeen," though it's hard to understand her through all the foam.

"But didn't you say crew members could get fired for hooking up with passengers?"

Mariah holds her finger in the air, pausing so she can rinse. Then she explains how Iain and his brother just bought a bar near Perth, so it's his last cruise with Aria. She leans toward the mirror, flashing a smile to study her teeth from all angles. "He still has to be careful," she continues. "He wants to leave with a good reference and all. But he doesn't have to be as careful as he normally would if he were coming back." She removes the clip from her hair, separating the long blond waves with her fingers. "Hey, could I have the bathroom to myself for a minute? I haven't been able to use it all night."

"Oh, right. Sorry." Lucy hates the idea of moving but knows that she has to now. She gathers her shoes and wraps one of the oversize towels around her like a shawl. When she stands up, she catches a glimpse of herself in the mirror. She looks sickly and pale, tinged a shade of greenish gray that she didn't think was possible for her skin.

The door closes behind her as she walks stiffly into the hallway, stepping around a shopping bag from the Villa. She'd actually forgotten about her purchase and is relieved to see it there. At the very least, she has a clean change of clothes for the day. She shuffles into the living room, where the stark morning light takes a moment to get used to. As she blinks back spots, she notices that the twin beds have been pushed together, and there's a thick tangle of sheets hanging off the edge. Lucy wants to lie down, but not there. She's about to settle for the chaise on the balcony when someone knocks on the door. It's an annoying knock, tapped out like a song she knows but can't put a name to.

"Could you get that?" Mariah shouts. "I called the steward for you."

Lucy isn't sure what this means, but she doesn't have the energy to ask. Simply walking across the length of the suite again exhausts her. When she opens the door, she finds the same man who showed them around their cabin the day before, standing rigidly at attention like he's in the military. He's dressed in a variation of his all-white uniform from yesterday, with his polo shirt tucked into his shorts and his tube socks pulled up to his shins.

"Good morning, miss," Jimmy says. "I understand you're not feeling well?"

He asks the question too brightly, given what the question is. She shakes her head and leads him into the living room.

"I have the supplies that Miss Mariah requested. Motion sickness pills." He hands her a pale blue box of something called Bonine. "An acupressure band, and also a tin of dried ginger to help settle the stomach."

Lucy thanks him and tears open the box of pills. She's about to swallow one of the tablets dry when Jimmy offers a bottle of water that she didn't see him bring in.

"Allow me, miss." He twists off the cap before handing it to her.

The more Lucy drinks, the thirstier she feels. She keeps tipping her head back farther and farther, dribbling water down the front of her stained shirt. Normally, she'd be embarrassed to behave this way in front of a stranger, but she's too sick to worry about appearances.

"Any news about my bag?" she asks, out of breath when the bottle is empty. The waterlogged feeling she was afraid of hits her immediately. Lucy imagines her stomach as the ocean and the *Sonata*, small and white, pitching in its depths. She slowly lowers herself onto the sofa, clutching the armrest until the sensation begins to pass.

"I'm very sorry, miss. It hasn't turned up yet, but your bag is our number one priority."

Again with the same script, she thinks. The staff on the *Sonata* all seem very obedient, always toeing the company line.

"Hey, Jimmy." Mariah walks out of the bathroom, greeting him as if they've known each other for years instead of having met just yesterday. Her robe is wide open, revealing her new strawberry-print bikini.

"Good morning, Miss Mariah."

"Thanks for coming so quickly."

"Of course, Miss Mariah."

"Any idea what the weather's supposed to be like today?"

"Oh, it's going to be another perfect morning. Eighty-three degrees and clear."

It embarrasses Lucy to see a man her father's age behave with such exaggerated deference while Mariah tries to chat with him like they're friends. Lucy suspects there aren't many reasons, other than tourism, in which the two of them would ever have cause to interact, much less be actual friends.

Mariah picks up the empty Bonine box and squints at the label. "They didn't have the nondrowsy kind in the store?"

"Unfortunately, no. That was all they had."

"Well, I suppose it's better than nothing."

Wait, Lucy wants to interrupt. *What did I just take, then? Is it going to put me to sleep?* But Mariah rubs her hands together and looks at her eagerly.

"Are you ready to go to breakfast now?"

Lucy instinctively covers her stomach at the thought of food. "I can't—"

"It's a beautiful buffet, miss," Jimmy says. "And you can even sit out by the pool with your meal."

"Oh, come on." Mariah squeezes her forearm and shakes it. "Let's go hang out by the pool."

Lucy doesn't want to leave the sofa, much less the suite, but she recognizes that something about her situation has to change or else she's going to miss it. The beautiful weather, the beautiful buffet, the break that she came here for but has yet to actually experience.

IAIN—*EEEEN*—IS apparently a writer. That's why he started tending bar on cruise ships, to have something to write about. Hearing this only makes Lucy dislike him more, though she knows she's being unfair, possibly even a little irrational. She has no reason to dislike him at all. He's nothing but a disembodied voice and a pair of black sneakers to her, someone she hasn't had an actual conversation with yet. She suspects she's just projecting her annoyance onto Iain because Mariah won't stop going on about him—how they met, who made the first move, how athletic he was in bed. Lucy isn't interested in any of these details, especially the intimate ones. They aren't close enough to talk like this, about men or anything else.

As Mariah continues her animated summary of last night's events in between sips of a mimosa, Lucy tries to focus on how much her situation has improved in just the past hour. The view, for starters. From their poolside table, she has a choice of pristine blue skies and ocean on one side and prime people watching on the other. The motion sickness pills and acupressure band are also working faster than she expected. She has an appetite again and can even keep down a few bites of dry toast. For the first time since boarding, Lucy doesn't feel queasy or look so out of place, dressed as she is in her new bathing suit and cover-up. She considers this progress, or what passes for it in her case.

"Earth to Luce." Mariah waves a piece of melon at her. "Did you hear that?"

"I'm sorry. What?"

"I said you're starting to get some of your color back."

Two little boys in matching swim trunks shriek as they run past the table. One of them is carrying a beach ball over his head, threatening to throw it at the other, but there's no mistaking how much fun they're having. All around them, people are having fun. The family shouting "Marco . . . Polo" in the bleach blue pool, the senior citizens at the high-top drinking round after round of Bloody Marys, the sweet young couple playing shuffleboard like they're a sweet old couple. The more Lucy observes the people around her, the more she understands what she finds so curious about their behavior, and Mariah's too. They're all carrying on like it's September 10, not September 17. Maybe this is what she wanted when she accepted the invitation to Bermuda. Not a respite so much as a chance to rewind to the world as it was before.

"That Bonine must be making you spacey," Mariah says.

Lucy startles, not certain if she drifted off again. "I'd usually have at least four cups of coffee by now, but I doubt my stomach could take it."

"Maybe doing something active would help wake you up?" Mariah rummages in her beach bag and pulls out two copies of the ship's daily newsletter. She hands one to Lucy and begins to flip through the other. "Anything jump out at you?"

In keeping with the *Sonata*'s Italian theme, the newsletter is called *Le Notizie del Giorno*. The interior pages are devoted to activities, scheduled every hour on the hour from dawn to midnight. The offerings are organized by exuberantly punctuated categories—DO! PLAY! WATCH! LEARN!—that are probably meant to convey energy but feel more like commands. There's a Tuscan cooking class, a wine tasting, aqua aerobics, an info session on time-shares in Bermuda, cha-cha lessons, movie screenings, bingo, mah-jongg, happy hour with the hypnotist, figure drawing, Jazzercise, something called Disco Beats, and the list goes on. Lucy is still getting used to the idea of being outside, sitting upright, and taking in small amounts of food and fluids. She's not prepared to make any sudden changes yet.

"Maybe we can just do more of this," she says lightly.

"Oh, I know." Mariah taps on the schedule. "How about this watercolors class at eleven? You were so artsy in college. I still remember that mural you did in the student center."

Lucy hasn't painted in the past few years, a state of inactivity that now feels like a loss. At first, she wasn't sure who to blame for this—Dr. Jimoh, who demanded so much of her time, or her father, who begged her to focus on her studies and not break his heart. As graduation approached, both of them kept reminding Lucy that her spider research had long since evolved away from art museums toward more practical, profitable business applications. She could sense them pushing her, often not very subtly, toward the kind of wealth that neither of them would likely achieve in his lifetime. But despite their outsized influence, Lucy eventually decided that the only person she had to blame was herself. How much could she have loved painting if she was willing to let it go?

"I don't really paint anymore."

"Why not?"

Lucy shrugs, taking another bite of toast. "No time."

"But you were so talented. You should make time."

Again, this isn't the compliment that Mariah seems to think it is. It's painful to be reminded of something she was good at once. Lucy also rejects the idea of "making time"—a suggestion usually offered by people who never had to try. After working, writing, researching, commuting, eating, sleeping, and getting ready for work, she rarely has anything left. She can't just paint on empty. Mariah, whose parents pay her rent while she writes poetry and works in a bookstore, seems to think that not being able to paint is an existential problem, whereas Lucy sees it as a mathematical one. How are people supposed to make time for art when a day has only twenty-four hours and all of hers are already taken?

"I'm not really up for a class," she says.

"Are you sure? We dock in Bermuda tomorrow, so today's the day to do all the ship stuff before we get into port."

"If you want to go, don't let me stop you."

"Oh, no. It's fine." Mariah finishes off her mimosa. "They'll probably offer the same schedule on the way back to Boston. Besides, it's so nice out. Let's just enjoy the sun and talk."

When Dr. Jimoh says they have to talk, there's usually a problem that he wants her to fix on his behalf. A proposal due in days that isn't up to snuff. An undergrad lab assistant who needs to be disciplined or retrained. Lucy's anxious reaction to hearing this phrase is now borderline Pavlovian. "Talk about what?"

"Anything, really." Mariah raises her empty glass at a passing waiter, signaling that she wants another.

There's an elderly woman trying to coax a toddler into the shallow end of the pool. The boy is red-faced and wailing, flapping his arms in the air like a bird. From a nearby chaise, a woman in a bikini is slathering herself with suntan lotion and shouting, "Mom! *Mom!* He doesn't want to. Stop trying to make him." The three of them continue on like this for a while—cajoling, crying, and screaming—to no effect. Lucy watches the impasse for as long as she can before she finally feels the need to say something.

"Why did you invite me on this cruise?"

Mariah seems taken aback by the question. "Why? Are you sorry you came?"

She was when she woke up this morning, but that hardly seems worth mentioning now. "No. It's just that you always had an easy time making friends. I remember that about you from school. You probably could have invited anyone."

"Well, sure." Mariah smiles at her like the answer should be obvious. "But I'm trying to get to know you, Luce. I mean, don't you think it's kind of weird?" She nods at the waiter as he deposits a fresh mimosa on the table. "We've lived together since the middle of July, but we never really see each other or hang out. I guess I didn't expect that when I moved in. I've always been friends with my other roommates."

Being friends with Mariah isn't something Lucy has ever considered. She's not sure if it's something she even wants. "I'd like that," she says anyway.

"Okay then, so tell me about yourself. Things I don't know already." Mariah wiggles her eyebrows mischievously. "Maybe things you don't want me to know."

Lucy's mind spins with possibilities that she quickly rejects. The nail polish she shoplifted in the fifth grade that her mother made her return to the store. The first guy she had sex with on a moldy basement futon. The way she resents showing up at interviews, dressed as professionally as she can afford, only to find the white people interviewing her in jeans and T-shirts. Her desire to travel. Her desire to paint. Her desire to be a different person than who she's allowing herself to become.

7.

The Edible Garnish class is scheduled to begin at 11:00 a.m. Franny arrives a few minutes early, only to discover that Ma and Esther are already there, sharing a workstation in the far corner. When she tries to join them, the instructor—an older man dressed in chef's whites and a ridiculous toque—asks her to move to an available station. Franny scans the brightly lit room, which contains twelve identical stainless-steel tables, most of which are occupied by women who already seem to know each other.

"But I'm here with them." She points at Ma and Esther.

"Each station has enough supplies for two guests," the man says, his accent indeterminate. He gestures at the array of paring knives and bowls filled with vegetables. "Why don't you work over here, miss?" He taps on the table one row behind Ma where an elderly woman is standing by herself. "You'll still be nearby."

It seems rude to keep insisting that she wants to stay where she is when the woman doesn't have a partner. Ma and Esther also haven't made any sort of protest on her behalf. She moves as directed, trying not to appear sullen about it.

"Celeste." The woman extends her hand.

"Franny."

As they make the usual small talk, Franny wishes she hadn't stopped to use the bathroom after the last class, an hourlong session on arranging tropical flowers. Although she was sandwiched in between Ma and Esther while they worked, the instructor kept going on and on about color palettes and petal textures, stem heights and filler leaves. It felt like they were listening to a lecture rather than spending quality time with each other, which was the whole point of taking these classes. And now here they are, not even standing at the same table together.

"You seem awfully young to be a *Starlight Voyages* fan," Celeste says.

"Excuse me?"

"The reunion cruise."

"Oh, I'm not a fan."

Celeste looks so dismayed that Franny feels the need to clarify. "I watched the show when I was little, but that's not why we picked this cruise. It was more about Bermuda and the schedule working out for my family."

Franny had seen all the *Starlight Voyages* signage when she boarded but didn't register that it was a reunion cruise until the variety show last night. She vaguely recognized the actor who appeared onstage, the handsome one who asked the audience to applaud for all the missing firefighters and their families, which struck her as unplanned and off message. Tom seemed to appreciate it though, going so far as to stand up while he clapped. Afterward, he leaned over and whispered in her ear, his breath laced with wine and cigarettes: "Well, at least *someone's* trying to acknowledge what happened."

"So you're here with your mother and sister?" Celeste asks, motioning toward Ma and Esther.

"She's not my sister," Franny says too abruptly.

She's been annoyed with Esther ever since she arrived at breakfast with a copy of the daily newsletter, highlighted to show Ma all the activities that might interest her. The two of them spent most of the meal huddled over the schedule while Jae talked to Tom about his ringtone business, how cell phones were the future. Franny glares at Ma's and Esther's backsides, huddled once again over their workstation, talking about how small some of the knives are. If Esther were more traditional, she would have offered to trade places with Franny since daughters outrank daughters-in-law in Korean families. But Esther, now dressed in a black Rage Against the Machine T-shirt and tattered jean shorts, is far from traditional and not part of the family yet, if she has any interest in marriage at all.

"Are you traveling with anyone?" Franny asks.

"My husband." Celeste smiles sheepishly. "He didn't want to come to this. He's probably off napping somewhere."

This is another source of annoyance for Franny, how quickly the men peeled off after breakfast without any discussion, leaving the women to entertain Ma. She wonders what they're doing now and imagines Jae sitting in the casino behind a dwindling pile of chips, which worries her. But then she imagines another possibility—Jae and Tom having a drink somewhere, talking about Jae's ringtone business—and this worries her even more. Her détente with her husband is precarious. It won't survive if Jae mentions that she loaned him the money for the cruise, something she didn't tell Tom in the hope that the amount was just insignificant enough to escape notice.

"Ladies." The man in the toque claps his hands. "May I have your attention, please? It's time to get started." He knits his fingers together in front of his chest until the chatter dies down. "My name is Arthur, and I'll be your instructor today. If you went to the midnight buffet last night or the breakfast buffet this morning, you probably saw some of my team's creations, including two edible garnishes that you'll learn how to make during this session."

Franny is surprised to learn that Arthur is an actual chef employed by the cruise line rather than a paid instructor. The hours these people must work, she thinks. The breakfast buffet was elaborate, with huge ice sculptures of palm trees, intricately carved melons filled with fruit salad, and hundreds of decorative flowers made from fruits and vegetables. She wonders how many of Arthur's minions are cutting and peeling away in some windowless kitchen at this very moment, just so the food for the passengers can look pretty. It's sad to think that Ma probably has more in common with the people trapped belowdecks than she does with her own daughter. That's partly why the *chilsun* seems so necessary. Without Ma's hard work, Franny never would have gone to Columbia as an undergrad or NYU for law school. She never would have married Tom or moved into his Upper East Side aerie, a distance of only ten miles from where she grew up, though it feels much farther. The effort it takes to avoid falling down this familiar rabbit hole is so distracting, Franny misses most of Arthur's instructions for the first project, a cartoonish-looking penguin fashioned out of a hard-boiled egg.

"Now be careful, ladies," he says. "Cut slowly so you can get a feel for how sharp and sensitive the knives are."

It seems like a terrible idea, gathering two dozen women—many of them elderly like Celeste, and some who probably tossed back a Bloody Mary or two at breakfast like Esther—and then giving them access to knives. But this is what the class is. Upon Arthur's cue, everyone starts on their penguins, following the step-by-step photos taped to their workstations. Franny works absentmindedly, worried about Celeste's trembling hands. She's certain that the poor old woman is about to slice off a finger.

"Rheumatoid arthritis," Celeste says when she notices Franny staring at her knuckles, which are red and bulbous. "I've had it since I was around your age. I probably should have realized this class might be a little hard for me."

"Well, I can help, if you want. Should I do the cutting for both of us?"

"Oh, how sweet you are." Celeste seems genuinely grateful for the offer. "Thank you, if you really don't mind."

Franny turns black olives into wings, capers into eyes, and carrots into beaks and feet, making double sets of everything. Celeste sticks the tiny pieces onto her peeled egg herself, creating a cockeyed penguin that looks like it was constructed by a child. Still, she appreciates the help and says so repeatedly, which Franny isn't accustomed to. It's a nice feeling, she thinks—to help and actually be acknowledged for helping.

"Yours is perfect," Celeste says, peering down at Franny's finished project. "It's exactly like the picture."

Arthur, who's been circling the room while the women work, seems to agree. He nods approvingly at Franny's penguin, which does look like the example photo, not that she takes much pride in its resemblance. She can't imagine any circumstances under which she'd ever make something like this again. When she and Tom entertain at home, they always hire the same caterer, an imperious Frenchman whose style is traditional and elegant, without a single edible garnish in sight.

"Excellent work," Arthur says. He glances at Celeste's penguin with a polite smile. "Both of you. Excellent work. You've done this before?" he asks Franny.

She shakes her head, intending to offer a longer response, when she notices the noise coming from Ma and Esther's station. The two of them are laughing all of a sudden. Not chuckling or giggling, but really laughing, clutching their stomachs and wiping the tears out of their eyes without a hint of self-consciousness.

"What's so funny?" Franny asks.

Esther turns and holds out her penguin, which doesn't look anything like the photos. Hers has angry black slants for eyebrows, big bug eyes, and—Franny realizes this is what they must be laughing about—a tiny penis made out of the thin tip of a carrot. Arthur lifts and lowers his eyebrows and then mumbles something about being glad that his students are having such a good time. Celeste, meanwhile, offers a timid grin and quickly turns her attention to straightening up their workstation.

Franny isn't surprised that Esther chose to do something off script and off-color. But what surprises her, wounds her actually, is the sight of her mother laughing out loud, like she's genuinely enjoying herself. Franny can't remember the last time, or if there ever was a first time, when Ma did that with her.

"Esther," she says. "Switch places with me?"

Esther trades glances with Ma, a gesture that contains some sort of question, like she's not sure if she should move, or if Ma wants her to move.

"Switch places with me," Franny says, not asking this time.

ARTHUR CLAPS HIS hands and gathers all the women around his workstation for a demo. He says their next project might seem more complicated than the first, but he assures them it's not. Using a vegetable peeler, he shaves long, thin ribbons of cucumber, carrot, and yellow squash. Then he rolls the ribbons tightly—sometimes alone, sometimes together—pinching and pulling the edges until they resemble petals. When the women return to their stations to try making their own, a chorus of lighthearted moans and laughter begins to sweep through the room.

"Practice, ladies," he says airily. "You know the old saying about practice."

The strips of vegetables are watery and quick to fall apart. Franny's first attempt results in a lopsided clump of squash that looks nothing like a flower.

"This is hard, isn't it?" She tacks on a laugh because it feels like she should.

Ma is bent over her cutting board, frowning at a spiral of carrot that refuses to stay in place. When she doesn't respond, Franny shaves another ribbon of squash and tries again. Her second attempt is an improvement, but not by much.

"He made this look easy, didn't he?"

"Ay, you've only done two," Ma says. "Keep trying."

She sounds annoyed, probably because Esther had to move. But she often sounds annoyed with Franny, who handles all the things in life that she can't. Medicare claims, estimated taxes, social security benefits, life insurance—complicated, bureaucratic tasks that are usually unpleasant to talk about and hard for Ma to understand given her limited command of written English. Franny initially agreed to the cruise because she thought a radical change of scenery and subject might help them get along better, but as they continue to work in silence, turning out increasingly flowerlike creations, she realizes her optimism was misguided.

"Once you've mastered your rolling technique, ladies, try making roses," Arthur calls out. "Or peonies. Or carnations. Don't just settle for one kind of flower."

Ma's soft spot for Jae isn't hard to understand. Franny always assumed that she treated him differently because he was a boy and the baby of the family, the only son she had left. But the more she observes Ma's relationship with Esther, the more confused she feels. All her life, Franny has tried so hard to be good, to be a source of pride and stability and security. She thought that was what her mother wanted, but clearly, Ma prefers the company of someone like Esther—barely employed, no college education, green-thong-visible-over-the-waistband-of-her-shorts Esther. Franny still can't believe how Ma laughed and laughed at the lewd penguin, something Franny probably would have been slapped for making, rather than rewarded.

After several long minutes, she looks back and forth between their cutting boards, trying to find something, anything, to talk about. "Do you think the customers at your restaurant would have liked these?" she asks.

"I'm retired now," Ma says with a shrug, as if Franny didn't know, as if she didn't handle the sale of the building and every piece of equipment inside it on her mother's behalf.

Arthur stops in front of their station, nodding at the volume of Ma's output. His toque bobs up and down as he counts, silently at first and then out loud as he nears the end. "Fifteen . . . sixteen . . . seventeen flowers!" he exclaims. "Such efficiency! This must be how the Japanese build so many cars."

"Korean." Ma is quick to correct. "Not from Japan." Usually, she makes allowances for strangers' ignorance, hardened as she is by decades of restaurant work. But the suggestion that she's Japanese is clearly too much.

Arthur, red-faced and chastened, says, "Yes, of course," and quickly resumes his loop around the room.

"You're very quiet," Franny says after he leaves, more statement than attempt at conversation this time.

Again, Ma doesn't look up from her cutting board. "I'm concentrating."

"I think you've made enough now, don't you?" Franny pauses, wishing this didn't have to be so hard. What more does she have to say or do to draw her mother out? "Are you having a good time on the cruise so far?" she asks hopefully.

The tip of Ma's tongue is sticking out of the corner of her mouth, straining with the effort of not wasting any cucumber, even though her blade is about to graze her skin. Franny wants to tell her it's all right if a little stub of vegetable goes to waste, but her mother is nothing if not frugal. Whenever Franny visits her in Fort Lee, she's struck by how every windowsill in the kitchen looks like a collection of grade school science experiments, with plastic to-go containers filled with water and floating stubs of carrots and onions that Ma's trying to regrow out of scraps.

"Are you having a good time?" she repeats.

"Yes, yes," Ma says impatiently.

Franny goes back to assembling her flowers, sorry she asked. A few minutes later, Ma turns and looks at her.

"Why are you sighing like that?"

She wasn't aware that she was sighing at all. "I was just trying to make conversation." She lowers her voice so people won't overhear. "Like everyone else."

Ma looks around the room, finally noticing what Franny already has. All the women are talking or laughing or listening to each other. The garnishes are just an activity to keep their hands busy while they enjoy their time together.

"It's hard to do two things at once," she says.

"You didn't seem to have any problem before." The words are barely out of Franny's mouth before she regrets them.

Ma makes her usual sour face. She's never had any patience for sensitive or delicate women. She raised Franny to work hard, to do what needed to be done, to try even when others failed. Although she's grateful for Ma's example, which helped Franny go far—farther than either of them could have imagined—she can't deny the obvious anymore. The way Ma treats Jae and Esther proves that she's capable of showing affection. Love, even. She just chooses not to show it to her. The difference confirms something she's long feared but never dared to bring up. Franny was in the backseat of her father's car when a delivery truck plowed into it, killing her father and older brother in the front. She feels responsible for the accident, however indirectly, and is convinced that her mother blames her for it, for the way their lives unraveled afterward.

"Are you and your husband okay?" Ma asks, tossing the paper-thin cucumber into the waste bowl.

The question feels loaded. Clearly, she's witnessed something that makes her think they're not.

"We're fine." Franny resists the urge to follow up with "Why do you ask?" "It was just a stressful week," she says instead.

Ma nods. "You'll both go back to work soon?"

"At some point. I'm not sure when."

Their offices are in the Financial District, in buildings still awaiting clearance before the tenants can return. Even if the engineers deem hers structurally sound, Franny isn't certain if she wants to go back, if she'll be able to. Her coveted office, the one she moved into when she became a junior partner, has a western view. How can she ever work there again, helping people plan for an orderly death when it overlooks a new skyline that proves there's no such thing? Franny catches herself sighing, frustrated that Ma is finally talking to her, reminding her of the very subject she wants to avoid.

After another interminable silence, Franny finally asks the question that she knows she shouldn't. "Did you call me on Tuesday?"

"What?"

"On Tuesday, after the planes hit the buildings. Did you call me?"

"You called me," Ma says.

Franny doesn't mean to slam her knife down on the cutting board, but she does.

Ma stares at her strangely. "*You* called *me*," she repeats, stressing the pronouns.

"Right," Franny says, as if she didn't remember. "Okay."

Her cell phone wasn't working that morning. Later, she'd learn that it was because of the transmission antennae on top of the towers. But she didn't know that then, so she kept trying to call. When she finally made it home, she picked up the landline in the foyer and attempted to dial out. The phone beeped loudly and then made a series of noises she'd never heard before. Ma had worried enough for a lifetime. Franny wanted to spare her more stress, so she dialed and redialed for over an hour until she got through, and Ma picked up on the first ring.

"There was a terrorist attack near my office this morning," she said evenly. "I'm home though. I'm fine." She didn't consider any of this a lie. Being fine that day simply meant being alive. Franny didn't mention what she'd just experienced or that she was standing in her entryway, covered in dust from head to toe. Perhaps she was still in shock. Perhaps she knew that if she talked about the dust, she wouldn't be able to stop thinking about what was in it.

"Is your husband there too?" Ma asked.

"No, he's out of town. I called you first."

"You should get off the phone then. In case he's trying to reach you."

Ma hung up without saying goodbye, but Franny continued holding the phone against her ear long after the line disconnected. How many times had she tried to get through, only to exchange a handful of sentences with Ma, who didn't sound happy, or even relieved, to hear from her? And what did it mean that twice in one lifetime, Franny had survived something that other people didn't?

BY THE TIME the Edible Garnish class ends, Franny is feigning seasickness again. Neither Ma nor Esther seems surprised when she tells them she's skipping their next planned activity—a bingo game—because she needs to rest. Esther just nods, her mouth full of penguin, and reminds her to hydrate. Ma, meanwhile, almost looks relieved, which is as painful to Franny as watching them walk off without her. She realizes that Tom was right. If she really wanted to show Ma a good time for her birthday, she should have just written a check and stayed home.

On her way back to the cabin, Franny passes through the crowded atrium, recalling the argument they had the first time he suggested this to her. She was sitting in bed, drafting a memo to a client, when he appeared in the doorway.

"What's that old quote again?" he asked, waving a rolled-up newspaper at her as if he'd just read something that he wanted to discuss. "The definition of crazy is doing the same thing over and over but expecting different results?"

It was September 13 and the city was slowly starting to reopen, but they were still staying indoors, held captive by their shuttered offices and an unspoken fear that something terrible might happen again. Although their apartment was large by New York standards, the kind of large that registered on people's faces when they first entered, they'd sequestered themselves in their own little corners—Tom in the den with the TV, Franny in the bedroom with work or a magazine. Time had such a strange quality then, like water dripping from a tap. It was collecting rather than passing, with each new hour bringing another fit of sadness or fear or grief to accumulate with all the rest.

Whenever they tried to share a meal or even a room together, they ended up returning to the subject of the cruise and arguing about it, which was so unlike them. Usually, Franny was content to let Tom have his way because his opinions about where to eat or vacation or give money were almost always stronger than her own. But this wasn't some minor difference of opinion that she could afford to give in on. This mattered to her deeply, and the fact that he couldn't see or didn't care how much it mattered was ringing every internal alarm.

Franny distinctly remembers bracing herself when Tom appeared in the doorway, asking about the definition of crazy. What had he just read in the paper that prompted him to get out of his chair? What new travel advisory had he come armed with that he wanted to read aloud? She was tempted to tell him that the quote—one of Einstein's—didn't actually use the word "crazy." It was about "insanity," but she wasn't about to start a fight over such a minor, meaningless correction, not when she sensed a much larger fight on the horizon.

"Is this about the cruise again? Are you saying I'm crazy because I still want to go?"

"No, I'm saying it's crazy to keep doing all these things for your mom when she's never been the least bit grateful. Why not just pay for the trip and let Nancy go on her own?"

"It's not like that in Korean families," Franny said, repeating something she'd already told him countless times before. "The children are supposed to show how grateful they are. That's why we have to be there for her birthday, to actually have a celebration this time."

She didn't mention that on Ma's sixtieth birthday, the year of her *hwangap*, Franny had offered to host a party, but Ma refused. Even Jae offered, but there was no changing her mind. Later, Franny was mortified to learn that Ma had spent her birthday catering someone else's *hwangap* at the restaurant. She claimed the money was too good to turn down.

"You know she'd probably enjoy it more without us," Tom said.

Franny didn't respond, aware that something else was forming on his tongue. She couldn't predict the words so much as the sentiment, which she knew would have the quality of a knife.

"Tell me again what your goal is here. Do you actually think you're going to take her on this trip and she's going to be all kind and loving all of a sudden?" He smacked the newspaper against the palm of his hand. "Honestly, Franny, why do you insist on trying when you know that's not who she is?"

Because her mother had worked fifteen, sixteen hours a day to keep a roof over their heads. Because despite growing up poor, Franny couldn't remember having to go without a school uniform, a field trip, a book, or a hot meal. Because she had memories, long faded but real memories of Ma holding her and smiling at her before the car accident. Because so much of Franny's now-gilded life was built upon her mother's shoulders, and it all could end at any moment, for either of them. She knew that better than ever now.

Franny didn't share any of these reasons with Tom. She didn't think she should have to. She was also afraid. If she explained and he still refused to understand, that would confirm something she'd been trying to ignore about her husband, about the state of his vow to love and honor and care for her. It was easier to just end the conversation, so she climbed out of bed and slammed the door in his face, which probably surprised them both. She'd never been angry enough to do that before. And now she's angry with him all over again because maybe he was right. Maybe they should have just stayed at home.

For the hundredth, possibly the thousandth time, Franny imagines what might happen if she simply told everyone where she was on Tuesday. If they knew what she went through to be here, would Tom understand why she kept insisting they had to come? Would Ma appreciate how much she wanted to honor her and give her the celebration that she deserved? She wants to believe they'd soften. She hopes they'd try to provide comfort. But then she remembers the quote again—how insanity is doing the same thing over and over but expecting different results—and she knows that she made the right choice. She would rather live with the weight of the lie than deal with the consequences of the truth.

"Excuse you, sweetie," someone says as they brush shoulders.

Franny looks up, momentarily disoriented. She passed the elevators she was heading toward some time ago. Her choice is to backtrack or walk through the casino, where there's another set of elevators. Franny wonders if Jae is hiding out somewhere inside, spending money that he doesn't have. Part of her wants to catch him in the act—proof that Ma's love is misguided and always has been. She enters through the brightly lit arches, squinting at the double row of chandeliers running down the length of the room. At first, the mirrored walls and ceilings appear to be making the space more crowded than it really is, but as her eyes adjust to the assault of light, she realizes that the casino is actually full, that despite the beautiful weather and long list of class offerings, so many people just want to sit inside and gamble away their money. She doesn't understand this impulse; she never has, although the taste for it runs in the family.

She passes through the smoking section, fanning away thick, stagnant clouds of smoke as she searches for Jae at the tables. Blackjack was his preferred game in college. Once a math major with a full ride to U Penn, he was both smart enough and dumb enough to teach himself how to count cards. After some indiscreet wins, the Indian casinos in rural Pennsylvania with single- and double-deck blackjack tables started turning him away, so he went to Atlantic City, where the standard eight-deck games were too difficult to count, even for him. When Ma called in a panic, telling Franny that Jae had to appear before a disciplinary board at school, she drove to Philadelphia without stopping. There, she learned that he'd been taking other students' stats and physics exams for hundreds of dollars apiece to support his habit. The offense, combined with his increasingly poor grades, resulted in a semester-long suspension, which cost him his scholarship. But rather than punish Jae for being kicked out of school, Ma welcomed him home, never complaining about the string of marginal jobs that he's cycled through in the years since.

According to Jae, he no longer gambles. He said so the first time he asked Franny for a loan. She barely remembers what that one was for now—something involving phone cards, she thinks—but as she scans the players at all the blackjack tables, she realizes that she never believed him. Maybe she didn't even want to believe him because when she reaches the end of the last row, she's almost disappointed not to have caught him in the act. Her brother is wholly unreliable this way, never living up to anyone's expectations, whether good or bad.

Franny leaves the casino and returns to deck seven. As she approaches the turn toward her suite, she hears two men talking loudly.

Before she can even make out their words, she senses that one of them is complaining to the other, perhaps even arguing with him. When she rounds the corner, she sees their room steward, Jimmy, halfway down the corridor, speaking to someone through an open door. She shouldn't be able to hear their conversation from such a distance, but the man in the cabin is yelling. She doesn't have to see his face to recognize his voice.

"Yesterday, you told us the satellite would be fixed soon," Tom shouts. "You said we'd get a newspaper too, but I haven't seen one anywhere."

"But, sir," Jimmy says pleadingly. "I have no control over the—"

"You're telling me this ship doesn't have access to another signal? I don't believe that for a second. It's like you're trying . . . actively trying to withhold information from us."

"Sir, we would never do—"

"Now I want to make a phone call. I don't care how that happens, but I expect you to make it happen."

"Please, sir. I'm not an engineer. If the equipment isn't working, I can't simply make it work for you. Tomorrow, we'll arrive in Bermuda and then you'll have access to—"

Tom lunges at him, reaching his hands through the open doorway. Franny stops and presses her back against the wall, certain that Tom is about to hit him, but he clutches Jimmy's shirt in his fists instead.

"Please. I need you to listen," he says, his voice unfamiliar now, weak with desperation. "Someone I know . . . someone I care about . . . She went missing last Tuesday. Please. I just need to find out if there's been any news about her."

8.

Doug keeps his eyes on the clock as he spins his partner to "Get Down Tonight," a song he hasn't danced to since the seventies. The name of the band escapes him, as does the name of his partner—Molly? Mary?—an older woman who's always a step or two off the beat. When he reels her back toward him, she grips his hand tightly. Her bones feel fragile, practically birdlike, but she's spry and spirited for her age, which he appreciates.

"How do you still remember how to do all this?" she shouts over the music.

"It's just muscle memory, I guess."

"What?" She turns her good ear toward him.

"*Muscle memory,*" he enunciates into her hearing aid.

It's 3:50 and he has ten more minutes of Disco Beats until the hourlong break he's been looking forward to all afternoon. Doug stares at the clock, trying to make time move faster. Molly or Mary is a perfectly nice woman, but he's tired of having to be on for everyone, pretending that he wants to be doing the things he's doing. His scheduled appearances for the day have included a bingo game, a shuffleboard tutorial, a skeet shooting lesson, and a wine and cheese tasting minus the wine—activities he didn't care for but had to smile his way through as participants came by to take pictures and say hello. This session, however, is by far the most taxing. Not only does dancing require uncomfortably close physical contact with strangers, but they all want to make small talk while they do it.

"I'm so glad they thought to have a photographer here," Molly says, mugging at the ponytailed man who's been following Doug from session to session. "My friends won't believe who I got to dance with on this cruise."

Doug holds still and they both smile for the camera. He wonders how much Aria charges passengers for their photos and whether his contract entitles him to a cut.

"So, where's home for you?" he asks, and then, remembering her hearing aid, he repeats the question again, louder and slower this time. "*Where do you live?*"

Molly's shoulders tense. "My real home's in Birmingham, Alabama. But the old folks' home my kids just put me in is near *their* home in Atlanta. I suspect this cruise is my reward for letting them. Like I had a choice," she adds indignantly. "Really though, can you imagine someone like me in an old folks' home?"

He thinks it must be comforting to have children who care enough to put her anywhere. If he had some of his own, he might be able to turn down jobs like this—jobs so anxiety inducing, he can't get through them without popping Xanax like mints. "You must be the youngest one there," he shouts, which coaxes back a smile. He turns to the side and lightly bumps his hip against hers, then turns and bumps the other.

The lyrics, "get down tonight," have been repeating for some time now, alternating with short bursts of horns. If he remembers the song correctly, he doesn't have long before it ends. Doug braces himself for another partner change. Unlike the signing session, there aren't any crew members present to help manage all the people vying for his time and attention. Whenever he has to pick a new partner, at least a dozen women crowd and clamor around him, reminiscent of his clubbing days when hazy scenes like this played out everywhere he went. Adding to the sense of frenzy during the changeovers is the noticeable shortage of male partners. Poor Gideon, who insisted on accompanying Doug to this session, is the only young person in the room and almost as popular as Doug is. He turns and spots Gid easily, a full head taller than everyone else, gamely dancing with someone who's old enough to be his grandmother.

"All right, ladies and gentlemen . . ." The DJ has a surprisingly baritone voice that doesn't match his face. "That was KC and the Sunshine Band—"

Aha, Doug thinks.

"—and now, let's hear it for Kooooooool and the Gang."

As the trumpets blare, signaling the beginning of "Celebration," Doug says goodbye to Molly and quickly surveys the half-moon of women that's assembled around him. There's one in particular whom he finds absolutely terrifying. She's wearing an oversize *Starlight Voyages* cast T-shirt, red jeans, and a matching red bow in her hair like Minnie Mouse. Even if her outfit wasn't so distinctive, he wouldn't be able to miss her. She's presented herself at every changeover, waving frantically to get his attention. Under different circumstances, he'd feel too guilty to snub someone so desperate to be picked, but he worries that she's the woman he heard shouting "We love you, Mack" over and over again during last night's show. Doug turns to his right, ignoring the overly eager and borderline lusty women his age in favor of the oldest one he can find. When he offers his hand to her, some of the other women sigh and grumble, but what can they do? He's chosen the eldest person in the room—it would be impolite to complain.

His new partner introduces herself as Ada, and within seconds of taking his hand, she tells him she's eighty years young.

"Very nice to meet you," he says, glancing at the clock again. It's 3:54. If there's a God, this will be the final song of the session.

Ada moves surprisingly well for an octogenarian. She's also much easier to lead than some of his previous partners. Doug asks if she's taken lessons before and she says she learned from her husband. She adds that until recently, the two of them went dancing at least once a month at the Rotary Club in Springfield, Illinois. Doug smiles stiffly, noting her use of the past tense.

"You're very good at this too," she says.

"Am I?"

He can't quite remember the last time he danced in public. It feels odd now, probably because he's not coked out of his mind. Confidence was always so much easier to manufacture under the influence. He glances at the DJ, who's surveying the room, nodding to the beat of the music. Although his expression is neutral, almost impassive, Doug senses that he could break out into laughter at any time, an impulse he'd actually understand. How foolish they all must look to him, doing stiff variations of the hustle and the slide, reminiscing about an era long past. The DJ is young and movie-star handsome, too young to be spinning records from the seventies for such a geriatric crowd. The fact that Doug is part of this crowd—maybe even the center of it—makes him feel old and intensely irritable.

As soon as the ship docks in Bermuda, he plans to find a phone and call Annette. He wants her to know what a disaster the cruise has been and how hurt he is by her recent behavior. These days, Annette is the closest thing to a friend that Doug has, so he can't decide what disappoints him more—the way she misled him about certain details of the job or the fact that she took advantage of his need to accept it.

Earlier this year, he had a scare. A baby-faced doctor, fresh out of his residency, told him that he had prostate cancer. "The best kind though," the doctor quickly added.

Doug was devastated. Ever since he got sober, he'd been working so hard to take care of himself. His days always included some combination of running, hiking, yoga, or meditation in the hope of reversing whatever damage he'd done to his body when he was young. As far as Doug was concerned, all cancer was cancer. He didn't realize it could ever be anything other than bad. But the doctor said he was in a very low-risk group and simply recommended regular blood tests and exams to ensure that it didn't spread. "Active surveillance," he called it. Doug had always assumed that a cancer diagnosis meant months of debilitating chemo and radiation. At times, he even wondered if he might prefer that route over this wait-and-see approach, which seemed cruel in an entirely different way. Once, when he mentioned this to Annette, she snapped at him, as she was prone to do with everyone in her life, whether the topic was personal or professional. "Doug, I love you," she said, and he knew that she genuinely meant it. "But don't be such a fucking idiot."

"My husband and I never missed an episode of *Starlight Voyages,*" Ada says, spinning clockwise in a butterfly. "Actually, your show was the reason why we started going on cruises back in the eighties."

"Well, thank you. That's such a nice thing to hear." He pauses for a beat and then switches the direction of the spin. As they turn counterclockwise, he catches a glimpse of the clock. It's 3:58 and the song has started to wind down.

"Oh, look." Ada stops and pats him on the shoulder. "My family came to pick me up. Would you mind if I introduced you?"

He doesn't even have a chance to reply before she's leading him by the hand toward the door.

"This is Sarah, my daughter," she says, motioning toward a middle-aged woman pushing a much older man in a wheelchair. "And this is my husband, Edgar. Of course, you two know who this is."

Doug shakes hands and tries to smile during the introductions, but his expression feels frozen in a rigor of surprise. Edgar sat in the wheelchair, his legs covered with a thin plaid blanket. As the photographer encourages them to gather around for a picture, Doug replays their earlier conversation and realizes that he jumped to the wrong conclusion again. Ada's husband is infirm and incapacitated, but he's very much alive. It's a morbid habit, one that he's been catching himself in the act of more and more lately. How quick he is to assume that anyone who ever cared about the show, who cared about him, is dead.

DOUG FINDS GIDEON on a bench outside the rec room, watching people walk down the corridor. He has a smear of coral lipstick on his cheek that he clearly doesn't know is there—a parting gift from one of his dance partners, most likely. Doug wipes it off with his thumb and shows him the offending smudge of color.

"Gross." Gid rubs his face with the backs of his hands. "No wonder everyone's been looking at me."

"Sorry to keep you waiting."

"Are you done signing autographs now?"

"Yes." Doug almost tacks on a "thank God," but there are too many stragglers nearby who might overhear. He was tempted to sign a few things and then say he had to go—something he's seen celebrities do in L.A.—but he didn't have the heart. On some level, he knew it was sad that any of these people wanted his autograph. For him, a D- or C-list celebrity at best, to refuse such a request would have been even sadder.

"I didn't realize that would take so long. I thought I'd be able to leave right after the last song."

"It's no big deal. What do you want to do now?"

But it is a big deal, Doug thinks. A very big deal. He was hoping to spend some quality time with his nephew on this cruise, not squeeze him in during breaks. "Let's go somewhere quiet and get a drink," he says.

If he hadn't turned at just that moment, he probably would have missed it. The almost imperceptible flick of Gideon's eyebrows, registering concern or maybe even judgment. It reminds him that despite fifteen years of sobriety, he's still being watched. Doug wouldn't put it past his younger brother to worry about him being back on the *Sonata* again. He wonders if he encouraged Gid, maybe even forced him, to accept the invitation to Bermuda so he could keep an eye on his uncle.

"I meant soda," Doug says. "Something with caffeine, or maybe sugar," he adds, trying to sound casual instead of hurt.

They consult a map and head toward a gelateria on deck five. People from other sessions are still filtering out of the multipurpose rooms, crowding into the long corridor. They pass Renee, who's standing in a huddle of women, chatting pleasantly while signing autographs. Doug tries to pretend that he didn't notice her, but how could he not? She's dressed in one of her leotards again. A lavender one with a long flowy pink skirt over it, similar to what she used to wear on the show. He assumes she's coming from another dance class that just let out. The only mercy of his appearance schedule is that they seem to have different ones, dividing and conquering all the various sessions to maximize the passengers' time with them.

"So, what do you have to do after your break?" Gideon asks.

"Dinner. The early crowd."

Gid looks disappointed. "Will it be like last night?"

"Unfortunately, yes."

To Doug's horror, he discovered there's actually something worse than being assigned to sit at a table full of people he doesn't know. It's being forced to rotate to a different table every night, meeting a new group of people each time—another special benefit for members of the Captain's Club. "You don't have to come though. You can just order room service if you want. And again, I'm sorry about—"

"It's okay, Uncle Doug. It's not your fault." Gideon stuffs his hands into his pockets. "Can I decide about dinner later? I'm not really sure what I want to do yet."

Doug can't blame his nephew for being on the fence. Their dining companions last night included a man with yellow dentures who chewed his steak like a savage and a pair of elderly sisters who insisted on telling them about their favorite episodes of *Starlight Voyages,* summarizing the plotlines as if they'd asked.

Instead of waiting for the elevators, they take the main staircase in the center of the ship. Doug keeps a firm grip on the polished brass rail and stares at his feet while they walk down two floors. Either the Xanax or the long, looping spiral is making him uncomfortably dizzy. Passengers walking up the stairs keep turning their heads as they pass and whispering his name to each other. He hopes that avoiding eye contact will send a signal that he wants to be left alone now. His break is only an hour long, which the Disco Beats autograph seekers have already cut into.

If Gideon came on this cruise to serve as his uncle's unofficial chaperone, then he's not the only one who has another motive for being here. Over the summer, when Doug was shuttling back and forth between doctors' offices, he couldn't help but notice how all the other patients, especially those waiting for the oncologist, were always accompanied by a spouse or an adult child. He was the only one who showed up for his appointments alone, a condition that seemed to register on people's faces, usually in the form of pity or concern. Although his prostate scare was relatively minor, he knew that wouldn't always be the case. At some point in the not-so-distant future, he was going to need help.

Annette, who's also unmarried and childless, frequently encouraged him to develop a close relationship with a younger relative, someone responsible enough to step up to the task of caring for him in his old age. Years earlier, Annette had chosen her eldest niece and spoiled her with lavish trips and gifts, and now Nina, in her thirties with kids of her own, effectively tends to her like a daughter. Although Doug disliked the idea of imposing on Gideon in this way, the fact remained that he couldn't think of anyone else. It was his nephew or the state. Whenever he was about to buy a Christmas or birthday gift for Gid that was slightly more extravagant than he could afford, he had to remind himself that he wasn't trying to buy his nephew's love. He genuinely liked Gid and always had. His nephew was kindhearted and earnest, so different from most of the people he'd surrounded himself with in the industry. His disposition often reminded him of Peter's, which only made Doug like him more.

On the landing, Doug spots Kevin near the Excursions desk, doing his best Jekyll and Hyde routine and enthusiastically high-fiving a group of passengers. Doug slows down, almost coming to a full stop. They didn't speak after the show last night, and he worries that Kevin is still upset that he forgot to introduce Renee, who walked onstage to a smattering of confused applause—such a letdown for what was supposed to be the grand finale.

Doug falls several feet behind before Gid eventually notices and turns to look for him. "Everything okay?"

"Oh, I'm fine." He waits for Kevin to disappear from view. "Maybe just a little tired from all that dancing."

Gideon winces. "Man. Disco . . . That's what people were into in the seventies, huh?"

"Every decade has some embarrassing trend. When you're my age, your kids will probably make fun of you for listening to . . ." He pauses, trying to think of a band that's popular now. "In Sync," he ventures, hoping he got the name right.

Gideon bursts out laughing. "Uncle Doug, that's a boy band. Only girls like NSYNC."

"Yes, well . . ." He reddens, feeling ancient all over again. He wants to change the subject already. "Whatever it is that boys are into now. By the way, you were a good sport about dancing with all those women."

"Every time a song ended, some random new lady would just grab me."

"They probably weren't expecting someone your age to be there. They were excited."

"Not as excited as they were to see you."

Doug can see a question forming on Gideon's face, just as he has so many times before. He braces for a topic that he probably doesn't want to talk about, adding to the long list of slightly uncomfortable discussions they've already had. Unlike the occasional friendly stranger he meets at a retreat or on set, he tries to be receptive to

Gid's curiosity about his life. He feels grateful that his nephew even wants to get to know him.

"What?" Doug asks. "You look like you have something on your mind."

A crew member walks by with a large stack of beach towels that seems sure to fall. Gideon is momentarily distracted, turning his head to watch the man pass. "Do you . . . enjoy it?" he asks, returning to their conversation. "The way all those ladies were like . . . kind of throwing themselves at you?"

Doug shakes his head. "No. Not at all. Not in the slightest." It feels like he could keep going, adding one more refusal after another. "Actually, I'm embarrassed for them," he says in a whisper. "I'm embarrassed for me."

"Then you don't like it, the attention?"

"No, but it's my job to pretend that I do."

Doug can tell that something about this answer isn't sitting right with Gid, but he stops short, noticing Kevin talking to another group of passengers nearby. Thanks to Kevin, Renee, and some of his more ardent fans, the *Sonata* has turned into a minefield of people he's trying to avoid. He's desperate to arrive in port tomorrow morning so he can get off the ship, if only for a day of freedom.

"I mean, that's what acting is," Doug tries to clarify. "It's all just pretending."

They continue on as Kevin rounds the corner, but Doug can tell that this explanation isn't sitting any better with Gid than the first.

THE GELATERIA IS nearly empty when they arrive. Aside from the woman behind the counter and a couple sharing a sundae in the far corner, Doug and Gideon are the only customers. With its out-of-the-way location and small, nook-like booths, Doug makes a mental note to return if he ever needs a place to hide, especially before dinner, when most people aren't thinking about dessert.

He slides into a booth, taking care not to spill his espresso. Above him hangs a large black-and-white print of Italian women churning milk while two men look on. All the walls are decorated like this, with old photos of farmers and their wives and cows. He'll never understand why Aria spent so much on every aspect of the ship's décor except the art. He glances around, trying to remember what this space was when they were filming the series. All he knows is that it wasn't a gelateria, and the walls weren't so pink.

Gideon joins him with a cup of pistachio gelato that's already melting. He scrapes at it with a tiny wooden spoon that's no match for the giant double scoops. When the ice cream starts to drip down his hand in milky rivulets, he licks the sides, rotating the cup to get ahead of the melt. Doug has a vague memory of being a kid and eating soft serve while his younger brother, Gid's father, did something very similar. It was the same mix of pleasure and panic that he sees now—pleasure to be eating ice cream and panic that it's about to make a mess.

"Be right back." Gideon sets his cup on the table.

Doug fishes the Xanax out of his pocket, staring at the bottle as he attempts to do the math. He took one after lunch, which was less than four hours ago, but he can already feel the knot inside him tightening again. If he expects to get through dinner and the show in one piece, he should probably take a few more now, just to be safe. He shakes out two pills as Gideon returns with a fistful of napkins.

"Are you supposed to be taking so many of those?" Gid asks.

"It's a prescription," Doug says, making sure to turn the label so it's visible.

"I know, but that thing was almost full when we boarded and now you only have half."

The bottle is amber and hard to see through. Gid has obviously been keeping close tabs on it, much closer than Doug. He chases one down with his espresso and puts the second pill back as he feels the grit of silty coffee grounds on his tongue. His nephew isn't entirely wrong. He is going through his supply much faster than usual, but if there were ever a time to double or triple his usual dose, it's now. Doug examines where the line of pills falls when he holds the bottle upright. He should probably try to get a refill in Bermuda since the thought of running out at sea is enough to induce another panic attack.

"You're right, Gid. I'm not supposed to be taking so many." He presses his back against the wall and takes a slow, calming breath, aware of the prickly heat of defensiveness rising within him. "But you've seen how people are on this cruise. It's hard not to feel overwhelmed by all the attention, and this stuff—well, it just helps."

Gideon twists his mouth into a shape that Doug doesn't recognize. Then he picks up his gelato and puts a layer of napkins on the table, blotting the sickly green pool of melted ice cream. Doug is about to tell him that he appreciates his concern, but he doesn't. Not really. He feels like a man in a fishbowl being watched by everyone on the ship, including his nephew. He decides to change the subject and ask what Gid would like to do in Bermuda, when he sees Tabby sidling up beside them, dressed all in black like she was the day before. She stops several feet away and waves her hand in an exaggerated circle like she's washing a window.

"Hello! I didn't want to scare you this time."

"Yes, hello, Tabby," Doug says, wondering how she managed to even find them tucked away here. He makes a conspicuous gesture of looking at the clock on the wall.

"I know you're on break, so I won't take up too much of your time. I just wanted to pass on a quick note from Kevin about tonight's show."

Doug braces himself. He wishes she'd asked to take him aside rather than do this in front of his nephew. But to be fair, he'd probably be upset that she interrupted his break, no matter her approach. "What's the note?"

"Well, it was really great how you got the crowd so pumped up, but Kevin says . . ." The apples of Tabby's cheeks redden. "Maybe this next time . . . Kevin says you might want to keep the tone a little more, um, upbeat? Like, maybe don't mention Alan not being here or anything related to that."

What's the *that*? he wants to know. The fact that Alan failed to show up? Or the reason why he didn't? Doug can't think about one without thinking about the other. *That,* he'd like to point out, was a tragedy. *That* killed hundreds, maybe even thousands, of innocent people. *That* is the one thing the crew clearly doesn't want the passengers talking about at the risk of ruining their collective good time. It dawns on him that maybe there's nothing wrong with the satellite link at all. Maybe it just makes everyone's job easier if the phones and TVs and Internet appear not to work. He wouldn't put it past the executives at Aria to do something like this in order to give the passengers what they think they need—a vacation free of any reminders of what they left behind.

None of this, however, is Tabby's fault. He reminds himself that she's just a nice girl doing an impossible job during an impossibly difficult time. He has no reason to take his frustrations out on her.

"Yes, I understand," he says. "Thank you."

Tabby looks relieved. Clearly, she expected a different kind of response. "Oh, great. Great." She backs away from the table as if she doesn't want to press her luck. "I'll tell Kevin we talked then. See you at call time."

She gives them a quick wave and then she's off again, her radio squawking. Doug turns back to Gideon, only to find his nephew staring at her rear end, making no effort to be discreet.

"*Gid,*" he says pointedly. "You can't do that."

"What?"

"Are you serious?"

Gideon shakes his head as if he genuinely doesn't know what Doug is talking about. "Can't do what?"

He wonders if his nephew is still a virgin. Maybe that would explain the exaggerated, almost cartoonlike leering. Then again, he knows firsthand how early this kind of behavior starts, how quickly boys are conditioned to act a certain way in order to be considered men.

"The way you look at Tabby." He lowers his voice. "The *very obvious* way you keep staring at certain parts of her body." Doug realizes that he's talking with his hands, waving and circling them around in the air like he's kneading dough. "You really shouldn't do that."

The crease in Gideon's forehead is now a deep furrow. He looks mad or embarrassed or both.

"I'm not saying this to judge you or shame you. She's a pretty girl . . . there's nothing wrong with noticing her, but if I'm uncomfortable seeing you do that, well . . ."

Gideon takes a bite of his gelato and immediately sets the cup down, pushing it away as if the cream has gone sour. "It's kind of hard taking advice about this from you, of all people. I mean, my dad's told me some stories—"

"Which is exactly why I'm bringing this up now. That actress who's on board? My former costar? She told me not to come anywhere near her." Gideon's eyes widen with curiosity, but Doug doesn't want to get sidetracked with an explanation, not that he could even provide one. "This kind of behavior—it just leads to things, Gid. It has consequences that you can't even imagine."

He pauses, trying to figure out how to talk about what could happen without going into detail about what happened to him. But before he can continue, he hears someone say, "Excuse me, Mr. Clayton," followed by an insistent tap-tap-tap on his shoulder. He turns to find the woman with the Minnie Mouse bow standing behind him.

"I'm *so* sorry to interrupt," she says. "I kept trying to get a minute alone with you during that last session, but you were always surrounded. Then I had to go to the bathroom so bad at the end—" She laughs out loud, cupping a hand over her mouth as if to contain herself, but the hand doesn't stay there for long. "By the time I finished, you were already gone."

The number of things Doug finds off-putting about this woman begins to tally. In addition to her outfit, there's the mile-a-minute way she speaks, the oversharing of information he doesn't want to know, the laughter that reminds him of a goddamn parrot. But what bothers him most is her nervous, overly reverent tone, like she's talking to someone important instead of an old, washed-up actor hiding out from his fans.

"You have no idea how long I've been waiting for this cruise. After those buildings got bombed last Tuesday, my husband said we shouldn't go anywhere, but I told him I just couldn't miss this. It turns out, I get pretty seasick, so I couldn't stop by your signing line earlier. I was hoping you could . . . Oh, no. Where'd that thing go?" She rummages through her giant purse, which sounds like it's full of loose change and keys. "Okay, here it is." She holds up a pen that has a large bug—a ladybug?—dangling from the cap on a metal chain.

"Maybe I should just get going," Gideon says, wiping off the puddle of green on the table with his last wad of napkins.

"Wait. Don't go. It's my break." Doug reaches out and grabs his nephew by the forearm, only to watch his face contort angrily, making an expression he's never seen before.

Gid shakes free from Doug's grip and walks off, leaving him with the woman.

"Oh, I hope he didn't go because of me. I just wanted to get a quick autograph. I'm so sorry—"

"Yes," Doug snaps. "You said that already."

"I didn't mean to interrupt."

"But you did interrupt, didn't you?"

The woman's face falls and she lowers her pen, revealing the image of the *Starlight* cast printed on her T-shirt. There he is, standing in the second row with his big hair and short shorts, smiling back at his older self without a care.

"My God. What is *wrong* with you people?" Doug shouts. He tries to squeeze out of the booth to go after his nephew, but before he can get up, the woman runs away.

9.

The scene at the *Monarca* reminds Lucy of a Toulouse-Lautrec painting. Dark swipes of color; kind, diffuse light; faces smeared softly with shadow. Now that it's late, more people her age—or at the very least, people closer to her age—have come out to gather, crowding into the *Sonata*'s ancient disco. The floor, which glows and pulses in sync with the music—mostly Top 40 hip-hop and R & B—invites passengers to get up and dance. Some do, but most huddle in the dark, nursing their drinks while eyeing each other.

"Oh, hey. Ten o'clock."

Whenever Mariah spots someone attractive, she calls out a time instead of a direction, which makes her sound like a sniper. It confuses Lucy, forcing her to rotate her head like an owl. Then again, everything feels slightly confusing after a long day of drinking, starting with the mimosas by the pool, then wine with dinner, followed by a round of tequila shots at the Grotto, courtesy of Iain. Now here they are, camped out with their cosmopolitans at a prime stretch of the *Monarca*'s S-shaped bar.

"Not my type," Lucy says, not certain whose ten o'clock Mariah is talking about, but not interested enough to ask.

By her count—though she's quickly losing count—Lucy has consumed more drinks in a single day than she usually does in a month. She's lucky that most of them were weak or served over too much ice, which quickly watered them down. Still, the combination of motion sickness pills and alcohol has a sedative effect, which her newly acquired sunburn only worsens. Lucy's skin is prickly with heat from lying out on a chaise all afternoon and falling asleep for long stretches, something she wishes she were doing now. Whenever the urge to yawn rises from her throat, she turns away from Mariah, who's having the opposite reaction to all the alcohol. With each new drink, she becomes happier, livelier, more excitable. And what excites her most is the prospect of finding someone for Lucy, like the cruise won't be complete until she too hooks up with a man.

Lucy didn't ask for this and tries not to encourage it. She hears enough matchmaking advice from her mother, who often questions why she doesn't have time to date.

"Lou, a date isn't necessarily dinner," Mom is quick to remind her whenever the subject comes up. "You could just go have coffee with a boy or two so you're not totally out of practice after you graduate."

Among her parents' circles, which include the people they know from church, the sorority and fraternity they rushed in college, and her father's friends from pharmacy school, there's no shortage of enterprising young Black men whom Lucy's mother would like to see her have coffee with. Usually, membership in this pool of potential suitors requires being well educated, having a good job in a major city, being reasonably attractive and God-fearing, and not having a reputation for getting around too much, whatever "too much" actually means. Being tall is a plus, as is being lighter-skinned, although this preference seems to be changing since her parents' courtship, when Lucy's maternal grandparents initially disapproved of her dark-skinned father. Had he not been from a well-respected family that put both their sons and daughters through college, Mom said she probably would have been forced to let him go.

"Aren't you lucky we don't put that kind of pressure on you?" she always asks, oblivious to the other kinds of pressure they apply.

It doesn't escape Lucy's attention that everyone in this prospective dating pool—men and women alike—has a similar background. Private schools, top colleges, impressive jobs, and above all, parents who did well despite the odds and expect their kids to do better. It seems like the adult kids are being married off to one another in order to protect the gains made by the previous generation, and those who fall short need not apply. She doubts she's seen even half a dozen Black men on the ship who are passengers instead of crew, and of those, few—maybe not even any—would be considered a good match by her mother's standards. If Lucy were interested in marriage, particularly her parents' kind of marriage, these ratios might bother her. But this is what no one seems to understand. Dating, marrying, having children—she's never wanted any of it. She just doesn't know how to say so without offending people who do.

"Then what about him?" Mariah nudges her in the side. "Five o'clock."

Lucy turns her head, capturing another yawn in her fist. The disco is stifling now, crowded with too many bodies. She makes no effort to figure out who Mariah is talking about. "He's not my type either."

"I'm starting to think I don't know what your type is."

Lucy pauses, thinking about the next three days, what it will feel like to keep up this charade for the rest of the cruise. "Well, he'd be Black, to start."

This quickly puts an end to the conversation, probably because Mariah has noticed the same dismal numbers that Lucy has. She wishes she'd gone down this route earlier—how much time they could have spent talking about something, anything, else. Mariah quietly finishes off her cosmo, siphoning the dregs through a thin plastic straw, while Lucy scans the dance floor. More couples are dancing now, grinding to a Ginuwine song with scrunched-up faces and bitten lips that make them look like they're in pain.

"So why did you move back to Boston?" Lucy asks, taking advantage of the silence to discuss something other than men. "Didn't you like New York?"

"Are you kidding? I loved it there. I still miss it, but I had a pretty bad breakup." Mariah raises her empty glass at the bartender, mouthing the words *another please*. It's hard not to notice her unusual way of ordering, which assumes that people are always looking at her, waiting to be beckoned and asked to do something on her behalf.

"New York's a big city though." Lucy hopes there was more than just a breakup that prompted Mariah to move.

"Not big enough. I kept running into my ex everywhere."

"So you left a place you loved for Boston, which is so . . ."

"Provincial, I know."

Lucy doesn't understand how someone who lived in New York, who says she loved it, could be sitting so casually on a ship, ogling men like there's nothing more important going on in the world. The only benefit of drinking so much is that it's easier not to think about recent events, which is probably why Lucy keeps doing it. In Boston, shortly after the attacks, she often found herself fighting two competing urges. One was to sit in the lab and cry, and the other was to paint what she saw on the news and in the papers, to give all the horror a color and shape and dimension. It startled her, how the desire to put brush to canvas had been locked down so tight for years and what finally reawakened it, what made it seem urgent again, was destruction. Neither impulse felt remotely appropriate considering how distant the events were from her life, how they happened in places she never lived in, involving people she never knew. Being American was Lucy's only real claim to grief, but she was distrustful of the surge of flag waving she'd witnessed in recent days. She worried about the violence that might result in the name of patriotism.

"Boston's fine though," Mariah continues. "It's familiar because of school. And it's smaller, so at least it's easy to meet people."

Mariah and her mother would get along, she thinks. Unlike Lucy's father, who encourages her to move wherever the job market eventually takes her, Mom is always trying to convince her to come back home, arguing that if Lucy wants to put her education to good use, surely she could do that in the nation's capital. She probably assumes that once Lucy returns to D.C., with its large Black professional community, she'll meet a nice young man, marry, and have children. "You can still have a career and a family," Mom's quick to add, as if employment is some grand concession made by an older generation of women to a younger one. It's impossible for Lucy to explain to her mother, a homemaker who aspired to and achieved a white, middle-class ideal of domesticity, that she doesn't want the life her parents worked so hard to build.

"By the way, Iain's going to come over after his shift ends tonight. You're okay with that, right?"

It takes Lucy a few slow blinks to understand what this really means. "When do you want me out of the cabin?"

"He'll be done at two, so he said he'll come by at about two-fifteen."

It's half past midnight. Usually, Lucy is asleep by now. She can't remember the last time she was awake at this hour, much less two. What is she supposed to do so late at night? Where should she go? She's about to ask when she looks around the sparkling disco, which is across from the sparkling casino, which is one floor above the sparkling Grotto. She realizes the whole point of being on this glittering ship is never having to worry about what to do.

"He doesn't have a cabin of his own?" she asks casually.

"It's on the staff deck. No passengers allowed. Besides, he said it's one of those little closets without a window, and he has a roommate. I figured since Gran splurged on a suite . . . You don't mind if I have him over, do you?"

Mentioning who paid for their cabin makes the conversation feel like nothing more than pretense. Mariah is simply going through the motions of asking if Lucy minds. She already said that Iain would be coming by after his shift, even though she has a roommate too.

"It's your suite." Lucy picks at a patch of skin near her wrist to avoid making eye contact. "I'm just a guest."

"Oh, no. Are you peeling already?" Mariah presses her thumb against Lucy's forearm and a pale white print blooms against the red. "Jesus, Luce. You really got burned, didn't you? I guess I couldn't tell earlier because you're so . . . dark." She says the word tentatively, like she's not sure if she should. The bartender deposits a fresh drink in front of Mariah and gives her a wink that she doesn't return. "You need to put some aloe on that. I have a tube next to the sink if you want."

The thumbprint continues to sting and fade slowly, as if it's being absorbed into Lucy's skin. She gets up from her seat, hoping Mariah won't follow. "Maybe I'll go do that now."

"You want me to come with you?"

"No, you just got a drink."

The sentence is barely out of her mouth before Mariah turns away, scanning the room to see who else is in it, as if Lucy is already gone.

SHE TAKES THE long way back to the cabin, walking up to the Lido Deck for some much-needed air. There's an elderly couple slow-dancing by the pool, taking advantage of the Muzak that's always playing over the ship's sound system. If she didn't know any better, she'd assume they were shooting an ad for the cruise line. Lucy walks past them quickly, mindful of their privacy, and chooses a stretch of rail on the far side of the deck. She leans over it, staring at the black water, seemingly endless and bottomless, dappled with light. It's cool outside, a few degrees shy of cold, and the breeze is a welcome relief. It makes it easier to ignore how painful her skin feels, like it's being pulled tighter and tighter over her body—a sensation that's getting worse by the hour.

She wonders at what point she'll finally admit that the cruise is a disaster. Then she second-guesses the impulse, loath to use the term too lightly. Even with the sunburn and seasickness and missing luggage, "disaster" seems like an exaggeration, insensitive to the actual disasters going on in the world.

Lucy barely has a minute alone with this thought before she notices a man walking toward her. He all but announces his presence, stopping to admire the elderly couple and shouting "Beautiful! Beautiful!" at them in an accent she can't quite make out over the engines. Out of the corner of her eye, she can see him as he continues his beeline approach—white shirt, blue pants, white skin. He doesn't have to say another word for her to dislike him. The whole setup makes her dislike him. She tenses, waiting to hear whatever dumb line he's about to try on her.

"So, I am not your type because . . . ?" He's now leaning over the same railing that she is, their elbows just inches apart.

Between what he said and how he said it—with an accent that she now clearly recognizes as Italian—she didn't expect to be surprised, which forces her to turn and look at him.

"What?"

He smiles. "You say to your friend that I am not your type."

The man is dark haired and olive skinned, maybe ten or fifteen years older than she is—too old to wear his white linen shirt unbuttoned rakishly to midchest. She doesn't remember him from the *Monarca*, but it appears they've already crossed paths.

"Were you the one she was pointing at? I just said that to change the subject. I couldn't see who she was talking about."

"It's okay. It's okay," he says, laughing. "I just tease. My name is Dario."

As he introduces himself, he gently places his fingertips on his chest like he's touching something precious. Dario seems to think he's handsome, and in a certain way he is, but his teeth are a mess. Misshapen and crooked, stained from coffee or cigarettes or both. A poor man's teeth, her mother would say. Lucy hates that she notices these types of things about people, a habit she inherited from both of her parents.

Against her better judgment, she shakes his outstretched hand. "Lucy," she says, and then without thinking, she adds, "*Piacere.*"

"*Piacere,* Lucia." He pronounces Lucia the Italian way, with the hard "chee" sound cracking through the middle. "*Parli Italiano?*"

She's tempted to ask why he did that. Why did he call her by a different name when she just told him what her name was? But his question still hangs between them unanswered. Does she speak Italian? Does she really want to get into that now?

When Lucy was younger, she used to take such pride in defying people's expectations. She enjoyed witnessing the not-so-subtle change in expression when strangers learned that she'd attended Sidwell Friends and then Wellesley and MIT. But now she understands that when people react with surprise at her education, her expertise in information extraction and data mining, her near-encyclopedic knowledge of major artists and art movements, her ability to speak conversational Italian and French—it's not because they're impressed. Maybe there's an element of that, but more often than not, she understands that it's because they took one look at her and assumed something different, something less.

It's exhausting to work so hard to excel, to be exceptional, and then have to explain herself to others. Lucy is attuned to a certain kind of inflection when people ask about her background. "So how did *you* develop an interest in programming?" "What made *you* apply to MIT?" Dr. Jimoh, who immigrated from Nigeria as a teenager, apparently still experiences the same, even in his late fifties. He freely admits that this is why he pushes her so hard compared to his other grad students. She can almost hear the pride in his voice whenever he tells her she'll have a thick skin after working in his lab, as if his idea of being a good mentor is to prepare her for hardship, rather than question why the hardship has to exist. How many times has Dr. Jimoh called or emailed since she's been gone? she wonders. How many times have her parents tried to get in touch? What else has she missed while she's been on this ship with Mariah, whom she's actively beginning to dislike? The more time they spend together, the more she suspects that Mariah feels the same.

"Lucia," Dario prompts again.

He seems overly eager to speak with someone in his native tongue. But Lucy doesn't particularly feel like talking about her junior year abroad in Florence or how she's able to read Pirandello and Calvino in their original Italian, albeit with a dictionary in hand. She doesn't want to watch his face go through the mental calculus, trying to figure out how a Black girl learned to speak his language so well.

"I don't really know Italian," she says. "Just some words and phrases."

"And my English is not so good," he says, pleased with his rickety joke. "It's too hot to dance inside, no?" He pinches his almost see-through shirt and pulls it away from his body, flapping the fabric to circulate air. "Their idea, it's much better." He throws a thumb back at the couple, who are still doing their slow box step under the lights.

Lucy can't tell if this is an observation or an invitation. She scans the deck again, wondering if there are hidden cameras somewhere, waiting to capture passengers in the act of doing something spontaneous and unguarded.

"You and your friend don't dance?"

She shakes her head.

"But you're on vacation, no?"

No, she thinks.

"In Italy, we dance and eat and enjoy on vacation."

Despite the *Sonata*'s aggressively Italian theme, Lucy doesn't think Dario fits in here any better than she does. Maybe it's because he's European and cruises seem like such an American way to travel. Or maybe it's because he's starting to sound like a shill for the cruise line, a secret employee paid to encourage people to have a good time, if such a position really exists. She's curious to know how he ended up on board, but doesn't want to prolong the conversation by asking questions.

"Tell me something about your friend," he says. "*La bionda.*"

Lucy can't help but roll her eyes. "Like what?"

"She has a boyfriend?"

She doubts Dario would understand the term "shipboard crush" and doesn't particularly care to explain it to him. "She's seeing someone, kind of."

"Beautiful women are always seeing someone. What about you? Do you see someone too?"

"Nope," she says loudly, raising her hand at him like a stop sign. "We're not doing that. I'm just standing here, trying to get some air, okay?"

"Tone," her parents would say. Neither of them appreciated what they referred to as "that tone," which was really just a euphemism for sounding too aggressive, too angry, too Black. If Dario picked up on it, she can hardly tell. He just smiles like it's all a numbers game to him and if he hits on enough women, one will eventually say yes. Lucy probably feels more rattled by her response than he does. She tries not to let on when she's irritated, something she learned from watching her mother and older female relatives—women who had to put up with not only the world's ideas about who they were, or who they should be, but their fathers' and husbands' too. Lucy is certain that if she allows what she feels on the inside to break through to the surface, people will quickly reduce her to a stereotype, and then everything else she is, everything she's worked so hard to achieve, will no longer matter.

"Could I please have some privacy?" she asks, but her voice disappears under the sound of water churning through the engines.

He brushes the hair out of his face and raises a cupped hand to his ear. "Come again?"

"Could—I—have—some—privacy?" she repeats. "I'm trying to think."

Dario nods, still pleasant, still gracious. "Of course. Enjoy your vacation, Lucia."

He taps the railing twice and walks off in the direction from which he came, shouting one last "Beautiful!" at the dancing couple. Lucy is left to stare out at the water again, startled to realize that she feels sober all of a sudden. Sober and very much alone.

AT FIRST, SHE doesn't notice it. Her mind is too focused on relief. She enters the suite and heads straight to the bathroom, where she slathers herself with cool, sticky aloe gel. It's pleasant for a while, but as soon as it dries, Lucy feels itchy and uncomfortable all over again, her skin as taut as a drum. She follows up with a handful of Mariah's body lotion, a heavily perfumed brand that fills the small bathroom with a bomb of roses. As she massages it into her forearms, she catches a glimpse of her watch and immediately regrets knowing the actual time. It's ten past one and she desperately wants to go to bed, but Iain—*Eeeen,* she thinks bitterly—will be stopping by in about an hour, and Mariah simply expects her to walk around the ship while they have sex.

Lucy flicks on the hallway lights when she leaves the bathroom and sees a black suitcase standing upright against the wall. She assumes it's Mariah's until she notices the small handwritten card hanging from the handle, tied with lavender ribbon. WE'RE SO SORRY FOR THE INCONVENIENCE, it says. PLEASE ENJOY A $100 DRINK CREDIT FROM YOUR FRIENDS AT ARIA.

A sound escapes her throat. An involuntary yip or yelp of joy. She spins the bag around, recognizing the missing zipper pull on the side pocket and the worn-out wheels that squeak whenever they roll. Lucy assumed her suitcase was long gone, forgotten at the pier or perhaps even dropped overboard, never to be seen again. She unzips the cover quickly, thrilled to be able to change out of the T-shirt, bathing suit, and sarong she's been wearing all day.

In the main compartment, she finds a Ziploc bag of toiletries, some of which have leaked, leaving oily smudges of pink and white inside the plastic. She also finds a bathrobe, a swimsuit, a sundress she's surprised to see because she hasn't worn it in years, and a single green flip-flop. Beneath this layer are four thick manila folders and several notebooks that usually sit on her desk—materials for her final dissertation chapter that she doesn't remember packing. She also doesn't remember packing two books on evaluating natural language processing systems; a folder with information on Intel's data science division, where she has an interview next week; and a fistful of pens and highlighters held together with a rubber band that's about to snap. The rest of the suitcase's contents are similarly useless: three pairs of socks but no sneakers to wear them with; some white tank tops, the see-through kind that are good only for sleeping in; a strapless bra to go under the sundress she probably can't fit into anymore; zero pairs of underwear; no phone charger; not even the matching flip-flop.

Lucy can't believe this is what she packed. This is all she packed. She examines the contents of her suitcase, now strewn across the floor. Half of her brain was clearly preparing to go to campus while the other half was preparing for Bermuda. Neither lobe seems to have been very committed to the act. This is the only explanation she can come up with for the random collection of things she's been waiting so anxiously for the crew to recover. She slams the suitcase shut as she hears the familiar knock on her door.

Jimmy has changed out of the shorts and midcalf socks he was wearing earlier today. Now he's dressed in a lavender sweatshirt with an Aria logo on the breast pocket and heathered gray slacks.

"Good evening, miss. I just came by to make sure your suitcase was in proper order."

Although he smiles as he says this, Lucy senses something slightly different about his demeanor compared to this morning. It's not fatigue, she thinks. He almost looks worried, or sad. She knows the difference well.

"Are you all right?"

Jimmy seems surprised by the question, and suddenly, his whole face adjusts—subtly, so as not to cause alarm—as if someone just poked a bony finger into his back and reminded him to smile. Smile for the guests.

"You're very kind to ask, miss."

Noticeably, this isn't a yes or a no. Lucy opens the door wider. "Would you like to come in?"

He takes a few tentative steps into the cabin, carefully avoiding the contents of her suitcase on the floor. He follows her into the living room, where there's evidence that someone—probably Jimmy—freshened up the suite while she and Mariah were out. Only now does Lucy see the full extent of it: the perfectly dimmed lights, the fruit basket newly filled with pears, the turned-down beds with a foil-wrapped mint on each pillow. He scans the room slowly, searching for a detail he might have missed.

"Was something wrong with your bag, miss? Or your suite?"

There's no use telling him about the manic assortment of things she packed, so she shakes her head.

"Are you still feeling ill? Would you like to speak to a doctor?"

She shakes her head again, not entirely certain why she invited Jimmy in. Maybe she's not as sober as she thought she was. Or maybe she's just desperate to talk to someone who might be able to relate.

"Do you like your job?" she asks.

"Of course, miss," he says without hesitation. "It's a very good job."

"Yes, but do you *like* it?"

Jimmy stares at her for a moment. Up close, he appears older than she thought he was. Once she gets past his youthful energy and bottle-black hair, she suspects he's even older than her father. When he narrows his eyes in concentration, a latticework of wrinkles appears across his forehead. It looks like he's taking her question seriously, but it also looks like it might be the oddest question he's ever heard.

"Aria is an excellent cruise line, miss. Rated number one in customer satisfaction for the past five years."

She wonders if crew members are trained to say things like this whenever passengers start poking around the edges of their experience. Are they allowed to have any autonomy at all? As soon as she asks herself the question, she realizes there's something wrong with her definition of the word. The very nature of autonomy is that people have it independently of others. It's not something that has to be granted or given or allowed.

"I understand that it's a good company. I'm just curious to know if you like what you do, or if you'd rather be doing something else."

Jimmy rests his hands on the back of a chair, giving thought to her question, but it's clear that something about it doesn't compute.

"I don't think about liking or not liking, miss. I just do my job well, I hope you'll agree, and I like what I can do because of my job." He sees the look on Lucy's face, accurately predicting what she's about to say before she even opens her mouth. "I helped my parents buy some property in the country, and I send my daughters money so my grandchildren can go to private school. I don't get to be with any of them enough because I'm gone for many months at a time, unfortunately."

"That's nice," she says. "Nice that you can do those things for them, I mean."

Although Lucy is at least a generation removed from this man and separated from his culture by an ocean, his response reminds her so much of her father. How pragmatic and focused he is. How unselfish. How totally unlike her. For the past few days, she's been quietly judging Mariah, observing all the ways in which her roommate is oblivious to her many privileges. But here she is, guilty of the same offense, thinking about a job as something she should love, or even like, when most people in the world simply have a job to do and a family that relies on them to do it.

"Are the phones working yet?" she asks.

Jimmy smiles weakly. He seems tired of answering the same question over and over again. "I'm very sorry, miss. The onboard system still isn't online, but we have a team of specialists waiting to meet the ship in port. And of course, you'll have access to phones and the Internet once we arrive in Bermuda."

Lucy glances at her watch and feels a sinking sensation of dread. In seven hours, the *Sonata* will arrive in port. In seven hours, she'll find the nearest phone and learn the full extent of all the damage she's done.

Tuesday, September 18

ROYAL NAVAL DOCKYARD, BERMUDA

10.

The passengers descend, five and six abreast down the ramp, feet tentative as they reacquaint themselves with land. Within minutes, they funnel through the arrivals building, collecting maps and brochures by the handful even though they have only a day to explore.

Outside the arched doors of Heritage Wharf, dozens of Bermudians—"Onions," the guidebooks call them—await the ship's arrival. The women stand with their arms outstretched to display their hand-painted sand dollars and necklaces strung with seashells—mass-produced souvenirs they neither painted nor strung themselves. The men, meanwhile, scan the crowd for the most well-to-do-looking passengers, offering their clean taxis with eager smiles and promises of honest, reasonable fares.

The exodus quickly splinters. A small group wanders off to explore the grounds of the Dockyard, following the ancient white clock tower in the distance. Some hire drivers and head to the neighboring parishes, lured by rumors of the turquoise blue water at Elbow Beach or the fine pink sand at Horseshoe Bay. Many gather with their prepaid excursion groups for an afternoon of golf, fish-ing, snorkeling, or scuba diving. The more historically inclined opt for guided tours, led by locals wearing unironic Bermuda shorts. Together, they visit the quaint seventeenth-century buildings in St. George's, painted in sherbet-like colors, or the capital in Hamilton, home to Parliament, old stone forts, and stately churches. Many remark that Bermuda seems so British, with street names that remind them of past trips to England: Victoria Street, King's Square, Chancery Lane. None of the guides mention that Bermuda was the first British colony to use African slaves.

The Onions say they're lucky. September is an unpredictable month for rain. But the day is as fine as any during the height of peak season. Seventy-eight degrees with a light northwesterly wind, the kind of weather that makes the passengers happy to be alive. They're tempted to close their eyes and let the sun warm their faces, but they can't, not when the sky demands their full attention. It's bright blue and clear, without a cloud or contrail in sight. It's the same sky that everyone was talking about a week ago, which reminds them that it's been exactly one week. One week since the world changed, and yet here they are.

Their desire to explore this beautiful, vibrantly colored country is at odds with their growing awareness of what they left behind. Among the things they learn soon after their arrival: Lower Manhattan is still burning, and what was once known simply as "the pile" now has a new name. Ground Zero. All over New York, shop windows and subway stations are papered with flyers that ask HAVE YOU SEEN MY SISTER? DO YOU KNOW THIS MAN? CAN YOU HELP US FIND OUR DAD? The faces of the missing stare out from street corners. Headshots and candids, wedding photos and family portraits, color and black and white. Blood banks have swelled with unused donations, offered in states of shock when people allowed themselves to hope for injuries instead of deaths. The funerals have begun. Firefighters and police officers and EMTs whose bodies were among the first recovered are laid to rest with full honors. The streets ring with elegy, real or imagined.

In Washington, D.C., commuters stuck in traffic on I-395 stare at the Pentagon, at the blackened, gaping maw in its side. National Guard troops stand armed and ready at locations that might be considered targets. In a city filled with monuments and museums, they appear to be everywhere. From the White House, the president addresses the people, intent on projecting strength, unity, clarity, and calm. Gone is the boyish grin, the accent calibrated to charm. He sits against the backdrop of the Oval Office, blinking often into the camera's void, as he recites Psalm 23: "Even though I walk through the valley of the shadow of death, I fear no evil for You are with me."

Near Shanksville, Pennsylvania, a makeshift memorial rises near the cordoned-off field where United Flight 93 went down, crashed by the hijackers when the passengers tried to take back control of the plane. Flowers, stuffed animals, crucifixes, and flags spread like mushrooms across the pale green grass, bordered by a grove of hemlocks. Handwritten signs thank the passengers for their bravery. HEROES, one simply says. Upon recovering the two black boxes and listening to the recordings, veteran air safety investigators reportedly weep as they listen to the flight's chaotic last moments. The shouts in Arabic, the fights breaking out near the cockpit door, the prayers to Allah, the lone woman's voice repeating, "I don't want to die."

All across the country, flags are flying at half-mast. It seems impossible to imagine when they might be raised again. Events are canceled. Moments of silence are observed. Condolences and donations pour in. Acts of patriotism surge alongside acts of Islamophobia.

The rhetoric of war begins. This is what the passengers' loved ones tell them when they call home and ask, What's going on? What's happening now? Then they answer the questions lobbed at them in return. "Bermuda's amazing." "We're having such a nice time." "The weather is perfect." They hurry off the phones because it all sounds so wrong. They know it as soon as their words hit the air.

The passengers do their best. They can't change the fact that they're here, so they sun themselves and shop and take photos and buy trinkets by the bagful. But there's simply no escaping the news. BBC broadcasts crackle from radios hanging in artisan market stalls. At expat cafés, copies of *The Royal Gazette* and *The New York Times* are spread out on every table, their worn pages smeary with ink from being turned and turned again. At swim-up bars, television sets tuned to CNN play in the background. Somber anchors report the death count in New York at 218—just 218, which hardly seems right. The anchors are quick to clarify that this is the number of bodies recovered by authorities. Nearly 5,000 more people are still missing.

A week has passed, and yet the attacks are all anyone on the island can talk about. It's impossible not to overhear. The Onions sit in public gardens lush with oleander and hibiscus, playing mah-jongg or cards. "Did you read about the man who went back up to find his friend?" one of them says. The others hold their breath, hoping for good news for a change, then shake their heads gravely when it's not. Expats gather at beach clubs to enjoy the elaborate lunchtime buffets. "What about that poor solicitor general?" one asks. The people at his table didn't know that the United States had a solicitor general, but it hardly matters. What matters is that the solicitor general's wife delayed a business trip so they could wake up together on his birthday. Then she boarded one of the doomed flights.

The flights. The flights. What terror they imagine in the air. And how wrong it feels to imagine it while they're sitting in the shade of a cabana or visiting one impossibly blue beach after another. Despite this, it's hard not to wonder what it was like for those passengers on the hijacked planes, calling home from the air only to learn about the other hijackings, the way planes were being turned into missiles and flown into buildings. How did it feel, knowing what they were a part of? That their lives were about to end?

On the easternmost point of the Bermuda Triangle, a place filled with strange, uncanny stories about disappearances, more uncanny stories begin to circulate. The accountant who narrowly averted death because she was laid off the day before the attacks. The Pentagon assistant who went into labor a month before she was due. The analyst who stormed downstairs to smoke after a fight with his boss. Travelers who were supposed to board one of the four hijacked planes but didn't because of illness or lateness, good luck or dumb luck.

For many passengers, it's too much all at once. A man renting scuba equipment for his family simply snaps. "Turn it off! Turn it off!" he shouts. The bewildered teenage boys behind the counter don't know what he's talking about until he stabs his finger in the air, pointing at the television mounted from the ceiling. Later, the man sinks into the azure water with his scuba gear, surrounded by honeycombs of coral, listening to the sound of his panicked breath. At an upscale oceanfront restaurant, an elderly woman begins to cry two courses into her meal. "What's wrong?" her family asks. "What happened?" But she's unable to speak, seized by the image of the man she saw on the news, the one whose wife and daughter both worked in the towers. It could have been me, she thinks. It could have been any of us. Another woman stands thigh-deep in Hog Bay, staring due west for nearly an hour, wondering if she can see the smoke still rising in the air. She knows that she can't; she knows that she shouldn't. There's only horizon here, and seemingly nothing beyond.

The passengers return to the ship in droves. The crew has never seen anything quite like it. Usually, there are nail-biters—careless or clueless people who push the far limits of their time in port, boarding only minutes before the ramp is pulled up. But these passengers are different. The majority of them return well before they're due with suntans and shopping bags and vaguely guilty expressions. They talk of being tired, of seeing and doing too much while onshore. They do not admit that they are frightened. They do not mention feeling ashamed.

The twin horns blow, and the *Sonata* departs again.

Wednesday, September 19

AT SEA

11.

Esther is going on about the food again, twisting open giant crab legs with her bare hands. "The return-to-ship buffet's usually the nicest one on every cruise," she says, glancing at the pool. "I think they do it that way because people are sad about heading home." She sucks the meat out of a claw and tosses the hollowed-out carcass into a bowl piled high with shells. "Empties," she calls them.

Noticeably, the mood around the table has changed since coming back from shore. Everyone is a little quieter. Everything feels a little more strained, adding to the strain that was already there. Esther keeps filling the dead air with travel tips and commentary that no one asked for, but Franny is actually grateful for the noise. Today is Ma's birthday. She wants it to feel like a celebration, or at the very least, she wants it to feel more celebratory than this.

"So, Ma, what did you think of Bermuda?" Franny asks.

Ma is wearing dark sunglasses and a denim bucket hat to protect her skin from the sun. It's hard to tell whether she's looking at Franny or something else. Reflections of children playing in the pool streak across her mirrored lenses.

"Did you hear that, Nancy?" Esther chimes in. "What was your favorite thing that we did onshore?"

Their time in Bermuda was brief, but they tried to make the most of every minute, taking walking tours of the capital, watching local artisans make pottery, visiting a botanical garden in Paget, and shopping for Ma's weight in souvenirs, all of which Franny paid for without being asked. Staying busy distracted from the strangeness of being back in the connected world, which kept offering unwanted reminders of the one they'd left.

"Ay, I don't know," she says mildly. "We did so much."

Franny glances across the table at her brother, who's draining his third gin and tonic since lunch started. She wants him to encourage Ma to talk like Esther did, but Jae just sits there, poking the lime wedge in his glass with a straw. During their excursions he was even quieter than usual, and he always made it a point to disappear whenever it was time to pay a check. Franny looks away, trying to put him out of her mind. Ever since she overheard Tom's conversation with the room steward, she's been trying to put so many things out of her mind.

Tom cheated once before. Once, that she's aware of. The "transgression"—his word—happened at one of his company's holiday parties, back when they were dating. He said his older brothers kept encouraging everyone to do shots and blamed his bad judgment on alcohol. Then he vowed to not drink like that again, a promise he frequently breaks. Franny was moderately consoled by the fact that he told her what happened without being forced to, and the transgression wasn't actually sex, just ten minutes in a coat closet with a company intern who'd been nursing a crush. For a week, Franny tried to contemplate a future without him. But marriage had seemed like their natural next step, and she couldn't get past the idea of starting all over again with someone new, someone who might disappoint her in other, perhaps even more damaging ways. She was also clear-eyed about the comforts that Tom's considerably larger income provided. The apartment, the vacations, the total absence of struggle. A month later, they wed at City Hall.

Briefly, Franny considered the possibility that the missing woman was just a friend or an employee, albeit one she'd never met or heard Tom mention before. But it made no sense. He'd subjected her to every other excuse and guilt trip he could come up with to get out of the cruise, so why not tell her that someone he knew was missing? The omission, she thinks, is the equivalent of a tell.

Franny sets her wineglass down, alarmed by how quickly she drained it. She wants to keep steady, to control herself and hold her tongue. At some point, she expects Tom to join them for lunch. She hasn't seen much of him since Bermuda, where he disappeared on a preplanned golf excursion by himself, which was how she'd finally convinced him to come. "More world-class golf courses per square mile than any other country," she remembers telling him. "You're always saying that golf is good for stress."

Yesterday, he played nine holes at each of the four top clubs in a single day. By the time Franny returned to the ship from her excursions with Ma, Tom was fast asleep on the couch. He was still there when she left this morning to meet with the catering manager. It's better this way, she thinks. She has no intention of talking to him about what she overheard until they're back home. All she wants to do is get through Ma's birthday. Everything else has to wait.

Two busboys arrive and ask for permission to clear the table. As they whisk away the empty dishes and glasses, Esther asks Jae to run up to the buffet and get her another plate of crab legs.

"You serious?" he asks. "You ate like a dozen already."

"Pleeease?" Esther clasps her hands together in mock prayer. Across her knuckles are more tattoos. A small letter on each finger that Franny could never make out clearly until now. H-E-L-L, the faded black ink says on one hand. Y-E-A-H, it says on the other. Who raised you? Franny wonders. She's not certain if Ma has ever noticed what these tattoos say, and if so, why she doesn't seem to care.

"Okay. Fine." Jae sighs and gets up from the table.

"Make it a big plate," Esther calls out after him.

Franny has never met anyone so thin and yet so motivated by food. Esther seems determined to eat as much as she can of whatever is offered to her. When they first sat down, she even explained her system for navigating the buffet lines, opting for what she described as the "big-ticket items" and forgoing things she could get anywhere, like salad. Franny refills Ma's water glass before her own, only half listening to the story that Esther is now telling them, something about how she once ate two pounds of shrimp by herself.

The list of preparations for Ma's *chilsun* is long and keeps getting longer. She wonders if she should remind Jae to iron his *hanbok* before wearing it, or if he's sensible enough to do it without being told. Renting one had been the full extent of his involvement in the party planning, and only after she enlisted Esther's help to make sure that he did. She hopes they went to a reputable rental store with good quality *hanboks,* not the old-fashioned kind made of cheap satin. Franny decided to have hers made by a seamstress in Queens who imported bolts of silk from Korea. She's never owned or even worn a *hanbok* before, but it seemed like a thoughtful thing to do for the occasion. She only wishes that Ma had more people around to witness it.

The main drawback of hosting the *chilsun* on a ship, other than being on the cruise itself, is the absence of an audience to see how grateful Franny and Jae are, how well Ma raised them. That always seemed like the real reason for the sixtieth and seventieth birthday celebrations she saw at Ma's restaurant—evidence of a life well lived. Franny had hoped that Ma would take her up on her offer to bring a friend along on the trip. More than once, she told her that an extra fare or two would be no trouble, but Ma seemed annoyed by the idea. *Who would I even ask?* she demanded. It occurred to Franny that her mother's friendliness toward customers, which had been good for business, didn't extend into her personal life, and it saddened her—the thought that Ma didn't have anyone close enough to invite on a free cruise to Bermuda. Then again, when Franny had found out about Tom's transgression with the intern, she couldn't bring herself to confide in any of her friends, most of whom probably considered themselves Tom's friends first.

This is what she's thinking about, or trying not to think about, when Jae returns from the buffet with Esther's crab legs. Several feet behind him, she notices Tom. He's wearing shorts again, navy blue this time, which make his white legs appear even whiter. It's a sight she still can't get used to. When he arrives at their table, he doesn't say "hello" or "happy birthday" or even sit down.

"Who's Mike Flatto?" he asks.

Franny doesn't recognize the name and assumes the question was meant for someone else, but when she shades her eyes from the sun and looks up, she realizes he's talking to her.

"I don't know who that is."

"Are you sure about that?" Tom asks, his expression stony. "He seems to know you."

Franny doesn't like the tone he's using in front of her family, or the way they're all glancing at each other now, like something is wrong. She smiles at him with as much affection as she can, trying to telegraph a message that only he can hear. *Behave, Tom. Please behave.*

"I don't know who you're talking about."

"Mike Flatto is the guy who found your briefcase."

Franny presses her back against the hot metal chair. The edges of the slats feel sharp against her skin. "Oh? I must have misplaced it," she says casually. "It's not a big deal though. I usually don't put anything important in it." Technically, everything she's saying is true. She did misplace it somewhere. She doesn't use it for more than a take-home file or two. If Tom drops the subject, it doesn't have to be a big deal, at least not now. Not today. Franny is thirsty all of a sudden. She eyes the glasses of wine on a passing waiter's tray, wishing she could reach out and grab one.

"I checked our answering machine when I was onshore." He slides a small piece of paper in front of her, torn from the corner of a map. "Mike Flatto" is scrawled in the white space above a phone number with a 718 area code, somewhere in Brooklyn or one of the other boroughs. "This guy left a message saying he had your briefcase, that you got separated last Tuesday. I called back because it sounded important and he'd obviously dialed the wrong number. But he said he found some of your business cards in the pocket, and then he described you, Franny. He said you ran into a building together after one of the towers fell."

When Franny closes her eyes, she sees the thick cloud of black hurtling toward her again, disappearing everything in its path. She reopens them before the cloud hits, only to find that everyone is staring at her.

"You were there?" Jae asks, like he suddenly has something to say, as if he hasn't been ignoring her for days.

"What do you care?" she snaps. At this, Jae looks away.

"Why, Franny?" Tom asks, more calmly than she would have expected. "Why didn't you tell me?"

"I don't understand. What's he saying?" Ma takes off her sunglasses. Her voice is considerably sharper.

"It's nothing, Ma. Don't worry about this today." Franny reaches across the table to touch her hand. "It's your birthday," she adds pointedly, glaring at Tom.

"It's not nothing," he says, more forcefully this time. "If you were there, I don't understand why you didn't tell me. We talked on the phone at least two, three times that day. You said you hadn't even left the apartment when it happened."

It's as bad as she imagined. Worse, because it's real. No one is trying to comfort her. No one is saying thank God she's all right. They're upset because she lied. Franny gets up from the table, backing her chair away too quickly. It clatters onto the deck, drawing the attention of nearby passengers and one of the pool boys, who hurries to pick it up for her. Suddenly, she's walking without a direction or a destination, desperate to remove herself from the conversation as quickly as she can. If Tom is following her or calling after her, she doesn't notice or care. Her instinct, once again, is to flee.

SHE WOULDN'T HAVE guessed that the man's name was Mike. All the Mikes she knew were frat-pledging, sports-playing boys from college or law school. She considered it a jock's name, and the man she met that day certainly wasn't a jock. The first time she saw him, he was standing in a crowd on the corner of Church and Fulton. The streets were empty of moving cars and littered with debris and paper, like a ticker tape parade for the Yankees had just rolled past. Occasionally, a stray scrap of paper or an envelope would flutter down from the sky and Franny would follow it until it landed, wondering which floor of the building it had come from.

The crowd at the intersection was large and growing larger. The only reason she noticed Mike at all was the way he kept talking to himself. It seemed almost manic, out of character for a such a buttoned-up-looking man in his boxy gray suit and unfashionable white sneakers. Whenever Franny returned her gaze to street level, she always landed on him. She attributed this to where he was standing—in front of a streetlight, at an angle that actually made it seem like the pole was protruding from his head. There was also something about his face that she couldn't stop looking at—the huge, unblinking eyes, the mouth in constant motion.

When Franny really concentrated, she found that she could almost read his lips. *Going . . . come . . . fall . . .* The longer she studied him, the clearer the words became. He was saying the building was going to come down. It was going to fall. He kept repeating this over and over, suggesting something she'd never considered before, something that didn't seem physically possible. It contradicted her understanding of buildings, their sturdiness and permanence, especially in the Financial District, where so many structures had been standing for over a century. She returned her gaze skyward, not thinking about him again until they were lying on the floor of a bank some minutes later, their faces only a few inches away from each other.

"Are you all right?" he whispered.

She didn't understand why he felt the need to lower his voice. She still doesn't. But there were so many other things she didn't understand in that moment, including how she'd gotten from the street corner into the bank.

"Hello?" He waved his hand in front of her. "Can you hear me?"

The emergency lights were on, casting the dim lobby in a faint wash of amber. Sirens were going off in the distance. Car alarms and ambulances and security systems, all beeping and blaring at once.

"How did you know?" she asked, her breath still ragged from running.

One of the lenses in Mike's glasses was missing, and the thin wire frames were bent at the bridge. When he frowned at her, they tilted sharply on his nose. "Know what?"

"You said it was going to fall."

"I did?"

She nodded.

"I don't remember saying that."

"You did though. I saw you."

Mike offered no explanation other than a bewildered shake of his head.

By then, most of the dust and debris that had followed them into the building had settled on the floor. As her eyes adjusted to the light, Franny noticed there were other people in the bank with them—at least a dozen or more, slowly sitting up or getting to their feet. Someone she couldn't see was crying. Not the muffled kind of crying that Franny occasionally did at home so her unhappiness could go undetected. Someone—a woman, she thought—was releasing a long, unbroken wail while another woman was trying to shush her like a baby.

Mike sat up. He touched the side of his face where the lens was missing and poked his fingers through the opening, confirming that the glass was no longer there.

"I just bought these," he said, as if it were the saddest thing in the world. A pair of new glasses, broken.

Franny eased herself up to a sitting position. Her neck was stiff, like she'd whipped it too quickly from one side to the other, and her left hand stung. She turned up her palm and saw that she'd scraped it, and the skin was dirty and glittering with bits of glass, too small and deeply embedded to remove without tweezers. When she examined the rest of herself, she was surprised to find nothing else cut or bleeding or broken. She was just covered in a thick layer of dust, the same as Mike and all the others. She tried to brush herself off, but it was hard to tell if what she was seeing was more dust or the fabric of her jacket—a light, heathered lilac she'd picked out that morning because it felt right for the weather.

"You're all right?" he asked again.

She nodded, and they helped each other up, blinking their dust-covered lashes as they took in their surroundings. All the windows in the trio of heavy bronze doors were blown out. One of the doors, which must have weighed hundreds of pounds, was hanging askew from its frame. There was paper everywhere. Small, confetti-like bits, as well as brochures and deposit slips that had flown off the racks. Outside the bank, people were on the street, moving in a slow, uncertain caravan through air that was thick and gray. She had never seen air like that before, so full of particulate that it actually had a color. It was the kind of air that she knew she shouldn't breathe, but what choice did she have? Franny and Mike held hands as they gingerly made their way across the shattered glass, each step through the lobby releasing a *crunch, crunch, crunch.*

"It's so dusty," she said, wiping her face once they stepped out into the street.

"That's not dust."

Franny spit, trying to expel the bitter taste of it from her mouth. She wondered what else it could be. What was all the gray in the air and in the streets, if not dust?

"I'm guessing it's ash," he said, clearing his throat.

In retrospect, she's grateful that he didn't explain any further, that he was kind enough to let her come to the realization on her own. What are cremains, if not ash? And what did the ash contain, if not cremains? She would have torn off her clothes right there if she'd known.

They made no agreement to walk together, or to walk in silence. They just did—Franny, with her briefcase in her unscraped hand and her purse slung diagonally across her chest; Mike, with his broken glasses and white sneakers that were no longer white. When did she give him the briefcase? She doesn't remember asking him to hold it or even deciding to put it down. When did she have the time? Mounted policemen and emergency workers kept shouting at everyone in the streets. *Move, keep moving, let's go.* So they obeyed, following the crowds north along Broadway, which had been cleared of traffic. There was so much to look at, so much to listen to. People were talking about where they'd been when the first or second plane hit, when the South Tower fell, what chaos they'd witnessed. They retold their stories haltingly, as if they couldn't believe them and didn't expect anyone else to either.

"Did you vote this morning?" Mike asked after several blocks.

Franny startled at the sound of his voice and the strangeness of his question. She'd been eavesdropping on a pair of men walking nearby. One of them was talking about a vice president who worked several floors above him. "A clotheshorse," he called her, not very kindly. "Always dressed to the nines, you know, with the shoes and bag and jewelry." He explained how she was staggering down the darkened stairwell of the North Tower along with everyone else from their company, carrying her jacket draped over her arm. "I don't know why, but I got mad when I saw that," the man said. "I kept thinking, *Just put the fucking jacket down.*" When they reached the street level and he finally saw her in the daylight, he noticed that half her body was burned—her clothes were literally fused to her flesh—and her entire right arm, the one holding the jacket, was charred black and frozen at a ninety-degree angle.

"I haven't voted yet," Franny said. "I was planning to go later today."

"My cousin works for the Ferrer campaign."

Freddy Ferrer wasn't her candidate, but he was still a better choice than Michael Bloomberg, the Republican billionaire masquerading as an Independent who was Tom's pick. They passed a news crew filming a woman motioning toward the street, and then someone—an emergency worker, she assumed—directing pedestrian traffic so an ambulance could squeeze through. The man was wearing neon yellow, but as they got closer, Franny realized it was a biking jersey, not a safety vest. He was just a random person trying to help.

"I wonder if the election's postponed," Mike said.

She assumed that it was. It had to be. Everything was postponed, if not canceled outright. She thought of Ma's birthday, how the cruise was coming up and she'd put so much effort into planning something special for her this year. How many years did they have left to fix what was broken between them?

She was staring at the ground when she felt Mike's hand gently patting her on the back. He was telling her not to cry, and she was ashamed for letting a stranger witness what she only did alone.

"My husband voted absentee. For Bloomberg," she said. Franny found this disturbing, evidence of the rift growing between them that she was trying to ignore. When they first met, Tom had described himself as a moderate Democrat. But the longer they were together, the more he seemed to tilt toward the right. Recently, he said he would have gladly voted for Rudolph Giuliani again if it wasn't for term limits, and she fixated on that word, too worried to ask what it meant. *Again?*

"Sometimes, I don't like him very much," she admitted. "My husband."

"I've always hated my cousin."

There wasn't anything particularly funny about what either of them said, but they both laughed—relieved, perhaps, to be so honest. Or relieved to feel something other than terrified, if only for a moment.

"Hang on," Mike said.

He veered off toward a small crowd gathered in front of a bodega. People were using the hose to wash the dust off their faces or helping themselves to bottles of soda and water that the owner was pulling out of a cooler, giving away for free. "Take it, take it," he kept shouting. "God bless you! God bless America!" It was hard not to notice how agitated he was, how frantic his generosity, but Franny understood. The owner was brown. He sounded like an immigrant. He probably remembered what it was like after the parking garage bombing in '93 and was expecting to be blamed.

Mike returned from the bodega with two bottles of orange soda. Franny wasn't a soda drinker, but the minute the sugary Sunkist hit her tongue, she couldn't stop drinking until the bottle was empty.

"Look out," he warned.

He pulled her off to the side just in time to avoid stepping on a stray bike tire that had been crushed flat. Women's shoes—some that she recognized as very expensive—were strewn across the street. Franny had a sensible pair of Ferragamos on, which was unusual for her. At work, the two older female partners favored stilettos, so she wore them too. Her closet was filled with the kind of perilously high heels that went from car service to office and rarely touched a sidewalk for more than a few steps. The only reason she'd chosen the low, block-heel pumps she was wearing that morning was that she expected to wait in line at the polling station after work. How would she have walked all this way in her regular shoes? she wondered. Even the ones she had on were starting to hurt.

They continued north, surveying the total abandonment of Broadway, which was filled with haphazardly parked cars and shuttered businesses. Shopping bags and packages littered the street, their contents deemed too heavy or unimportant to carry. She didn't question if she and Mike were going in the right direction because they were always following someone else, always being yelled at from the sidelines to move, move, move. They slowed down only once: when news of the second tower's collapse made its way through the caravan like some terrible, crushing wave. People began to stop, to scream, to sit down on the curb, covering their faces. Franny looked behind her, searching for another black cloud that might overtake them, but there was nothing. Just smoke in the sky and an emptiness where none had existed before.

"Let's keep going," Mike said. "We shouldn't just stand around."

Did he hold her up by the elbow then? Was this when he took the briefcase to help lighten her load? They walked in silence for so long that she just assumed Mike was there until he wasn't anymore. Franny wishes she knew when they got separated, but she doesn't. All she remembers is looking around at one point and realizing that she was alone and had been for some time.

THE KEY IN the lock turns, announcing Tom's arrival. When he enters the darkened suite, he flicks on the lights in the living room, where Franny is sitting on the sofa. He sits down across from her without saying hello and plucks an orange from the fruit basket, tossing it back and forth between his hands.

"Did you even remember that it's Ma's birthday today?" Franny asks, her voice tight and controlled. Usually, she'd let him be the first to speak so she could gauge his mood, but she's too upset to wait.

"That's what we're all here for," he says, which isn't an answer.

"I should be spending time with her right now."

"Then you shouldn't have run off."

A few months into their marriage, Franny went to a therapist who told her to ask people for what she needed, rather than hint or hope that they'd understand. "No one can read minds" was her favorite line. Although Franny lasted only three sessions before the self-examination became too much, she tries to recall what she'd learned from those conversations, desperate for any trick or technique to get her through the day.

"Can we talk about the briefcase later and just focus on getting through Ma's birthday? Please?"

"Franny." Tom sets the orange down on the coffee table and presses the heels of his hands into his eyes. She can't see his face, but it almost sounds like he's laughing. "You can't possibly . . . Do you really think . . ." When he lowers his hands, it's clear that he wasn't laughing at all. "You need to explain what's going on here."

"I've already told you so many times. The *chilsun* is one of the most—"

"No! Not that."

"But it's context—"

He slaps his hands against his thighs with a sharp crack. "Are you okay? Are you still in shock or something?"

"I'm fine!" She raises her arms in the air, turning them in all directions. "See? No scars, no bruises, Tom. Nothing broken. I'm *fine.*" She wants to add that she's alive and that's what matters, but she can't bring herself to say it.

"Jesus, Franny. You're a grown woman. I shouldn't have to explain that there's more than one way to be hurt. You saw things that day. Terrible things, probably. And the fact that you didn't tell me— Why did I have to find out like this?"

His voice is raised. Not quite a shout but close. Tom seems more upset about how he discovered, rather than what. As usual, he isn't speaking to her like a person for whom he cares deeply. But that's always been the quality of Tom's love. Less than what it should be but better than what she's known, which was probably why she was willing to accept it. How different he sounded when he was telling the room steward about the woman who went missing, so desperate and distraught.

"Do you remember what you said when you came back from Philly?" she asks, vaguely aware that the phone in their cabin is ringing. "You weren't home for even five minutes before you insisted on canceling this cruise, probably because you never wanted to come in the first place. But this was important to me, Tom. That's why I didn't tell you. My fam—"

"You could have just said that."

Franny glares at him, refusing to argue the point.

"Okay, fine," he concedes. "Maybe you did. But I didn't want to come because your family's not exactly welcoming, Franny. To either of us. And if I'm being totally honest, my family—with my brothers and their wives and all their kids—that's enough for me to deal with. I don't need another group of people that makes me feel like I don't belong."

Honest. She turns the word over and over in her head, tumbling it like a stone. What do you know about being honest? she thinks.

"Well?" Tom asks.

"Well, what?"

He stands up and walks around and around in small circles, as if his body suddenly has more energy than he knows what to do with. "You're just going to sit there and tell me you lied because of a *birthday party*?"

Lied. She can't even begin to count or catalog all the lies, the times she said she was happy when she wasn't, or that she liked something when she didn't. She'd made so many concessions to Tom over the years, always folding up her desires until they matched the shape of his. At first, they were just little things. What movie to go to. Who to socialize with. Where to celebrate their anniversary. And then they grew bigger and bigger. A wedding at City Hall because he didn't think their families would get along. Skipping Korean holidays in Fort Lee to avoid the discomfort of spending time with Ma and Jae. She even allowed him to convince her that she didn't want children, although he must have known this wasn't true. Whenever they got together with his family—people who treated her kindly but coolly, like someone they expected to refer to as "the first wife" one day—Franny spent most of her time playing with the nieces and nephews, preferring their company over the adults'. He must have seen her tenderness toward them, her desire to nurture children of her own in a way she'd never experienced. But what she wanted always mattered less, and the biggest lie she told herself was that she didn't mind. Until recently, this had seemed like a small price to pay for a quiet, comfortable life.

Franny lowers her eyes to her lap. Her hands are knitted together; the fingertips are almost blue. The phone is ringing again, but she can't be bothered to pick it up. She releases her fingers and looks over at Tom, who's frowning at something on the bed. It's a swan.

Two of them, actually. Two swans twisted and shaped out of white bath towels with their necks intertwined. She hadn't noticed them in the dark, or the heart of pale pink rose petals surrounding them on the bedspread. More of Jimmy's handiwork while they were out.

"What the—? I can't deal with these . . ." He picks up the swans by their necks like he's trying to strangle them and pulls the towels apart, throwing them back on the bed in a heap. "There's something really wrong with us, Franny. You know that, right? For you to go through an experience like that and not tell me . . . to lie about it so we could come on this cruise with your family. I don't . . . I mean, I think there must be something seriously, seriously wrong with us."

She nods, unable to disagree. But his words don't strike the terror in her heart that she thought they would. It feels more like an opening.

"That woman you're worried about—the one who's missing—how long have you been seeing her?"

He turns from the bed to Franny. He doesn't seem surprised or afraid or even guilty. There's just a pause, and then a flicker of something that she suspects might be relief.

"A year." He blinks several times, as if he's trying to count with his eyes. "Actually, about eight months."

Franny looks him over. Why is it only occurring to her now? He's not sunburned from playing golf yesterday because he never went. "Were you able to track her down when you were onshore?"

He shakes his head and lowers himself onto a corner of the mattress. "Still missing," he says, grabbing a handful of rose petals.

Franny sits down on the opposite corner of the bed, imagining how Tom spent his day in Bermuda, making phone calls and sitting in Internet cafés while she and her family were taking walking tours and buying souvenirs. "You tried her employer? Her family?"

"It's . . . complicated." He clears his throat. "She's married too."

"Oh."

He picks up more petals and shreds them into pieces. The air fills with the sickly smell of roses. "How long have you known?"

She thinks before she responds, "Not long." But she questions whether this is really true. Maybe she registered how he'd started showering at the gym, or how he was traveling even more than usual lately. Maybe she noticed, but it was easier not to see.

Tom continues shredding petals and throwing them on the carpet next to his feet. "You're not mad?"

"Do you want me to be?"

"No. That's not what I'm saying. I just thought . . . Most people . . . they'd be upset."

She noticed this too, the total absence of anger. She thinks it all must have seeped out over the years, taking with it whatever modest ideas of love she started with and leaving only this vast emptiness inside her. She suspects this is why she didn't think about Tom that day, not in any meaningful way. She was relieved that he was safe in Philly, but she wasn't in a rush for him to come home. When they spoke on the phone for the first time, she didn't start the conversation intending to lie about where she'd been when the planes hit or the towers fell. She simply found herself saying what she wished had happened instead. *I woke up late. I hadn't even left for work yet.* And the more times she repeated this version of the story, the more it felt like she might be able to change what she'd experienced, distancing herself from it until it took on the quality of something she'd watched on the news, something that happened to other people.

"I hope she's okay," Franny says, but this seems unnecessarily cruel. If there's anything she learned from her time in Bermuda, glancing sideways at TVs and eavesdropping on the locals' conversations, it's that the kind of hope she's talking about doesn't exist anymore. That's why she can't bring herself to be curious about this woman. She can't even be jealous of her, or upset about what they did. The woman is dead. "I hope you're able to find out what happened to her."

The phone continues to ring, but neither of them moves, not even to take it off the hook.

"So, what do you think this means?" he asks, staring at the pile of towels on the bed. "For us?"

The skin on Franny's palm is still streaked with pebbly scabs from where she had to pluck out sliver after sliver of glass. If he ever held her hand, he would have noticed them by now.

12.

When Doug reports to the Lido Deck for his three o'clock event, he feels a hard thump on his back and hears someone shout, "Dougie!"—a nickname he deeply dislikes. The only person who ever called him that was Alan Dennehy, who insisted on having a nickname for everyone on the *Starlight* cast and crew. Doug turns, annoyed by both the force of the thump and the familiarity, only to find that the person responsible does look a lot like his former costar, but not entirely. The Alan Dennehy he remembers was muscular and tall. Taller than Doug even, with skin that was perpetually tan. He used to tell the makeup artists on set that the color he was going for was "Italian bricklayer." But the man standing in front of him is stoop-shouldered and liver-spotted, with teeth so straight and white, they're obviously dentures. And his face has the appearance of a walnut under a woolly-comb-over of dyed brown hair.

"What?" The man spreads his arms. "No hug for an old friend?"

Doug embraces him tentatively, taking in the scent of alcohol, cigarettes, and strong piney aftershave. Alan's scent. He steps back, confused. "But I thought— Renee told me you couldn't come because of your brother."

"We found him," he says, in a distracted way that doesn't suggest whether the news was good or bad.

Doug sits down, struggling to shift from one surprise to the next. He hopes that Alan will elaborate so he doesn't have to ask, but he's too busy staring at a brunette spilling out of a bikini, running his eyes up and down her body. The same old Alan.

"You were saying, about your brother . . . you found him?"

"We did, thank God. He got hit by a chunk of falling concrete and ended up in Bellevue. For some reason, poor Davey wasn't listed on the ride-in sheet, so every time we called around to the hospitals, no one could ID him."

"He's okay, then?"

Alan considers the question. "Well, they patched up his head and he's not unconscious anymore. But he's totally distraught, which is understandable. I mean, can you imagine? He woke up in the hospital and found out that half the guys from his firehouse are either missing or dead." He glances over at the pool. "Hold on. Be right back."

He gets up from the table and walks toward the elevated stage, where two female crew members are hanging a banner for the upcoming event. MEN'S SEXY LEGS CONTEST, the sign reads in alternating red and yellow letters. Doug winces at the sight of it. He can't believe he has to do this. He can't believe anyone else would want to, especially after returning from shore. What they're doing here—it all feels so frivolous, so disrespectful to people like Dave, with whom they should be mourning. Doug also hasn't shaken off the sadness he felt in Bermuda, sitting on the beach by himself, requesting a table for one at restaurants, surrounded by so many happy couples and families. He felt foolish for wanting people to leave him alone and then spending his one free day ashore feeling lonely because Gideon had ditched him. He couldn't even get through to Annette to complain because her voicemail was full, a once-infrequent annoyance that now happens regularly.

Doug watches Alan sidle up next to the crew members and offer to help them hang their sign. He leans in too close to their faces, prompting them to lean back, far back, smiling nervously at him and each other. Doug shakes his head. He knows he did the right thing by telling Gid not to leer at Tabby, but a small part of him wishes he'd just kept his mouth shut.

"Cuties," Alan says happily when he returns to where Doug is standing. He seems pleased with himself for the interaction, even though the women declined his help. "Those two look like milk-maids."

"Why are you even here?" Doug asks. "Shouldn't you be with your family right now?"

"Yeah, try telling that to Aria." Alan attempts to hail a passing waiter. "You know those people have been calling and calling, threatening to sue for breach of contract if I didn't get on a plane and meet the ship in Bermuda? Me and the wife—I don't think you ever met this one—we're in the process of splitting and her lawyer's going through my financials like it's a prostate exam. I can't exactly afford to have any more lawyers coming after me, you know what I mean?"

"But that's—that's terrible. Did you explain what was going on with your brother? Would they actually try to sue you?"

Alan seems to think this is funny. "Don't be naïve, Dougie. You can't put anything past a big company like Aria. You know how much money they make off these reunion cruises?" He grins and gives him another thump on the back. "Hey, it's really good to see you, bud. When I heard you were finally coming on one of these, I couldn't believe it. Weren't you the one who said you'd never set foot on this ship again?"

"Did I?" Doug doesn't remember saying this, but it sounds like him.

"I'm pretty sure that was you, wasn't it?"

They shrug at each other, their memories addled by a decade of booze and drugs, and now faded over time. Although only a year or two separates them, Doug thinks that Alan appears much older than he does, which suggests that he continued to party long after Doug stopped.

"I honestly wasn't sure if we'd ever be in the same room again," Alan says. "I figured for sure that I'd see you at Petey's funeral, but—"

"Let's not . . . Can we please not talk about that?"

"Yeah, I get it. Still fresh. Fifteen years ago feels like yesterday sometimes, doesn't it?"

Another waiter walks by with a tray full of drinks. Alan waves him over, even though the tray looks large and heavy.

"Hola, my friend. I'll have a double vodka soda, and this guy over here will have . . ."

Doug glances at several tumblers of whiskey and bourbon on the tray. "Just the soda, please. Thanks."

When the waiter leaves to deliver his drinks, Doug can feel Alan examining him.

"On the wagon, huh?"

Doug nods.

"For a while now?"

He nods again.

"Good for you, bud. Good for you." He stares past the railing at the water for a moment. "You know, I gave it up once. For almost a whole year, actually."

It's hard to imagine Alan not drinking or smoking or doing all the things that made him Alan. But Doug realizes he must be thinking the same about him.

"It didn't quite take?"

"Eh. I had a young wife who liked to party. I think she liked me more when I could party with her."

A pair of middle-aged women in bathing suits keep staring at them and whispering excitedly to each other. Now they're both getting up from their table and walking over, all hips and cleavage and freckled, sagging skin.

"Yoo-hoo," the taller one calls. Doug wonders if he misheard her. Did she really just wave at him and say "yoo-hoo"?

"Could we get your autographs, please?" the shorter one asks.

Alan flashes them a ready smile. "Of course, ladies. Of course."

He's quick to turn on the charm for them, which the women—perhaps being their contemporaries—actually seem to find charming. Alan asks where they're from—Toronto; how they're enjoying the cruise so far—loving it, the shorter one says; and whether it's their first reunion cruise—first, but not last, the taller one chirps. Doug signs their books like he's signing a credit card receipt for something he can't afford and returns them to the women without so much as a word. Unlike Alan, who seems to revel in being adored, Doug can't help but notice the types of people they're being adored by. How old they all are, how long past their prime. And now that Alan's reminded him of Peter's funeral, he can't stop thinking about it, how he couldn't even sober up long enough to show his face and say goodbye. It remains one of the greatest regrets of his life.

The waiter returns with their drinks and offers to take a photo of the foursome, which the women eagerly accept. Alan wraps one arm around each of them, while Doug stands a few inches off to the side. The waiter asks him to move closer, so he takes a step in and feels one of the women's hands curl around his waist, settling low on his hip. Afterward, Alan encourages them to vote for him during the contest.

"Remember these legs!" he shouts, pointing at his knees as they head back to their table, giggling as they look over their shoulders.

THE MILKMAIDS, AS Alan keeps referring to them, finish setting up the stage for the contest. In the center, there's a blue velvet curtain, about twelve feet wide. Alan, who's already on his second double vodka soda, explains that the contestants are supposed to roll up their pants, take off their shoes and socks, and assemble behind the curtain. When the emcee gives the signal, the milkmaids will lift the curtain to knee height so the audience can vote. Whoever gets the most applause will be crowned sexiest male legs.

Already, there are half a dozen men kicking off their sandals and getting ready to compete, and the milkmaids are roaming through the pool area in search of more. It bothers Doug to see the crowd gathering around the stage, light beers and margaritas in hand, so eager for the show to begin. Why would anyone want to do this, especially now? To make matters worse, he notices Renee—impossible to miss in her hot pink caftan and wide-brimmed hat—sliding into her seat at the judges' table with two other women.

Alan notices her too and elbows Doug in the ribs. "Wow. That Ray-Ray just doesn't age, does she? What a difference from Kitty Cat."

Catherine was the youngest member of the regular cast—a baby at twenty-two when *Starlight* first aired. After the show wrapped, she remained in the spotlight, mostly as the girlfriend of an A-list actor with a drug problem and a violent temper. The tabloids fed off their very public arguments for years until they broke up in spectacular fashion and Catherine eventually faded from view. Doug often wondered how being on the show at such a young age affected her, if she was one of the people he'd recruited on a long downward spiral who couldn't find their way back.

"So . . ." He's almost afraid to ask. "How is Catherine these days?"

"Pretty good, actually." Alan leans across their small cocktail table. "She's a llama farmer," he says conspiratorially.

"She's a what?"

"She raises llamas." Alan leans in closer. "And grows weed. She's got this huge farm in New Mexico, out near Taos. Apparently, she makes big money from the weed, but you should see her now. All flabby and out of shape, hair completely gray. She's like, what—ten years younger than Ray-Ray?" He looks over at the judging table again. "But man, put the two of them side by side and everyone would think Kitty Cat was the mother. Anyway, let me go over and say hi real quick."

He walks over to Renee, stretching his arms out as he shouts hello. She jumps up and the two of them hug, all air kisses and chatter until Alan motions toward where Doug is standing. Renee's entire body—face, spine, fists—tightens at the sight of him. She quickly recovers with a wide, unconvincing smile as Alan continues yapping at her for several minutes.

"I was telling her they should do a contest for sexiest women's legs," he says when he returns. "Equal opportunity, right?"

Doug swallows hard. Something that tastes like pure bile slides back down his throat. "I don't want to do this," he says, though he wouldn't be able to explain why if someone asked. He's just desperate not to.

"Oh, it's no big deal. I've won this contest twice with my knock-knees. You just got to ham it up a little behind the curtain. You know, give a little twirl so the audience knows you're into it."

Alan takes a long swig of his drink and wipes his mouth with the back of his hand. The gesture—the wetness, the sloppiness of it—brings back a mirror shard of memory that Doug can't be certain is real, but it feels real as he sees the split-second flash of their younger selves. Alan, Doug, and some random woman going at it in the greenroom. Three-ways involving two women happened from time to time back then, but Doug had never been that close to a half-naked man before, and he was so ashamed of his arousal that he tried to focus all his attention and energy on the woman, possibly treating her more roughly than he should have. He wishes he knew who she was.

"I'm serious, Alan. I don't think I can do this."

"Why? What's the problem?"

Doug can feel the blood pumping violently in his chest. It courses through his body; the drumbeat of it floods his ears. He's convinced he can't breathe, which is how it always starts. He inhales and exhales slowly to prove that he can and pats himself down in search of his pills. He's relieved to hear the bottle—newly filled in Bermuda—rattle in the pocket of his slacks. "Tell them I'm not feeling well, okay? Tell them I had to go."

"You all right, bud?"

Doug speeds toward the elevators without saying goodbye. In the vestibule, he fishes out two Xanax and swallows them dry, but the pills catch in his throat, causing him to gag. He sits down on a bench and folds over his knees, coughing fitfully until someone thumps him on the back—not the friendly kind of thump that Alan gave him earlier, but more forceful ones that actually manage to knock the pills down his throat. When he looks up, Gideon is standing over him.

"God, are you okay?"

"Oh. It's you," he says weakly. He reaches up and takes his nephew's hand, relieved when Gid lets him. "Just . . . just give me a minute." He folds over his knees again while the drumbeat continues to pound in his ears, but the longer he sits there, the more it begins to recede. It's almost gone entirely when he sees a pair of brown suede loafers stop in front of him. He looks up at Alan, who's grinning like the lech that he is. Doug quickly drops Gid's hand.

"You're dating 'em kind of young these days, aren't you, bud?"

"Alan," Doug says sharply. "This is my *nephew*."

"Seriously?"

"Yes." Doug wants to scream. "Seriously. Gideon, this is Alan from the show."

"Hey, sorry about that. I didn't see the resemblance."

They shake hands, and Gid mumbles something to the effect of "nice to meet you," but he keeps looking back and forth between them, still processing what he heard. "I was going to a class by the pool," he eventually says.

"Oh, sure. Have a good—"

"But it looks like you might need me to stick around?"

Doug springs to his feet, ignoring the dizzying constellation of floaters now shooting across his field of vision. "No. You go on. I'm fine." He rests his hand against the wall casually, as if he's leaning on it for no reason, rather than depending on it to stay upright. "Alan will look after me," he adds.

Gid hesitates, but—perhaps remembering their argument earlier—decides to move on. "Okay. I'll see you later, then."

Doug watches him leave the glass vestibule and disappear around the corner. When he's gone, Doug grabs Alan by the lapels, shaking him roughly. "What is *wrong* with you? Why in the world would you say something like that?"

"What? What'd I say?"

"Are you drunk already?"

The vodka on his breath is answer enough. Doug lets go of Alan's shirt and pushes him away, furious. His most closely guarded secret, held tight for all these years, blabbed by a careless old drunk. He wants to shout, Why? Why would Alan out him in front of his nephew like that? But to use that word—"out"—would effectively admit that he was in.

The elevator opens with a ding and several passengers stream out, funneling through the vestibule toward the pool. Doug pretends that he and Alan are having a private conversation, leaning in to shield their faces until everyone has dispersed.

"Your nephew didn't know already?"

"Know *what*?" Doug says, screaming though his voice is no louder than a whisper. "What do you think he's supposed to know?"

The second elevator opens and they both freeze again until the passengers leave the vestibule. Alan stands up straight, smoothing out the pinched fabric of his shirt.

"Sorry, bud." He shrugs. "I just figured . . . I mean, you know people aren't so closed-minded about that kind of thing anymore, right? Not like they used to be. It's okay for you to be . . ."

Doug digs his nails into his palms. "Okay for me to be what, Alan? *What?*" He leans toward him, almost daring him to say the word out loud. "You know my career—my entire career—was built around me being straight, right?"

Alan may still be a drunk, but he's not a mean drunk. He's not mean enough to ask "What career?" Or "Why are you trying to protect something that barely exists?" He just stands there while Doug asks the questions of himself, unable to come up with an answer other than he's afraid, and he always has been.

"It's been such a long time though." Alan takes a step back, putting some distance between them. "You're telling me no one knows? Not even about you and Peter?"

Doug wishes there was something nearby that he could break. If there was, he'd grab it with both hands and smash it against the wall until there was nothing left. He didn't realize that Alan knew about him and Peter. That was supposed to be private, meant for them alone.

When the elevator opens to unload another group of passengers, Doug quickly steps in.

"The contest . . . you're really not staying?"

The doors close, but Doug can still hear Alan shouting, "I'm sorry, bud. Sorry!" as the elevator descends.

THERE'S AN AIR-CONDITIONING vent inconveniently positioned near his bed. Doug slides down several inches to avoid the cold air blowing on his face, forcing his feet to dangle off the edge of the twin-size mattress. During shooting weeks on board the *Sonata*, the cast was assigned to accommodations in direct proportion to their celebrity, as determined by the show's producer and locations manager. The Royal Ocean Suite that Doug used to stay in was at least ten times the size of his current cabin, a narrow, windowless interior decorated in island pastels to make the space seem bigger and brighter than it really is.

When they first boarded and Doug saw his sad little room, he told himself it was fine. He assumed he wouldn't spend much time in it. But now he doesn't want to leave, not until they're back in Boston. With room service, he thinks he could probably pull it off. Once they return to port, he and Gideon will take the train back to

New York. Then Gid will fly home to his parents in San Francisco and Doug will fly to LAX. From there, he'll take a cab to his condo in Sherman Oaks, hit the AA meeting at the local library or the NA meeting at the rec center—whichever one meets first—and return to the life he remembers before all this. Small, solitary, uncomplicated.

Doug lifts his hands, which have been folded over his chest. Underneath them is the photo of Peter that he stole from the greenroom. He lifts it gently by the corners, careful not to smudge the print. They'd been so discreet, or so he thought. Discreet with each other, at least. They both had very public affairs and one-night stands with women, which was easy enough to do. There were usually plenty of willing fans and would-be starlets hanging around wherever they went. Doug should have known though. How many times had he woken up after a party, only to hear stories about all the crazy things he'd done—things he had no memory of? In that state, it was entirely possible that someone from the cast had seen him and Peter being unguarded with each other.

The only person they ever told about their relationship was Annette, whose judgment Peter trusted. He reasoned that she was their agent and confidante. Of all the people in their network, she should be able to help. This was back in the early eighties, when she still had the office in L.A. with its huge windows overlooking Studio City. Doug and Peter were both fresh from a stint in rehab, which is probably why his memories of this conversation are clearer than most. Annette was sitting at her big glass desk, smoking a cigarette and doing three different things at once, as usual. She started paying attention only after Peter told her, and she laughed along in that phlegmy way of hers until she realized no one else was laughing with her. Then her expression turned serious.

"You two can do whatever you want on your own time. It's a free country. But if you're thinking about making that public . . . I'm not exaggerating when I say neither of you will ever work again."

"But we're not gay," Peter said. "We're bi. We sleep with women too—lots of women," he added. "As you well know." He was referring to the countless conversations in which she'd had to reprimand one or both of them for some glaring indiscretion that had gotten back to her through the grapevine or the tabloids. Annette looked upset all of a sudden, as if she wished they were still talking about something simple, like the difference between being a marketable sex symbol and behaving like a pig.

"If you sleep with him," she said, pointing at Doug, "then you might as well be gay because that's all anyone will ever remember about the two of you. Also, if you haven't noticed, gay men aren't exactly popular right now. Everybody's saying you're responsible for that disease that's going around."

A man who lived in Doug's building had gotten sick with the virus and died, quickly and alone, in a hospice facility. The neighbors said his family refused to claim his body for a proper burial, so he ended up being laid to rest in a potter's field out in Boyle Heights. The landlord went through his belongings, cherry-picking a few expensive items to sell, and a cleaning crew carted away the rest in garbage bags and metal bins. Doug could easily imagine a similar kind of fate for himself if he wasn't careful, so even though it bothered him to see the sadness spreading across Peter's face, he was grateful to Annette for discouraging him.

"How many gay men in Hollywood can you name who are out and still getting jobs?" she continued.

"We're *bi,*" Peter repeated.

She ignored this and went on to list several actors who were quietly rumored to be homosexuals. Rock Hudson, Cary Grant, Anthony Perkins, Raymond Burr, Robert Reed. She counted them off on both hands, eventually running out of fingers.

"You think any of these guys would have had the careers they did if they came right out and said they liked men?"

Doug regrets not telling her in that moment that he didn't just like Peter. He loved him. By that point, they'd loved each other privately for nearly seven years. There was no one who knew Doug better, no one who accepted his faults and insecurities and vanities with as much empathy as Peter. And he was funny, so incredibly funny. All Peter had to do was cross his eyes at him to call back a thousand private jokes, and Doug would have to stare at his feet to avoid dissolving into laughter. They partied too much, which they sometimes recognized was a problem. But when they were drunk or high and all that energy was swirling around them, they both felt free of the small-town boys they used to be, so deadened by the thought of spending the rest of their lives in the places where they'd been born. For a while, there was no one Doug wanted to enjoy his success with more than Peter, which felt like a middle finger to their fathers—cold, disapproving men who'd expected them to be good farmers like they were and eventually died not knowing what to make of them.

Peter, however, was growing increasingly tired of how careful they had to be, how they often felt the need to carry on publicly with women for the sake of appearances. It was unfair to the women, unfair to each other, he said. He kept insisting that all he wanted to do was go to the grocery store together, which in retrospect was probably his way of signaling that he was ready for a different kind of life. Doug wonders what, if anything, would have changed if he'd spoken up during that meeting with Annette and said that he didn't care about his career. Maybe he and Peter would have fought less. Maybe they would have stayed clean that time. Maybe Doug wouldn't have felt the need to end things soon afterward because he couldn't give Peter the honest life he wanted, and worse than letting him go was continuing to deny him.

He raises the fading photograph, staring at what remains of Peter's face. He wonders how long the Polaroid will last until the image fades entirely and he loses him all over again. Doug has never loved anyone, has never even been with anyone, since Peter's death. Why would he? He'd experienced what it felt like to be known and cared for so deeply once, and he threw it all away. Being alone is his penance, he thinks. His punishment for the chance not taken.

Someone raps loudly on the door, prompting Doug to scramble out of bed. He pauses, realizing that his first instinct after getting up was to hide the photo in the pocket of his sports coat. He didn't even think. He understands why Peter took their breakup so badly, why he called Doug a coward and refused to be on speaking terms with him, much less be friends.

The person at the door knocks even louder. He assumes it's the room steward or Gideon coming to check on him and makes no effort to hide his disappointment when he finds Kevin standing at the threshold instead.

"Oh. Hello."

"You skipped the contest," he says, not bothering with a greeting.

"I'm not feeling well. I told Alan to let someone know."

Kevin's eyes wander past Doug's head, taking in the cabin behind him. "I'm actually here to discuss something else."

Doug waits for him to explain until the silence stretches on for too long "Yes? And?"

"We've received a complaint about you," he says, this time without hesitation.

Doug opens the door wider, not certain if he wants to have this conversation out in the hallway, but Kevin remains where he is. "Who complained?" he asks, even though he already knows. He's just trying to imagine what in the world Renee would have to complain about. He hasn't said a word to her since the day they boarded. He's been keeping his distance, exactly as she instructed him to do.

"We had a report that you were leering at one of the guests."

For a moment, Doug is so relieved that Renee wasn't the source of the complaint that he doesn't actually register what the complaint is. Then he circles back to the offending word. "*Leering*? Who was I supposedly leering at?"

"One of the female passengers. We were told that you were staring at her breasts and then you yelled at her."

The idea of this is so ridiculous that Doug begins to laugh until he realizes that he did raise his voice at Minnie Mouse. "Wait. Are you talking about that woman who was wearing the old cast T-shirt? The one with the big red bow in her hair?" Kevin's expression is impassive. It neither confirms nor denies. But Doug is certain that must be who he's talking about. "I wasn't *leering* at her, for God's sake. My face—my actual face—was on her shirt. It was hard not to notice. It didn't even occur to me that I was looking at her chest."

"All right." Kevin still seems unconvinced. "Maybe I can understand that. But did you yell at her?"

Did I? he wants to ask. But of course, he did. He just doesn't know how to account for his behavior. "Is that what she told you?"

"No. It was Mr. Hamm, her husband, who told us. Apparently, his wife is a huge fan of the show and they've been saving up for this reunion cruise for several years. You really upset her, which upset him, so now we have a problem with the Hamms that the company will probably have to resolve by—"

"Look. That woman, she wasn't entirely right in the head. I know I shouldn't have snapped at her, but she was being intrusive."

"Perhaps so, but she's the guest, Mr. Clayton. We exist to show our guests a good time."

Doug refuses to be lumped together in this collective "we." He wants to believe that he has more reasons to exist than this. "Maybe that's your job," he says. "But I thought mine was to show up for the events I'm assigned to. And when I'm not scheduled to be somewhere, my time is my own, right? That woman you're talking about had been throwing herself at me during the dance session, which was embarrassing, frankly, and then she followed me during my private time when I was with my nephew. Are you telling me I don't have a right to respond when someone acts like that?"

"Of course you have rights, Mr. Clayton. But you also signed a contract to entertain. Between yelling at a passenger and skipping the contest this afternoon, it seems like you're not entirely clear about what your responsibilities are."

Kevin pauses as if he expects Doug to protest, to insist that he does know what he's supposed to do, but Doug won't give him the satisfaction.

"Maybe it would be helpful if I contacted your agent to review your contract with her, particularly the legal consequences of not meeting your obligations to the company. Then the two of you can talk."

The suggestion is thinly veiled in corporate speak, but there's no mistaking the threat. "Go ahead," Doug says. He resists the urge to add, "Good luck getting in touch with her."

13.

"You've done this kind of thing before?" the woman sitting next to Lucy asks.

"You mean plein air?"

She nods.

"Not with watercolors. I usually paint with oils."

The woman's eyes widen. "You must be an expert, then."

"No." Lucy wishes she'd sat somewhere else. "No. Definitely not."

The instructor for their three o'clock class is running late. A nervous young crew member keeps telling everyone not to worry, her voice straining with cheerful reassurance. The eight passengers waiting for class to begin are seated in a long row on the shady side of the ship, each with their own easel and painting supplies. Their deck chairs face the open water, which is smooth and granite-colored, flickering with afternoon light. Lucy wasn't sure if she wanted to take the class and has contemplated leaving at least half a dozen times. Now that her neighbor has started chatting with her, she considers it again.

"I'm Dottie," the woman says.

"Lucy."

They shake hands as a gust of wind nearly topples several easels, forcing people to lunge out of their seats. Dottie brushes a lock of hair out of her eyes and proceeds to tell Lucy an abridged version of her life story. She was born and raised in Chicago; she works at Loyola Marymount University as an assistant bursar; she likes her work but thinks students these days are so spoiled; she's recently divorced; the cruise was a gift from her kids, who aren't speaking to their father right now; she used to love watching *Starlight Voyages* and still knows the theme song by heart.

Lucy has no intention of sharing anywhere near this much information, so she offers the bare minimum of what she thinks she can get away with: she's never watched *Starlight Voyages* before and she's traveling with a friend. It's easier to refer to Mariah this way rather than explain who she really is: someone who invited her to come on a cruise, and then ditched her as soon as she hooked up with a guy.

Shortly before the ship docked in Bermuda, Mariah said that Iain's friends who lived in Tucker's Town had invited him boating, but their catamaran could seat only so many. "You don't mind if I go with him, do you?" she asked. Lucy recognized the insincere phrasing. It was the second time Mariah had mentioned something that was about to happen and then asked if she'd mind, like Lucy really had any say in the matter. She responded as casually as she could, trying to ignore the contradictory feelings battling inside her—annoyance at how rude Mariah was being and relief to be rid of her company.

After overhearing a family discuss their plans to take a short ferry ride into Hamilton, Lucy copied their route, arriving in a city much larger than she'd expected, but like no city she'd ever seen. She was accustomed to the historic buildings of D.C. and Boston, all white marble or gray travertine, with their grand columns and stately port cocheres and the occasional gilded dome. The buildings along Hamilton's Front Street were squat one- and two-story wood structures that looked more like houses than the banks and shops they actually were. Most were painted flamingo pink and lime green and topaz blue, their façades all windswept and weathered from their proximity to the harbor, which the street signs referred to as "harbour." As Lucy walked, startled by the strange sensation of returning to land, she grew increasingly embarrassed by her own ignorance. She didn't know if Bermuda was a former colony or a current one. A sign near Queen Elizabeth Park proclaiming the country the oldest self-governing territory of the British Commonwealth didn't make its status any clearer.

"So which beaches did you go to yesterday?" Dottie suddenly asks.

"Beaches?"

"Yes." She glances at Lucy's arms, which are covered with flaky white patches that are starting to peel despite her liberal use of Mariah's lotions and gels. The effect is unsightly, almost reptilian.

"None."

"You didn't go to any? But then how did you get burnt like that?"

Her tone is so skeptical, it makes Lucy feel like she did something wrong or missed out on something good, which she probably did. She explains that she was sunburned from sitting by the pool so she explored the capital instead. This seems to satisfy Dottie, who goes on to tell her about the wonderful snorkeling in Horseshoe Bay. Lucy looks around, wondering if the instructor is ever going to arrive and whether this is a sign to just get up and leave. But leave and go where? The suite feels off-limits, and the pool and Grotto do too. She could go to another session, but most of them have probably started already, and she has no interest in magic shows or dancing or bingo games. All she really wants to do is avoid Mariah, who she still has to live with after the cruise ends. She doesn't want to say or do anything that might jeopardize such a reliable source of rent, but she doesn't entirely trust her impulses right now.

"I'm still trying to decide which beach I preferred," Dottie continues. "The sand at Horseshoe Bay was actually pink. But the water at Hidden Beach, oh my God . . ."

Lucy smiles and nods, her head bobbing like a bird. She catches only bits and pieces of what Dottie is going on so rapturously about—something about neon-yellow fish darting in and out of a reef.

In Hamilton, Lucy walked a few blocks along Front Street in search of a place to buy a charger for her dead phone. Finding none, she stopped at a café called the Pelican. The entrance was decorated with a large, parrot-like creature that looked like it had been painted by someone who didn't know what a pelican was. To the left of the door was a sign in alternating pastels that read INTERNET, and to the right was another that read INTERNATL. CALLS. She stood outside for several minutes, weighing the immediate, heart-palpitating terror of going in and checking her messages versus the slow-growing terror of waiting until she returned to Boston. She walked away and returned. Then walked away and returned again, annoyed with herself and the fear that now seemed to govern every decision she made, or didn't make, no matter how big or small.

Finally, she went inside, spurred on by the sight of an elderly woman watching from her window with a bemused expression. Lucy purchased a pot of tea and a one-hour phone card from a teenage boy who looked surprised by her arrival. He showed her around the empty café with too much ceremony and then directed her to the private phone carrels, which resembled the red British phone booths she'd seen on television. Among the twenty-eight answering machine and voicemail messages that she retrieved: requests for second interviews from Cisco, IBM, Microsoft, Google, the Department of Defense, and two Internet start-ups. The relief she should have felt upon hearing these invitations was muted, in large part because they were interspersed among messages from her mother, father, and adviser, whose voices sounded increasingly agitated.

"What do you mean, 'I'm going to Bermuda'?" Dad shouted.

"Lou, honey, how could you do this?" Mom asked.

"Why on earth would you do this now?" Dr. Jimoh demanded. "Are you having some sort of a nervous breakdown?"

Lucy purchased another hour on her card and requested a second pot of hot water. Then she returned to her carrel and followed up with every company that had called her, making arrangements to interview again in a week or two. She was relieved that she'd managed to reach everyone on the first or second try. The only problem was the Google recruiter, who wanted her to come to New York on September 20. The vice president of engineering was going to be in town that day and had a rare opening on his calendar. Lucy recognized what a big deal this was. The recruiter was effectively offering her a chance to jump a full level or more of interviews with junior management by setting her up with this man. She felt sick to her stomach when she explained that she was traveling and couldn't be in New York on the twentieth. Then she braced herself, accustomed to feeling like she had to go along with everything people asked of her or else the rug would be snatched out from under her feet.

The recruiter was surprisingly understanding. He suggested a phone interview instead, which she knew was meant to be an accommodation, although it didn't really help her. She considered admitting that she was on a cruise ship and she wasn't sure if the satellite phone would be up and running on the twentieth, but it sounded like such a ridiculous excuse. If she were responsible for hiring people, wouldn't she question the judgment of someone who went on a cruise in the middle of recruitment season? After a terrorist attack had just killed hundreds—possibly thousands—of Americans?

Lucy agreed to the phone interview, feeling the slippery flip and flop of her stomach as she scribbled the details on her ferry schedule. What if the phone system still wasn't fixed when she returned to the *Sonata*? What if she had no way of contacting the executive and just stood him up? She knew she was taking a major risk, the kind that her candidacy wouldn't recover from no matter how many times she apologized or explained. But she was motivated by the idea that her parents and Dr. Jimoh would be less upset with her if she returned from the cruise with an invitation to interview at Google's headquarters in California. That was what passed for hope in the moment.

DOTTIE'S INCESSANT CHATTER is making it hard to hear, so Lucy assumes that she misunderstood the first time. But then the instructor apologizes again.

"Mi dispiace, a tutti."

She wonders if the *Sonata* has permanently damaged her brain, and now she's just imagining everything in Italian. She leans back in her chair to glance at the instructor and doesn't know whether to laugh or cry. The man who's breathlessly apologizing to the group is the same one she met on the Lido Deck two nights earlier.

Instructor Dario looks so different from Lothario Dario, which is how she still thinks of him. Gone is the nearly see-through linen shirt unbuttoned to midchest and the unkempt locks of hair worn loose and flowing. He's now dressed in a heavily stained denim painter's apron over a T-shirt and khaki trousers, and his hair is pulled back into a low, neat ponytail.

"So sorry, so sorry," he says, switching to English. "*Allora,* you're here for outdoor painting, yes? Plein air, from the French."

"Don't you love his accent?" Dottie whispers under her breath, like she and Lucy are now old friends.

He's laying it on nice and thick for them, she thinks. Much thicker than she remembers, like it's a role he's playing for their benefit. He doesn't offer any explanations about why he's late, which no one except Lucy seems to mind. She assumes a woman was involved and imagines Dario scrambling out of a warm bed to get to class. If Iain considers himself quietly exempt from the company's "no fraternizing" rule, then surely there are others like him.

When Dario looks down the long row of chairs and finally makes eye contact with Lucy, he seems confused for a moment, and then his expression warms with recognition. She's not charmed by his crooked smile and doesn't return it. After a break of nearly three years, she just wants to paint already.

"The ocean, it's perfect plein air subject for beginners," he says, gesturing toward the water. "Such nice big shapes, you add as much or little detail as you like. Some people say, 'It's only ocean and sky. It's all the same.' But the light and color—they're different everywhere. Look closely now. Don't be afraid to do this." He holds his index fingers and thumbs in the shape of a rectangle, scanning the horizon.

Everyone in the class follows suit except for Lucy, who doesn't need to pretend that she's holding a camera in order to see what's possible. She opens her metal palette of watercolors and finds three cheap brushes and twelve square wells of paint, all previously used. The two blue shades are particularly worn down, exposing the bottom of the tray.

"You find what you want to paint, and *guardate qui,* watch here." He angles his easel toward them so they can all see. "You start like this."

Dario sounds like a caricature with his accent and halting speech and occasional retreat to Italian. Lucy tries to block him out, and her neighbor too, which is easier said than done.

"You're skipping ahead," Dottie observes. "See? I knew you were an expert."

While Dario shows the class how to do their first wash of color, Lucy is already moving on to her second. She brushes a layer of purple over the damp paper, blending it into her base of blue in order to form the basic shapes of the sky and the ocean. She quickly recalls why she never liked painting with watercolors, which are a much fussier medium than her beloved oils. She's not accustomed to paint that needs to be diluted with water, which makes it hard to achieve the right intensity.

Somewhere on the other side of the ship, probably somewhere near the pool, a crowd begins to whistle and applaud. Lucy distinctly hears the words "Limbo! Limbo!" being shouted through a microphone and then the tinny ghost notes of a xylophone. She scans her palette for options, wishing she had more than twelve shades to work with.

"You're using so much purple," Dottie says, her eyes traveling from Lucy's painting to her own to the water. "You must see color differently than I do. I'm not getting any purple."

Dottie reminds her of the bursar at Wellesley, a campus official best known for shutting off students' accounts when their tuition checks didn't arrive or their federal loans were delayed. No hardship could move her—not deaths in the family or sudden job losses, and definitely not tears. Lucy didn't have to interact with her very often, for which she was grateful. But whenever she learned that a dreaded flag had been placed on her account, she approached the bursar's desk with trepidation, bearing messages from her father that she knew weren't convincing.

"I'm only a few weeks late," he'd shout over the phone, money being the rare topic that caused him to raise his voice. "Just tell her I mailed the check already and she should let you register for classes!"

Until now, Lucy had assumed that the bursar's personality was hers alone. But it occurs to her that maybe all bursars have to be like this—rigid and rules-driven—in order to do their job. To someone like Dottie, the tuition is probably either paid or unpaid. A student is either eligible or ineligible for work study. The sky is either purple or blue. There's no room for nuance, which makes it hard for Lucy to explain that she's never cared for still life or portraiture or other styles of representational painting that involved fidelity to something that's already there. That's why she's using the purple. Like Gertrude Stein, she prefers to pretend there's no *there* there, and the urgency of painting for her—the challenge and the joy of it too—is to produce physical images that are faithful only to the ones in her head.

The watercolors, however, are making this exceedingly difficult. Every shade comes out less saturated than what she envisions. The purple becomes lavender, the black turns to gray. Although she's quickly produced a respectable rendering of a moody seascape, it's not the image that appears in her mind. Not even close. With the largest of her three brushes, she tries to go darker, frustrated with the cheap bristles, the crappy middle-school-grade paint.

"Now you're using black?" Dottie seems incredulous. She leans over to examine Lucy's painting. "Oh . . . well, that's interesting."

"Thanks," she says, more focused on what she's looking at than what she's hearing. It takes a full beat to realize that Dottie doesn't mean "interesting" in a good way.

"But . . . you're kind of just doing your own thing, aren't you?" She waves at the sky, which is blue and streaked with flat white clouds.

Dottie's painting attempts to depict these colors as they truly are. Lucy scans the row of easels, seeing similar works in progress done in various shades of blue. Robin's egg, Tiffany, cornflower, cerulean, teal. None of them is right. None of them looks real. Lucy's version, flawed as it is, is an attempt to capture a feeling instead of a color. She shrugs off Dottie's remark, aware that Dario is walking toward them, checking on his students' progress and offering words of encouragement. She hopes he'll keep walking if she appears deep in concentration.

"It's excellent," he says, now hovering over her shoulder, arms crossed like her old studio instructor from school.

"She says she's not an expert, but I think she's just being modest," Blabbermouth Dottie tells him. "Usually, she paints with oils."

"You did not mention you paint," Dario says, as if the subject should have come up earlier.

"You two know each other already?"

"We meet a few nights ago. I should realize she's an artist from how she stares and stares at the water. Very deep concentration." He imitates a person with intense, unblinking eyes, which draws a laugh out of Dottie before she starts in again.

"Her painting's really interesting, but I'm kind of confused. Aren't we supposed to make it look like what's out there?"

Dario shakes his head. "In art, there is no 'supposed to.'"

For once, Lucy doesn't want to roll her eyes at something that Dario has said or done. With his fake broken English and exaggerated accent, he's actually managed to land on something that she hasn't been able to articulate for herself, the reason she suspects she's always been drawn to art. She wants to sit with this idea while she paints, but she's trapped between two people who won't stop talking to her and about her.

"So this is hobby for you, Lucia? Or did you study in—"

"Lucy," she snaps, unable to hear her name being mangled like this any longer. "My name is *'Lu-cy,'* not *'Lu-chee-ya.'*"

Her abrupt change of tone momentarily silences them. But unlike the sour-faced Dottie, Dario glides right past it, offering the same warm, irritating smile he flashed when she asked him to leave her alone.

"*Mi dispiace,* Lucy."

THE SESSION IS winding down when she decides to try a different approach. With her fingernail, she digs a chunk of black paint out of its well and crushes it on the lid of the palette, mixing the hardened powder with a single drop of water to turn it into a paste. Then she dries off the largest of her three brushes and applies a thick sweep of black to the middle of her painting. The paper is well past the point of damp now. It's soggy and the fibers are starting to pill from being overworked, but finally—Lucy begins to see something approaching the right intensity of color.

Dottie hasn't spoken to her since her outburst. Normally, Lucy would feel guilty about losing her temper in front of a stranger, worried about what kinds of conclusions Dottie might be making about angry Black women or Black people in general. But time is the more pressing concern now. She isn't ready for the session to end yet, an irony that isn't lost on her as she digs out another chunk of paint.

"You know, someone's going to have to use that set when you're done with it," Dottie says disapprovingly.

"There's still plenty of black left."

She's tempted to add "Don't you worry" or "Mind your own business," but she's distracted by what's materializing in front of her. By now, her painting looks like an inversion of the scene that everyone else has been trying to reproduce. A bottom to their up. A hell to their heaven. The intensity of the black paste transforms the image in just a few thick strokes, pushing it toward an edge that Lucy didn't know was there. It's obviously no longer a seascape. It probably never was.

Dottie makes a noise that sounds like a "humph" as the female crew member thanks everyone for coming to the session. Lucy races to brush on more black, convinced that she might be able to finish if she just had more time, even though it's unrealistic to think so. It used to take her months to finish a single painting. Whatever she hopes is going to happen isn't going to happen here.

"I still don't understand why you'd do that," Dottie says, now standing and looking over Lucy's shoulder. She seems almost angry as she stares at Lucy's painting, a morass of black and gray, tinged with vestigial blue. "It's such a beautiful day. Why not just paint what's there?"

Because Lucy can't stop thinking about the people on the plane—the one that crashed in Pennsylvania. At the Pelican, she read articles about how some of the passengers secretly used their Airfones during the hijacking and learned about the other planes. They knew what was going to happen to them, that's why they decided to fight.

Until she sat down at her easel, Lucy had been able to put them out of her mind, but then she started replaying their last minutes over and over again until all she could think about was the desperate courage of what those people did, how they risked the possibility of their lives to save countless others. She didn't know how else to express her grief but this.

Someone touches the back of her chair. She turns to find Dario in a low crouch beside her, using the top rail for balance while he looks at her painting. "It reminds me of smoke," he says, almost admiringly.

The area behind him is empty. All the other members of the class, including Dottie, have now dispersed.

"You should take the paints and paper," he says. "So you can keep working."

"Don't you need them for your next session?"

"Eh." He stands up and folds a nearby easel into thirds. "It's a rich company. They don't miss these small things."

The panic of trying to finish instantly lifts. Lucy snaps the metal palette shut and tucks it into her bag. Her right hand is painfully stiff. She tries to knead the gristly palm, but her thumb quickly gives out. Dario moves down the row, collecting supplies and breaking down easels, so she gets up and places hers in the rolling cart where he's stowing all the others. She continues helping him, grateful for not only the paints but also the silence while they work. It's obvious he won't be the first to disrupt it this time.

"Do you mind if I ask you a question?" she asks.

"Ask me anything, Lu— *Lucy.*"

"What's with your accent?" She's not sure why she wants to know this; she just does.

"What do you mean?"

"It gets thicker when you're teaching."

Dario smiles. "The older passengers usually like it."

Lucy thinks it must be nice to have the right kind of accent when there are so many wrong ones in the world. "So . . . is this what you do for a living? You teach painting on ships?"

"I paint for a living," Dario says. "I also teach at schools and tutor some children. Twice a year, I work for Aria, mostly to travel."

This is the existence that Lucy is afraid of, how she fears she'd have to survive. She's inherited too much of her parents' pragmatism to have romantic ideas about the life of an artist. Whenever she allows her mind to wander toward that possibility, she tends to catastrophize it, imagining dingy apartments and degrading part-time jobs, unpaid bills and no health insurance. Dario just confirmed some of her fears, albeit inadvertently. If he actually earned enough from his painting, he wouldn't have to teach or tutor. He could afford to take real vacations that didn't involve work, however modest his duties might be.

"Can I ask you a question now? You studied painting, yes? Because you're very good."

It's been years since anyone noticed her abilities, years since she last exercised them so publicly. Lucy feels herself blooming a bit, but she tries to keep the compliment in perspective. Lothario Dario is full of lines.

"My neighbor didn't think so."

Dario blows the air out of his mouth. "She's an old woman. She confuses painting and photography. But you, clearly you learned somewhere."

"I studied painting in college." She adds "Not seriously," because she doesn't want him to launch into the same lecture that Mariah did about having talent and making time. She knows what life after grad school has in store for her, particularly if she opts for the private tech firm route. If she's offered a six-figure salary and stock options somewhere, she'll have to work a hundred hours a week to keep them.

"*Allora* . . ." Dario claps and rubs his hands together, which reminds her of a fly. "I put these things away and then I'm free. You'll join me for a drink at the Grotto?"

"No," Lucy says, so quickly and emphatically that both of them seem surprised by the force of her reply.

His smile, she realizes, might not be the infuriating display of confidence that she initially assumed it was. Maybe it's more like armor. It has to be, because there he is, displaying those crooked teeth of his like she just told a joke.

"You confuse me, Lucy. I'm nice to you. Friendly. I admire your art. But you are . . ." He genuinely seems to be searching for words now, not just fumbling for them in order to charm the older passengers. "I don't know. To me, you are so . . ."

She braces herself to hear him say "angry," which will only make her angrier. She's tired of people implying that women like her aren't entitled to their rage. "What's so hard to understand? I don't want to have a drink with you because I don't like you."

"Yes, but what do I do to make you not like—"

"You act like you're God's gift to women. You milk your accent when some people learn English and spend their whole lives trying to lose theirs. You show up fifteen minutes late for class without so much as an explanation. You think flirting and teaching are the same thing. You get away with shit that I could never, not in a million years . . ." She pauses, aware that she's about to jump the track and needs to right herself before she pulls too far away. "You want me to keep going?"

Dario shakes his head. He's not smiling anymore. He actually appears gutted, which isn't the reaction she expected. She was beginning to think he really might be impervious. Lucy has never spoken to anyone so harshly before. It's not the release she thought it would be, in part because she knows that Dario isn't what she's upset about.

"I'm sorry," she says quietly. It feels like she broke something out of spite and now she has to put it back together again out of guilt. "I'm sorry. I appreciate the paints, I really do. I'm just not myself right now."

"I'm not myself too. I'm usually never late to class, but my father, he had surgery in Naples this morning. I had to check on him, and my mother—she does not understand how expensive it is to call from the ship, but what can I do? I have to listen."

He continues telling her about his parents, probably to justify his lateness, but Lucy's mind is racing, replaying something he said that she was too afraid to confirm on her own. He called to check on his father before class, which means that the phones on the *Sonata* are finally up and running again.

14.

Franny goes to the private dining room an hour early to oversee setup. When she arrives, she's both relieved and disappointed to find that everything has already been taken care of, and the catering staff followed her instructions to the letter. There's a banquet table in the center of the room and a buffet table off to the side, both draped with red linens and decorated with red and pink flowers. Across the length of the table are the items that Franny rented in Koreatown and carried onboard in an extra suitcase. From a distance, the tall faux pillars of whole fruit and plastic spirals of bean cakes look surprisingly real, glistening under the overhead lights as symbols of a plentiful life.

The arrangements are Franny's best attempt to re-create the *hwangap* and *chilsun* celebrations that took place at Ma's restaurant, which had a large rental room upstairs for private events. Although the guests always seemed to enjoy themselves at these parties, Franny still remembers how nervous the adult children looked in their role as hosts. They barely ate except to ensure that the food tasted good and spent most of the time stealing glances at their parents for signs of approval or disapproval.

Franny didn't particularly mind the sons. They were stern and stiff, but they left her and the other waitresses alone, relying mostly on their sisters or wives to communicate with the staff. In retrospect, this was probably why the women were always so demanding. Not only were they communicating their own complaints, they were also responsible for their families'. Franny's instinct was to hide whenever she saw one of the daughters or daughters-in-law walking toward her, usually to point out some detail that was amiss or some expectation that wasn't being met. As a teenager, she thought the women seemed so unpleasant and unreasonable, but as she examines a pair of floral arrangements displayed on white plaster pillars, she understands the kind of pressure they must have been under.

She calls out to the catering manager, who's standing at the buffet table, centering a large tower of finger sandwiches centimeter by centimeter. The woman turns and claps her hands together as soon as she sees Franny. "Oh, what a beautiful dress!"

Franny feels ridiculous in her shiny rose pink *hanbok,* which looks even shinier under the lights. She wishes she'd packed a coat to throw over herself, though she doubts any coat would be long enough or big enough to hide the bell sleeves of her jacket or the fullness of her floor-length skirt. On her way from the cabin to the private dining room, Franny felt thoroughly examined by her fellow passengers, who seemed to regard her as some sort of charming novelty. The ones who spoke to her were complimentary, but a few just couldn't stop themselves from asking what kind of dress was she wearing, what country was it from, what country was *she* from? This time, Tom wasn't around to run interference for her.

They'd agreed that he should sit the *chilsun* out, a decision Franny isn't looking forward to explaining to her family. She still isn't entirely sure how. But better to make up an excuse about Tom's absence than allow his presence to ruin the event. Once his affair was no longer a secret, he simply deflated with grief. Franny is torn between her own grief and a kind of anger that she can hardly articulate. If she focuses on it for any length of time, she's certain it will burn her alive.

"Will you be wearing that to Formal Night afterward?" the catering manager asks.

Franny shakes her head, unable to think one minute past Ma's party. "Could I talk to you about these flowers, please?"

Before coming over to Franny, the woman retreats to the corner and hoists a small rolled-up rug onto her shoulder. Franny wishes she could remember her name, but her mind is racing. It's been racing ever since Tom learned where she was last Tuesday and then proceeded to tell everyone. She clings to the delusion that she'll be spared her family's shock and anger, at least for the next few hours. However unlikely, she wants to believe that none of them, not even Jae, would ruin such an important occasion by asking questions about what happened and why she lied. Now that the event is finally upon them, Franny hopes they'll understand, and maybe even respect, the lengths she went to to preserve this moment, to make it all about Ma.

"I talked to a crew member about Korean customs after our meeting this morning. It's my first time doing one of these, so I really wanted to get it right." The woman unfurls the rug at Franny's feet. It's a red and black kilim. Turkish, most likely, with a fringe of ivory tassels on the ends. "I know it's not Korean, but if you're planning to do the bow, I was wondering if you wanted something like this on the floor to protect your clothes."

Franny cycles through all the events at Ma's restaurant. The *keunjeol* was customary at Korean New Year celebrations, but she frequently saw adult children perform it at birthdays too. She can't recall anything being on the floor when they got down on their hands and knees to pay their respects to the guest of honor.

"That won't be necessary. But thank you for asking." She's impressed that the catering manager even knows about the bow, and relieved that she can see her name tag now that the rug is no longer covering it. "Actually, Lindsay, I wanted to talk to you about these floral arrangements . . . This isn't what I ordered, is it?"

She recognizes the question as soon as she says it out loud. It's the same one she heard from so many customers. She hated it then and hates herself for asking it now, but it can't be helped. Although *hwangap* and *chilsun* celebrations were meant to be symbolic displays of gratitude, they were also material ones. For hosts like her, who could afford to be extravagant, it was considered shameful to skimp on any details, big or small. Even for hosts of more modest means, a parent's significant birthday was supposed to be an occasion to stretch.

Lindsay removes a notebook from her back pocket and quickly flips through the pages. "It says here 'four extra-large tropical floral arrangements, red and pink, display on pillars for height, no white flowers or baby's breath.'" She looks at the flowers again. On the face of it, they appear to be everything that Franny asked for. "Did you want them to have more height?"

The arrangements, which are lined up in a row behind the banquet table, are gigantic. Including the urn-like vases, they're taller than some of the children Franny has seen playing by the kiddie pool upstairs. Including the pillars, they're probably taller than Ma, but it's not the height that bothers her.

"I paid for 'tropical,'" she says. "But these are just red roses and pink carnations. I'm not sure what's tropical about that."

Lindsay's name tag says she's from Kissimmee, Florida, and she's a member of the Catering and Hospitality team. She gives Franny her most hospitable smile. "Well, the designers are limited to what they have on board the ship—"

"Yes, but I took one of those floral arrangement classes a few days ago, and we had lots of tropical flowers to choose from. Lilies," she says, not certain if lilies are actually tropical. "And birds of paradise."

"Lilies are white though, and you said white is for funerals in Kor—"

"I know," Franny says, a little too sharply. "I was just using them as an example." She smooths out her skirt, feeling the itch of the thin crinoline layer underneath. She wishes she had pockets to shove her hands into. She has too much energy all of a sudden and doesn't know what to do with it except this. "Arrangements with only roses and carnations just look . . . cheap. And I know what I paid for all of this. It definitely wasn't cheap."

Lindsay is still smiling, but it seems like she's making more of an effort than she was before. She reaches for the radio clipped to her belt. "All right. Let me step out into the hallway and try to reach someone downstairs."

She says this pleasantly enough, the same way Franny had to speak pleasantly to customers at the restaurant, then professors at school, and now clients at her firm and Tom's extended family. She doesn't want Lindsay to think she's being difficult or rude, but if that's what happens, she decides it can't be helped. In her lifetime, she's seen so many *hwangaps* and *chilsuns,* but very few *palsuns*. There's no guarantee that Ma will live to be eighty. She needs to show her mother how much she appreciates the hard life she led, just so she and Jae could have their comfortable ones.

Franny walks over to the buffet table and scans the four-tier displays of finger sandwiches. Beside them are matching towers filled with ornate little pastries, enough to feed a party three or four times their size. Surrounding them are familiar edible flowers made of beets and carrots and squash. Korean food wasn't an option on the catering menu, so she ordered an elaborate English tea service, hoping the novelty of it might compensate for the inauthenticity. On each level of the towers, there's a small handwritten sign explaining what the items are. CUCUMBER AND WATERCRESS SANDWICHES, EGG SALAD WITH DILL, PEACH SCONES WITH CLOTTED CREAM, LEMON POPPY TEA CAKE. She knows how strange it is to celebrate a *chilsun* without Korean food, but it was a calculated risk. Ma never liked other people's cooking more than her own anyway.

"Success!" Lindsay shouts, returning from her conversation in the hallway. "The assistant floral designer's going to bring up some more stems to add to the arrangements. I told him to make sure they're tropical, so let's see what he can do."

Franny nods and scans the room again, disappointed that there's nothing left to fix or focus on. The staff is ready for her family, even if she isn't.

"I think I followed all your other instructions," Lindsay says, looking around the room with her. "Aside from the flowers, is everything else what you hoped for?"

The poor woman is waiting for a compliment, Franny realizes. No different from the way she used to wait at the restaurant, just wishing for a kind word from the daughters or daughters-in-law that almost never came. The women couldn't open their mouths except to say something negative.

"Thank you. You did an excellent job," Franny says, hoping it will all be enough.

* * *

IT DOESN'T SURPRISE her that Ma, Jae, and Esther arrive nearly ten minutes late. What does surprise her is how they look when they walk in. Franny blinks several times, certain that she's having some kind of stress-induced nightmare. But no. She's very much awake, and the three of them are still wearing the same clothes they had on at lunch.

"Why—why are you dressed like that?" she asks.

They trade glances, each waiting for one of the others to respond.

"We weren't really sure what we were doing anymore," Esther finally says.

"But how could you not be sure?" Franny snaps, glaring at Jae as she says it. "We had an agreement. We said we were going to wear *hanboks*."

Jae shakes his head. "It just didn't feel right, Franny. It's kind of a weird time to be getting dressed up and doing something like this."

"But that was the whole point! That's why we came!"

Ma sighs. "Ay, lower your voice. People will hear."

It's her seventieth birthday and she looks upset and uncomfortable, no different from her usual state. Franny is beside herself. She takes a deep breath and smooths out her skirt again, trying to focus on the stiff, expensive silk.

"The room is really nice, Franny," Esther offers quietly. "And you ordered—high tea," she adds, registering the oddness of the choice like a question.

"Come on, Franny. Why don't we just sit down and enjoy it?" Jae says.

"No!" She stabs his chest with her finger. "You're not the one who gets to decide that!"

In the background, she sees one of the waiters briefly enter and exit the room through a swinging door without putting his teapot down. He probably heard them arguing and decided it was best to leave, which is mortifying. Worse still, he probably caught the tail end of what Franny said and assumed that she was the source of all the tension. Franny is distraught. Months and months of planning, for this.

"I can't believe you," she says, though she's not certain which part of the situation is hardest to believe. She focuses on the most immediate, obvious issue. She's dressed in traditional clothes while Jae is wearing his usual uniform of ripped jeans and a T-shirt. "If you weren't sure what we were doing, then you should have asked me. You shouldn't have just assumed . . ."

"I tried calling your cabin, but no one—"

"Then you should have tried harder!"

Ma waves her hands in the air like she used to when they were children and she couldn't stand the sight of them. "Ay, stop fighting. Let's just eat. Where's your husband?"

Jae and Esther suddenly seem to notice that Tom isn't there. Although no one has particularly warmed to him during the five years that he and Franny have been together, Ma does recognize the obligation of inviting Tom to family gatherings, even when she doesn't want him around and he doesn't want to be included. Franny can feel everyone staring at her now, waiting for an answer to Ma's question. She considers the possibilities. *He didn't want to come.* Or a softer alternative: *I'm not sure where he is.* She wonders if the satellite phone is working yet. If it is, then she has a reasonably good guess. *He's trying to find out what happened to the woman he was sleeping with. Or in love with.* She doesn't know which version is true.

"Tom's not feeling well," she says instead. "He's sorry he couldn't make it." She assumes they all know she's lying, but they don't react except to nod or avert their eyes, as if they never believed he was coming in the first place. Franny thanks God he's not here to see this—the big celebration they fought over, the one he said Ma wouldn't appreciate.

Through the porthole-size window in the swinging door, she notices two sets of eyes staring out at them. Franny waves the men in. "Let's just start."

Tuxedoed waiters arrive with individual china pots of hot water and sachets of tea arranged in large wooden boxes for them to choose from. The presentation is over the top, but after so many decadent dinners and elaborate buffets, high tea doesn't feel particularly special or even appetizing to Franny. Everyone else seems to feel the same. They help themselves to small, obligatory portions, including Esther, who limits herself to just three small triangles of sandwiches and a single éclair. Once they sit down with their plates, they all make quiet, inane observations about the food. "It's so good." "They did a nice job." "Everything's very pretty." Franny senses the larger topic looming over the table, but strangely, her whereabouts after the attacks never come up. It's the only surprise of the day for which she's actually grateful.

Directly behind Ma are the flower arrangements that Franny complained about, now spiked with birds of paradise. As she studies the clumsy, last-minute addition of the bright orange stems, she continues to fume—at Tom, for telling everyone what happened; at Jae, for not doing what he agreed to do; at Esther, for not being able to convince him; and most of all, at Ma, for not appearing to care whether they celebrated her or not. Lindsay checks in to ask how they're enjoying the tea service, to which they mumble a chorus of "fine" and "thank you," but no one, not even Esther, gets up for a second helping, which makes Franny feel guilty about all the food that's about to go to waste. The words spin around and around, circling the drain in her head. *What a waste.*

She sets her cup down too hard, and a dark brown splash of tea blooms across the tablecloth. Ma and Jae, who are seated across from her, don't seem to notice. They're looking at something behind her. She turns to find a ponytailed man holding a giant camera. He's tall but hunched over, creeping toward them the way a wildlife photographer might when he doesn't want to spook his subjects.

"Hello, so sorry . . ." He directs his comments at Franny. "So sorry to disturb, but Lindsay said you'd requested a family photo?" British people always sound so apologetic to her, but the man's tone is even more apologetic than usual. One of the waitstaff probably warned him that they were arguing. Or perhaps he just observed their funereal interactions and came to that conclusion himself.

Franny doesn't know how to respond. It's customary for families to take group photos at these events while everyone is dressed up. But what kind of picture would this be? Why would anyone want to document what happened here today?

"Should we take a photo?" she asks Ma.

Ma, who's still wearing her mirrored sunglasses perched in her windblown hair, shakes her head no, confirming what Franny suspected. The photographer looks relieved to be sent away.

The nervous clink and clank of silverware subsides soon after. As a busboy clears away their dishes, Franny decides it's time to get on with it. She removes Ma's gift from her purse and slides it across the table. She didn't bother to wrap it. The signature red box from Cartier seemed like wrapping enough.

"This is for you."

"But I thought the cruise was the gift."

"I wanted to get you something special for your birthday. In addition to the cruise." Franny glances at Jae, daring him to protest.

"But it's already too much," Ma says, even before she opens the box to find the watch inside. It's a Panthère de Cartier. Eighteen thousand dollars' worth of rose gold and glittering diamonds surrounding a petite, rectangular face—perfectly sized for Ma's small wrist. For someone who appreciates fine watches, the sight of it would probably elicit some kind of reaction, a gasp even. But Ma just stares at it for a while, her mouth a thin, flat line.

"It's engraved," Franny says.

Ma pulls the watch out from its casing and examines the backside. "I can't read this." She stretches her arm out, trying to hold it farther away.

Esther wipes her hands on a napkin before gently pinching the face between her fingers. "To Ma," she reads, squinting. "Thank you for everything. Franny." She exchanges a look with Jae before handing the watch back.

"It's nice." Ma clears her throat. "I don't know where I'll wear it, but it's very nice."

Wearing the watch was never the point. Franny just wanted to show Ma that she was worth it, that maybe their whole lives had been worth it if one of her children could afford to do this for her. Jae finishes off his tea, his expression unreadable. If he's upset that she got Ma an extra gift without discussing it with him first, he doesn't let on.

Ma returns the watch to its box, which has a clamshell lid that closes with a loud, sharp clap. "It's very nice," she repeats, tucking the box into her beach bag. "Very heavy."

The *chilsun* feels over now. Although Franny didn't think Ma would weep or beam or hug at the end of the event—those were other people, other types of parents—she realizes that she'd allowed herself to hope for some sort of reaction to the watch, even a very small one. She feels foolish now, embarrassed that both Tom and Jae were right. No one wanted this except her.

"So, should we go?" she asks, trying to put everyone, herself included, out of their misery.

"But the bow," Jae says. "We haven't done the bow yet."

There's a crudely scribbled drawing on the front of his T-shirt. A single continuous white line that could be an electrical current or a figure playing the guitar. Jae has been wearing the same shirt for several years. It's faded now, with tiny holes in the sleeves that allow his newly tanned skin to peek through. As soon as Franny saw him walk in, she assumed they wouldn't bow, which infuriated her. It was the thing she'd looked forward to doing most. At birthday celebrations at the restaurant, she used to watch how everyone, especially the parents, seemed so proud when the adult children, dressed in their *hanboks*, stood in front of the guest of honor and slowly lowered themselves to the floor. Franny studied their movements—how they rested the backs of their hands against their foreheads and then bowed so low and deep, their heads touched the floor as a sign of their respect and gratitude. This was usually the moment when she saw the parents cry, or at least wipe their eyes to avoid crying.

"Franny," Jae repeats. "Shouldn't we do the bow?"

Everyone is looking at her now. It seems disrespectful for Jae to do this dressed like he's about to perform in his old grunge band. But he wants to, and Ma—Franny can't tell what she wants. She gets up from the table, gathering her voluminous skirt in one hand. Jae follows her as they stand in front of Ma, who's staring at both of them impassively. Franny puts her right hand over her left, her left foot in front of her right, and lowers herself to both knees. Out of the corner of her eye, she can see Jae performing the same motions, but with his hands and feet reversed, the way men are supposed to do.

As she drops her forehead to the ground, the room begins to disappear. The overhead lights fade, replaced by darkness. Franny feels the cold tile against her skin and closes her eyes, returning to the place that she's been running from. There's no avoiding it anymore, no pretending that it happened only to strangers. A noise escapes from her mouth that barely sounds human, and suddenly she's sobbing. Wailing. Unable to quiet herself or stop the tears. All those people, she thinks. All those people, dead and lost and taken, and here she is, living this miserable, miserable life.

ONE OF FRANNY'S earliest clients at the firm was a retired architect named Alex Tuttle. Over the course of his career, Alex had accumulated several investment properties that had grown significantly in value, but he had no will, which was alarming for someone of his age and net worth. At their first meeting, Franny learned why he'd never made it a priority, despite being financially savvy enough to know better. His parents were dead, and he had no partner, children, siblings, close friends, or even distant relatives to name as his beneficiaries—a fact that didn't seem to bother him when he mentioned it.

Franny prepared a will and trust on his behalf that addressed Alex's most immediate concern, the one that had seemingly prompted his interest in estate planning—arranging for the care of his newly adopted rescue dogs in the likely event that he predeceased them. The rest, he decided, would be divided between Yale, his alma mater; and three regional animal shelters whose work he supported. Once all the paperwork was finalized, he seemed relieved, possibly even content, but Franny didn't understand how he could be. The act of planning for his death had made the truth so glaringly obvious, at least to her. Alex was alone. He had no one. He was the person she most feared becoming.

When Franny finally lifts her head from the ground, she expects to find herself alone. But Jae is sitting a few feet away from her, cross-legged on the floor with his hands folded in his lap.

"Where—where did she go?" She turns around, confirming that she and her brother are the only people left in the room.

"Esther walked her out."

Franny sits up and wipes the tears from her eyes. Her hands look dirty when she pulls them away, zebra-streaked with runny mascara.

"Please don't say 'I told you so.'"

"I wasn't going to."

"But you're thinking it. I know you are."

Jae doesn't respond. He just stares at his lap. Franny does the same, counting all the watery dots of eye makeup on her skirt, which has billowed around her like a mushroom. She worries that the mascara stains won't come out of the delicate silk, but realizes it hardly matters. She doesn't think she'll ever wear her *hanbok* again.

Behind the service door window, several waiters and busboys are crowding around to get a better look, no longer trying to be discreet. Franny can't blame them. What a sight they must be, sitting on the floor—Jae in his jeans and flip-flops, she all in pink, the guest of honor nowhere to be found. The servers have probably never witnessed a party like this one before.

"Get away from the door!" a woman's voice hisses. Franny catches a brief glimpse of Lindsay through the window, shooing away the staff. She seems frustrated, apologetic, worried—all the same things that Franny feels.

"Disaster," she mumbles, drawing a knee up and resting her chin on it. The crinolines under her skirt itch, but she can't be bothered to do anything about them.

"What did you say?"

"Ma's *chilsun*. It was a disaster."

Jae makes no effort to confirm or deny this, but Franny doesn't need him to. "You were right," she says. "I never should have done it. Any of it."

He studies his fingernails, which are short and ragged, bitten down to the quick. An old habit from childhood that he hasn't been able to break. He appears to be considering his next words very carefully. "Why did you, then? Why wasn't it enough just to take her on the cruise like we planned?"

If they were close, Franny would tell him. But they haven't been close in such a long time, not since their older brother died and the trio they used to be was reduced to a pair, their roles suddenly and violently recast. Franny as the eldest child, Jae as the only son. It feels like their orbits have been moving further and further away from each other ever since. She gives him the simplest answer she can think of that still feels true.

"It's tradition."

"But that's what I don't understand, Franny. Ma's not really traditional. You always acted like she was, like she expected these kinds of things from us—"

"Just because she doesn't talk about what she expects or deserves doesn't mean she's not traditional. She's still Korean. We may have been born here, but we are too."

"Franny," Jae says emphatically. "I live at home and I never finished college. Plus, I'm dating Esther, who's great. Really great," he quickly adds. "But you've seen what Esther's like. If Ma were some old-school, traditional *umma,* you think any of this would ever fly?"

That's because she loves you, she thinks. Franny can even imagine the way Ma justifies her leniency with Jae. Why alienate the only son she has left? Why not keep him close, baby him, let him do whatever he wants so he never grows up or goes away—especially since she has Franny around to do the hard work of being the adult child?

"If she doesn't care about tradition, then why did you want to do the bow?"

Jae looks at the floor, breaking the longest stretch of eye contact they've had since the cruise began. "I figured it was the least I could do. You know, since I couldn't afford to pay."

"Well, I didn't tell her that." But even as Franny hears herself saying these words out loud, she knows it's just a technicality. The part of her that's wounded and resentful has considered telling Ma that he didn't pay his share at least a dozen times, and wanting to do something but not actually doing it is different from what she's claiming.

"That almost makes it worse, Franny. Besides, she probably assumes. I've been out of work since June."

Like his grand scheme to start a ringtone company, this is also news to her. She wants to ask what happened to the job he was so excited about six months ago—overseeing the renovation of a large Korean supermarket in Leonia—but she already knows. It's the same thing that happened to his last job, and the job before that, and every job he's ever had. Her brother has always been an impossible combination of smart and impatient, with an allergy to hard work that's followed him through brief stints in retail, tech support, property management, and construction—jobs that he considered beneath him, which probably made him an awful employee.

"When are you ever going to change, Jae? Ma's seventy now, and you're not—you're not reliable. You can barely take care of yourself much less her." She notices him straightening up as if he's about to protest and raises her hand to stop him. "I'm the one who always has to deal with her doctors and the accountant and the insurance company. I'm the one who handles all the things she doesn't know how to do on her own. But what if I wasn't around, Jae? What if something happened to me?"

"Stop yelling. I'm sitting right—"

"No! No, I won't stop. What would you do if I hadn't . . ."

Franny leaves the sentence unfinished, but they both know how it ends. She unfolds her legs, feeling the savage itch of the crinolines against her skin. She scratches herself through the fabric while Jae stares at his hands in his lap.

"I'm a lot of things, Franny. But I'm not stupid. When all that shit went down last week, I had this thought. And I'll be the first to admit—this is probably going to make me sound like an asshole, but I'm trying to be honest here. I knew your office was in that area, so all I could think was—what if you were gone? How was I ever going to live up or take your place if that's what I had to do? And then to find out that you were actually there . . ."

Jae is still talking, but Franny is too busy replaying what he just told her. She's shaken by his string of admissions, particularly the last. She recognizes that it was simultaneously the most selfish thing he's ever said and the closest thing to an acknowledgment of the weight she carries for them both.

" . . . I'm sorry. Sorry that happened to you. It must have been scary as hell. I mean, it was scary for us, and we were just watching it on TV, trying to call you."

"You and Esther called me?"

"What?" He looks confused for a moment. "No. Esther wasn't there. I'm talking about me and Ma."

"Ma called me?"

"Of course she did."

"She told you that?"

"She didn't have to. I was there. I turned on the news during breakfast and saw what was going on, so we both started calling, but the phone lines were all messed up and we kept getting busy signals."

Franny doesn't understand. If the two of them had been trying to reach her, then why didn't Ma sound relieved when Franny finally got through? Why didn't she say they'd been trying to call instead of insisting that Franny was the one who'd called first? She asks Jae, who looks at her like the answer should be obvious.

"She was scared."

"But then why didn't she just say so instead of hanging up?"

"*Franny.*" His tone is incredulous, almost exasperated, but his expression is pure pity. "Since when do any of us talk about the things we're afraid of?"

15.

It's Formal Night on the *Sonata*. All the men in the dining room are dressed in tuxedos or dark suits, while all the women sparkle and glitter and shine in their evening gowns. Doug's tux, a rental from a wedding store in L.A., smells like a toxic blend of dry-cleaning chemicals and plastic—something he didn't notice until he unzipped the flimsy garment bag it came in just minutes before dinner. Twice now, the woman seated to his left has wrinkled her nose and looked around the room with a bewildered expression, asking no one in particular, "What on earth is *that smell*?" The wording of her question, coupled with the sharpness of her tone, brings back the hot flicker of shame that Doug used to feel in church as a boy, scrubbed clean and dressed in his good Sunday suit but unable to rid himself of the all-permeating stink of the farm.

Adding to Doug's discomfort is the woman's husband, who's been interrogating him for the past ten minutes like he bought the right to with the cost of his fare. Among the many things the man wants to know: which guest stars were the most fun to work with, which ports of call were his favorite, what he's been up to since the show went off the air, how he likes living out in California, why a good-looking guy like him isn't married, what the dating scene is like in Hollywood for men their age. The onslaught of questions reminds Doug why he tries to avoid situations like this, meeting strangers who assume his life is an open book because he was on TV.

Doug scrapes the candied pecans off his salad with a fork, moving them to the side of his plate in an attempt to buy a moment of pause. The husband keeps using Doug's name in conversation, tacking it on to the ends of his questions like they're old friends, but for the life of him, Doug can't remember his. After dining with a different group of Captain's Club members every night, names are like water through a sieve.

"Are you sure I can't pour you a glass of this wine?" Chatterbox asks, holding the bottle menacingly over Doug's empty glass. "It's a terrific merlot."

"Oh, no. No, thank you." He turns his glass upside down, exchanging a glance with Gideon, who's sitting across the table. He wishes one of the servers would take the glass away because he doesn't put it past the man to insist. "I'm emceeing the karaoke contest tonight. I have to stay sharp."

Chatterbox makes no effort to hide his disappointment, and Doug understands why. He enjoys drinking more when others are doing it with him.

"Now tell me . . ." Mrs. Chatterbox drains her glass, which her husband fills without being asked. Doug has a good guess about what's to follow. So far, all she's wanted to talk about are the elaborate Bob Mackie evening gowns and Gloria Vanderbilt sportswear that the actresses wore on every episode. "Did you get to keep any of the clothes they made for the show?"

"I think the ladies got to keep some of their pieces from Wardrobe, but I didn't." He considers adding that his character mostly wore tank tops and tight shorts but decides against it. How could anyone forget?

A few tables away, an animated Renee is telling her rapt Captain's Club members a story, while Alan has his group in stitches, holding their stomachs and wiping away tears. Doug hopes the Chatterboxes don't feel cheated. He doesn't have Renee's natural charm or Alan's comedic talents, but he's committed to being as interested in his tablemates as he can, ready to talk or just listen like his character on the show. He senses that's what everyone on the ship wants from him, the whole reason why Aria brought him back.

His conversation with Kevin earlier today spooked him. He hasn't been able to stop thinking about it all afternoon. Doug was paid fifty percent of his appearance fee up front. It's the biggest check he's seen in a while—a rare source of financial security for him. The acting jobs have been dropping off year after year, and like most ensemble players who were on television in the seventies, his residuals are a joke. If Aria decided to withhold the balance of his payment for violating his contract or harassing a guest, he wouldn't be able to hire a lawyer, and he doubts he can rely on Annette to help. The lawyers in her once-considerable Rolodex probably aren't even practicing anymore.

Even though Doug knows he didn't leer at anyone, the accusation is still unsettling. It reminds him that he escaped judgment for his bad behavior all those years ago, but maybe the universe has a dark sense of humor and a delayed sense of justice. Doug is convinced that if he could just talk to Minnie Mouse—he should probably start referring to her as "Mrs. Hamm" instead of "Minnie Mouse"— if he could just talk to Mrs. Hamm and explain that he was staring at his face on her T-shirt, not her breasts, she'd probably understand. Maybe she'd even laugh at the irony of the situation. He was short with her because she'd interrupted an important conversation in which he was telling his nephew *not* to leer at women.

"So, who did all the men's costumes on the show?" Mrs. Chatterbox asks.

Doug has no idea. On any given shooting day, he just wore whatever the wardrobe assistants told him to wear, but that's clearly not what she wants to hear. He plucks a vaguely familiar name buried deep in his memory, hoping he pronounces it correctly. "I believe Pierre Cardin was responsible for some of them."

"Oh, my. And did you ever meet Mr. Cardin?"

Was there a Mr. Cardin? he wonders. "I'm afraid not."

"Well, that's too bad." She pauses, waiting for something else to follow. When it doesn't, she makes an observation about the wine, which she says has hints of blueberries. Her husband stares unhappily at Doug's upturned glass, wondering aloud if she's confusing blueberries and blackberries again. They go back and forth about this for a while, but it's clear that neither of them really cares.

The salad course isn't even over yet and the conversation feels like it's about to dead end into silence. Doug wishes some of the other people at the table would jump in, but Gideon is busy talking to the Chatterboxes' granddaughter, which is nice, actually—he finally has someone his own age to connect with—and the Asian family looks like they're attending a funeral. The three of them—an elderly woman and an oddly dressed pair in their twenties or thirties—have barely said a word since introducing themselves and taking their seats. There are two empty chairs between the young man and woman, who don't seem to have any interest in talking to each other, much less to him. He worries they might not know who he is and they're confused by the addition of new people to their assigned table so late into the cruise.

"So, were you all fans of the show when it was on?" He makes an attempt to engage them anyway. "*Starlight Voyages*," he adds, just in case.

The man in the T-shirt and wrinkled blue suit nods without enthusiasm. "It's been a while since we've seen it," he says. "But yeah, we remember you."

Doug is relieved to be spared the humiliation of explaining who he is, though he can't help but parse the man's language. Seeing the show isn't the same as liking it. And remembering him isn't the same as wanting him around. "Well, tell me about yourselves, folks. How long have you been in the Captain's Club?" He turns to the elderly woman, who's been fussing with a loose thread on her jacket. He assumes she's the frequent cruiser because she's in the right age demographic for it, so he's surprised when the young woman with several piercings raises her hand.

"This is her first time," she says. "I'm the Captain's Club member."

"Oh." It was impossible not to notice Nose Ring when she first approached their table. Unlike the other women in the dining room, floating around in their airy silks and satins and chiffons, she was wearing a dress that was little more than a long black tube of fabric, so tight that he could see her hip bones jutting out underneath. "If you don't mind me saying, you're . . ." Best behavior, he thinks. *Be on your best behavior.* Doug realizes it might be offensive to tell her that she doesn't look like the typical cruiser, so he opts for a more benign alternative. "You're much younger than most of the people who usually take cruises."

She shrugs like she's heard this before. Her biggest earrings, a pair of long, needly spikes, graze her bare shoulders. "I like to travel," she says, yanking her dress up to cover more of her chest, which Doug takes care not to watch. "Cruising's the cheapest way to do it if you know how to look for a deal. Plus, once you book, someone else does all the planning for you."

"Isn't that the truth?" Mr. Chatterbox butts in. "We've been in the Captain's Club for eight years. It's nice to just pick the dates we want to travel and then let all these good people take care of the rest. They're such pros at it."

Doug realizes that the comment was probably made at that moment for the benefit of Johannes, their headwaiter, who mercifully has a name tag affixed to his lapel. He's hovering over their table, studiously watching the busboys clear the salad plates. If he overheard the compliment, he doesn't let on. He just inquires about the first course—"You all enjoyed it, yes?"—like he's asking a question, but he's not. Not really. It sounds more like a statement that they have to affirm by nodding and dutifully mumbling "yes."

As the entrées arrive from the kitchen to replace the salads, Doug catches himself staring at Blue Suit and Nose Ring, trying to understand their strange energy. It seems like they're both upset about something, possibly each other. Or maybe they're upset with the people missing from their group, the ones who should be sitting in the empty seats between them. At first, Doug expected a pair of stragglers to run in, apologizing for their lateness. But at this point in the meal, he doubts anyone else is going to join them.

"Are we missing some folks tonight?" he asks, nervously throwing in a lame joke before he can stop himself. "I hope we didn't leave anyone onshore."

He laughs only once before the stiffness of their expressions stops him cold. Doug quickly picks up his napkin and coughs into it, as if he'd been coughing all along.

* * *

THE CHATTERBOXES, WHO have consumed two bottles of wine on their own, are now having a debate with their granddaughter about college. The girl keeps insisting that a bachelor's degree isn't really necessary anymore. She reminds them that Bill Gates and Steve Jobs dropped out of college in order to start their companies, and now look at them. This clearly irritates her grandfather, who asks if she thinks she's a genius like they are, a question that she doesn't dignify with a response.

"Gideon, you just graduated from Pomona. What do you make of all this?" Mrs. Chatterbox, the softer touch, asks.

Gid shrugs, chewing thoughtfully on a roll. "Most people would probably benefit from going, but I think it really depends on the person and what they want to do."

Both the granddaughter and the Chatterboxes seem satisfied by this, as if each believes his answer supports their point of view and cancels out the other. Doug has to hand it to his nephew, who's more politic than he was at the same age. He's also smart enough to take a large bite of his dinner, filling his mouth with mashed potatoes so the Chatterboxes can continue their debate without him.

Doug glances at his own dinner, not entirely sure what to do with it. He ordered his prime rib "medium," but the plate-size slab of beef in front of him barely looks cooked, and there's a well in the middle collecting an oily pool of blood-red juices. He saws off a slightly darker piece of meat from the end, tempted to send the whole thing back.

The Asian family isn't eating much more than he is. He wonders if the kitchen got their orders wrong too.

"Is yours a little . . . blue?" he asks, leaning toward the older woman beside him.

Her untouched prime rib almost appears raw in the light. Doug can't believe anyone would want to consume meat like this, but the woman is so quiet. He suspects she wouldn't complain unless someone else did.

"Blue?"

"Rare." He pokes his fork into the center of his meat, forcing more bloody juices to ooze out. "Mine's pretty rare. Is that how you like yours?"

The woman isn't listening. The question is barely out of his mouth before her attention begins to drift. Her children are finally talking to each other, furtively whispering across the two empty seats between them.

"I told you . . ." Nose Ring says. "She's not coming."

"What am I supposed to do—"

"You should have apologized."

"For what? She said it was a bad idea."

Their voices are low, and occasionally, Doug thinks he might have missed a few words here or there, but he understands the gist of their conversation. He can tell how upset they are. The Chatterboxes too. His dining companions all seem like people who have been stuck with each other for four days and are barely keeping it together anymore. He glances at Renee and Alan again. The two of them are still holding court, giving their Captain's Club members a nice memory to share with their friends when they return home. Doug knows he should be doing the same, but instead, he's listening to arguments break out on both sides of the table.

"Absolutely not, Allison," Chatterbox snaps. His wife immediately touches his forearm, patting it several times to calm him, which seems to have little effect. "We put that money away for your education. We're not just giving it to you to buy a car."

"But how am I supposed to get a job if I can't drive anywhere?"

"Who's going to hire you without a degree? Some store at the mall?"

"Maybe. People work at the mall, Grandpa."

Doug and Gideon smile weakly at each other—relieved, perhaps, that they don't belong to either of these families. They're just visitors passing through. Doug turns his head from left to right, stretching the stiff muscles. All the day's tension has collected in his neck. He's tempted to sit quietly and count the minutes until dinner is over, but the words "best behavior" continue to ring in his ears. He reminds himself to do his job. Be kind, be gracious, be interested in his fellow passengers. Talk.

"So what brought you on this cruise?" he asks the woman, who may not be listening to him, but she's listening more than anyone else is. "Just a vacation, or are you celebrating something special?"

"It's my birthday."

"Today's your birthday?"

She winces and raises a finger to her lips. "Ay, I don't want those two to hear."

Her visible distaste for the still-squabbling Chatterboxes suddenly endears her to him. "Well, I hope you're having a nice day?" He says this as brightly as he can, even though it's obvious she's not.

"My children gave me this cruise for a gift." She pretends to wipe her mouth, covering it with her hand so that only he can hear. "What a headache."

Doug looks back and forth from the son to the daughter. The smooth, unlined faces they arrived with are now all sharp angles and lines as they continue arguing under their breath. He wonders if they might be half siblings. He doesn't see any resemblance between them, aside from their taste in clothes.

"She's my son's girlfriend," the woman says. "My daughter and her husband aren't here tonight."

Doug understands who the empty chairs belong to now. He can't imagine going to all the trouble of booking a cruise as a birthday gift for someone but not coming to dinner on their actual birthday. And on Formal Night, no less. Judging from the effort put into the décor, the second to last night of the cruise is clearly meant to be the high point of the sail. The pink and silver dining room has been transformed into a dramatic black and-white-ballroom, complete with a ceiling lit up like the night sky. There's a live band in the corner, twelve men in lavender tuxedos playing quiet jazz standards until dinner ends. Afterward, the signage around the ship proclaims, everyone will DANCE UNDER THE STARS!

"Birthdays can be stressful," he says weakly, thinking of his own.

Gideon is always good about sending a card, although Doug suspects his mom picks them out because a boy his age would never be drawn to such terrible poems. Sometimes his brother remembers to call. Sometimes he doesn't, but who could blame him? Doug was absent and irresponsible for most of their adult lives, particularly when their parents were old and needed care. It will take a long time to get back into his brother's good graces. The only other person he hears from on his birthday is Annette, who calls and asks how he's planning to celebrate. Every year, Doug tells her the same thing: his friends are taking him out for dinner. In case she asks "Which friends?" he's always ready to recite the names of his therapist, yoga instructor, AA sponsor, and book club leader.

"I think I might send my food back to the kitchen," he says. "The meat's too rare. Would you like me to ask them to do the same with yours?"

The woman shakes her head. "The people who made it will be upset."

Doug's instinct is to protest, but she adds, "I owned a restaurant for thirty years." She takes a bite of her blue prime rib, chewing it slowly until a great big lump of it labors down her throat. Doug wants to tell her that she doesn't need to do that, to suffer through her own birthday dinner, but the arguments on both sides of the table are getting louder and louder. Judging from her expression, the woman is suffering already.

"She has every right to be mad," Nose Ring says.

"But the three of us decided—"

On the other end of the table, Mrs. Chatterbox sets her empty wineglass down too hard. A piece of silverware falls on the floor and a busboy appears out of nowhere to collect it. "That's enough, Allison. Stop upsetting your grandfather."

"I'm just talking, Grandma. Why can't I talk without him getting upset?"

"Because you're not saying anything remotely sensible," Chatterbox grumbles.

Doug turns his attention back to the Asians, catching Nose Ring in mid-sigh.

"I really think you need to apologize to her," she says.

"Why?"

"Because she paid for everything! Because she paid for us to be here."

"Jesus, Esther. Lower your voice." The son's eyes dart around the table. Doug averts his just in time to avoid being caught eavesdropping.

Esther abruptly turns to the woman. "Nancy, shouldn't I go get her, at least for dessert? Jae doesn't think so, but I worry she'll regret missing this."

Everyone, including Doug, watches her and waits for a response. She frowns at her lap for a while, holding a napkin tightly in both hands. Just when it seems like she's decided to ignore the question altogether, Nancy nods her head yes.

BY THE TIME the third course begins, Doug is both hungry and anxious. Hungry, because he barely touched his prime rib, and anxious, because Jae and Esther have been gone too long—at least fifteen minutes and counting. He worries that dinner will be over before they come back with the missing daughter—a thought that Nancy probably shares, judging from the way she's continuously scanning the room. Adding to the tension is Johannes, who treats the sight of uneaten food on his tables like a personal affront. He keeps needling them with questions about the temperature of the beef, which Doug chose not to send back, opting to graze on string beans and potatoes instead.

"I ate before," Nancy finally says, looking as anxious as Doug feels. "I was full."

Johannes turns to Doug, who doesn't know what to say except the same. "Me too. I had a very late lunch."

"Well . . ." Johannes smiles, but he doesn't seem convinced. "I hope you both have room for an extra-special dessert." He checks his watch and hurries off like he's late for a meeting.

Their table has noticeably thinned out since the dinner service began. Jae and Esther were the first to leave. Then Allison, fed up with her grandfather, decided to skip dessert and dragged Gideon off to the arcade. Now it's just the four of them, and Doug gets the distinct impression that Nancy doesn't like the Chatterboxes. She may not even like him. What a birthday, he thinks. It occurs to him that people who have children can be just as lonely on their birthdays as people who don't.

The band plays a loud trill, and the light operator who's projecting stars onto the ceiling swings one of his spotlights toward a set of double doors. Accompanied by the frantic, reedy notes of the "Flight of the Bumblebee," two dozen servers suddenly stream out of the kitchen, rolling shiny metal carts. In perfectly choreographed time, they form a circle in the middle of the room, and then pinwheel out to their assigned stations. Everyone cheers, applauding the effort at showmanship. When Doug sees what the carts contain—dozens of individual soufflés in small white ramekins—he realizes why they're making such a production out of the rush to serve. He's about to remark to Nancy that it will be a miracle if they can get so many soufflés out before they collapse, but she's not paying any attention to them. Instead, she's staring at Johannes, who's approaching their table at the opposite speed, taking slow, intentional steps. Balanced on his silver platter is a cake with a tall, firecracker-like candle burning brightly in the center that he's trying to keep lit. Johannes sings the first few words of "Happy Birthday," which is all it takes to get everyone in the dining room to join in, their voices rising toward the ceiling.

The closer he gets, the more Nancy stiffens. She looks like she's about to burst into tears. As Johannes sets the cake down on their half-empty table, Mr. Chatterbox suddenly seems to take notice of his surroundings.

"Hey, where'd your kids go?" he asks. "They should be here for this."

Nancy ignores him and blows out the candle with an anticlimactic huff before the song even ends. Johannes finally seems to register that there's more going on here than undercooked beef, but he doesn't know how to respond any more than the rest of them do. Doug thinks about his character Mack, how the writers made him too good to be true. He always knew what to say or do when people were down, so much so that two minutes of screen time with Mack was usually enough to trigger a change for the better in another character's arc. Doug tries to channel that spirit now, to be possessed by it as he gets up from his seat and approaches the bandleader.

"Could you play something slow?" he asks, grateful that the man seems to know who he is.

Heads turn and voices whisper as Doug returns to his table. When he extends his hand to Nancy, nearby diners begin to applaud. She gawps at him, confused, but Mrs. Chatterbox catches on immediately.

"He's asking you for a dance!"

Nancy shakes her head. "Ay, no. No. I don't—I don't know how."

"Don't worry," Doug says encouragingly, just as Mack would. "I'll teach you."

The lighting operator is now shining his spotlight on them. Nancy is either squinting because of the glare or flinching because of the attention. Doug's hand remains extended. His heart is about to burst through his chest. *What if she refuses to get up?* But before the humiliating possibility of this begins to sink in, he remembers what allowed him to play Mack for all those years. The part was so ridiculous, the lines so corny and predictable—the only way the character worked was to commit to him fully.

"Come on. It's your birthday," he says. "You deserve to have at least one good memory of it."

Nancy looks at him with dark, wet eyes—eyes that he doesn't know well enough to read. He's not sure if it's Mack who convinces her or the unrelenting sound of applause surrounding them on all sides—applause that simply won't take no for an answer. The diners murmur with approval as she puts her small hand in his and they walk to the center of the dance floor. In response to his request for something slow, the band is playing "Unforgettable" by Nat King Cole, which is more romantic than he'd like, but easy enough to dance to. Despite her initial protests, Nancy has a decent sense of rhythm, and she's a surprisingly pliable partner. After a few initial missteps, she allows herself to be led around the floor in big loops and she even gets the hang of the occasional spin, which delights the onlookers. Doug can tell from the rigidness of her face and posture that she's not enjoying this any more than he is. They're both just playing parts now.

Halfway through the song, the bandleader invites all the other diners to get up and join them. Once the dance floor begins to fill, Nancy quietly asks if they could please sit down. Doug escorts her back to their table, searching the room for her children, who are still nowhere to be found. As he helps her into her chair, the Chatterboxes applaud and compliment them, the unpleasantness with their granddaughter seemingly forgotten. Doug is so distracted by how slurred their speech sounds that he doesn't notice the middle-aged man approaching him, dressed in clothes for the pool instead of a tuxedo.

"Are you Doug Clayton?" he asks.

He nods, wondering how he could be mistaken for anyone else after that display on the dance floor.

"I want to talk to you about my wife."

As soon as Doug hears the word "wife," he knows who the man is. "Oh, I'm—I'm sorry, Mr. Hamm . . ." he stammers, and the man doesn't correct his assumption. Doug wants to explain that he was staring at his wife's shirt, not her breasts, but he fears that even using the word "breasts" will set Mr. Hamm off. He also senses that nothing he says will actually matter. The man's breath is yeasty and warm, and his skin bears the shiny, red-cheeked flush of someone who's been drinking for a while.

"Just shut up," he says, loud enough to turn heads. "You just shut up and listen."

Although they're both standing, Doug has to tilt his head back to get a good look at him. It's hard not to notice that Mr. Hamm is at least a foot taller and nearly a whole person wider. Nancy and the Chatterboxes, who have all gone quiet, have clearly registered this too. Their eyes are wide and unblinking as they alternate between Doug and Mr. Hamm and back again.

"You know, my wife loved your show. Loved it since before I met her. I don't know why. It always just seemed like a bunch of nonsense to me, but she was crazy about it—owned all the videos and everything—so when she heard we could take a cruise on the ship where the show was filmed, and some of the actors would be there too, I knew there wasn't any point arguing with her about whether or not I wanted to go. We were going." He almost laughs as he says this, but then his expression quickly darkens again. "Three years we saved up, and she was so excited when we finally booked, especially when she heard you were coming because she always said your character was her favorite. You know how disappointed she was to find out you're just some stuck-up Hollywood phony—"

"No, Mr. Hamm. It's not like that—"

"—some stuck-up Hollywood *phony* who actually looks down on the very people who line his goddamn pockets? She hasn't come out of our cabin since Monday! She wouldn't even get off the ship in Bermuda."

"Sir, please. Let me explain . . ." Doug drifts off, realizing that his defense for leering isn't what's needed here. Mr. Hamm is upset about the disrespect.

In the background, two uniformed security officers are approaching, summoned perhaps by the eagle-eyed Johannes, who's standing nearby. Doug wants them to keep their distance. Maybe if Mr. Hamm says everything he needs to say and gets it out of his system, he'll just wander back to whichever bar he came from.

"Sir, I'm very sorry I upset her. If you'd like me to apologize to your wife directly—"

"No! You think I want you going anywhere near her again? No way."

Mr. Hamm is shaking his head when he notices the officers lurking behind him. Doug knows what's about to happen before it even does. Their presence has given the man a reason to act out. Every muscle in Mr. Hamm's body tenses as he winds up to throw the punch. In the milliseconds that follow, Doug suddenly feels his breath get away from him. All the air is forced out of his diaphragm, his lungs, his throat, while a pain starts to swell in his gut. People are shouting now. As they scramble to get away, chairs tip over and thud, coffee cups and wineglasses shatter on the floor. The officers attempt to restrain Mr. Hamm, who's yelling things that Doug can't fully comprehend. He falls to one knee, trying to catch his breath, but the pain is too much to stay upright. He goes down like a tree and rolls over onto his back. The last thing he sees before he closes his eyes is the ceiling full of stars.

Thursday, September 20

AT SEA

16.

The woman at the Guest Services desk with the charming Irish accent—the one Lucy first spoke to about her missing luggage—doesn't sound quite so charming when she's annoyed.

"You want to know how long it'll take to *dial the phone*?" she asks, repeating the question in a way that suggests it's idiotic.

"No. That's not . . . Didn't you just say I'd have to enter my credit card number and then wait for the system to connect?"

The woman nods, but uncertainly, like she's missing something.

"So, what I'm asking is: *How—long—will—it—take—to—connect?* What kind of lag time should I be expecting?"

Lucy doesn't think this line of questioning is so strange. The *Sonata* is an older ship. Judging from the technical problems of the past few days, it's reasonable to assume that its communications system is older too. She probably shouldn't have enunciated her words so slowly—the woman doesn't seem to appreciate that—but they've been talking for almost ten minutes and Lucy has no more clarity than she did when she first arrived.

"It's just like using a calling card, miss."

A pair of passengers walk by and wave at the woman. They thank her for recommending the wine-tasting class.

"Fabulous!" they shout in passing. "We loved it!"

"Oh, I'm so glad," she shouts back, in a voice completely different from the one she resumes with Lucy. "All you have to do is enter your card number and dial, and your call will go through pretty much immediately."

Lucy pauses on the words "pretty much." The left half of her brain rejects this description as too loose, too prone to human interpretation and error. "But what does 'pretty much' mean?" she asks. "I don't want to dial and then sit through a delay while the system connects. I have to be on time for this call."

"Apologies, miss," the woman says tightly. "What I meant to say is that the call will connect immediately, assuming everything works as it should."

Assuming everything works as it should.

Lucy failed to inherit her mother's natural ease with people; she's much more her father's child in this respect. She tries to channel her mom now, recalling how she could ingratiate herself with almost anyone—irritable bus drivers and unhelpful shop clerks, nervous parents of Lucy's classmates who weren't sure if their daughters should sleep over at their home. Unlike her father, who assumed that racism was at the root of almost every negative interaction in their lives, her mother preferred not to think about the cause and focus on the corrective. A little kindness, Mom believed, could go a long way. Usually, she started by just saying the person's name over and over again like they were old friends, and then sharing something in confidence with them.

"Siobhan . . ." Lucy begins hesitantly, pronouncing the unfamiliar combination of letters on the woman's name tag as "see-oh-bawn."

"It's shiv-VAWN."

"Yes, Shiv-VAWN. Sorry about that, and sorry to keep asking you all these questions. I'm just nervous about the call. It's a job interview—a really important one."

Siobhan looks startled for a moment. "Miss, you understand that ship-to-shore calls are fifteen dollars a minute, right?"

Lucy has already done the math. If the interview lasts thirty minutes, she'll be out $450. If it lasts an hour—which would actually be a sign that things are going well—it will cost her $900, an amount that makes her queasy. She tries not to think about how that's more than her share of the rent, or how her card will be close to maxed out afterward, with no hope of paying it off anytime in the near future. In moments like this, she understands why her parents are so uptight about money—making it, having it, putting so much away. The best thing money can buy is freedom from worry.

"It's not like they gave me any choice about the meeting time."

This is the first thing Lucy has said that elicits anything remotely resembling sympathy from Siobhan.

"If I want this job, I have to talk to them when they want to talk to me," she adds. "It's a big company. You know how it is."

"But that's terrible." Siobhan almost seems offended by the idea. "They probably didn't even think twice about interrupting your vacation."

Lucy is reminded that her mother used to do this too—find a common enemy. The supermarket manager who walked around the store like a little emperor; the careless, inconsiderate drivers on the road. "I suppose if I get the job, it'll all be worth it."

Siobhan lifts and lowers her eyebrows, seemingly unconvinced. "You should probably start entering your credit card info a couple minutes before the call. If there's any delay at all—and I'm not saying there will be—but if there is, it's usually on the payment processor's side. They might need a minute or two to accept the charge. After that, it's just like dialing a phone on land, assuming everything works as it should." Siobhan correctly predicts that Lucy is about to interject again. "The system's online and working now. That's all the guarantee I can give you, miss."

"Probably," "if," "usually," "might, "assuming." Lucy can't help but replay all the vague words, none of which inspires confidence. Still, she recognizes it's more information than she had before the conversation began. She also suspects it's the best she's going to get. She thanks Siobhan, embarrassed by her rude, impatient behavior. An old Sunday school lesson buried deep in her memory makes its way up to the surface. Something about a farmer and his crops. Although the details of the story have faded over time, the moral stayed with her—how the true nature of a person is revealed not when things are going well but when they're going poorly. She apologizes to Siobhan again.

Lucy returns to the empty suite an hour before the call is scheduled to start, mentally checking off the list of things she wanted to do beforehand: confirm that the phones are working and learn how to use them, make sure her suit is back from the cleaners, hang the DO NOT DISTURB sign on the door so the maids won't enter, ask Mariah to let her have the cabin to herself during the call. On her way back from Guest Services, she even stopped by the Grotto and asked Iain if he'd mind not coming by while she was on the phone. He seemed slightly surprised by the request—his daily visits to the suite have always been nocturnal—but Lucy wanted to anticipate every possible source of interruption.

It hasn't escaped her attention that she's going through an unusual—and expensive—amount of trouble for a job she's still not sure she wants, a job that will demand everything from her, probably for as long as she has it. But this is when she has to channel her father and remind herself not to reject a position that hasn't been offered to her yet. Also, how upset can anyone be about her trip to Bermuda if she aces the interview and advances to the next round? Other than missing some writing time and hours in the lab—hours that she'll make up and then some—the cruise actually won't have a negative effect on her work or future career. If she does well this afternoon, it will be as if she didn't go on the cruise at all.

Lucy removes her Brooks Brothers suit from the dry-cleaning plastic, relieved that she didn't damage it on the first day of the cruise when she fell asleep on the bathroom floor. She can't say the same for her button-down shirt, which is permanently stained with waterproof makeup. She puts it on because it's clean, at least, and the jacket covers the pale, brownish-orange streaks on the sleeve. On some level, she knows it's ridiculous to get dressed up for a phone interview. She could do the call with Rahm Mohan in her bathing suit and he'd never be the wiser. But the suit makes her feel confident and professional, which she hopes to convey through the sound of her voice.

Half an hour before the call, Lucy is dressed and sitting at the desk in the living room. All the lights in the suite are on, and the curtains on the balcony door are drawn to prevent any distracting glances at the ocean. Arranged in front of her are a copy of her résumé, a notebook and pen, and the folder of information she compiled before her meeting with the recruiter. Lucy is good at interviewing, always has been—probably because she's accustomed to explaining herself to different audiences—so she knows the nervous feeling in her gut isn't about the activity. It's more about where she's doing it and how many things outside of her control could go wrong. Also, going to such lengths to take the interview suggests that she's made some sort of decision about her future, but she hasn't yet.

Lucy looks at her reflection in the mirror above the desk, wondering if she'll ever get past the age when everything she does or doesn't do feels so momentous, like she's about to alter the course of her life. She tries to smile, just as she would during a face-to-face interview. Smiling, she's convinced, is something that people can hear through the phone, but her skin is still so dry from the sunburn. Just lifting the corners of her mouth makes her face feel like it's about to crack. She straightens up and tells herself to smile anyway.

"Thank you for speaking with me today," she says brightly, practicing a line she's used so many times before.

AT DR. JIMOH'S urging, Lucy spent weeks preparing for her first-round interviews, studying thick folders that she'd assembled about each company and their senior leadership. In comparison, she knows almost nothing about Rahm Mohan, an executive who's apparently high on the corporate ladder but not so high that his name came up in her earlier research. What little information she has about him is limited to his title—vice president of engineering; his current whereabouts—New York; and his interest in indexing and artificial intelligence; all details that were supplied by the recruiter.

Upon learning that both phone and Internet access on the ship had been restored after docking in Bermuda, Lucy tried to visit the business center to look Rahm up before their scheduled call. But every time she stopped by the sad little room, painted in a sickly shade of yellow, the lone workstation was occupied. Only this morning did she realize that it was always occupied by the same person.

Although the man had his back to the glass door, she recognized him by his posture, which she remembered thinking was odd during her previous visits. He was slumped so low in his chair that it almost seemed like he was sleeping.

Lucy felt a petulant flare of injustice, similar to the kind she experienced as a child when a classmate commandeered a certain piece of playground equipment, oblivious to anyone else's desire or right to use it. The business center was supposed to be a public space; it was rude to just camp out there. She pushed open the door without knocking and cleared her throat, intending to ask if she could have half an hour to prepare for a job interview. It didn't seem possible to sit in such a tight space for much longer than that.

The business center had proportions similar to a deep but narrow closet. Upon entering, Lucy was standing over the man in a way she would have found menacing if their positions had been reversed. She didn't intend to look at his screen, but it was impossible not to notice the open browser window with the words "CNN Special Report" written in bright red letters. Below this headline was a photo of one of the World Trade Center buildings in midcollapse.

The man looked up at her, his eyes red and glazed, probably from hours of reading under the glare of fluorescent lights. He turned back to the screen and clicked on a link, opening an article with a photo of the site where the towers used to stand.

"They haven't found any survivors for days," he said flatly, like he was telling her about the weather.

The laminated sign next to the workstation read INTERNET ACCESS: $4 PER MINUTE. PRINTOUTS: $1 PER PAGE. It seemed like the unpleasant room, combined with the high prices, was meant to encourage a speedy return to vacation mode. But this man obviously didn't care about being on vacation. Scattered across the table were several piles of paper that he'd printed, easily half a ream of articles about the attacks. How many thousands of dollars had he spent here in recent days? It made her phone call seem like nothing.

"I'm sorry," Lucy said, and she meant this in every possible way. She was sorry for intruding, sorry for assuming that her needs were more important than his own, sorry for his loss because it was clear that he'd suffered one far more personal than the confused, generalized loss she'd been carrying around for days.

As Lucy picks up the phone, she doesn't regret backing out of the business center and leaving the man alone. Although it's unlike her to be so unprepared for an interview, she's not convinced the interview will actually happen. By now, she's imagined and reimagined all the things that could go wrong—her credit card will be rejected, the system will go offline again right as she's about to dial, or maybe the call will go through but the sound quality will be so poor that she and Rahm won't be able to hear anything. They'll just shout at each other for a few minutes before he loses patience with her and hangs up.

Lucy enters her credit card number slowly, careful not to make a mistake that will send her back to the beginning. An automated voice tells her to wait, followed by nearly a minute of dead air. The longer she hears nothing—no music, no static, not even a hint of noise—the more convinced she is that the call failed. Lucy is about to hang up and try again when a prompt instructs her to enter a phone number, which she obeys. Afterward, she glances at her free hand, wondering why it feels so odd. She unwinds the cord wrapped around it, shaking out her numb, purpled fingers as a woman picks up and asks for her name. Lucy is startled to hear the voice on the other end, not only its presence but also its clarity, as if the woman is just in the next room. It takes all of ten seconds for the assistant to transfer the call to Rahm, who greets her warmly, and suddenly, Lucy is on. The interview that she didn't think would happen has begun.

"It's too bad we couldn't get together in person," he says. "Remind me, where are you calling from?"

By this point, Lucy has done so many interviews that she has an answer and an elevator pitch for everything. Almost everything. But not this ship. She's decided there's nothing she can do about where she is except tell the truth.

"I'm on a cruise, believe it or not."

Too many beats of pause follow.

"Seriously?"

"Yes."

In the background, Rahm's computer pings, followed by several clicks of a mouse. She assumes he's opening the message that just arrived or turning off his notifications.

"That's one way to make yourself memorable, I guess. Would you mind me asking why?"

She explains that she had a last-minute opportunity to travel to Bermuda for free, something she doesn't get to do very often as a graduate student. It actually sounds reasonable when she says it, plausible at the very least. "Plus, I was curious," she adds. "I've never been on a cruise before."

"Curious" is exactly the right word to use with Rahm. Curiosity, he says, is his language. He moves on with a laugh, noting the irony of interviewing someone who's finishing the same program he left after two semesters. Lucy wasn't aware that Rahm ever attended MIT, but she tries not to let on.

"Who was your adviser?" she asks.

"Tilman Perry. Is he still around?"

For the first time, Lucy is relieved to be talking on the phone instead of in person. Dr. Perry is an emeritus now, someone she hasn't thought of in a while. His last year of teaching was her first in the program, an overlap that was mercifully brief. At a reception to welcome new graduate students, she overheard him complaining to another faculty member about all the international students the program was letting in, how their accents were nearly impossible to understand and whenever they showed up in his lab, they always smelled of curry or garlic. Lucy went out of her way to avoid him afterward. If Dr. Perry spoke like this out in the open, in front of other people, she could only imagine what he might say about her behind closed doors.

"He's retired now."

"I figured. I left in eighty-nine and Perry was old even back then."

There's a pause, one that Lucy knows she's supposed to fill. The candidate should always be prepared to fill the silence, she can hear Dr. Jimoh telling her.

"He used to get drunk at receptions and say the most terrible, racist things about people," she says. "I was glad when he retired."

Without intending to, Lucy has wrapped the cord around her hand again. Her fingertips are almost white from the loss of blood. She stares at them, horrified, and then looks at herself in the mirror. *What are you doing? What are you doing? What are you doing?* she wants to shout.

"Sorry about that . . ." she stammers. "I don't know . . . I'm sorry."

"No, no. Don't be. Perry was one of the reasons I left. Just zero support from that guy. Zero empathy. I'm guessing it hasn't been easy for you either . . ."

Rahm drifts off before his words take the form of a question. She senses that he wants to hear about her struggles in the program, perhaps to reinforce whatever story he's told himself about why he couldn't finish. Lucy, however, can't allow herself to do this. It's hard enough to study something she's good at but doesn't feel inspired by. If she starts thinking about the small indignities and huge obstacles and deep, cutting hurts she's experienced along the way, she'll never be able to get out of bed, and then what? All the Dr. Perrys in the world, the people who assume she's had it easier because she's a woman, because she's Black, because their field is trying to diversify—they'll finally get what they wanted. Proof that she didn't belong in the first place. Lucy isn't about to give any of them that kind of satisfaction.

"I just put my head down and do my work," she says, hearing Dr. Jimoh's voice in her ear again, reminding her to focus on her research during interviews, always bring the conversation back to her research. "Would you like me to tell you what I've been up to lately?"

LUCY KEEPS WISHING Rahm would say something disturbing or problematic. But the longer they talk, the more conflicted she feels. He's not the unkind, unreasonable, or unbearable tech evangelist that she wants him to be. Judging by her mother's standards—standards that Lucy has been raised by and reminded of at every turn—Rahm demonstrates one of the main qualities of a person who's been brought up well. He's both interesting and interested in others. He asks thoughtful questions and tells excellent stories and occasionally makes Lucy laugh in a way that almost lets her forget that she's doing an interview. He seems to like her too, even more so after her comment about Dr. Perry, who Rahm explains had a major impact on his ideas about mentoring and the importance of being a good mentor to his team.

A future is taking shape, one in which she can actually imagine working for this man, doing cutting-edge research, moving further into the artificial intelligence arena, perhaps even getting rich one day, depending on what happens to the company and her stock options. Google began hiring only three years ago, but some industry analysts are already talking about the possibility of an IPO. Judging from Rahm's enthusiastic descriptions of the culture, buying into the idea of long hours today in exchange for big rewards tomorrow is a condition of employment. If Lucy joins them, she suspects she'll be too busy to paint except on occasional vacations, assuming she ever takes any. She'll definitely be too busy to devote the time necessary to grow as a painter while she's still young. But maybe this is just what adulthood is—a series of choices made and doors closed, one after another, until she ends up in the room that is her life. Maybe this is how bursars become bursars and pharmacists become pharmacists. Maybe this is why aspiring artists eventually stop making art.

They're forty-five minutes into the conversation when Lucy hears someone jiggling the key in the lock, and then the door to the cabin opens and closes. From her seat at the desk, she can't see who's entered. She can only make out small movements in the bathroom, followed by the click and clack of someone picking things up and putting things down. Lucy feels a flare of annoyance, wondering what's the point of putting a DO NOT DISTURB sign on the door if the housekeepers don't stop to pay attention.

"God damn it. This whole thing's gone."

Annoyance quickly turns to alarm as Lucy cups her hand over the receiver to muffle the sound of Mariah cursing in the bathroom. She can't remember if she told her how long the interview would be, but wouldn't it be common sense to stay out for at least an hour? She stands up and moves toward the hallway, stretching the phone cord out as far as it will go so she can signal that the interview is still in progress.

Mariah enters the living room area with a lime-green tube of aloe vera gel. "If you're going to use up my things, the least you could do is replace them," she says hotly. "Or at the very least, tell me so I can replace them myself."

Lucy blinks at her. Mariah has eyes, she thinks. Mariah is looking right at me. She can see that I'm on the phone. *Stop,* she mouths at her violently. And then more lightly to Rahm: "Oh . . . sorry about that. My roommate just came in. I don't think she realized I was doing a *job interview.*"

The emphasis on the words "job interview" only seems to aggravate Mariah more. She flings the empty tube onto the coffee table, skipping the plastic off the surface before it clatters onto the floor.

"Right, well, it's probably time I got off the phone anyway. It was great speaking to you, Lucy. Stay tuned, okay?"

She barely has a chance to get the words "thank you" out before there's a sharp click and the line goes quiet. Stay tuned? *Stay tuned?* Lucy remains standing, stock-still with the phone pressed against her ear. She's trying to decide what she heard in Rahm's voice in the seconds just before he hung up. Was it surprise? Or impatience? Or possibly even disappointment? She shakes her head in disbelief, not sure what it was, but she knows with absolute certainty what it wasn't. It wasn't the invitation to headquarters that she was hoping he'd extend at the end of the call, the thing that would have made all her efforts worth the trouble. It wasn't even a hint that any such invitation would be forthcoming.

Lucy slams the phone back into its cradle. "What the hell is wrong with you?"

"Wrong with *me*? Oh, I don't know. Let me think." Mariah puts her hands on her hips, flaring her arms out to the sides in a way that reminds Lucy of a cobra. "I invite you on a free cruise to be nice to you, to get to know you, but—"

"But what? I got sunburned and used up all your lotion? I'll buy you another one! You didn't have to go acting like—"

"—but then you take over my suite, *my* suite, and start telling people when they can and can't be in it."

Lucy feels like she's talking to an insane person, or possibly a drunk person—someone whose memory of the events is deeply flawed. "Mariah," she starts, as calmly as possible, "I *asked* you, and you said it was fine. There's a big difference between asking someone and telling them. And you know perfectly well that that wasn't just any call you interrupted. It was a job interview."

"Well . . ." She sniffs. "One job for another, then."

Lucy shakes her head. "I don't know what that means."

A flash of something darkens Mariah's face. "Did you go to the Grotto and tell Iain not to come here while you were on the phone?"

"No! Is that what he said? I *asked* him, politely. I didn't tell—"

"Did you notice that he wasn't alone?"

She had just left the business center a few minutes before going to the Grotto. She was distracted when she stopped by, still thinking about the man sitting at the computer and who he must have lost. Lucy remembers what she said to Iain but didn't take note of much else. "He was getting ready to open," she says uncertainly. "There weren't any customers yet."

"No, just another bartender doing setup who sold him out to their boss."

Mariah flops down on the sofa, putting her bare feet on the edge of the table. Lucy doesn't know what to do but sit down beside her.

She doesn't recall seeing another person behind the bar. Then again, she wasn't looking. She just wanted to get in and out so she could go back to the suite and change. Her mind is racing now, as quickly as it was before the interview. She's no longer cataloging everything that could go wrong for her but everything she might have screwed up for someone else.

"Did I get him in trouble?"

"Lucy, I told you—these ships, they have strict no fraternizing policies. You didn't just get him in trouble. You got him fired."

Noticeably, she's not "Luce" anymore. She hasn't heard that nickname in a while, probably because she's proven herself wholly incapable of being the fun girlfriend, the easygoing travel companion, or even just the good roommate. She pulls her hand away from her mouth, aware for the first time that she's covered it with her fist.

"But didn't you . . . I thought you said he was quitting to run his own bar after this trip, so it doesn't really matter now, right?"

Mariah glares at her, and Lucy is forced to listen to the lengthy explanation that follows—how there's a difference between walking away from a job and being let go; how contract employees like Iain are ineligible to collect severance; how Aria now has cause to withhold the bonus he was expecting at the end of the sail for working on his twenty-fifth consecutive cruise. And worst of all: how he was relying on that bonus to make repairs to the bar he bought. Lucy is gutted. She thought she was being so careful, preventing every possible source of interruption. How many doors have slammed shut for Iain because of what she did?

"Can I talk to someone?" she asks. "Can I fix this for him somehow?"

"I doubt it. I wouldn't even know who to talk to, and he'll probably never speak to me again. He just screamed at me in front of a bunch of people and stormed off."

"I'm so sorry," Lucy says.

Mariah's posture softens. She rests her hand on Lucy's, patting it reassuringly. "It's okay. The whole thing with him was running its course anyway. But, God, it was embarrassing."

She realizes that Mariah thought the apology was for how Lucy's actions had affected her, rather than how they'd affected Iain. All that anger was about her embarrassment, not his injury. Lucy looks around the suite, scanning the walls as if she might find visual proof of the signs she already knows are there. For the first time, the space seems small and claustrophobic, as uncomfortable as the cramped little business center.

"When we get back to Boston, I think . . . I think it would probably be best if you moved out."

Mariah smiles at first, then narrows her eyes upon meeting Lucy's. "Are you serious?"

"You can take your time, until you find the right place. And we can prorate the rent if you end up—"

"No. Wait." Mariah snatches her hand away. "Are you serious? You want me to move out?"

Lucy wishes she had a glass of water. Conflict feels like sand in her mouth. "I appreciate you bringing me on this trip, I really do. But it seems pretty obvious that we're not compatible . . ."

Mariah gets up and paces the room as she shouts at Lucy, who hears only bits and pieces of the barrage being leveled at her. "Joyless," "antisocial," "workaholic," "dull." Clearly, Mariah took offense at her description of them as incompatible. She probably assumed it was some sort of insult or judgment against her, which it wasn't. Lucy was actually trying to point out that they're more alike than they are different. They're both selfish and self-involved. They should be around people who make them better than what they are. She wants to tell Mariah this, but there's no moment of air in which to interrupt.

"You know, if you're kicking me out of our apartment, then you can just fuck off and find somewhere else to sleep tonight."

Lucy has never seen Mariah like this before. She doesn't know her well enough to understand how serious she is. "But it's not a hotel," she says, examining her face for clues. "I can't just get another—"

"That's not my problem. You're not my problem anymore." Mariah stands up and returns to the bathroom, shutting the door behind her with a loud, hollow bang.

17.

Franny isn't sure how many laps she's walked. Twelve, maybe? Possibly thirteen. Enough to know that it takes roughly fifteen minutes to do a full loop around the Lido Deck. Enough to recognize certain landmarks along the way: the spirited mah-jongg tournament taking place under the starboard-side canopy, the couple in his-and-hers gold swimsuits sunning themselves near the swim-up bar. Enough to make her legs feel elastic and rubbery, on the verge of collapse, as they did that day. And yet, still not enough to forget why she's out here like a lab mouse on a wheel.

At home, Franny never walks like this despite living so close to Central Park. She can see the vibrant expanse of color from every window of their apartment, filled with tiny dots of walkers and joggers, whom she has no desire to join. Her mind tends to drift when she exercises. She'd rather spend her spare time reading or catching up on work—things that require her to focus. But here on the *Sonata*, time is all she has. She's just biding it until she can get off the ship, and then a whole different kind of worry sets in.

As Franny walks, she imagines the drive back to New York in the morning. There are at least two possible versions of it, both equally uncomfortable—one in which she and Tom attempt to work things out, and another in which they sit in silent acceptance of the end. She knows what she wants to do, which isn't the same thing as knowing what she will do. Leaving a marriage is complicated. Who will she have if he's gone? Lap after lap, Franny keeps thinking about her life after the cruise as a series of choices between one bad option and another, and she doesn't understand how it turned out like this, or why she continues to accept the terms.

Near the hot tubs, she notices a large, noisy family that she's seen around the ship, always traveling in a pack. Now they're dragging chaises from different areas, forming a single long row in the sun. The eight of them are clearly related, either by blood or by marriage. The elderly parents have strong Italian features, and their three adult sons resemble them in different ways, each having inherited a variation of their mother's prominent brows or their father's Roman nose. There are girlfriends or daughters-in-law too—fair-haired, freckled women in full-length cover-ups and big, floppy hats. The sight of them reminds Franny that this is what some families do. They vacation together, willingly. They consider it a good time.

This trip that she had such high hopes for has gone wrong in ways she never could have imagined. Worse still, it stirred something inside her, beyond any disappointment she's ever felt, like she asked a question that she already knew the answer to, and now she can no longer pretend that being content is the same thing as feeling happy, or that being married is the same thing as feeling loved.

Franny finds herself at the elevator banks again, the starting point for a new lap. She's exhausted and wants to stop doing this, but where would she go? The upside to being in constant motion is not staying in one place long enough to be found. She's trying to decide whether to start another lap when she spots Jae quickly walking, almost running, toward her. It's the first time she's seen him since yesterday's *chilsun*. She's about to reverse course when he reaches out and touches her shoulder.

"Come with me," he says.

It's a rare invitation. The only other time Jae asked her to join him anywhere was on this cruise.

She eyes him warily. "No. Just leave me alone."

"Come on. You're going to miss it."

"Miss what?"

"You have to see for yourself. Let's go." Jae grabs her arm and starts pulling her along, which he's never done before. Franny allows herself to be dragged toward the stepped section of the deck, if only because she's curious about what could possibly be so important. As they descend the stairs toward the largest of the two pools, she spots Esther sitting on a chaise in a tiny black baby doll dress and enormous combat boots. There are two empty chaises, one on each side of her, but despite being exhausted, Franny has no intention of sitting down.

"It's the pool," she says. "So what? I've seen the pool before—"

"Do you see who's in it?"

Franny shields her eyes from the sun and searches the blinding water. Through mirrorlike shards of light, she can make out a few kids congregating in the shallow end and some swimmers doing laps. Their white, glistening arms occasionally appear, slicing through the air in midstroke. "Who am I supposed to be seeing?"

Jae points toward the deep end, where a dark-haired figure is bobbing up and down, treading water. "There," he says. And as soon as he says it, the figure darts toward the shallow end like a fish in a pond.

Among the many things that Franny never expected to see in her lifetime: her mother in a bathing suit. Her mother in a pool. Her mother doing the backstroke. Franny assumed that Ma was afraid of water and couldn't swim, but as she thinks back, she doesn't actually know where she got these ideas or how they lodged so firmly in her mind.

Jae and Esther both look as confused as she feels. Neither of them can take their eyes off Ma, who alternates between doing laps and floating buoy-like in the deep end, surrounded by seniors batting around an oversize beach ball.

"Could I get another beer?" Jae hails a passing waiter, raising his empty cup at him.

"Me too," Esther says.

"Just water, thank you." Franny realizes how dehydrated she is after hours of walking. "Two glasses, please. No ice." She lowers herself into a chaise, feeling her aching muscles melt into the warm plastic.

The three of them sit stretched out on their loungers, fully dressed in regular clothes. Everyone else near the pool is dressed like Ma, except for the waitstaff. As odd as the sight of Ma swimming is, Franny realizes that she, Jae, and Esther probably look like the odd ones here.

"So . . ." She's not even sure where to begin. "She has a swimsuit?"

"It's new," Esther says. "She told me she got up early and bought it at one of the shops downstairs." She explains how they were heading to the four o'clock bingo game when Ma noticed the pool wasn't busy. Unbeknownst to them, she'd been wearing the swimsuit underneath her shirt and pants all day, just waiting for the opportunity to strip down, which she did—in front of Esther and Jae, in front of complete strangers—revealing the plain black one-piece. It was apparently one of those modest suits for older or overweight women with the high neckline and built-in skirt, and yet Jae said it was more revealing than anything he'd ever seen her in. Now Ma is doing a slow but steady breaststroke across the length of the crowded pool, and Franny isn't sure what surprises her more—the fact that Ma can do the breaststroke, or the fact that she's skilled enough to avoid crashing into people as she does it.

"Did you know she could—" She turns to look at Jae.

"No. I had no idea."

"I suppose it makes sense," Esther says. "You can't grow up near the sea without learning how to swim."

Franny knows only the barest plot points of Ma's life. How she lived in her hometown of Busan until the age of eighteen, worked as a cook for an American missionary in Seoul until she married, had her first child shortly before immigrating to the United States, and then two more after they settled in Fort Lee. She didn't talk about herself like a person who had a history and responded to Franny's occasional questions about Korea with annoyance. Franny realizes that's what's missing in this moment. Annoyance, impatience, worry, fear. All the things she observed in Ma's face during those years when the restaurant was barely hanging on, and then later, when it was doing well but she was still bracing for life's next disaster. Now the restaurant is gone, sold off in big chunks and small pieces by Franny, and Ma is swimming in a pool on a ship in the middle of an ocean.

She wipes her eyes, turning her face away so her brother won't see, but it's too late.

"What are you crying for?" he asks.

Esther smacks him on the arm. "She can cry if she wants to."

"What?" Jae scowls. "I'm not saying it's bad. It was just a question."

Franny lets them bicker while she takes one last look at the strange and strangely beautiful sight of Ma gliding through the water. This is all she cares to remember about this trip. She wants to slip away before her memory of it is ruined or interrupted, but when she tries to stand up, her muscles have turned into concrete.

She actually has to grab her legs and pull them off to the side just so she can put her feet on the ground. She makes a few discreet attempts to get up from the low chaise—rocking into an upright position, reaching for the ground so she can tip herself forward—but her legs simply won't cooperate. She wonders if this is what it's like to grow old, to lose the ability to do things that once came so easily. Yet despite her rising panic about being stuck in a lounger, she feels a newfound respect for all the senior citizens on the ship, her mother included, carrying on as if the body never betrays.

BY THE TIME Ma finally gets out of the pool, the sky is turning pink with the approach of sunset. Esther, who's been going on and on about the amazing buffet on the final night of a cruise, is eager to return to their cabins and start getting ready for dinner. As Ma approaches, she springs out of her chaise, her combat boots landing on the deck with a thud, and hands her a giant lavender beach towel emblazoned with the Aria logo. Ma covers her head with it, rubbing her hair in rough circles.

"Did you enjoy yourself?" Esther asks.

"I didn't know you could swim," Jae adds.

From under the towel, there's a muffled, economical "yes" that could be a response to one or both of them.

Franny hasn't seen Ma since the *chilsun*. It feels like something they should talk about—all of them—but she knows better. They'll probably never discuss it again.

"I thought you were afraid of water," she says, blurting out the first thing that comes to mind.

Ma hugs herself with the towel like a cape and frowns, as if the idea of being afraid of anything is offensive to her.

"I don't know where I got that idea from," Franny says, still disturbed by the falseness of her memory. "Do you?"

She shakes her head, flicking water everywhere. "You and your brothers always wanted me to take you to the pool when you were little, but I had to work."

Franny pauses on the word "brothers," having not heard the plural form in so long. She glances at Jae, who's registered it too. She can tell by the slight lift of his eyebrows, the small "o" of his mouth.

Esther, who's both hungry and oblivious, hooks her arm around Jae's. "We should probably start getting ready for dinner now, don't you think?"

"You go." Ma waves them away. "I want to talk to Franny."

Like so many things that have happened today, this is new. The declaration, the desire. The reason seems obvious though. Either Ma's upset about how the *chilsun* ended or she's upset that Franny didn't tell her what happened on the day of the attacks. She prepares to be scolded for both. If asked to explain why she lied on the phone, Franny will say that she didn't mean to. She was in shock and she didn't want Ma to worry. That was how she justified it in the moment. But some part of Franny is actually touched that she did. The thought of Ma and Jae trying to call her while she was trying to call them is the closest they've come to behaving like a family in some time. She doesn't know if this should make her feel better or worse.

Once they're alone, Ma sits down sideways in a chaise, mirroring the awkward position that Franny is stuck in. They're facing each other; their spread knees almost touch. If Franny could move, she'd be tempted to back away, to put the usual distance between them because how they're sitting now—it's too close. She senses that something strange is about to happen. She can see it in Ma's expression, which no longer looks peaceful like it did in the water. But she doesn't look angry or annoyed either.

"I want to talk to you about that watch," she says.

"The watch?" Franny repeats dumbly.

"Yes."

Suddenly, her ears flood with all the permutations of the conversation before it even begins. Franny is so desperate for acknowledgment that even a hint of gratitude or understanding about the gift's meaning would make this fiasco of a cruise worthwhile. But she knows better than to hope. Didn't the spectacle of the *chilsun* finally teach her that lesson? She steels herself to be chastised about how the watch was too expensive. How Franny shouldn't have bought it. How Ma will never have anyplace to wear it.

"I wanted this birthday to be special for you," she says, cutting her mother off before she has a chance to start. "The watch was part of it."

Ma looks down at her bare feet and nods. Water continues to drip from her hair, dotting the weathered gray deck between them.

"I want you to return it and get the money back—"

"Oh, God, Ma." Franny reacts much louder than she intended, surprising even herself. "I can afford it. I don't need the money. Plus, the watch was engraved. The store's not going to take back an engraved watch." She resists the urge to remind Ma that it was engraved especially for her. Why point out something she already knows and clearly doesn't care about? "Do you really not understand how anything works?"

Ma's face, taut from pool water and chlorine, suddenly turns pale. Even in the warm, golden pink light of sunset, her skin looks ghostly. Franny has finally said the obvious out loud. All the education that Ma worked so hard to provide has allowed Franny to surpass her, to move about freely in a world that confuses Ma with its language and confounds her with its customs. Franny should feel terrible for giving voice to this reality, but she doesn't, not when she believes Ma is being equally terrible to her.

"Then sell the watch to someone else."

"Ma! I already told you. I don't need the money. The watch was a gift."

She waves her hands at Franny, trying to quiet her down. "Ay, ssh! Listen. Listen to me. I want you to sell it and give *me* the money. That would be my gift."

The pool area is mostly empty now that the light has faded and the temperature has dropped. Only one couple remains nearby. They've made no effort to hide the fact that they've been eavesdropping, which would normally bother Franny, but she's grateful to have a third party listening in. She makes eye contact with the woman, who takes a slow, uncomfortable sip of her cocktail, confirming Franny's instincts that Ma's request is disturbing, even for her.

"What are you saying? Do you need money or something?"

Ma shakes her head, flustered. "No, it's—"

"Because I can just give you—"

"Ay, no. It's not for me. It's for Jae. So I can invest in his business."

If Franny had a glass in her hand, this is the moment when it would shatter. Then she'd hold the jagged pieces in her palm until she squeezed out all her anger or all her blood, whichever came first.

"Did he put you up to this?"

"No."

"Did Esther?"

Ma says nothing.

Franny shakes her head. She should have known. "She's as bad as he is, isn't she?"

If Ma contradicts her or tries to stand up for Esther, Franny thinks she'll snap. But Ma continues to sit in silence.

"Why do you like her so much?"

"She's young."

"I know she's young. But you actually seem to *like* her."

"You should be nice to Esther. Her father was a minister. She's had a hard life."

Franny imagines how badly the bleached hair and tattoos and edgy clothes might go over in a traditional Korean family, much less a religious one. It's not a great leap to assume that Esther's parents disowned her, and the reason she's so attached to Ma is that she no longer has a mother of her own.

"Also, you should be nice because she's your brother's girlfriend. He doesn't bring many around."

Air forces its way out of Franny's chest, violent and quick. The sound that accompanies it is neither laughter nor surprise, but something more bitter. Tom was the first man she ever brought home to introduce to Ma. She understands on some level that she chose him because he was well educated and wealthy, the kind of person that Ma always wanted her children to become. Franny thought that a husband like Tom was what was expected of her, yet despite his early—now abandoned—efforts to charm and impress, Ma never took to him the way she did to Esther.

"What's so funny?"

"I'm not laughing. I'm trying to imagine how you would have reacted if I'd brought home a guy who barely has a job and spends all his free time playing music. Do you even understand how differently you treat me and Jae? Can you really not see it?"

"You're the oldest. I expect—"

"No, Ma! I'm not the oldest. I *became* the oldest." And because their last night on the cruise feels like a door that might be closing, Franny finally says what she's been holding on to for all these years, the fact that has governed and guided most of her life. "I think you've always hated me for that."

SECONDS PASS. POSSIBLY minutes. Franny isn't sure how long she's been sitting there, cupping her face with her hand. At first, the slap stunned more than it hurt. But now a burning sensation is blossoming across her cheek, unequal parts anger and embarrassment and pain. The couple nearby gather their things and scurry away. Eavesdropping on a minor disagreement was probably their idea of an innocent pastime. A fight is more than they care to witness.

"Don't say things like that," Ma shouts, no longer self-conscious about raising her voice now that they're alone. "Mothers don't hate their children."

Ma has never struck her before. Franny lowers her hand, imagining how many times she's wanted to, the restraint it must have required to wait all these years. "It's okay, Ma. I understand. We don't have to pretend anymore."

Ma looks at her blankly, prompting her to continue.

"I'm sorry about Joonhee and *appa*."

"Sorry why?"

"I'm sorry I missed the bus that day and had to call *appa* for a ride."

"Ay, what's wrong with you? Why are you talking about this?"

They were well trained as children, independent because they had to be. Franny now knows the term for what they were—latchkey kids—but she didn't back then. It was just the way they were raised. While their parents worked, she and her brothers packed their own lunches, caught the bus to and from school on time, set the table and folded the laundry without having to be reminded. On the day of the accident, both of her brothers were home sick, so Franny had to find their teachers after school to collect their assignments. One of them wasn't in her classroom, and by the time Franny found her, the bus was gone and a heavy diagonal rain had begun to fall.

Even at the age of eight, she knew she wasn't supposed to do things like call her parents from school to ask for a ride. They were too busy for their children to make mistakes. While a secretary waited with her at the entrance, Franny cried and cried until she saw her father's station wagon pull up. To this day, she still doesn't know why he brought Joonhee with him. The only person who might be able to explain his decision is sitting right in front of her, but the topic has always seemed off-limits, cordoned off by some imaginary tape that separates the time before the accident from everything that followed.

"I know you blame me for what happened to them, and I'm telling you I understand, and I'm sorry."

Ma looks at her intensely, so much so that Franny has to drop her eyes to the floor for a moment before she has the nerve to lift them again.

"You were little and you missed the bus. Why would I blame you for that?"

"It seems like you—"

"Ay, stop talking about this. Why are you talking?" Ma almost gets up to leave, but like Franny, she struggles to lift herself out of the chaise. She grips the metal frame for leverage, her papery, freckled hands shaking with the effort.

"Are you cold?" Franny asks, suddenly aware that Ma is still dressed in her wet swimsuit, wrapped in a damp towel.

"No," she says, even though her teeth are starting to chatter. "Now stop this."

In another time, in another place, Franny—always observant of her mother's darkening moods—would likely obey. But they're stuck here on this ship, stuck in the very chairs they're sitting in. She'll never get a chance like this again.

"But we have to, Ma. We have to talk about this while we can because we don't know what's going to happen next."

"What does that mean, 'next'?"

Franny can't explain what she doesn't fully understand yet. But the longer she sits here, the more convinced she is that something has to change. She didn't survive two disasters only to return to the life she had before this. To retreat to the emptiness of that existence would betray the people whose bodies she saw falling from the sky, people who fought so hard to live until they couldn't anymore.

"Tomorrow," she says. "We don't know what's going to happen tomorrow, Ma."

"You're talking nonsense now. Stop bringing up these old things. And never say your mother hates you. Mothers can't hate their children. You'd know if you had any."

Maybe "hate" is too strong a word. But what Franny has felt all these years surely isn't love.

"You've been angry at me for so long, Ma, and I'm telling you I understand why. But I can't spend the rest of my life trying to change your mind. I'm not going to do that anymore," she says, hearing the decision before she's fully thought through what it means to make it.

"I'm not angry," Ma insists. "I'm just— I'm just . . . upset."

"Isn't that the same thing?"

"No! I'm upset because you're so . . . you're such a sad person. Every time I see you, I think how sad you are."

Franny is tempted to protest because she doesn't like to hear herself being described this way, but she can't scramble together a defense.

"And then I think—this is what I worked so hard for? For you to live in that big apartment with such a fake nice man? To spend your days helping people plan to die? You have no babies—" Ma seems to sense that Franny is about to cut in, so she holds up her hand to stop her. "I don't care that you don't have babies, but then what do you have? Just work and that man and all your beautiful clothes and expensive things, and every time I look at you, ay, I think you're so sad." Ma shakes her head. Franny is stunned by the number of consecutive sentences her mother has just spoken to her. She doesn't think Ma will continue, but now she can't seem to stop. "I worked hard my whole life for you to have better."

Again, Franny wants to protest. She does have better. She does. Even a stranger taking one look at her life would agree. But the insistent voice inside her doesn't say any of this out loud. She realizes they've been operating under such different definitions of "better," and somehow, Franny twisted hers into the shapes of money and things, while Ma's jumped the track onto an entirely different plane.

"Then what about Jae?" she asks. "Is he sad too?"

"Your brother . . . he's just lost. Jae and Esther, they're both lost little children. You're not like them."

If the comment was meant to be a compliment, it doesn't land that way. Franny waits for more, hoping the words that follow will explain why Ma's expectations of her are so different, why her disappointment has always felt like disdain. But Ma just shivers and hugs the towel around her tighter.

"So what am I like, then?" Franny asks.

"You're more like me. You do what you have to do." Ma frowns.

"I worry, maybe, you're too much like me." She hesitates, then reaches over and pushes the hair away from Franny's forehead, something she hasn't done to her since she was little. "You're good, but I want you to have better, understand? Now let's go," she says, her face reddening with the effort of getting out of her chair. "Dinner's starting."

Franny doesn't care about dinner. She wants to stretch this moment out for as long as she can, but Ma looks like she's going to hurt herself as she tries to stand up, reminding Franny that her original problem still hasn't been solved.

"I'm stuck," Ma says.

"So am I. Here . . ." Franny reaches out and grabs Ma's forearms. "Maybe we can pull up on each other at the same time."

They lock arms, and together, they awkwardly, unsteadily attempt to lift themselves into a standing position. On their first try, they're almost able to rise, so they try again without agreeing to, their hands scrambling for purchase against each other's skin. If anyone were around to watch, Franny might be embarrassed about how silly they look—two women, climbing each other like ropes in order to get up from their chairs. But by the third time around, the maneuvering actually works, and the strange upright position they find themselves in almost feels like an embrace, the first one they've shared in some time. They're so close that Franny can smell the wind and chlorine in her mother's hair, the fruited trace of suntan lotion on her skin, and maybe something else, something unidentifiable that Franny will forever try and fail to name. Stranger still is the fact that even though they're standing, they remain where they are, holding each other tightly, and for once, Franny isn't sure who won't let go.

18.

One more night. One more night and he can get off this ship and never come back. All he has to do is smile his way through the talent show, be a good and charming emcee, and then he can collect his paycheck and be free of the *Sonata* forever.

Doug surveys the backstage of the *Avventura!*, which is once again teeming with activity. Tonight, however, it's filled with passengers instead of members of the repertory. He hovers in the wings, going mercifully unnoticed as the amateur performers do vocal warm-ups and practice their steps and talk to themselves as if onstage. It looks like a scene from a mental hospital. He flips through the index cards he was given when he arrived, this time written in large block letters.

MEL HARRIMAN FROM TEANECK, NEW JERSEY—

"BEST OF BILLY JOEL"

JUDY MEYERS FROM POUGHKEEPSIE, NEW YORK—

ORIGINAL POETRY

MR. AND MRS. STANLEY BRICE FROM DES PLAINES, ILLINOIS—

TANGO

HOWARD NOONAN FROM SARASOTA, FLORIDA
—STAND-UP COMEDY

There are at least a dozen more cards after that. Doug carefully puts them back in order and returns the deck to the pocket of his tuxedo, wincing with the effort. He's convinced that his ribs are broken. He keeps imagining the sharp, jagged tip of one of them poking into an organ. But twice, the ship's doctor said no. If that were the case, he wouldn't be able to stand or walk or do much of anything.

A couple brushes past—the tango dancers, he assumes, judging from the woman's voluminous red skirt, which forces Doug back several steps. There's a full-length mirror in his line of sight now, so he gives himself a final once-over, adjusting his bow tie. He thinks he's lucky that Mr. Hamm hit him in the stomach instead of the face and then immediately chastises himself for having such a vain, vapid thought. Where is he now? Doug wonders. What does security do with a passenger who commits an assault while on board? And what will happen to him when they return to Boston in the morning? No one has bothered to ask Doug whether he wants to press charges. He knows better than most that crimes committed at sea—drug possession, for example—are difficult to prosecute and often go overlooked because of questions about jurisdiction.

In the mirror, he catches a glimpse of Kevin. Doug has been actively avoiding him since last night, hiding idiotically behind columns and people and plants, but this time, he's too late. It's obvious that Kevin has already spotted him. He's walking in his usual quickstep with Tabby trailing close behind. Judging from the stern, serious looks on their faces, news of yesterday's disastrous Formal Night dinner has finally caught up to them.

"It was *not* my fault" are the first words out of Doug's mouth. And as soon as he says them, it feels like he's regressed to a time when he refused to take responsibility for his actions. But for once, he thinks his defensiveness might actually be justified. Mr. Hamm hit *him.* Kevin and Tabby, however, don't look particularly convinced of his blamelessness. They glance at each other and then back at Doug.

"You can ask anyone at my table. I'd just finished dancing with one of the ladies and when we came back to our seats, Mr. Hamm was just standing there, shouting at me. I have a huge bruise on my stomach now." Doug touches his side, tempted to lift his cummerbund and shirt as proof. "I'm lucky he didn't break my ribs—"

Kevin raises his hands, patting them against the air in an aggravating, infantilizing gesture that's the opposite of calming. "All right, let's just take this into the greenroom, shall we?"

Doug squints at his watch. "But the talent show is about to start." When he looks up, he notices Alan approaching them with a cordless mic and a guilty expression.

"Good. You're here." Kevin consults his own watch. "Alan will be taking over for you as emcee tonight. Please give him the cards. Quickly."

Doug didn't even want to host Talent Night, but now he's not sure if he should relinquish the role so easily. Can they argue breach of contract if he was willing to go on and they wouldn't let him? And what's worse—listening to someone's original poetry or being lectured at in the greenroom for being the victim of an assault? Usually, he's careful not to throw that word around too casually, but in this instance, that's what he believes he is.

"Quickly," Kevin repeats. "It's showtime."

"Dougie, please. I have to go on," Alan says, holding his hand out. "I got a job to do."

He's also been avoiding Alan since their argument by the pool yesterday, grateful for the careful scheduling that's allowed them to keep their distance. Doug is still angry with him, and now he's angry with Kevin too. But what will he actually miss if he doesn't host? The forced banter with the performers, passengers whom he assumes are all oddballs and exhibitionists. And the dreadful finale—a group singalong of "We Are the World"—that he's been trying not to think about. He slaps the deck of cards into Alan's open palm and watches him take his mark behind the drawn curtains.

"This is ridiculous," he huffs, embarrassed by how petulant he sounds about something he never wanted to do in the first place.

"All right, let's go," Kevin says, trying to steer him away from the backstage area, but Doug is having none of it.

"I don't want to go to the greenroom!" He curls away from Kevin's touch, sending a sharp, stabbing pain through his side. "Whatever you have to say to me, you can say it right here." He glances at Tabby—suddenly mute Tabby, who's just standing there, staring idly at her feet. "You believe me, don't you? I was having a perfectly nice time with my Captain's Club group when that man showed up, reeking of beer. Ask the people at my table if you don't believe me."

Tabby can barely make eye contact, a reaction he's witnessed countless times before—that breaking point when people are so completely fed up, they just want him out of their sight. But he hasn't done anything to earn it this time, he thinks. *Mr. Hamm* punched *him*.

"I was finally able to reach someone in your agent's office," Kevin says.

Of all the things Doug expected to hear, this isn't it. Panic starts to flutter through his chest. He never imagined that Kevin would get through to Annette. Can they fire him on the last night of the cruise? And do they have any cause to? How many times does he have to say it? He was the *victim* of an assault.

In the background, Alan's voice booms "Hello! Hello!" through the loudspeakers. After he welcomes the audience to Talent Night, there's a long, loud round of applause, punctuated by hoots and people shouting "Bring it on, Howie!" or "Let's go, Mel!" for their family and friends. Doug waits for the noise to die down before asking Kevin what he and Annette discussed.

"I spoke to her niece."

"Nina?"

"Yes. Ms. Fischette. She was the one who finally answered." Kevin looks down at a slip of paper that he's discreetly cupping in his hand.

Doug hasn't seen or spoken to Nina in years, not since that disastrous visit to New York when he landed in rehab. "I don't understand. Why would Nina be picking up Annette's business line?"

Kevin and Tabby exchange another look, and it dawns on Doug that they're not here to talk about Mr. Hamm punching him at dinner.

"She was trying to find some paperwork in the office. I'm so sorry to tell you this, Mr. Clayton, but your agent passed away." Kevin pauses. "Ms. Fischette said it was very sudden."

Doug doesn't check to see if there's a chair beneath him. His knees simply go out and he lands on the hard edge of something. He sits there for some time, feeling like he just had the wind knocked out of him again. Instinctively, he holds his hand over his stomach, as if the locus of the pain is there, when in fact it's everywhere. Annette has passed away. Annette, the person who knew him better than anyone. His last real friend.

"I'm so sorry for your loss, Mr. Clayton."

"Would you like me to walk you back to your cabin?" Tabby asks.

"When? When did this happen?"

"Last week," Kevin says. "Tuesday."

"Tuesday?" Doug counts backward. "It wasn't because— She wasn't in the one of the towers, was she? She never goes downtown."

"No, no. It had nothing to do with that. It was a heart attack." Kevin consults his notes. "Her niece said she was at home when it happened. She called the doorman for help, but apparently, it took so long to get an ambulance that day—she was gone before it finally arrived."

Someone is playing the piano onstage. Not badly, but not well either. For every few notes of "The Entertainer" that Doug recognizes, there are several more slightly off-key ones fumbled in between. And then a man begins to sing the first lines of the song, sounding nothing like Billy Joel. His voice is even more off-key than his playing, giving their conversation the quality of a very bad, very surreal dream.

"I can't. I can't listen to this," he says, getting up from the wardrobe crate he landed on.

"Let me take you back to your cabin now," Tabby offers.

"No, no." He brushes her hand away from his elbow. "I'm not sitting in that coffin again. I just want to get out of here."

As he leaves the backstage area, his foot catches on an electrical cord that isn't fully taped down. A microphone stand topples to the floor, but he continues walking as Tabby scrambles to right it. Behind him, he hears Kevin calling out in a stage whisper that almost sounds like a scream, "Again, I'm so sorry for your loss, Mr. Clayton."

EVERY RELAPSE BEGINS the same way. The just-one-drink game. *Just one drink, and then I'll stop. Just one drink can't hurt. Just one drink, be-*

cause I'm _____________ now. He's played this game too many times to act like he doesn't know how it ends. But maybe it doesn't matter anymore. Maybe he'll walk down this path and not come back again, because what does he really have that's worth returning for?

Doug rotates his glass of whiskey to the right, tuning it like a knob. He keeps touching it, turning it, smelling it, staring at it. He does everything but actually bring it to his lips. A pair of couples walk past his table to throw coins into the Grotto's lagoon. He hears his name whispered under someone's breath and catches a shy backward glance from one of the women. He must look strange to her, just sitting there with the same drink he ordered several hours ago. The bartender didn't notice the hesitation in Doug's voice when he asked for a double Jameson, neat—his usual. To him, it was just a transaction, not a retreat he's been fighting off for years.

Beside his glass of whiskey are two Xanax capsules, a familiar and tempting combination. Doug knows exactly what will happen if he mixes benzos and booze. Time will speed up as it lulls him into a deep and dreamless sleep for the rest of the night. But in the morning, he'll leave the *Sonata* and return to land, to a life in which Annette is no longer his agent, no longer his friend, no longer alive. The loneliness of being the last person standing is almost too much. How is he the one who outlasted everyone he ever cared for, who cared about him?

Shortly after Peter's death, Annette convinced Doug to visit her in New York. She insisted that keeping busy was the antidote for grief, so she sent him on auditions for roles that all felt like long shots. Doug was aware that she'd probably gone out of her way to arrange the meetings, so he tried his best, but the combination of sadness and pressure proved to be too much—something Annette later said she should have known. He quickly succumbed to the just-one-drink game, and when he finally spiraled to that storied rock bottom that he'd heard about during previous rehab stints, it was Annette who picked him up and paid for his stay at a facility upstate. For the life of him, Doug can't remember if he ever thanked her for that. He suspects he was too caught up in his own problems to express the gratitude she deserved, which is an awful thing to know about himself.

He moves his glass another quarter-turn, looking around the Grotto. He'd forgotten how much he used to love being here late at night. When it's busy, the hum of activity is just the right volume. The atmosphere is the perfect balance of dark and light. He assumes the talent show must have ended because there's a steady stream of people walking into the bar now. He's looking at the door when Renee enters, dressed in a filmy caftan that resembles liquid gold. They make eye contact, and he's surprised to see her leave her group to approach him. She puts both of her bejeweled hands on his table and leans down to talk over the Muzak.

"I was sorry to hear about Annette," she says. He must look confused by how she knows this because she adds, "I ran into Alan after the show. I'm really sorry. I remember how close you and Peter were to her back in the day."

He doesn't expect this kind of sympathy from Renee. He also doesn't expect her to sit down at his table. At any point before this, he would have welcomed a second chance for her company, but he's not in the mood for it now.

"I don't really think you want this," she says. Her rings glitter as she slides his whiskey away. She's about to do the same with his pills when he catches her wrist.

"Leave it," he says. "All of it." He drags his drink back, reclaiming the possibility of it for himself.

Renee glances at his other hand.

He realizes he's touching her. He shouldn't be touching her. "Sorry," he says, releasing her wrist.

"No. It's fine. It's probably not my place to get involved. But Alan told me you're sober now. You've been sober for a long time, he said. You don't want to give all that up, do you?"

What's the "that"? he wonders. He has no real career anymore, no family of his own, no circle of friends who know and love him for what he is. Beyond the fact that he has so little to show for himself, he's racked with a kind of blunt-edged guilt that being sober only worsens. He'd been having such terrible thoughts about Annette lately. She was old. Incompetent. Losing it. He was embarrassed by her. Frustrated with her. He would have left her for another agent if someone had even remotely given him a chance. These past few days, he's been blaming and cursing her for convincing him to come on this cruise, but she was already gone. The last friend he had left, and he didn't even sense the loss of her in the world.

"I don't really have much to give up, Renee."

"What kind of nonsense is that?" she snaps. "Everyone has something."

He looks up at her face, haloed by the Grotto's soft lights. She's so pretty, he thinks. Even now, when she's clearly annoyed with him, she's still such a beauty.

"Renee, did we . . . did I . . ." He can barely bring himself to ask the question. All the words he could use feel like knives in the pit of his stomach, ready to slice his insides into ribbons.

"Did we what?"

He suspects that Renee knows what he wants to ask. He wishes she'd just fill in the blanks, but why should she make this easy for him? "Did we ever have sex?" he blurts out. "Or did I— Please tell me I never tried to have sex with you?"

Her face shrivels. All the lines he hasn't been able to see suddenly appear, wrinkling with distaste at the thought of what he's asking. "No! I was with Ron during most of the show. You know I didn't sleep around."

He should be relieved to hear this, but he's not. The tension he's been carrying in his gut remains exactly where it is. Her answer isn't really an answer. It explains nothing. "But you told me not to come near you again. You didn't even want to share the greenroom with me—"

"Because you and the guys used to have your disgusting little sex parties in the greenroom! Why would I want to be reminded of that?"

"Okay, but . . . it still feels like there's more to it, so I keep thinking I must have done something to hurt you, to harm you in some way. I just don't— It sounds like an excuse, but I can't remember what."

He's tempted to tell her about the electroshock therapy—twelve sessions he underwent during the worst of his depression in the midnineties. When the doctor told him about the most common side effect—the possible loss of some long-term memory—it only made him more resolved to undergo treatment. There was very little Doug wanted to remember. And there was so much that the alcohol had already allowed him to forget.

"You hurt *Peter,*" Renee says. "You harmed Peter. And then he harmed himself. That's what I haven't been able to forgive. That man loved you, and you just tossed him aside. For what? To be an actor? A celebrity?" She laughs, but her eyes are suddenly wet with tears. "Look at where we are, Doug. Look at what we're doing, for God's sake. Are you telling me this was worth it?"

Doug sinks into his chair. All this time, he thought he and Peter were being so careful. He's devastated to learn that they were protecting a secret that wasn't even a secret. How much energy they wasted—effort that would have been better spent on simply loving each other.

"Did everybody on set know?"

She shakes her head. "I doubt it. No one talked about it, if that's what you're asking, and something like that would have gotten around." She removes a tissue from her pocket and dabs at the corners of her eyes, scanning the Grotto to make sure no one is watching. "No, it wasn't until the show ended and you broke up with him that Peter finally told me, and I was shocked . . . All those women you slept with, the way you both just used them . . . He was staying at our house in Palos Verdes when it happened, you know." She says "it" so gently, like she can barely stand to form the syllable, and Doug suddenly understands why she loathes him. "Peter said he wanted to take a drive that night, and for a second, I thought about offering to go with him, but I didn't. You know how many years of therapy it's taken to stop blaming myself for that? I mean, I can't be any more responsible for what happened than you are."

He should feel bad about what she just said, but he's already indicted himself for worse. A person can love someone deeply but still not care about them enough. And Doug didn't care about Peter more than the fear of losing his career, which felt like everything at the time, the source of all that was good and special about his life. He didn't understand that it only felt that way because he had Peter to share it with.

"I loved him, you know. I still do," he says, which is all the truth he can offer in return. "What I wouldn't give . . ." he begins, but there's no good way to finish the sentence.

She motions toward his whiskey. "That's not going to change what Peter did. It won't bring Annette back either." She shrugs. "I don't have a lot of experience with this kind of thing, but my guess is—if you don't think you have much to give up now, you'll have even less at the bottom of that drink."

Renee continues staring at it until Doug releases the glass from his grip. He pushes it into the center of the table, where it remains for several silent minutes. It's still there when Gideon walks over to them, his eyes wide with alarm.

"Is that yours, Uncle Doug?"

Before he can answer, Renee stands up and whisks the glass away. "No, sweetheart. It's mine. Excuse me," she says, extending Doug a kindness that he knows he doesn't deserve. "I have to get back to my group now."

THERE'S A GIRL lurking several feet behind Gideon, trying hard not to be noticed. When Gid calls her over, it takes Doug a moment to recall where he's seen her sad but pretty face. It's the granddaughter of the Chatterboxes from dinner last night. Aileen. Alice.

"You remember Allison, right?"

"Oh, yes. Allison. Hello."

She waves, and the light catches the bracelet on her wrist. Doug can't be certain, but it looks like the same friendship bracelet that Gideon was wearing at the start of the cruise.

"Would you two like to sit?" He realizes that the Xanax capsules are still on the table and quickly sweeps them into the pocket of his tuxedo, where he can feel his miniature AA handbook.

Allison shakes her head. "I'm avoiding my grandparents. They'll probably stop by for a drink now that the talent show's over." She touches Gid's arm, then gives the hem of his T-shirt a playful tug. "You want to head back to the arcade? They'll never think to go in there."

Doug is both hopeful that they'll leave and frightened that they'll actually go. He says nothing to persuade them either way. Alone, it would be so easy to go back to the bar and order another drink to replace the one that Renee took. *Just one drink.* He feels a strange pulse of energy in his chest at the thought of it, a familiar mix of excitement and terror and desire. He watches Gid whisper something in Allison's ear, slyly giving her a peck on the cheek. Then he tells her to go on, he'll meet her there.

"Okay," she says, and to Doug, another wave. "See you around."

As Gid sits down across from him, Doug is reminded of the reason he hasn't played the just-one-drink game yet. He doesn't deserve kindness, but people—a handful of people—keep extending it to him in spite of everything he is and all the wrong he's ever done. He wants to be worthy of the faith that his nephew, his brother, Annette, and even Renee have shown him. He doesn't believe he has any more chances left.

If Gid knows who the glass on the table really belonged to, he doesn't let on, and he doesn't ask twice. He seems more intent on keeping Doug occupied by telling him about the talent show he missed. Apparently, there was a juggler who couldn't keep his bowling pins in the air for more than a few throws. Every time one of them clattered onto the floor, he'd laugh nervously and say, "I've got this." There was also a woman who read original poetry inspired by her time in Bermuda. Her longest poem was about all the different colors that she observed on the island, rhyming words like "citrine" and "aquamarine."

"But the worst part was the end," he continues. "Everybody had to stand around in a circle and sing 'We Are the World' while holding hands, and it wasn't, like, a joke. That guy you were talking to at the pool yesterday, the one who was emceeing, he kept telling random people to join the circle. He even got the waiters to put their trays down and get in. You should have seen their faces." Gid sits up straight and smiles rigidly, making his eyes wide and doe-like.

They both laugh, but it's a nervous, hollow kind of laugh—a noise to fill the air rather than genuine amusement. Even the attempt at laughter makes Doug's side hurt. He wants to tell Gideon that it's not his job to cheer him up, but he appreciates the effort.

"You heard about my agent, I'm guessing?"

"I ran into Tabby after the show. She told me. Sorry, Uncle Doug."

"It's okay," he says, even though it feels far from okay. "It was just . . . 'Surprise' isn't the right word for it."

"You said she was pretty old though, right?"

Doug nods. He's said so many things about Annette that he wishes he could take back now. "Yes, but an old and dear friend, and I'm realizing I took that part of our relationship for granted. It's not . . . it's not a very good feeling."

They both turn their heads at the sound of people shouting. There's a group now gathered by the lagoon, tossing coins in. They appear to be aiming for the open mouth of a large frog statue. One of the men must have landed his coin because he pumps his fist in the air and shouts, "Two points!" while a busboy nervously looks on.

"There was a kid from my frat who died during my senior year. Killed himself in our basement—"

"Gid!" Doug snaps his head back. "What? Why am I only hearing about this now? How did—"

"He hung himself, so the school brought in a grief counselor, but I didn't really want to go because Mike and I never got along. He was kind of . . . I hate to say it, but he was kind of an asshole?" The question in his voice reveals how conflicted he feels about using that word, which speaks well of him—the fact that he wouldn't use it lightly. "Anyway, the school made all the guys—not just the ones who found him—but everyone in the frat had to do a one-on-one with this lady whether we wanted to or not, and you know what she said to me?"

Doug has no idea where this is going, but on some level, he's glad to not be talking about Annette anymore. "What?"

Gid eyes him thoughtfully. "She said that guilt compounds grief." He pauses for effect. "It makes us suffer twice."

He seems so pleased with himself for remembering this and being able to recite it in the moment. It's hard not to smile at his attempt to be helpful, this young person who has so much of his life left to live, who has no idea of the grief that might be coming for him one day.

"I'm sorry . . ." Doug starts. He doesn't know quite what to call the boy from the frat, who clearly wasn't a friend. "I'm sorry about your frat brother."

The forehead crease appears again, and Doug is grateful that the college made Gid speak to a counselor, even if he isn't yet. He scans the Grotto, looking for something to help change the subject when it occurs to him that he already saw it. "So . . . you and Allison? Was that your bracelet she was wearing?"

The dim lighting makes it hard to tell if Gid is blushing when he nods. But either he's too embarrassed to talk about her or unwilling to take the bait. "You know, I don't think I've ever heard you talk about your friends before."

"Really?" Doug asks, more reflex than question.

They're edging toward the rare subject that he'd prefer not to discuss with his nephew. To explain his self-imposed loneliness would require lifting the edge of something he's long kept sealed. How much damage he's done to people. How many mistakes he's made in the past. How he's denied the only part of his life that ever felt true.

"Was that guy I met at the pool yesterday your friend?" Gid asks tentatively, in a way that suggests he's asking something else.

"We used to be on the show." Doug thinks about all the photos of them together on the greenroom wall. "But Alan and I haven't seen each other in years."

"So what was he talking about when he said, 'dating 'em kind of young these days'? He was saying what? That you like men?"

The question is alarming in its directness but asked in such a neutral way, without the judgment or condescension that Doug used to fear when he was younger. He wonders if every instinct he ever had—to hide, to protect, to pretend—was wrong. What if the openness that Peter wanted for them both could have changed their lives for the better? What if he finally admitted that he loved a man for many years and then made a terrible choice that he's lived with every day since? Knowing Gid, he'd probably respond with something heartbreakingly thoughtful and kind, confirming the very thing that Doug doesn't want to acknowledge. What a waste of love. What a waste of life.

There's an unanswered question still hanging between them. Doug feels like he's inched his way to the edge of a cliff, toes out over the water with a view straight down. He reaches across the table, placing his hand on Gideon's forearm. Unlike the last time he did this, Gid doesn't pull away. Doug stares at his nephew's face, which is so similar to his brother's face, which is also a version of his own face such a long time ago. Inhale, he thinks. Inhale, one-two-three.

"I want to tell you about someone," Doug says slowly. "Someone you actually remind me of."

19.

Less than twelve hours of the cruise remain, but Lucy isn't sure how to fill them. Ever since Mariah kicked her out of the suite, she's been dragging her suitcase from one public space to another, dressed in the black pantsuit she wore during her interview, the same black pantsuit in which she boarded the ship. To pass the time, and to avoid the awkward looks and attempts at conversation by people curious about her outfit, she changed locations frequently, shuffling from the casino to the library to the gelateria to the pool. She could have gone to the Grotto, where the dark corners and dim lighting would have allowed her to hide out for longer, but she was too ashamed to return there after costing Iain his job.

Now, as the evening wears on, Lucy just wants to sleep. She's convinced there must be an empty cabin somewhere on the ship that she can stay in, but as she rolls her noisy suitcase toward Guest Services, the likelihood of getting access to it seems less and less certain. She imagines the use of a cabin, even for just one night, will probably be expensive. And thanks to her lengthy ship-to-shore call, her credit card is effectively maxed out. She steels herself to ask for charity, something she's never done before, something that would mortify her parents if they knew, even more so than her decision to come on this cruise.

At the sound of the suitcase's squeaky wheels, Siobhan looks up from her desk with a smile. How long are her shifts? Lucy wonders. When does this woman get to rest? Siobhan sets down her paperwork and caps her pen with a click. She asks how the interview went with the enthusiasm of someone now invested in the results.

Terrible, Lucy thinks, still blistering with anger at Mariah for interrupting the conversation. She's convinced this is what prompted Rahm to hurry off the line.

"It didn't end well."

"Oh, you're probably just being hard on yourself."

"No. It really didn't end well," she says, feeling the sting in her cheeks as she emphasizes the word "really."

Siobhan waits for more explanation. When nothing follows, she asks if there was a problem with the phone, grimacing as if she's afraid to hear the answer.

"No, the phone worked perfectly."

"Oh, thank God." Siobhan puts her hand to her chest, releasing a dramatic breath. "You went to so much trouble, after all."

Lucy doesn't want to be reminded of this. In fact, she would very much like to forget the series of events that led her back to Siobhan's desk. She runs her fingertips against the burled wood edge, not certain how to bring up the latest thing she needs from Guest Services. How many times has she come here during the cruise to ask for something? she wonders. Has she visited more often than the average passenger? She was raised not to be a bother to anyone, but she fears that's exactly what she's become. And now she's about to ask for a room, of all things. A free one, no less.

"So what can I help you with? Would you like me to arrange a car to pick you up in the morning?"

Lucy scans the rows of identical digital clocks hanging on the wall behind Siobhan. There are at least a dozen in all, each one with bright red numbers and the name of an international city underneath. LONDON, PARIS, TOKYO, SYDNEY. The largest clock in the center—the ship's clock—says it's 10:02 p.m.

"We're back on East Coast time already?"

Siobhan turns and looks over her shoulder. The ship's clock and the one labeled NEW YORK are finally in sync again, the same way they looked when the *Sonata* departed. "That must have just happened," she says. "We'll be docking in Boston before you know it."

Lucy is conflicted. She's both relieved by the thought of the cruise ending and anxious about returning to land. All week, she's been chafing against the strangeness of Mariah or Aria making so many decisions for her—when to eat, what to eat, how to be entertained, what to do with her free time. It makes her wonder why she allows people to do this to her at home with so much less resistance.

"Are you okay?" Siobhan makes the same gesture that Mariah did earlier, circling her face with her finger, as if to indicate that something about Lucy's doesn't look right.

"I'm fine," she says unconvincingly.

"Then what can I help you with?"

Siobhan doesn't sound annoyed when she asks. In fact, it seems like they established some kind of understanding during Lucy's last visit, a familiarity that almost feels friendly. But Lucy has been conditioned against handouts from an early age. It's hard for her to accept help, even when it's the very thing she needs.

"Where's the best place to look at the stars?"

The corners of Siobhan's mouth lift, and she leans forward as if to tell a secret that she enjoys sharing. Apparently, there's a small deck on level three that few passengers visit. A metal gate makes the stairway look off-limits, but Siobhan assures her that it's not. Because it's the highest public deck, it has a beautiful unobstructed view of everything above and below. "It's also nice and secluded," Siobhan adds. "I go there myself sometimes. It's a good place to daydream."

Lucy counts backward, realizing that she's spoken to Siobhan three times now, always at this desk. She's relieved to learn that she has off-hours to spend somewhere else. She was beginning to wonder if Aria ever let her leave her post.

"What do you dream about when you're up there?"

Siobhan looks at her curiously. "Me?" She starts to laugh. Fortunately, she appears more charmed by the question than offended by the intrusion; otherwise, Lucy would feel terrible for asking.

"Galway, I suppose."

"That's a city, right?"

Siobhan nods.

"Because that's where you're from?"

"No. My grandparents were. But one day, I wouldn't mind settling down there. I remember liking it as a child, the speed of things out that way, you know."

Lucy doesn't know, but she nods anyway, recognizing that this stranger has offered up something she didn't have to. She hopes Siobhan won't ask the same question in return, because she won't have a good answer. Or at the very least, she'll have a confused answer about working toward a successful career in tech while resisting an irrational, uncontrollable desire to paint. *Why can't you just do both?* a reasonable Siobhan will probably ask. And Lucy will be forced to explain the difficulty of becoming exceptional at two vastly different things, and why she can't risk being anything less.

The person who understands this best is actually her father. She's reminded of the conversation they had when he picked her up at Dulles after she returned from her junior year abroad. She'd flown from Rome to D.C. on a red-eye and assumed that he'd bring her straight home to sleep off the jet lag. Instead, he took her to the National Portrait Gallery. Lucy was so tired, as tired as she feels now, but she didn't complain about the outing, assuming a sweetness of intention that she later realized wasn't there. Her father, it turned out, didn't bring her to a museum to remind her that their hometown had plenty of art to look at, no different from Italy. He brought her there to discourage any ideas she might have developed during her time away.

"You see all those names?" he asked during the drive home.

By that point, Lucy was bleary-eyed after several hours of traipsing through the galleries, barely able to make conversation with her father, who often seemed mystified by the chalk-white faces on the walls and unimpressed by the lifetime of study needed to reproduce them so finely. She had no idea which names he was referring to. When she didn't answer for a while, he reframed the question.

"Was any of that art made by people who look like us?"

It was the National Portrait Gallery, she wanted to protest. Not a contemporary art museum. But even as the argument began to form in her throat, she knew it was a weak one. He could have taken her to any of the Smithsonians, or even the Guggenheim or MoMa in New York, but still, only a fraction of the art would have been created by people who looked like them. History was not on her side. Not then, not now, not yet.

THE THIRD DECK is exactly what Siobhan said it would be. Secluded, with an unobstructed view of the night sky. Lucy realizes that for most of the cruise, she's been looking out—at the horizon, at her surroundings, at her fellow passengers. Until now, she has yet to really look up.

The sky is pitch-black and unpolluted by light. A crescent moon hangs above the water, its pale, trembling twin submerged below. At sea, the stars actually twinkle—a word she's never used in a sentence before, only sung about as a child. She scans the darkness, surprised to locate the Big Dipper so easily, and then the Little Dipper just below it. When Lucy was younger, she had a fascination with stars that could only be indulged twice a year—once during her annual school visit to the planetarium and then again on vacation with her parents on Maryland's Eastern Shore. The skies in D.C. were rarely clear enough for stargazing without a telescope, and memorizing constellations in books could only hold her attention for so long.

Against the blank canvas of night, the constellations begin to announce themselves almost immediately. The dragon, which she's never seen outside of the Natural History Museum, is the first to emerge after the Big and Little Dippers. Lucy blinks, not certain if she's actually seeing Draco or just wishing she could. When she focuses on the area again, she recognizes his unmistakable shape almost directly above her. He's crouched low with his head bowed, but his long tail is held high. Right above the upward curve of it, there's Hercules, who slayed Draco, standing heroically with his arms and legs outstretched. Lucy's parents lacked the imagination to see images like this in the stars, even when they were very bright. They tried every summer, sitting with her on the porch of their beachfront rental, wrapped in blankets with their faces tilted up toward the sky. But despite all of Lucy's pointing and prompting, her parents could never make out what she did.

Perhaps for the same reason, they used to squint uncertainly at her paintings whenever she worked up the nerve to show them.

"You got this from your great-grandmother," Dad once said at her high school art show. He and Mom were standing in front of the piece that Lucy had entered, heads cocked in confused unison.

"Wasn't she the crazy one?" Lucy asked.

"No, no," her mother cut in, glancing at the parents and students nearby. "There wasn't anybody crazy in our family. He's just saying that she liked art."

That wasn't Lucy's interpretation of what he'd said at all. But there was no point arguing with either of them. She knew she'd learn more by simply watching her parents take in her work. The way they stared at it with their mouths suspended in nervous, uncomprehending smiles conveyed more than their actual words did.

"You matched up the colors really nice," Mom finally said, the strain of coming up with a response evident in her delivery.

The painting, an abstract titled *Comfort*, was inspired by the quilt that hung in their family room. As graduation approached and the move to Massachusetts for college felt less and less like a dream, Lucy was seized with nostalgia. It was hard for her to imagine waking up in the morning and not walking past the quilt, an heirloom that had been present for her entire life. It was in the background of nearly every old photo, capturing occasions both big and small. Her first steps. Her first Christmas. Her first father-daughter dance. And every night, she sat on the floor or sofa beneath it, doing homework or watching TV. The painting was her best attempt to reproduce how its constancy made her feel. But unlike the quilt, with its sharply geometric pattern repeating in squares of rust, gold, black, and beige, *Comfort* only reproduced the colors, rearranging them into large, amorphous shapes with no discernable pattern. Mixing the paint to create the shades—the one thing her mother found fit to compliment—had taken no time at all. It was the light she'd been obsessive about, angling and bending it across the canvas, referencing all the ways she'd seen it shine through the windows at home.

For her efforts, Lucy won first place that night. She even received a special citation from the head judge, a D.C.-area painter of some note and the parent of a fellow Sidwell student. After the awards were announced, he came over and shook her parents' hands before he shook hers.

"She's very talented for her age," he said. "Unusually talented. I hope she continues working on her craft."

The fact that he was saying this to her parents suggested that the decision to continue rested with them, not her. Lucy didn't realize she was frowning until she felt the gentle nudge of an elbow in her ribs. When she looked over, her mother smiled at her instructively and then scanned the small crowd of parents and teachers that had gathered around them, reminding Lucy that they were all being watched.

"Thank you," her father said, pumping the man's hand eagerly, the same way he did whenever someone in a position of authority told him that Lucy was special in some way. "We're very proud of everything Lou does." But even as he responded with the appropriate, expected amount of public enthusiasm, Lucy couldn't help but think that he looked a little panicked by the possibility that the man's assessment of her might be right. His response dulled whatever excitement she would have felt about either the prize or the compliment, something that must have registered in her expression, because all during the drive home, Mom kept saying how much she liked her art.

The painting, now almost a decade old, hangs on the family room wall. For this, Lucy gives her parents credit. They clearly didn't care for it. Nor did they like what it suggested. But the morning after the art show, their love for her compelled them to give it a place of honor next to the quilt, where it remains to this day. How Lucy wishes she had that quilt now. Not just for the comfort, but also for the warmth. The temperature is so different than it was a few nights ago—cold, instead of cool. The wind keeps curling down the open collar of her shirt, pebbling her skin with goose bumps. She buttons every available button on her shirt and jacket, then wheels her suitcase to a row of chaises beneath a staircase leading up to a restricted deck. The overhang created by the stairs provides some protection from the elements, so she stretches out on the chaise in the corner, aware that this is probably the closest thing to a bed she'll find tonight.

The stars continue to shine, offering a silver lining to the cold. Lucy rummages through her suitcase in search of more layers, making use of what little she packed. She drapes her bathing suit cover-up around her shoulders like a shawl, spreads her still-unworn sundress across her lap like a blanket, wraps her hands in tank tops like they're mittens. She tries to remember the date, wondering if they've officially crossed over into autumn yet. Her heart sinks when she realizes that it's the twentieth, something she quickly backed into by counting the number of days that have passed since the eleventh. Suddenly, this is her point of reference for time. Hers and everyone else's, she suspects. It feels like they'll always be counting the days, the months, the years since it happened.

Lucy exhales into her cupped hands, watching her breath turn into vapor. She looks for more stars to distract herself, angling her head to see past the overhang. Aside from Draco, Hercules, and the unmistakable Vega, other constellations are harder to identify. The anchor stars aren't as showy, and a streaky veil of clouds has started to blow in. This was always what frustrated her about stargazing when she was younger—how wanting to see didn't necessarily mean that she could. Sometimes, it was the weather that interfered. Or sometimes, it was the location of the stars. Most of the time, it was simply the limits of her vision.

She recalls a rare argument between her parents that she overheard a few months before her tenth birthday. They were trying to decide whether to finally buy her a telescope. Her mother said yes—how else could Lucy keep learning about astronomy? Her father said no—children outgrew their interests, and then what? They'd be stuck with a giant telescope taking up precious space in their home. As usual, he was right. Or maybe he put just enough obstacles and distractions in her path to prove himself right. Regardless of the reason, Lucy started spending her time in other ways—Westinghouse science competitions, quiz bowl, computer programming camp. She suspects her parents always assumed, or maybe even hoped, that she'd eventually outgrow her interest in art, but it never left her. Even when she wasn't painting, the desire to paint was always there. It's with her now as she looks out into the darkness and imagines how to render it in a way that others might be able to understand, that might help her understand the full depths of her grief.

MEN ARE TALKING. Two of them, possibly more. Lucy stirs awake, not certain if she's been asleep for several minutes or several hours. This isn't the languid, luxurious kind of waking that she experiences on the rare weekend when she lets herself sleep in. This is jarring and abrupt, an awareness that she isn't alone. Lucy lies very still, jaw clenched to prevent her teeth from chattering. At some point during the night, she pulled her sundress up to cover her face. Through the gauzy black fabric, she can see the shapes of two men standing by the railing, not far from where she's lying. As her eyes begin to adjust, she's relieved to make out bright white officers' uniforms, which lowers the volume of her alarm.

The men are looking out over the water with their backs to Lucy. Either they haven't spotted her yet, shrouded in black beneath the shadowy overhang, or they have and they're trying not to disturb. She suspects it's the former because she can hear their voices clearly. One is British. The other, European in some indeterminate way. They're not making any effort to avoid being overheard.

"Should we do an announcement, sir?" the British one asks.

"What? Now? Everyone's sleeping."

"It's something worth seeing though."

"It's not even light out. We'll give them all a heart attack."

"Respectfully, sir. I disagree."

"What are you suggesting, then? We make an announcement, wake everyone up and tell them to report to their muster stations? They'll think the ship is sinking."

"We'd probably have to soften it more than that. Maybe prepare them a bit for what they're seeing?"

The European makes a sneering noise.

"I know I'm new here, sir. Normally I wouldn't argue, but it just seems like a once-in-a-lifetime opportunity."

Lucy slowly pulls the dress away from her face. All the stars she was admiring earlier have faded. It's still dark out, but it's a grayish, diluted kind of dark that suggests morning is coming soon. From her angle, she can't tell what they're talking about.

The European, who sounds more Greek than anything else, shakes his head. "They can't actually see it though. And we don't have enough viewfinders or binoculars to go around. How can I justify waking everyone and scaring them half to death if they can't even see what we woke them for? No." He shakes his head again, more resolutely this time. "Can you imagine the complaints? Corporate will never let us hear the end of it."

The Brit says nothing.

Between them, the men have one large pair of binoculars. They take turns looking through them at something in the distance, handing them back and forth without conversation. Lucy thinks she might be able to wait them out if they leave soon, an idea that doesn't last for more than a minute because of the sound of footsteps lumbering up the stairs.

"I thought you were going to wait until 0600," a voice calls out. "Can you see it yet?" A third man joins them, his accent distinctly Australian. Lucy holds her breath, anticipating an awkward reunion. She's relieved when an older man comes into view, also dressed in officers' whites, with a potbellied silhouette that definitely isn't Iain's.

"Who did you leave on watch?" the Greek asks.

"Wilmer. Can you see it yet?"

"Not without these." The Greek hands him the binoculars.

The third man raises them to the horizon, taking a moment to adjust the focus. "And there she is," he says quietly, almost as if he's talking to himself. "Huh."

"What kind of response is that?" the Greek asks. He seems to be getting more and more agitated the longer the conversation continues.

"I don't know. I guess I wasn't sure what to expect."

"There's no preparing for this." The Greek shrugs. "This one here thinks we should get everyone to muster." He throws a dismissive thumb back at the Brit, who looks almost sheepish now, turtled into the collar of his shirt and jacket.

"At this hour?"

"That's what I said."

"Jesus, there's still smoke." The Aussie takes one last look before handing back the binoculars. "I thought that'd be gone by now. How can there still be smoke?"

"Remember this, if you're planning to have any sort of career with Aria," the Greek says to the Brit, who shrinks even further upon being directly addressed. "Our job is to show the passengers a good and safe time. That, out there? That's what they're going home to. They'll see it all soon enough."

"Can I see?" Lucy asks.

The men turn. Despite the darkness, the whites of their eyes gleam. She understands how she must appear to them, calling out from the shadows, dressed all in black. She considers giving them her friendliest, most ingratiating smile, but suspects that would make her presence seem even odder.

"I'm sorry. I didn't mean to startle you."

"You've been there the entire time, miss?" the Greek asks.

"I fell asleep. I wasn't trying to eavesdrop, really."

She can imagine the confusing stories the men must be telling themselves, the data that just doesn't compute. Her business suit and flip-flops. The cover-up draped over her shoulders. The white tank tops, which she quickly peels off her hands and shoves into her pockets. With her suitcase next to her chaise, she probably looks like a stowaway who managed to avoid detection during the cruise or a passenger who's unnaturally eager to disembark.

"My roommate and I are staying in one of the Royal Ocean Suites," she says, watching their frowns instantly soften at the mention of her cabin class. "We had an argument, so I just needed some space."

"But it's so cold, miss," the Aussie says. "You haven't been sleeping out here, have you?"

"I wasn't trying to. I just came to look at the stars. Siobhan in Guest Services told me there was good stargazing on this deck."

She gets up and walks toward them, taking stiff, careful steps to avoid stumbling. She's surprised to feel more numb than cold after so many hours outside. Needly pinpricks race up her legs, recirculating her blood as she joins them at the railing. Once Lucy is beside them, she extends her hand. "Can I see what you're looking at?"

The men glance at each other. Up close, she notices that the Greek has four gold stripes on the epaulets of his uniform. The Aussie has three. The Brit, only one. All of them are standing rigidly at attention, their posture as straight as boards.

"Are you the captain?" she asks the Greek.

"Yes. Captain Mallas. I'm sorry. You surprised us earlier. Very pleased to meet you, Miss . . . Miss . . . ?"

Gone is the surliness that she witnessed just moments ago. In its place is all charm and warmth. It's obvious that he's asking for her last name to address her more personally, but what does it matter now? she thinks.

"We're passing New York, aren't we?"

He hesitates, appearing almost guilty. "Miss, we're many, many miles from—"

She extends her hand again. "Can I see? Please?"

The binoculars are long and heavy. When he gives them to her, he's careful not to let go until she understands their full weight. She raises them to her eyes, struggling to hold them level. Captain Mallas wasn't lying. They're very far from shore. So far that it takes several scans to figure out where to look. When she finally locates land and focuses in, New York appears as a small, twinkling outline in the distance, its high-rises blurred into indistinct shapes, all jagged in height.

"Oh" is all she can manage to say, and she understands at once how the Australian must have felt.

There are too many details to remember. Too many sights that demand to be retained. Lucy does her best to take them all in. The faint amber glow of morning, still pale as the sun breaks over the horizon. The great absence from the skyline. The thin spire of smoke at the city's southern tip that marks where it happened, where so many people lost their lives. For the rest of hers, Lucy will always be thinking about the futures that ended here, about the beauty lost and the chances that would never be taken. And her fear of what lies ahead will subside with the knowledge that there is no forever. Only morning, fleeting and true.

Friday, September 21

RETURN TO ~~NEW YORK PASSENGER SHIP TERMINAL, NEW YORK~~
BLACK FALCON CRUISE TERMINAL, BOSTON

20.

The passengers descend, five and six abreast down the ramp, feet tentative as they reacquaint themselves with land. Before funneling through the arrivals building, they notice several crew members pointing, encouraging them to take one last look at the ship. When they turn around, they see the *Sonata*'s officers standing in a row on the upper deck, smiling and waving goodbye. Those who watched *Starlight Voyages* remember fondly and wave back. It's the last glittering moment of the trip, the long shot before everyone fans out and heads home.

Later, it will all seem like a dream. The officers in their dress whites with the sun behind their backs. The sight and smell of the ocean. The pastel-hued island with its pink sand beaches. Whenever the passengers stop to think about this strange, suspended time, they'll wonder if they were really there, if any of it really happened, because so much is about to happen. The world they're returning to has already begun to change.

Among the many things the passengers don't know as they disembark that morning: A war is coming. In a few short weeks, the first U.S. troops will arrive in Afghanistan after the Taliban-led government refuses to turn over the leader of Al Qaeda. This is what the president meant when he blinked into the camera and said, "We will make no distinction between the terrorists who committed these acts and those who harbor them." The United States will remain in Afghanistan for the next two decades to support a new government and fight off insurgents. Millions of Afghanis will be displaced by this war, which will claim the lives of nearly 3,500 American and Allied soldiers and 46,000 Afghan civilians. Not long after the symbolic U.S. troop withdrawal deadline of September 11, 2021, the Taliban will return to power.

In 2003, the attacks on New York and Washington, D.C., will be used to justify another war, this time in Iraq, to end a dictatorship and search for weapons of mass destruction that are allegedly being manufactured in the country. The WMDs are never found—an intelligence lapse, the history books will later say. This war will last eight years and result in the deaths of nearly 5,000 American and Allied soldiers and at least 185,000 Iraqi civilians. Again, millions of Iraqis will be displaced, and the violence and instability will help give rise to the Islamic State of Iraq and Syria. For the next decade, the United States will increase and decrease its troop presence in Iraq to combat ISIS before it formally withdraws from the country in 2021.

Terrorist attacks—seemingly more and more each year—will continue to claim lives around the world. There will be too many incidents to list, too many horrifying deaths to count. In time, the violence will lead to other, different kinds of loss. The loss of safety, which will be used to justify a global war on terror. The loss of privacy, as governments claim unprecedented new powers to surveil their citizens. The loss of dignity, experienced by peaceful Muslims around the world who will be scapegoated for the acts of a radical few. And the loss of humanity, as personnel at black sites and military detention centers attempt to extract information from suspected terrorists, using interrogation methods indistinguishable from torture. Decades after the war on terror begins, there will be no end in sight.

Strange things are on the horizon. The makings of sci-fi or satire, except all of it will be real. People will send letters laced with anthrax, shutting down government mail service, congressional office buildings, and news centers. Millions of travelers passing through airports will have to remove their shoes to be X-rayed because someone tried to walk on a plane with a bomb hidden in his. Conspiracy theorists will develop alternative explanations for the attacks that will spread widely despite a lack of evidence or common sense. The new U.S. Department of Homeland Security will categorize each day's "terror alert level" according to one of five colors. For reasons that DHS will rarely be able to explain to the public, most days will be orange.

It will take years to identify all the victims of the attacks on 9/11 and to declare the missing as legally dead. Eventually, the number of lives lost that day will be confirmed and recorded as follows:

> In New York, 2,753 people died when American Airlines Flight 11 and United Airlines Flight 175 struck the North and South Towers of the World Trade Center.
>
> In Washington, D.C., 184 people died when American Airlines Flight 77 struck the Pentagon.
>
> Outside of Shanksville, Pennsylvania, 40 people died when hijackers crashed United Flight 93 after passengers tried to take back control of the plane.

On each of these sites, memorials will rise. Austere, ghostly, beautiful memorials where people will gather annually to remember and honor the dead. When their names are read aloud, the muffled sobs that pierce the silence will convey all the grief that remains, many years and decades later. The people who visit these memorials will treat them like museums, places built to record and preserve our shared history. But the numbers engraved in marble and steel will not account for the slow, painful loss of additional lives—to respiratory illnesses from inhaling toxic fumes during rescue or recovery, to suicide by those who couldn't forget what they saw or lost.

Later, when the U.S. government is so divided and dysfunctional, it will be shocking to think about the speed with which Congress created a victim compensation fund after the attacks. Never mind that the fund was part of a bill to stabilize and protect the airline industry from litigation. What matters is that the fund will eventually distribute $7 billion to the families of the victims or those injured in the attacks. Before doing so, the government-appointed special master of the fund and his staff will meet individually with the loved ones of thousands of victims to determine the appropriate award amounts. When asked to recall what stood out to him about these conversations, the special master—a serious, bespectacled man known for mediating complex government settlements—will surprisingly mention love. A deep, enduring love for the people who died.

Sometimes, the passengers of the *Sonata* will randomly remember being on the ship or the island, and they'll feel a sharp pang of guilt at the thought of the breeze on their faces or the sight of their toes in the impossibly clear water. These memories will forever be at odds with the collective mood of mourning during that time, so the passengers will work hard to tamp them down and tuck them away, preserving them as private. But later, as the world continues to change and they witness so many things that disappoint and bewilder and terrify them, they'll realize that the seeds of all this chaos were already in the ground on the morning they disembarked in Boston, and it will be hard not to shake their heads at their innocence or ignorance.

For now, however, none of what is about to happen has happened. For now, the passengers are simply walking down the ramp toward the terminal building, dragging luggage heavy with souvenirs. Smiling crew members stop them on their way out and tell them to take one last look at the ship, so they oblige. When they turn toward the *Sonata*, the uniformed officers wave at them from the upper deck, outlined by a sky that will probably never be as blue as it was before. The passengers blink and shield their eyes from the sun, just long enough to let this image imprint somewhere deep in their memories. And then they move on, returning to the many possibilities of their lives.

ACKNOWLEDGMENTS

My husband, Joel Anderson, and I have been together since the start of my writing career. He's my forever first reader, most compassionate critic, and loudest cheerleader. Everything I write bears the deep imprint of Joel's love and encouragement, as well as his careful editorial eye. I'm so thankful to him and our families for supporting my work, including our seven nephews to whom *All the World Can Hold* is lovingly dedicated.

My editor, Dawn Davis, understood this novel from the start and was instrumental in helping me lean into its themes of regret, hope, and possibility. I am indebted to Dawn; my associate editor, Maria Mendez; and everyone at 37 Ink and Simon & Schuster who dedicated themselves to launching my third book with such thoughtfulness and care, particularly Ingrid Carabulea, Samantha Hoback, Carly Loman, Math Monahan, Matt Roeser, Maggie Southard, and Anne Pearce.

My agent, Jennifer Gates, has been a tireless advocate for my work since day one. I'm so grateful to Jen and her colleagues at Aevitas Creative Management—Mags Chmielarczyk, Shenel Ekici-Moling, Erin Files, Lauren Liebow, and Allison Warren—for their collective wisdom and investment in guiding my career. Meanwhile, Kate Lloyd of Broadside Public Relations has been an absolute gem in her efforts to help readers discover this book.

For nearly a decade, my colleagues and students at the George Washington University ("GW") have made coming to campus feel like both a pleasure and a privilege. How lucky I am to be surrounded by fellow readers and writers who believe in a spirit of honest inquiry and civil discourse. I also owe a special thanks to the Columbian College of Arts and Sciences at GW, which provided me with an invaluable Dean's Research Chair Award in 2022.

Some truly amazing women helped to sustain me during the writing of this book. My heartfelt gratitude to Hannah Bae, Jessie Chaffee, Jane Delury, Elizabeth Evitts-Dickinson, Julia Fleischaker, Krys Lee, Jeannie Vanasco, and Grace Yoojin Wuertz for the gift of their friendship. I'm cheering each of them on, wildly and proudly, as they pursue their individual literary and professional goals.

A final thanks to the Robert W. Deutsch Foundation, which awarded me a generous Rubys Grant in 2023. One of the most important things that this grant allowed me to do was conduct 9/11-related research in New York; Washington, D.C.; and Shanksville, Pennsylvania. The time that I spent in these locations, particularly at the memorial sites, served as a necessary reminder of the many innocent lives lost that day, and the countless lives that changed from that day forward, including my own.

My younger self never imagined that writing a book—much less sharing it in published form—was something that I would ever be able to do. I'm truly humbled by the opportunity and grateful to everyone who makes this dream of a life possible.

ABOUT THE AUTHOR

JUNG YUN was born in Seoul, South Korea, and grew up in Fargo, North Dakota. She is the author of *O Beautiful*, which was a *New York Times* Editors' Choice, a *New York Times* Group Read, and a *San Francisco Chronicle* Book of the Year. Her debut novel, *Shelter*, was a finalist for the Barnes & Noble Discover Great New Writers Award and was also long-listed for the Center for Fiction's First Novel Prize.